THE EXILES

GHALIB SHIRAZ DHALLA is the author of *Ode to Lata*, a novel critically acclaimed by the *Los Angeles Times*, and also an accomplished film-maker. He wrote and produced the film adaptation (*The Ode*) and has just completed his forthcoming film, *Embrace*. Dhalla's seminal work has been celebrated at The Lincoln Center for Performing Arts in New York and Yale University's prestigious Master's Tea.

PRAISE FOR *THE EXILES*

'A beautiful, sometimes joyful, yet heartbreaking exploration of love in all its manifestations. Here it is many days later, and I still find myself thinking about Ghalib Shiraz Dhalla's insights into the fierceness and frailty of the human heart. Oh, the things we will do for and in the name of love. Dhalla is a brilliant young writer, and his novel is exquisite, drenched in emotion, and timely.' – Lisa See, best-selling author of *Shanghai Girls* and *Snow Flower and the Secret Fan*

'. . . a novel filled with unexpected turns and beauty, Ghalib Shiraz has examined with perceptive compassion the complex and heart-wrenching ties that bind families, and the secret desires that pull them apart.' – Chitra Divakaruni, best-selling author of *The Palace of Illusions*

'Shiraz immerses us in his gripping narrative as he delves into the nooks and crannies of human desire and explores both its splendor and the havoc it can wreak. A formidably intelligent and adept writer, he has stretched my understanding of a world I know very little about with this touching and masterfully written novel.' – Bapsi Sidhwa, author of *New York Times* Notable novel *Cracking India*

'Ghalib Shiraz Dhalla writes with a voice that is both agile and compassionate. He renders scenes of great emotion with equal parts passion and precision. At its core, [this] is a classic tale of tragic, forbidden love, but Dhalla infuses it with an astute discussion of Hindu culture that should appeal to a broad cross-section of readers.' – Christopher Rice, *New York Times* best-selling author of *A Density of Souls and Blind Fall*

'A powerful, sure-footed novel of love, longing and loss that richly portrays life like no other work of fiction I've read. With his complex cast of characters and poetically drawn landscapes, Dhalla's talent shines and he shows us he's wise beyond his years.' – Mark Jude Poirier, author of *Goats* and *Modern Ranch Living*

The Exiles

GHALIB SHIRAZ DHALLA

HarperCollins *Publishers* India

First published in India by
HarperCollins *Publishers* in 2011
Building No 10, Tower A, 4th Floor, DLF Cyber, City Phase II,
Gurugram 122002
www.harpercollins.co.in

4 6 8 10 9 7 5

ISBN: 978-93-5029-062-0

Typeset in 10.5/12.5 PalmSprings at
SÜRYA

Printed and bound at
Replika Press Pvt. Ltd.

HarperCollins *Publishers*, Macken House, 39/40 Mayor Street Upper, Dublin 1, D01 C9W8, Ireland

For the Virjees –
Mama Kuba, Jomba, Gulshan and Bapa.

And Karsh Kale, whose music is the heartbeat of my words.

Book One

'O Dhananjaya, I bless you, my dear friend. There is none equal to you in the three worlds, as you know my secret. O Arjuna, you will curse me if you talk to anyone about the secret which you wanted to know and have experienced.'

– Krishna to Arjuna
Padma Purana (c. 12th century)

'The one and only wife should with internalized belief and total absorption, hold her husband as a God.'

– *Kama Sutra* (2nd century BC)

DESIRE IS INCAPABLE of hypocrisy. The thought broke through Rahul Kapoor's mind as he prepared to tell his first lie of the day. Sitting at his desk, Rahul stared at the framed picture of his wife and son, their laughter trapped beneath glass. His finger ran over the surface and he touched them, almost feeling the planes and curves of Pooja's beautiful face, the softness of her pink chiffon sari, Ajay's weathered leather jacket.

We can force ourselves to tolerate certain people, to acclimate to a job we detest, and for a while, even rein ourselves in with logic and common sense, he thought. But we are truly helpless against the heart and its obdurate desires.

Rahul's finger trailed off the pane of glass, leaving behind an oily smudge. He looked at his watch. It was three-thirty in the afternoon. If he left now, he could beat the evening traffic. He stood up and absentmindedly packed his leather briefcase, threw on a navy-blue suit jacket and called his assistant Amelia, sitting on the other side of the busy bank office, surrounded by her coterie of little stuffed toys.

He made his excuses about visiting important clients, about being unable to make it back in time due to traffic and she, in her typical, obsequious manner, assured him that everything was under control. Los Angeles, after all, was not kind to wayfarers or commuters.

Clutching his briefcase, Rahul left his corner glass office and cut across the lobby to pick up a few sales brochures for effect. A queue of impatient clients paying credit card and mortgage bills, making deposits, or just withdrawing money because they were untrusting of the ATM machine looked at him expectantly. He ignored them. He was a man in love, removed from the mundane. Rahul said his perfunctory goodbyes to a few employees, one of them too busy to notice, and made for the door like a convict for whom the prison gates had miraculously opened in the middle of the night.

As his Mercedes sped down the 405 Freeway, the lane markers morphing into a solid line, Rahul thought about how naïve he had been in thinking he could wrestle with his urges, simply vaporize them. In the end, years of deprivation had only served to nurture them.

Before long, Rahul approached an army of red lights, and a wave of sickness washed over him. The solid white line broke down into halting dashes again. He came to a complete stop, felt the acid drip in his stomach. Walled behind a massive white truck, there was no telling what lay ahead. He was going to be late.

Rahul was not a cruel man. His disbelief in a higher power – in karmic retribution – did not make him apathetic to the pain of others. But entrenched in the heat of traffic, Rahul couldn't help wishing that someone else also suffered. For this to cost him another second of delay there had better be damage, significant devastation, a bonfire of metal and flesh, not just some calm CHP officer completing a speeding ticket and throwing already paranoid drivers into apoplexy.

The heat surged. The digital temperature display on his dashboard reached the nineties and the gasoline indicator lit up. He restrained himself from cranking up the air conditioner. He loosened the noose – a deep-burgundy silk tie, clustered with wisps of turquoise paisleys that his wife had given him some years ago to celebrate a raise – and let it hang limply around his wet neck, granting him permission to unbutton the starched cotton shirt. His son thought the tie unfashionably ornate and Rahul often joked that one day he would pass it on to him as an heirloom.

The remnants of his Jaipur aftershave mingled with his sweat and produced the kind of pheromonal aroma that he knew would elicit excitement when he finally got there. The thought of it made him sweat even more. He rolled down the window and warm air barged in with the cacophony of traffic. Rahul's eyes glazed behind his sunglasses, as they often did when the world around became too harsh and the visual had to be blurred momentarily: a kind of expeditious meditation. Then Rahul could hear the deep, throaty laughter, feel the gnawing of teeth on his stubbly chin, see bare limbs and torsos undulating in pure white sheets. And for some inexplicable reason he heard the faint crackling of electrical wires overhead.

He reached out for the telephone headset but the cord was tangled on the parking brake. His frustrated tugs only strengthened its hold. *Calm down, calm down,* he urged himself. *You're making matters worse.* He uncoiled the cord gently, reminding himself to breathe evenly. An elongated press of '9' on his cellphone transported him to his destination. *If only I could fly over all this. Leap over it all and be there with you.* The answering machine came on, and then that voice filled his ear and made his heart jump. Rahul knew that preparations were being made – tuberoses being placed to crane out of vases to perfume the air; pungent powders in shades of earth and vermillion were being portioned out into bubbling pots of food; music being selected to set the mood, to score the soft moans of pleasure and grateful cries of release; and a volume of Rumi was being placed on the nightstand to celebrate the afterglow.

'I'm on my way. I'm coming. I'll be there soon,' he said. And then even after he had disconnected, he continued to say it to himself in a whisper, like a mantra, a reassurance that his life was waiting for him on the other side.

The barricade gave way. One by one, without rhyme or reason, the red lights of forbiddance were snuffed out and the cars began, almost with a moan of relief, to lurch forward. Rahul took a deep but shaky breath and stepped on the gas.

The whirl of the kitchen fan overhead drowned the simple solution to ages of rivalry between the Muslims and Hindus; so Pooja tempered the heat of the stove and rushed to the living room to rewind the ghazal by the Hussain brothers. She pressed a button on the CD player and after a jumble of quick words, there it was, her favourite verse:

Mandir aur masjid ka yun jhaghra mitaya jaye,
Beech mein dono ke maikhana banaya jaye.

The war between temple and mosque can be dissolved easily.
Just erect a bar in the middle.

She threw her hand up in the air in appreciation, a gesture that looked as if she had just freed a bird, and rewarded the verse with an effusive *wah-wah*. Then she went back to the kitchen, continuing to sing along in her undeniably flat voice, made worse by the drastic difference in the baritone of the brothers and her off-key falsetto.

In the long hours of the afternoon, while Rahul ran his fiefdom at the bank and Ajay was at college, no doubt flirting with all the girls who constantly demanded his attention on the little red cellular he'd sprouted from his hip, Pooja found a way to occupy herself by catering home-made Indian food.

Apart from the special orders that trailed in through word of mouth mainly from American families in the Palisades and Brentwood, Pooja's one consistent client was The Banyan, a yoga studio on Santa Monica's trendy Montana Avenue. The spacious indoor and outdoor facility offered day and evening classes in hatha yoga and was popular with the hip youth, although her son, sadly, was not among them. A small store at the front carried candles, exotic oils, yards of spirituality books by the likes of Deepak Chopra and Osho, CDs of Eastern music, overpriced clothing silk-screened with Indian gods and goddesses, chakra-enhancing nutrition bars and beverages, and Pooja's specially packaged savouries. In the back of the studio was a little meditation garden Pooja was particularly fond of, where banana trees and bamboo surrounded a burbling fountain, and graceful statues of bodies in various asanas posed blissfully. The studio was managed by Magda, an efficient girl in her twenties who bore a striking resemblance to its owner, Charlie Ackerman, and claimed to be addicted to Pooja's spicy 'Kali' trail mix.

On such afternoons, while trays of cashew marzipan solidified and spiced trail mixes cooled in large trays, the stereo kept her company. She loved listening to classic Bollywood songs from the 1950s and '60s, but her favourite were Indian devotional songs. To her, devotional music felt like the pure, cool water from the clay *matki*s back home. Because the imagery was personified on a human level, the emotion conveyed was easy and beautiful. The soul's yearning for God was portrayed in the lover's yearning for his beloved, as in Radha's craving for Krishna. With the balm of these melodious bhajans, she grew tranquil and patient.

But there were times, late in the day when the orders had been filled and picked up, when nobody else was home and even the lamps in the house and the television could not chase away the gloom, when she would think of when she had first met Rahul. Melancholy would seize her and she wondered why they couldn't go back to being close. *The tragedy of a lasting love story,* thought Pooja dolefully, *is that it must prove itself by outliving and enduring the loss of its youthful enchantment.*

Basmati rice had already been soaking in a large pan in the sink for hours. Earlier she'd moved through the aisles of Asia Bazaar in Culver City where the overzealous shopkeeper always compared her to a popular Bollywood actress, and selected her ingredients and produce with utmost care. At first she'd feared her successes were accidental, but after her clients had oohed and aahed repeatedly over the perfect balance of spices and flavours in her dishes, Pooja grew more confident. She ran fresh water over the grains and sifted them through her hands until the water ran clear and was no longer milky. She inhaled the starchy scent deep into her lungs, comforted by the familiar, raw fragrance of the earth. In a saucepan, she began sautéing the rice in clarified butter, cinnamon, bruised cardamom pods, peppercorns and a few drops of lemon to keep them from sticking. When the grains hardened and glistened like ivory filaments, she poured in double the amount of water and, covering the saucepan, let it simmer until the moment they would blossom into the light, fluffy pilaf for which basmati or 'scent of the earth' rice was famous.

In a non-stick pan Pooja churned a potpourri of spices – finely chopped yellow onions, hot green serrano chilies, minced garlic and cilantro, teaspoons of *garam masala* and turmeric – into thick aromatic gravy. Indian cooking, she had been instructed a long time ago by her mother, required non-stick cookware because the caramelizing and toasting was an essential part of its flavour. She tossed in the prawns from the colander and coated them, watching them turn into succulent pink tendrils. Her arms, like Shiva in motion, reached for one thing after another rhythmically and through pure instinct. She poured in some fresh cream and coarse sea salt to finish her most popular dish, *Jheenga Masala*. Poultry and seafood were Pooja's forte. As a rule, she never cooked red meat, even though as a Bhatt, she'd been brought up in a household where eating meat was not only accepted, but meat was served quite frequently. Her father had been an avid beef-eater.

Pooja consulted the artificially antiqued clock mounted on the wall above the stove. It was almost six. He would be here any minute. There was still the sari to change into, the *tika* to anoint her forehead and the incense. Although the ionizer tower Rahul had bought her and which sat suspiciously quiet in a corner of the kitchen, emitting a strange sterile smell, apparently did its best to expunge the aromas of her cooking, Pooja ritually lit a stick or two of incense at the end of a cooking session. So now the scents of sandalwood, jasmine and rose had become part of their home's breath, a perfume instantly noticed by visitors.

She was careful not to let the smells of cooking stick to the walls as they often did in the homes of other Indians who cooked generously with pungent spices and garlic and ginger, and at whom the rest of the Western world was so quick to wrinkle their noses. Pooja remembered how an apartment manager, whom she'd met at one of Rahul's bank holiday parties, had most indelicately confessed to having the toughest time renting out apartments vacated by Indians because the strong smells of cooking had refused to follow suit. 'I can't decide which one is worse,' he had admitted, scratching his profuse moustache. 'Indian or Chinese. All I know is it's never a problem with the Japanese.'

She knew that it was also the reason Rahul didn't take her food to the office with him, resisting the little Tupperwares she had tried to ply him with at first. 'Oh, Poo. You know these people with their subway sandwiches,' he said. 'They claim the microwave still smells of my curry from a year ago.'

Pooja lit a match and awakened the pair of incense sticks; she was never one to light them unceremoniously as from the top of the stove. She closed her eyes and dipped her face into the whorls of fragrance dancing up. Then she hurried off to get dressed.

From the glove compartment, Rahul fished out a permit that would allow him to park right in front of the apartment. It was located a stone's throw from Montana Avenue, the shopping area where celebrities were often spotted, lined with overpriced speciality boutiques full of prosaic fare and worn-out, 'distressed' rubbish that Rahul thought people paid absurd amounts for. It was also home to The Banyan, the yoga studio where Pooja made an occasional delivery.

As he hooked the plastic card onto his rear-view mirror, Rahul looked up and saw his abode through the filigree of heavily laden tree branches. The second-floor apartment had large French windows dressed with heavy burgundy velvet curtains and ivory sheer panels, and opened up to a private balcony overlooking the street upon which he stood.

Now that he was finally here, he didn't rush. The frenzy

subsided and Rahul took pause. He stood under a majestic magnolia tree that blessed shade intermittently on his face. A pair of solemn joggers sprinted past. He wished that darkness would engulf him. There was something starkly malapropos about such a rendezvous in summer's extended light.

When he first started to come here towards the end of last winter, darkness had cloaked his visits and the chill in the air was electric, serving to increase the hunger of his body. Although his mind had been laden with hesitation, his body had managed to move forward, knowing a different movement, an agility and vigour. The power of repetition could not be underestimated, thought Rahul. If repeated, action became purged of thought and awkwardness. Soon only gratification mattered and even the gnawing fear, however improbable, that he might run into Pooja making an unexpected delivery of cashew marzipan and spiced trail mix just a few blocks from here couldn't deter him.

A mother pushed a gurgling infant in a stroller and Rahul let them pass him on the pavement before crossing over. The baby delightedly shook a fluffy green monster at him. Rahul smiled at them and couldn't help but think of Ajay. He pictured his grown-up son standing there. His smile faded; regret twisted at his mouth.

The premium of old age, he thought, should be the peaceful ratchet of routine, the unwavering aura of predictability. Instead, as he approached his forty-eighth birthday, everything had been turned upside down. The boredom and conservatism that should have been the enduring hallmarks of his old age had simply vanished. Instead his world had bifurcated and at any given point, he found himself being hurtled back and forth.

A heavenly body shifted and an unexpected breeze came his way, blowing his dark hair softly. Branches above him stretched and rustled. He licked his parched lips, dissolving the thorny skin around them as he removed the tie from around his neck. Folding it gently, he pocketed it. He looked up and saw a figure move across the window and his heart jumped. Before he crossed the pavement, he slid the platinum band off his finger. The joint of his finger gave little if any resistance.

By the time she heard the doorbell chime, Pooja had donned a saffron sari and a teardrop-shaped bindi on her forehead. From her ears hung buttery gold *jhumka*s – 24-carat as was essential to any self-respecting Indian – and matching bangles that clinked delicately to the graceful movement of her arms.

Now, she thought, smiling to herself, *the illusion is complete.*

Earlier, as she had stood in front of the mirror and pressed the convenient sticker bindi encrusted with a little glittering stone on her forehead, Pooja had drifted to her childhood. The red mark, which in ancient Aryan society was applied by the groom with his own blood on the bride's forehead as recognition of wedlock, about which countless poets had written couplets, now came in self-adhesive versions made of felt. Pooja used them not as much to propitiate the gods or mark her love for Rahul any more, but to make her look more exotic for the benefit of her wealthy clientele.

Pooja knew, of course, that her adornments wouldn't make or break her makeshift business but she also knew the great importance of appearance. It had been ingrained into her that the visage was a reflection of the inside. If anything on the outside looked amiss, something on the inside had to be, too. As a result, she'd seldom seen her mother without heavy kohl-lined eyes, the most refined silk saris, a proud bindi. Performing duties and suppressing maudlin emotions were unspoken rules in the Bhatt household.

It seemed to her like only yesterday when her mother had sat her down at the dressing table covered with the instruments that transformed her into a film star. Imported perfumes – of which a stubby yellow bottle called 'Kiku' was her mother's favourite – and lipsticks and powders of various shades lined the marbled Formica surface like a miniature city.

After applying a dot of Vaseline on Pooja's forehead, to that area between the eyebrows which is the seat of wisdom and the sixth chakra, Savita Bhatt would dip the tip of her middle finger into an ornamental container of red turmeric and press it onto that same spot. When Savita Bhatt moved aside, like a curtain glissading away from the mirror, Pooja saw herself, her eyes widened, and her heart rejoiced. She was suddenly grown-up, a worthy consort for her Krishna. Her young mind, still cocooned from the sexual intimacies of matrimony, fantasized about the purely romantic aspect of their courtship. One day, he would come and take her away and she would dance to the music of his flute like no other Gopika could.

Many years later, just after she had turned eighteen, Rahul became her dark god. Pooja had read somewhere that we all carry in our minds a subliminal model of our ideal partner. When we recognize similarities between our lover and the model we created, chemistry is sparked off. We fall in love. In the adoration Rahul inspired in his friends and the amorousness in the girls, in the charismatic way he flirted and compelled others to do his bidding without asking, and the way flocks of people followed him on sports fields and in social gatherings, Pooja recognized her Krishna. He may not have been dark – in fact, he had the much sought-after fair complexion – or known how to play a musical instrument, let alone a flute, but in the way he looked at her, as if clearly able to see her burning from within, he made her want to swoon, just as the Gopikas must have swooned to Krishna's melody.

The doorbell chimed again. Pooja took another look at herself. Gently, she touched her bindi with her index finger, conjuring Rahul. 'I'll be right there,' she called out and rushed to the kitchen to survey her preparations. In her haste, she almost tripped over Ajay's chrome dumb-bells in the hallway, which Rahul had also been using of late. She could not understand why Rahul was concerning himself with such things. No doubt he had always been athletic in school, but decades had fleeted by and he had let himself go; although she had noticed with at least some regret how age had begun to mould and soften their physiques, she had got used to the idea of them transforming together.

Pooja took a deep breath and opened the door.

'Namaste, Mrs Kapoor.'

'Hello, Greg. Come in, come in,' she said, stepping aside.

'Parmesh, please,' he said, a bit wounded, his hands still folded.

'Oh, yes, yes, Parmesh, of course. Sorry,' she said. 'Come in, please.'

Parmesh was garbed in faded blue jeans and a psychedelic white cotton kurta crammed with every imaginable Hindu iconography from Om to the dancing Nataraj. Around the teenager's neck hung a necklace of *rudraksha* beads, and his golden hair was pulled back into a ponytail so that through his pale bespectacled face, he looked like he was practically gaping at spirituality. He inhaled deeply, looking as if he had entered a temple.

Pooja led him into the kitchen where a box of baked Indian savouries – *papdis, dhokdas,* Indian trail mix and such – waited with an invoice taped to it. Next to it, a sealed container of the shrimp curry for Charlie Ackerman.

'It's always so nice here, Mrs Kapoor. So tranquil,' he said.

Oh, that's an easy enough effect to achieve, thought Pooja, *when nobody's ever around and sufficient perfumed cones and incenses have been burned.* 'Thank you, Parmesh.'

She found him looking adoringly at the bronze statue of baby Ganesha on the mantelpiece, crawling along as it looked over its plump shoulder, holding a ball of rice in his hand. *I swear,* she thought, *this boy feels more for our gods than my own son does!* The thought made her bristle, as if personal wealth had been squandered on strangers.

'And how are your parents?' Pooja asked perfunctorily. She had seen the Goldsteins just once, in passing at The Banyan when making a delivery herself. Parmesh had just started working there and his bedecked parents had dropped by to inspect the studio on their way to some fund-raiser. She could still see them, ill at ease, scanning the lobby with displeasure.

'Oh, you know. Okay, I guess,' he shrugged, eyeing the Bollywood cassettes she had lugged from Kenya, stacked neatly next to the stereo.

Pooja glanced at him.

'Business is booming. But in the end, what good's all that?'

Pooja felt a tinge of envy even as she was surprised by his candour. How old was this boy, nineteen or ninety? Why wasn't he out there dating girls, staying out late, doing the things that displeased parents but which were normal at his age, more like her own son?

'I'm sure they work very hard to make sure you have a good life.'

Parmesh managed a smile, appreciating her attempt at vindication.

She motioned him towards the food and he obediently sprang to action. 'I'll help you with the curry,' she said.

It was clear just from the hankering on Parmesh's face as he embraced the box that he wished he hadn't had to skip a lifetime to be reincarnated into a devout Hindu home like the one he was standing in. *If he only knew,* thought Pooja, shaking her head imperceptibly.

Greg, also known by his own preference as Parmesh ('creator'), was the gangly nineteen-year-old son of Valerie and Mark Goldstein, two of the most sought-after dermatologists in Beverly Hills. They were responsible for the looks of much of Hollywood royalty, many of whom appeared in affectionate poses with the couple in the gallery of pictures lining the walls of their home and office. Parmesh, of course, was not impressed.

While Parmesh's passion for Hinduism vexed his parents, it was painfully obvious to him that he had been a Hindu in his previous life, and that skin colour – like the assortment of luxury cars and palatial homes his parents flaunted – got in the way of real advancement. He longed to chuck it all away, move to an ashram in India where he could learn from a guru.

His parents had balked. Having failed to persuade him to see a psychiatrist – another crutch indicating spiritual bankruptcy to Parmesh – they tried a different approach. First, they confiscated his credit cards. 'You want to be more like *them?* Running around in goddamn Halloween sheets? Well, we'll see how lucky you feel when you can't buy those goddamned Lucky jeans any more!' Mark

Goldstein hollered, pocketing the plastic that Parmesh coolly surrendered, the loss of this perk only enabling his renunciation of the material world. 'Next he'll want to shave off his goddamn head.'

'Mark,' Valerie Goldstein cried. 'Don't give him any more ideas!'

They took away his car keys. 'From now on you can just stay in your goddamn room, channel Buddha from there,' Mark Goldstein suggested smugly.

So Parmesh, further exasperated that the Buddha, who was not even the focus of his worship, had become both an embodiment of and a scapegoat for eastern spirituality to his parents, retreated to his room and spent all his time chanting and meditating, learning rudimentary Hindi, driving his parents crazy. When necessary, he enthusiastically hopped onto public transport for hour-long bus commutes, searching for true camaraderie with the masses, some of whom couldn't even manage a polite nod and looked either resigned to their deprivation or stared out of the windows enviously at the bevy of gleaming cars.

Fearing that one of these days Parmesh might simply hike his way up to some peak on the Himalayas and not return home, his parents settled upon a compromise. First, with Valerie Goldstein sobbing theatrically, they reminded him that honouring one's parents was paramount in every faith, and that the pain he was inflicting on them was a sin even in the eyes of the many-limbed creatures he thought of as gods. He must apply to colleges, delay his plans of trekking to some ashram. In return, he could keep his job at The Banyan and the Goldsteins would also fund any charities of his choice. As if on cue, Valerie Goldstein presented him with a brochure on a Kolkata orphanage.

'Surely you're not going to be so goddamned selfish and think only of yourself? You do want to help them, don't you, Pa-Pa-Pruss –' Mark Goldstein looked at his wife. 'Oh, whatever the hell is it he likes to be called these days?'

She threw up her hands helplessly.

The pained faces of malnourished children in scraps of clothing with matted, ropy hair and distended bellies cried out at Parmesh. He was unpleasantly reminded – as the Goldsteins themselves must have been when they conjured this little ruse – of the time during the Ethiopian famine when he had seen such harrowing images on television and found it impossible to eat; it was only when they promised to mail out a reasonable donation to Unicef that he could muster up an appetite for the veal and foie gras he would also end up renouncing some years later out of his concern for animal welfare.

Lovers, Rahul learned, created an orbit around themselves.

Within this sphere, they could come together with a kind of desperate hunger and the outside world and everything that didn't begin or end with their colliding bodies were erased or committed to pure oblivion. It was like that when Rahul sprinted up the stairs and entered the apartment.

The first thing that changed about his world was the smell. Wisps of perfume, like the *anchal* of an elusive apsara that had just left the room danced around him. It was always the same intoxicating scent, of ripe, effusive tuberoses. Tapering candles stood guard over an immaculate feast, illuminating the dinner table directly across the entry. Atif stood next to it with a look of such yearning on his face that his breathing had become laboured and it seemed that any moment his legs would buckle. A week passed since they had last met and his resolve was finally draining out of him like blood from a punctured heart.

'Sorry I'm late,' said Rahul. 'I can't stay too long.'

Atif managed an unconvincing shrug, expecting as much. Such was the nature of their relationship. An apology expressed regret but could never serve as reassurance that it wouldn't happen again. Atif's knuckles were white from gripping the chair. 'How much time do you have?'

Rahul approached Atif, looking down at him. Atif winced as if from a sharp punch. Rahul touched the scar on his lip and leaned forward to kiss his forehead, feeling the breath escape Atif in a sigh. Atif's bare feet climbed onto Rahul's polished shoes and he buried his face in Rahul's chest, his arms encircling the strong girth of Rahul's waist. At that moment, if Rahul had been able to hear Atif's heart, he would have heard, 'Thank you God for bringing him to me. Now I can feel the air in my lungs. Now the merciless counting of time can stop. He's mine, every bit of him. She doesn't exist here.'

They began to kiss and Atif began his ascent on Rahul, twining onto him like a vine. Rahul lifted him completely off the ground, against gravity and the commitments that had kept them bound to the heavy earth.

Afterwards, when they lay on the floor, temporarily satiated and peaceful, Rahul looked down at the much younger boy pinned under his weight. Atif's eyes were closed and a faint smile played around his lips. Ecstatic. Rahul had never been with anyone who knew how to give himself so completely to a moment, to a feeling, to him. The abandon in Atif was nothing less than mystical.

With their bodies clinging together, a pleach of sticky limbs, Rahul finally felt the symphony of an integrated self, no matter how fleeting or costly the feeling. Sweat and semen sheathed them, but Rahul didn't move.

Atif opened his eyes and looked adoringly at Rahul. He ran his hand over Rahul's face and then, after licking the salt off his fingers, coasted both hands over the film of sweat covering Rahul's strong back. Rahul turned his face away from Atif's adulating gaze, the naked tenderness, and rested it upon his own shoulder, his mouth pressed against his bicep. His eyes fell on the bedside clock. He would be unable to stay for dinner.

Atif caught this, looking at the clock and then up at Rahul.

Rahul smiled, reached overhead and pulled the quilt off the bed with one hand. He deftly arranged it around their adjoined bodies, covering them in a soft cloud. They continued to lie in silence for a while. Then Atif said, a distant look in his eyes, 'I wish I knew what it was like to spend a whole night with you. To fall asleep next to you, know what you dream.' The tremor of an expected refusal played in his voice and it broke Rahul's heart.

'Rent *"The Exorcist"*', he offered flippantly, stroking Atif's hair.

Atif stopped himself from saying more but couldn't bring himself to respond. Rahul's body tensed; he looked away. Claustrophobia invaded him. He wanted to say: But you knew going in that it was going to be like this.

He tried to move but Atif grabbed his arm, keeping their bodies joined.

'I'm sorry. Please, stay.'

Rahul looked at that face, remembering the sudden and disturbing attraction he had felt when he first laid eyes on Atif across the aisles of books at the store where Atif worked. He'd had the distinct feeling, however improbable, that they had met before, actually talked, got to know each other in a way more than just casual; the smiting, drug-like titillation, the anxiety and euphoria of being reawakened. Those eyes, the pain in them.

But at moments like this, when he was reminded of how much others were being made to suffer because of his selfishness, of his disregard not only for his wife and lover, but also his son whom he could barely face, Rahul grew disgusted with himself.

'I know, I shouldn't say such things but . . . It's just that sometimes I wonder, you know? I wish we could go away, just the two of us. Couldn't you just say you were going away on a business trip or some . . . Shit. Here I go again.'

Rahul broke away from Atif's grasp, rolled off to the side. He looked up at the stucco ceiling. 'There are certain things that I just can't do, Atif. You know that. You knew that.'

Atif turned his face away from Rahul, tears stinging his eyes. Yes, he had always known it would be this way. From the very beginning, even though the idea of having a married man for a lover had seemed sexy, a fantasy, he had also known that the trajectory of an affair inevitably passed through broken promises, hurried, hushed phone conversations with abrupt hang-ups, private meetings, self-loathing, incomplete nights. If Atif had wanted to build a home with someone, to be seen in public with his lover, take off on vacations together, even just feel the moisture of someone's breath on his neck through the night, this was not the man. Why, Rahul could scarcely even use the word 'gay' and perhaps he didn't even think of them as such. He was just one of those men who was comfortable loving you as long as he wasn't labelled, thrust into a movement or asked to give up the very things and people that kept him from doing the things Atif was asking him to.

Rahul propped himself up on one arm and looked at Atif. He touched Atif's face and forced him to look back at him, feeling his pain as if he were being lacerated himself. He fingered the scar on Atif's lip gently, wishing he could have prevented whatever had caused it along with what he was now inflicting. 'You deserve more than this. Someone who can give you more, do all those things with you.'

'Such selfless talk is hardly going to help me to get over you,' Atif said, trying to pull himself together, to compensate for his lapse. 'Waking up with someone is overrated anyway. Who needs bad breath, crusty eyes? And you probably snore.' Atif wiped the tears from his eyes before they could spill onto his cheek. 'I made you a promise. I intend to keep it. If you should ever decide that you don't want to continue . . .'

'No, you won't understand.'

'Okay, so maybe I won't. Stay anyway.'

'But one day . . .'

Atif pulled Rahul's lips close to his own. 'Better to regret what we've done than what we won't allow ourselves to do.'

Pooja remained outside for a little while after Parmesh left, lingering in the dying light. She was grateful for the extra hours of sunlight that the season bestowed because an overwhelming sense of melancholy pervaded her at dusk. Summer was her favourite time of year. Its heat and radiance took her home to the clamminess of Mombasa and the soporific afternoons when she and Rahul's sister Kiran would lie down in her in-laws' verdant garden, looking up at impossibly blue skies and eating *khungu* fruit until their lips turned purple.

Suddenly she became aware of her neighbour Sonali Patel, jabbering away on the phone, shuttling between shocked exclamations and wicked laughter. Unlike Pooja,

Sonali came from the motherland, the city they now called Mumbai in an ineffectual revolt against India's imperial legacy. 'Stupid people!' Sonali had said, jabbing the air with her hand for emphasis. 'Without the British they would still be squatting over pit latrines and riding bullocks to work.'

O-ho! Really? She did what? Hai Ram! Did you see how much weight she's put on? My God, she's become a house. At this rate, she'll be taking in tenants soon . . . And she has the nerve to tell Sonali she thinks she's lost a lot of weight. Ha-ha! Oh, my jaan, *you are really too, too much!*

Sonali had the irritating habit of using her name in the third person, as if she were not the person herself but a mere vehicle for the larger-than-life persona residing within.

Not too long ago, over a cup of masala chai at Pooja's, Sonali had brandished a copy of *Cosmopolitan* and excitedly explained the reason for Pooja's melancholia as being menopause. 'Hormone therapy, darling,' she had touted. 'It's the way to go these days, don't you know?' When Pooja pointed out that unlike Sonali, she wasn't 'quite up there' Sonali had wrinkled her nose and said, '*Hanh, hanh!* Fine! Do as you please then and don't eat my head when you become suicidal. Helping people has become such a crime these days I don't know why Sonali even tries! But what can one do? You know my heart – it's as big as the ocean. Sonali just can't bear it when others are suffering!' And then, without a moment to recover from her indignation, she glutted her face with cocktail-sized samosas with a clumsiness she abhorred in others.

As Pooja looked up at the pastel canvas of the sky, she tucked a wisp of hair behind her ear and said goodbye to Surya, imagining the plumes of colour as the dust the god's chariot kicked up as it receded into the heavens. The driveways were once again greeted with parked cars, homes were filled with the laughter and idle chatter of families over supper, and from where she stood on the porch, surrounded by the effusive blooms of intoxicating jasmine and roses, she could see the park at the end of the cul de sac, now brightly lit with floodlights. Little children in their sports attire were running around and although she was so far away, in her mind, she could hear their laughter, their innocence and abandon. This was where, in her loneliness, Pooja often found some solace, in the indistinct, anonymous sounds of life in the homes of her neighbours.

The blocks leading up to the park were lined with jacaranda trees in full bloom. Every now and then a slight breeze would cause the faintly fragrant lavender-coloured flowers to cascade from the tree's canopy and carpet the street. Come winter, she thought sadly, their purple rain would be depleted and the white star-shaped blooms of jasmine would wilt and take their fragrance with them. Night blanketed the sky but there was not a single star to be found. She went back into the sleeping house where the CD player shuffled and Ali Akbar Khan's poignant sarod fell upon it like a veil.

Loneliness ensconced Pooja. Minutes began to stretch like a roadway, uncoiling, driving the destination further from reach. The clatter of dishes, the rambunctious chatter of dinner conversation echoed from somewhere. Both father and son had found whole universes that took of all their time and none of hers. Their world had expanded, opened up. Hers had shrunk, reduced to the space within the boundaries of her home.

She cleared off Parmesh's glass of *nimbu pani* from the coffee table. There, in the stillness that had started to stifle her of late and remind her more and more of the home she had left behind, Pooja thought of Parmesh some more. Why, when the West had seduced even her own people, was he so lost to his own culture? Where her own people had whored out their gods, Americans were ready to renounce their luxuries, shave their heads, bang cymbals and accost people with portable Gitas.

These days, she thought sadly, nothing was sacrosanct, least of all our religion. We'd consigned our divinity to commerce. The same deities at whose altars millions of us still performed *puja,* to whom we implored for divine intervention, could also be found silk-screened onto vibrant stretch T-shirts and standing guard on toilet seat covers where we defecated. Laxmi, goddess of prosperity, love and beauty was no longer just in temples but could also be found blooming out of her lotus over our piss and shit. And Radha and Krishna were not just holding court in her altar but also stuck in convoluted poses over cans of Kama Sutra paraphernalia holding flavoured massage oils and clusters of feathers to tickle one another with.

Such a passion kit had been presented to Sonali at her birthday party. Everyone had oohed and aahed, but Pooja had just sat there with flushed cheeks. She tried to join in the bawdy laughter of the group but all she could think of was: Is this what it would take to reignite desire in Rahul – a stupid pail of toys? She could only imagine what Rahul's face would look like if she waited up for him under the covers one night, armed with a feather brush in one hand and chocolate-flavoured massage oil in another.

Pooja washed out the glass by hand, towel-dried it and returned it into a maple cabinet above the sink. Then she went to the living room and switched on a lamp before settling on the sofa to flip through the latest issue of *India Currents.* But tonight the personal essays, celebrity interviews and regional recipes didn't grab her. She tossed the magazine aside and leaned back into the sofa, looking up at the impassive ceiling. Everything seemed to be turning upside down, she thought, clicking her tongue. Perhaps this is what Charlie, who had travelled throughout

India and lived in an ashram in Pune, had meant when he had talked about the bartering of cultures and the arch of progress.

During one of their brief discourses at The Banyan, inspired when Greg had excitedly announced that he wanted to be called Parmesh, the store owner, with a youthful twinkle in his eyes for Pooja, had explained his theory: we were fatigued by what was culturally inherent.

Pooja, standing on the other side of the glass cabinet in which Charlie was displaying her baked goods, had looked at him inquiringly, and he had continued, 'Listen, love, we are all facing the exact opposite set of problems, don't you see? The East – you Indians, for that matter – has exhausted all methods of introversion. Yoga, fasting, meditation, all that, are no longer able to produce the same effect any more because the Eastern mind is now hungry for extroversion. It has mastered, gone – as far as it possibly can – on its spiritual journey, and to complete itself, it now needs the opposite.'

'Like what, Charlie? MTV?' she asked, wrinkling her nose.

'Modernity,' he said. 'Technology. By contrast, the West – all of us – has been practically desiccated by it. So now, we are hungry to learn about the soul. In order for us to feel complete, we now need less of technology and more of what you have to offer. The pendulum, love, has swung.' And then he laughed boisterously, and pointing in Parmesh's direction, said: 'That one's pendulum, however, might have shifted a little too far.'

As she surveyed the frozen house, she longed to be embraced by the warmth of her mother's puja room, to hear the clashing of little cymbals and hear her sing '*Jaago Mohan pyaare*' (which being a dedication to Krishna, Savita Bhatt only sang to pacify little Pooja). Her ears ached for her father's harping on the importance of being a progressive Indian and the pitfalls of perceiving religion simplistically; she missed Rahul's elder sister Kiran, their carefree days at school and their highly strung best friend 'Rotal Rukhsana' with her unpredictable crying spells.

Although Pooja knew that talking with her family back home would exacerbate her sense of isolation, she decided to call them anyway. From her purse, she fished out a visiting card that had been endorsed by a popular Bollywood film star. Various poses of him with generously moussed hair, tight clothes, and a penetrating gaze covered the little piece of plastic, making it appear as if the card was to serve as a beeline to the star himself. In the card's commercial which ran incessantly on the Indian satellite show, he had, in between flexing his formidable muscles, enthusiastically endorsed the visiting card and expressed how indispensably it had served him every time he was on tour and had to call his family back home. Although Pooja had immediately made a mental note to try that particular brand the next time, Rahul had scoffed, 'Now why the hell does this buffoon need a visiting card with the crores he makes on every film?'

'To buy more steroids,' Ajay said.

'Just look who's talking. I sense jealousy,' said Rahul.

'Or maybe another thumb for the freak.'

'Ajay,' Pooja cried. 'How can you be so mean? I didn't raise you to make fun of people's misfortune.' It was common knowledge that this heart-throb of millions had an extra thumb on his right hand, which even Pooja herself had tried to spot religiously in his films. But he always danced too fast and gesticulated with the other hand and it wasn't an easy task.

'Misfortune? Mom, most people in India don't have the limbs God gave them. He's got an extra thumb and money to boot. How's that any kind of misfortune? And by the way, Pop, I don't use any of that steroid crap, okay?' He flexed his arm proudly and knocked at the bicep with his fist. 'All one hundred per cent natural.'

'I don't know why you bother with those visiting cards, Poo, they're a nuisance. Just dial direct.'

'Yes, I know money grows on trees, so father and son can be as wasteful as they like. Somebody around here has to act responsibly.'

Their voices faded like spirits from the room and the walls withdrew from her. Pooja turned to the phone and punched in the number from the back of the card. When it asked for a pin code, she found she was unable to read the last fading digit and took a chance. The automated voice informed her that it was incorrect. Pooja tried again, this time experimenting with a different last digit. It worked and she was notified of the nine minutes left for redemption. Pooja balked. How was this possible? The card was good for at least forty minutes and so far she had used only ten. There must be a mistake. Pooja hung up the phone and looked at the card. The Bollywood star flashed his most winsome smile, promising much gratification.

She tried again but couldn't remember the correct pin code. Was it one at the end? Seven? She tried seven and it worked. This time the robotic voice told her she had six minutes left, upsetting her even more, but she held on, the vacuum of distance in her ear. Minutes went by and nothing. Mombasa seemed not only at the other end of the world, but in another realm. Pooja hung up, dialled again, waited, but this time she was informed that the balance was insufficient to complete the call. She slammed the phone down and threw the card with all her might but it fluttered weightlessly and fell rebelliously close to her feet, face up. The Bollywood star looked up at her, flashing his dimpled, impossibly pearly smile. Pooja broke down crying.

The rituals incumbent on infidelity are myriad.

After partaking in the forbidden, there are, most elementarily, the hours that must be accounted for with excuses of late client dinners, unexpected senior management meetings and overdue financials reports. The appearance has to be affected too, to attest to those hours spent in the drudgery of an unrewarding career instead of clandestinely in the throes of passion. One must wash but with water only since using a strange bar of soap would be tantamount to putting someone else's perfume on your body. Never scour oneself so clean as to look rejuvenated, but just enough to rinse off the residue of sex. Brush and tousle the hair, and then, drawing the knot of the tie just a few inches short of a neck that was as a rule deprived of rapturous bites, try and embody a state of industrial toil. Finally, most crucially, there is the attitudinal fix – guilt must never be overcompensated for with sudden, cloying attention to the deceived or, on the other hand, hostility for feeling compelled to do so. The skill in being unfaithful was ultimately about balance.

Rahul, having performed the rituals of infidelity, headed back to that place he still called home. The drive back through Santa Monica, now cleared of the claustrophobia of traffic, of denizens desperately manoeuvring their way through the city's clogged arteries in their glittering sarcophaguses, became the meditative part of Rahul's life. Unless he took the freeway back to Venice – there was no accounting for traffic when it came to the 405 – Rahul could enjoy the drive back through side streets and make it home in less than twenty minutes. A savvy Angeleno, he had pored over maps, dared to experiment and knew that there were always easier ways to get somewhere if you were prepared to give up the comfort of familiar routes.

Tonight, his mind travelled back to when it all began, just a couple of days short of Pooja's thirty-ninth birthday.

The irony was that she had inadvertently created the circumstances for them to meet. The warm wind blew through his thick dark hair as he leaned against his hand, his elbow resting on the open window, instantly wafting him back to Elton's Bookstore in Brentwood.

Rahul had ventured into the independent bookstore at Pooja's request, to buy a costly compendium of world cuisine books, an accompaniment to the bottle of Chanel No. 5 for her birthday present. Pooja, as was typical of her, was always rooting for the underdog, and in this case preferred spending her money at smaller privately owned businesses that she was sure were struggling against corporations. The formidably large cookbook which he knew Pooja neither needed nor would use (she cooked more from instinct than recipes) incorporated global award-winning recipes by notable chefs who he was biased to think couldn't awaken half the taste buds Pooja's cooking could.

They had been married for nineteen years and had been living chastely for at least the last seven. Rahul was aware that this abstinence was not by Pooja's preference but his own lack of sexual desire for her. On the rare occasions that she was able to overcome the awkwardness and tried to initiate any intimacy between them, Rahul tactfully dodged it. The fires of sexual desire got doused; a marriage inevitably turned more fraternal in the end, he tried to reason to himself.

Rahul found the bookstore, laid out in a series of wings named after literary geniuses, each intended to house a set of subject matters. But despite its best efforts, Elton's was a jumble, a dusty amalgam of tables, shelves and piles of books. So Napoleon could easily be found wedged between travel guides on Egypt, and a French cookbook simmered under a pile of Marianne Williamson's teachings on miraculous shifts of perception. None of this, however, could override the immense passion for books that was apparent in the conversation among the booksellers and tea-sipping customers at Elton's.

He took advantage of the coffee bar hissing away frothy coffee concoctions and grabbed a strong espresso that he loaded with sugar. He made his way through the maze and found himself in the courtyard, under a fecund tree that was being decorated with lights for some kind of literary event.

'Cookbooks?' He looked up and asked the worker who had climbed up the tree and was garlanding its branches with lights. 'For my wife. Which building?'

The teenage boy, clad only in jeans and a flimsy T-shirt, pointed to Shakespeare's home in the west wing. Once inside and closed in by books, Rahul looked around for a trash can but couldn't find one. He felt the urge to leave the cup on a pile of books but carried it to the counter. Save for the one lady who was perusing an oversized Taschen, Shakespeare's domain remained empty. *Nobody reads anymore,* he thought, remembering back to when he himself preferred to dive into non-fiction or a Henry Miller novel rather than HBO. Reading, like fine dining had become the casualty in a city that demanded astounding commutes. Nobody had patience to spare once the city was done with you.

Albinoni's 'Adagio in G Minor', one of the few classical pieces that Rahul recognized and which, from then on, he would forever associate with Atif, hung in the air. He approached the counter where a Goth salesgirl was talking intensely on the phone. She had short and spiky ink-black hair, pencil brows, a silver stud under her bottom lip. Seeing Rahul, she reluctantly ended her conversation.

Rahul told her what he was looking for and almost immediately spotted the set of pricey editions locked up in the display case behind her but the salesgirl, still in the grip of whatever conversation she was having, was unable to find the keys. He pictured someone like his own son at the other end of that call, remembering the time some American girl had shown up at his doorstep in tears over Ajay. His son had become quite the playboy and in a typically macho way this infused him with as much pride as it filled Pooja with disappointment.

She let out an unguarded expletive as she rummaged around the counter, in the process knocking over her cup. They both jumped back from the counter, Rahul still clutching his empty cup, the coffee splattering over the glass counter and soaking the fliers and magazines. He dabbed himself with the white monogrammed handkerchief that Pooja had given him and which he found stuffy but continued to carry in the inside pocket of his jacket to please her. The phone, which the salesgirl had probably kept blocked for hours, started ringing again. She ignored it, frantically throwing the soiled stuff off the counter.

Exasperated, Rahul abandoned his cup on a pile of books behind him, and inspecting his overcoat to make sure it was spared from coffee, turned around to walk away. That's when he heard that voice, gravelly like someone who had just awoken. Rahul turned around. A young Indian man was answering the phone while dispersing paper towels to clean the mess. He was so engrossed that he barely noticed Rahul, but Rahul, somewhat surprised at his timely appearance and finding strange comfort in the presence of another Indian, remained. He picked up his coffee cup again, barely looking at it, and exchanged his first glance with the man who seemed vaguely familiar.

Atif looked like he was in his twenties, athletic, and with a goatee which, in the political climate roused by 11 September, was definitely unwise. In many parts of the country, patriotism had taken a violent expression so that anyone who looked even remotely Middle Eastern was at risk. Many didn't know the difference between Hindu and Sikh or Muslim. Only last week Rahul had seen on CNN that a Sikh convenience store owner had been attacked because he had been mistaken for Muslim, and Rahul knew at least one Muslim co-worker who had shaved off his beard for fear of being targeted.

On Atif's upper left lip was a noticeable scar. *An accident? A fight?* Rahul wondered. Although he had never been to Elton's and had no recollection of ever meeting him, Rahul couldn't shake off the gnawing feeling that they knew each other. *Could he be one of Ajay's friends? A bank customer?* Rahul didn't even realize that he had been staring at him until Atif caught his gaze. Rahul turned away uncomfortably, deciding he would pay no further attention to him.

By the time Atif had replaced the phone, he had already covered the counter with yards of paper towels that had blotted up the coffee. The salesgirl, looking utterly helpless and confused, continued agonizing over the missing key. Atif, a bit embarrassed, smiled apologetically at Rahul and dived under the counter to look for it. When he came up again, he was holding the little silver key in his hand. The girl sighed theatrically.

'Why don't you to take a break, Becca?' Atif said to her. 'I'm here now.'

She thanked him with a hug and walked out, cellphone in tow, and Atif motioned for Rahul to give him the empty coffee cup, which he tossed in the waste-paper basket behind him. 'I'm really sorry about all this,' he said, and then looking at the key he was holding between his fingers, 'You were looking for . . .'

When Ajay walked into the house and found Pooja hunched over in tears, he pulled out the iPod headphones from his ears and rushed to her side. Under normal circumstances, Pooja would have rallied to pull herself together but this time she found herself unable to summon the strength that she had been able to depend on in far more turbulent occasions.

Ajay had never seen his mother so distraught. He huddled at her feet like he had when he was a child fishing for the toys she had playfully hidden within the folds of her sari. He looked up at her flushed face, the large, adoring eyes now smudged with kohl and swimming in tears, and asked, 'Mom, what happened?'

But his concern made her cry harder and she laid her face on his strong shoulder, finding it easier to let everything wash through her. In her son's distress, she found her own seeping away because finally someone was taking notice. She held on to him tightly, remembering the baby whose lower lip she tickled with her nipple to get his mouth to open wide, the little boy who nestled his head in her bosom before he could fall sound asleep. She longed to give herself to him in the same way again but of course, now he was a grown-up man and his need for her had changed.

'Mom, what happened? Speak to me. Why are you crying?'

Pooja shook her head, wiped her tears with her *chunni*. 'I don't know. It's nothing.'

'You don't know? Tell me,' he implored, pushing the dishevelled hair back from her face.

'Nothing. Nothing,' she said.

In the background, the carousel shuffled to another CD and an incongruous *masala* song started playing. Good old Asha Bhonsle made the whole situation feel quite ludicrous with her lustful *'Ye hai reshmi zulfo ka andhera'* so that suddenly Pooja started to feel foolish. Moments of sentimentality, she realized, didn't always find an appropriate score in real life. 'I don't know what came over me, *beta*,' she said with a dismissive wave of her hand. '*Bas*, let it go. It's nothing.' She grabbed the remote control and pointing it at the stereo killed off the siren.

'But it can't be nothing if you're crying,' he said. 'Did something happen with Papa? Where is he?'

Her eyes dropped and for a moment, it looked like she might start crying again. She carefully placed the remote control on the side.

'Mom?'

'Your father's busy. He's working. Always working, what else?' she sounded more bitter than she had intended to and it didn't go unnoticed by him.

He consulted the bulky diver's watch on his wrist; it was past seven-thirty. 'Working at this time?'

'Your father works very hard,' she said, tucking an errant wisp of hair behind her ear and slowly pulling herself together. 'How else are we going to put you through college? With my samosas? Besides, you're one to talk,' and she pinched his ear playfully as he looked away guiltily. 'He's just a workaholic, you know that.'

'Yeah, I guess that's all he cares about any more,' he said, some of his own sadness creeping in.

'Well, better workaholic than alcoholic, no?' she joked. Pooja's thoughts went quickly to Rahul's jovial father, Ravi Kapoor, who didn't have any reservations about taking nips of Black Label whiskey in the evenings. It was a wonder that given the liberal environment of his upbringing, Rahul never touched the stuff and had turned out as reserved as his father had been sprightly and expansive. 'Thank God, all of us have been spared from all those influences.'

'Mom, I've never seen you like this.'

What am I supposed to tell you? she wondered. *That I'm crying because of the phone card? Because Charlie's theories are coming alive under my own roof? Or because I miss your father?*

'It must be – what is it Sonali aunty keeps saying I have? Menopause,' she started laughing. 'Crazy woman.' Pooja noticed that she had sullied his neck and T-shirt with her crying and she quickly sprang to her feet, becoming her old self again. 'Oh, God. Just look what I've done now. Let me get something to wipe . . .'

'Mom, really, it's okay. It's only water. Just sit,' he said, grabbing her hand but it was too late. Pooja had closed up again.

'I won't be a moment,' she said and disappeared into the kitchen, relieved that the unexpected spasm of emotion had passed and that they wouldn't have to linger on it any longer. Just the fleeting moment of concern from her son had bolstered her so much that now she felt she could go on forever. 'You know what I made today?' she called out from the kitchen. 'Your favourite, well, it was your favourite when you were little. Channa masala with parathas.'

'Mom, you know I can't . . .'

'Yes, yes, I know all about your nutrition nonsense,' she said, returning with a moist hand towel. He rose to his feet and she smiled when she noticed how he was so much taller than she and that she had to reach up to him. 'I miss spending time with you, Ajay. You grew up so fast,' she said. 'Don't worry, I'll broil some chicken for you, nice and tasteless, just the way you like it, hanh.'

Two long insistent honks sounded in the driveway, and he glanced out through the living room window. 'It's Nicky,' he said. 'But I don't really have to go.'

She managed a smile. 'Nonsense. I'll be fine.'

'One sec,' he said, squeezing her hand with the towel and went out of the door.

Pooja walked over to the window and peeked out discreetly. She saw Ajay leaning into Nicky Cacioppo's shiny new jeep. Something in her stomach tightened. Like Ajay, Nicky was nineteen. Tall, imposingly built and covered with tattoos of the Virgin Mary and even the state of California, he was Ajay's closest friend from high school and gym partner. Although she had met him only a few times, more than once it had been under incriminating circumstances.

Once when another student had been beaten up by Nicky and because Ajay had also been present, the principal, Mr Flaherty, had demanded to see a parent; and another time, some weeks later when the same principal's car tyres had been slashed and obscenities spray-painted all over it, someone claimed to have witnessed Nicky and 'his partner-in-crime' in the act. Although the student had inexplicably changed his story in the end, Pooja had once again been summoned for a visit with Mr Flaherty. She had kept all this from Rahul. When it came to Ajay, she had found that she was able to handle things best by herself.

Pooja hadn't doubted Nicky Cacioppo's role in all this but like a typical parent, she doubted her own child was capable of such actions. In time, she refused to probe further, choosing instead to observe extra prayers for him, and Mr Flaherty's impassioned auguries about 'angel-faced Ajay' actually being a 'ticking time bomb' were dismissed from Pooja's mind, only to be revived at the ominous mention of Nicky Cacioppo's name once in a while.

She had tried to discourage Ajay from seeing too much of Nicky but was careful not to come across as domineering, aware that the one certain way of making young people rebel was to try and enforce absolute restrictions. She also suspected that in Rahul's absenteeism, something that seemed to have increased in the last year, Ajay must be thirsting for male camaraderie. Even the rare occasions of going to watch the Lakers together or just watching those noisy action DVDs at home had ceased now.

Pooja had read somewhere that there were some very specific psychological stages that a child went through on his journey to manhood. A son must negotiate the process of differentiating from his mother and she must be careful not to mollycoddle him. He had to stop seeing himself in her, develop a sense of his own identity, and eventually align with his father. She was saddened to think that while Ajay had successfully severed the umbilical cord, father and son had only managed to forge a distant affection for one another.

Even as she looked out at the street, Pooja stood next to Rahul at the edge of the Indian Ocean in Mombasa, his arm around her waist, contemplating their lives together in America; Rahul and she bent over little Ajay as he blew out the candles on a birthday cake – moments which now felt like they'd happened to somebody else. Pooja grew restless, wanted to ask Rahul if they could change things, go back. Slowly, what made her uncomfortable was growing familiar. *This is not the life I envisioned,* she thought. *This is not the family I want.* She backed away from the window.

The jeep roared away and Ajay jogged back in, throwing his hands up in the air. 'Okay, let's bust out that channa masala.'

'Really? Because if you'd rather not . . .' she found herself saying.

'Mom,' he said, walking up to her and putting a hand on her shoulder. 'I want to, okay?'

'Okay,' she said, beaming. 'Just the way you used to like it then, with lots of coriander.'

While she busied herself in the kitchen, he sat on the sofa and took the small statue of cherubic Ganesha, frozen in his crawl, from the coffee table and into the palm of his hand. His finger ran over the god's rotund belly, coiling trunk and broken tusk.

'I would rather you didn't mention anything to your father. I really don't want to worry him,' she said from the kitchen. 'Ajay?'

'Yeah, Mom.'

She glanced out at him, found him communing with the elephant god. 'You know, when you were little, you loved to hear the story of Ganesha over and over again. Just couldn't get enough of it. Sometimes, I'd trick you into eating all your food by telling you the same story.' Little Ajay, looking up at her with his wondrous brown eyes under a fringe of soft brown hair, crawled through her mind's eye. 'Do you remember?'

Ajay gave a short laugh, a bit embarrassed but basking in the attention.

She came out of the kitchen with place mats, napkins and utensils and started laying out the dinner table. 'I used to call you my little Ganesh. I think if your grandmother hadn't insisted on calling you Ajay or Arjun, you would have been called Ganesh only.'

'Which grandma?'

She looked up at him, realizing that she had unwittingly opened a door into the past. 'Your father's mother,' she said, hurrying back into the kitchen.

Ajay put Ganesha back on the table and walked over to the kitchen so he could see her. He stood in the doorjamb, watching her spoon out the golden curry onto a plate, her agitation palpable. 'I'm sorry, but it may be a little salty for you. I can add some lime juice.'

'You never want to talk about them.'

'Whatever do you mean, beta?' she said, her eyes fixed on the cilantro she was sprinkling over the hillock of chickpea beans.

'Papa's parents. We never talk about them. No pictures, nothing.'

'But what's there to talk about? You weren't even born when they passed away.'

Pooja removed parathas glistening with a film of clarified butter from the skillet, and stacked them on another plate. Finally, she looked up at him. He was not going to be discouraged. Her lips parted but there were no words. How do you describe to your son the horrors of watching your family degraded and annihilated? How to recall the hell without being dragged back into it, without robbing him off his innocence? Even now, she could hear the screams, see their faces, smell the charnel. No, it was better this way. Better he grew up untouched by the evil she had seen, just another normal, American boy.

'There was just a terrible accident, Ajay,' she said, blinking back tears. 'You already know this.'

Ajay saw the tears in her eyes, how much she missed them and the pain it was causing her. He let it go. As usual, it was a closed subject. His father never spoke much to begin with but when it came to the past, he was a stone, as if nothing existed before Ajay was born, and his mother was complicit in this. As a child Ajay had been inquisitive, often asking about their lives in Kenya: What was it like growing up there? How did their family end up in Kenya in the first place? How did they come to America? What had been the names of his grandparents and the aunt who had died with them in this tragedy? When he persisted, the answers were always without elaboration, tinged with discomfort. 'Kiran and your Mum were best friends in school,' or 'We were the lucky ones, won the lottery.' As he had grown older, Ajay had stopped asking completely, the curiosity dissipating with the distraction of his own life.

Holding a plate overflowing with steaming food in each

hand, Pooja paused by him on the way to the dining room. 'Your father – we,' she added almost as an afterthought, 'don't think it does much good to linger in the past, Ajay. The future – now that is much more important.'

After Rahul left, Atif gathered the soiled sheets to him with the care and reverence reserved for the truly sacred. He buried his face in the soft cotton, breathed in the mingled smell of sweat, semen and sticky lubricant, trying to relive the hours, to prove that they had actually been together. The human body shed so many skin cells every moment that in a few years a person could shed his entire body weight in them. Atif knew that so much of Rahul was still there, contained in those sheets.

After carefully rolling them up and depositing them into a hamper, he paused to look at himself in the mirror above the bathroom sink. There, coalesced with the thatch of hair on his stomach, he found Rahul's crusted semen. As he fingered the ashen remains of their lovemaking, bits of it flaking from his touch, he wondered if Rahul's wife held the same awe for her husband's seed. If she too, had tasted it on her tongue, touched it – not with repulsion but with wonder – and let it tarry upon her skin until it had altered into this. *How can any woman who has lived with a man, who has loved him for so long not know? Was deception just this simple?*

Through the paper-thin walls, he could hear his neighbour, Nona Nguyen, rummaging through her medicine chest as she prepared for yet another blind date through Matchmaker.com, to which she had become addicted. To date, Nona had been on some one hundred and thirty futile dates; she painstakingly compiled the entire correspondence – even the shortest liaison qualifying for some fifty emails – in hulking files alphabetized by the failed candidates' first names. Someday, she hoped to release them as a self-help book for serial daters who could learn from her experience.

Nona was Vietnamese, in her thirties (she was never specific), possessed a startling talent for make-up and freely told everyone within fifteen minutes that she had herpes. 'Don't use that glass, I have herpes! Oh, I'd better not kiss you because, you know, I have herpes. But then it's quite common, so you probably already have it too, right?' The other story she liked to tell, a bit more hesitantly, was how she remembered being picked up off the roof of the consulate building in Saigon by the US troopers, the smell of burning napalm and death all around her.

Atif wanted to bask in the afterglow. So he tried to be quiet, so that they wouldn't have to speak, since mere presence in the bathroom was enough to be alerted of goings-on on the other side. He would hear from her soon enough, if not at the end of the night, then the first thing tomorrow. She'd call out his name, announcing her arrival long before she got to his door. He expected her to come in slumping, looking as dowdy in her flannel pajamas as she had looked glamorous the night before in the shocking red mini and knee-high leather boots, without the contact lenses and squinting through bottle-thick glasses, to invade him with her litany on the shortage of quality, available men in 'this fucking plastic city'. She just might pop in to get a gay man's fashion take before unleashing herself on her next victim. Or maybe she had rear-ended yet another car. Nona Nguyen had rammed into more cars than anyone Atif knew and had totalled at least two of them, one being her own, because she was rummaging for the cellphone in her purse.

She had frequently and vehemently advised him against

Rahul. 'Atisha,' she was fond of feminizing his name, 'He's a married man, for Chrissake! What's wrong with you? I mean, wake up and smell the chai, baby. What do you think? He's going to leave his wife for you? You think he's going to jump out of the closet he's been hiding in all his life and – tah-dah! – run out to West Hollywood with you? Come on.' When he explained that he wasn't interested in all that any more, she said, 'Well, then take yoga, join a gym – hey, what about some kind of support group, you know, for people recovering from something? Those places must be perfect for meeting needy guys who've done it all and just want to fall in love.'

'Look, I don't want him to leave anyone, okay? I don't even want him to come out of any goddamned closet. In fact, I think I prefer it this way. I've been with single, gay men, trust me, they're overrated.'

'That's the problem,' she said, blinking vigorously like she was rapidly losing sight, 'you're a straight-hag. What you need to do is to put yourself out there, honey. In the whole of Weho, there's got to be at least one perfect guy for you.'

But he had already been out there – foraged through its nightclubs packed with impeccably sculpted bodies that offered little more than façades, spun like a drunken dervish in dank rooms marinating in sex only to feel lonelier and debased in the morning with a lice-picking comb at his crotch; grown elated about a new prospect only to feel bitter because they were either sexually incompatible with each other (exclusive top or bottom) or not mutually interested.

Without the enterprise of marriage and children, which kept even unfulfilled couples hanging on in tenuous relationships, there was also a discriminating consumer mentality so that gay men were always shopping for a new love, sampling new merchandise, finding it hard to commit or settle, refusing to grow up. Most of the gay couples that had made a go of it had, within a few years, evolved into an 'open relationship' where a third was brought in to fan sexual desire, or an understanding was reached about turning a blind eye to one-night stands.

Atif had ceased confiding and defending his point of view. Slowly he gave in to a hermetic lifestyle, growing tired of listening to how selfish Rahul was being, how he wanted to have his cake and eat it too, how he should be concerned about that poor woman; how, if he had no guilt about cheating on her, he would do the same to Atif as well. He knew better than to explain the complexity of love with commonsense.

The damned fools would never understand that love – that fatalistic, inexplicable attraction between two people – was not just the virtuous, purgative ingredient of some hackneyed fairy tale; love was savage, unrelenting. Not something clean or tidy. It trampled on logic. Passionate, archetypal love, the kind that had inspired great art and endured through time, never came in decorous, predictable packages. It was never free of the kind of tribulation that tested the mettle of one's very existence, and it inevitably became the target of contempt by those people who didn't possess either the imagination or the strength for its mysteries.

Pooja sat by Ajay, watching him eat the curried garbanzos with delight. As he parcelled little mouthfuls wrapped in the flaky leavened bread into his mouth, she practically felt her own stomach thank her. She wanted to hold him, but she knew that now this kind of affectionate display would embarrass him. She settled instead for the dimpled smiles he gave her and in which she could clearly see Rahul, making her miss him even more.

Children, she knew, were supposed to be physical and spiritual extensions of their parents. Sometimes though, save for a physical trait here and there, they turned out mystifyingly different, perhaps taking qualities from past generations lost to cognition. She herself had been no exception, famous in her father's eyes for what he saw as her peculiar eating habits and love for Krishna.

She looked tenderly at Ajay's shaved forearm where a burn mark resembling South America had been etched. He had been only three when it happened but she remembered it as if it was only yesterday. Then Rahul and Pooja had lived in a little two-bedroom apartment on Washington Boulevard in Culver City. One evening, Pooja realized she had forgotten to pick up black mustard seeds for the potato curry she was making for supper. Although Rahul offered to dash to the neighbourhood supermarket and pick some up, Pooja had insisted on the black variety that could only be found at Indian stores, and she'd driven to one nearby, leaving Rahul to give Ajay his milk bottle.

When she returned, barely fifteen minutes later, Pooja heard Ajay's painful wailing even before she had entered the apartment on the second floor. She rushed up, abandoning the sack of groceries on the stairs, its contents spilling out. She blasted in to find Ajay sitting in a puddle of the steaming milk from the uncapped bottle, Rahul helplessly trying to dab Ajay's scalded arm. They rushed to the emergency room just a few miles away but feeling like it was across the world, Pooja pacifying Ajay in her arms; but the fight between them – a rare occurrence – had been terrible.

'You're so self-absorbed!' she cried. 'How could you let this happen to him? How could you endanger our child's life? Can't you watch him for five minutes?'

'Are you insane? Do you think I did this on purpose?' Rahul, while regretful, grew equally incensed. 'Why are you talking this way?'

'Why? Why? Look what you've done to him! Look!' she said over Ajay's crying, 'And all because you couldn't get your eyes of that bloody television set!'

At the end of the night, after a bandaged Ajay had been put to bed and the chaos had subsided, Pooja sat down next to a depressed Rahul at the dinner table. She laid her head against his chest, broke down crying in regret over her furor. He put his arms around her, understanding of the maternal instinct, but she had hurt him. The damage had been done.

'Don't you think I love him just as much?' he asked.

She didn't answer because in her heart, she suspected nobody could love Ajay more than she did. There were times when she felt jealous when she saw Ajay bubble up with laughter when Rahul tickled his stomach or kissed and licked Ajay's nose, as if she was competing for Ajay's attention with his father. The love Pooja felt for her son, the euphoria she experienced every time Ajay tugged at her breast or felt his hands and feet clamber over her lifted all her despair over leaving her family behind, and she felt as if she wanted to absorb him back into her where there would be no separation.

In time, the scar had become a part of Ajay much like the broken tusk of Ganesha, but for Pooja it signified much more. It was proof that she was indispensable to Ajay, that he could only truly be safe with her.

'Mom,' Ajay's voice brought her into the present. 'So tell me. Tell me the story.'

'Story?'

'You know, about Ganesha.'

'Oh, you don't really want to hear it,' she waved her hand dismissively. 'Do you?'

He gave an approving grunt, continued relishing the meal.

'Well, you know when Shiva, in his anger, had –'

'No, no,' Ajay said, shaking his finger. 'From the very beginning, Mom. The beginning.'

'Okay, okay. *Vinayaka,*' she said, smiling and touching his hair. 'Vinayaka because he was born without the help of a father. Parvati, the beautiful, fair daughter of Himavat, the god of the mountain, created Ganesha by rubbing herself with scented oil and from the dirt of her body. She created him because, you know, when Shiva went away for such long periods of time in his quest for enlightenment – men,' she said, rolling her eyes. 'She became so lonely in his absence. And sometimes when he returned, he refused to recognize her space, expecting things to remain just as they were. You know this is where you would ask, "But, Mom, why did he leave her there? Why couldn't they go together?" And I'd say, "Because the path to enlightenment, to find out who you truly are, has to be taken alone."'

Ajay found himself drawn into the tale as if he was listening to it for the first time. He started eating more slowly, his eyes glued on the theater of her face.

'Ganesha was flawless. Big and strong, so handsome,' she said, her face now glowing, 'just like you. And Parvati gave him all kinds of precious ornaments and robes. She told him that he was created just for her. That he belonged to her and that from that day on, he would be her gatekeeper, protecting the honour of his mother from one and all. And Ganesha bowed to his mother, and taking a large stick in his hand, stood guard outside her door.'

Ajay's cellphone began ringing, piercing through them. He quickly unclipped it from his belt, and barely giving it a glance, pushed a button to silence it.

'Then one day,' she continued, 'Shiva returned from his long absence when Parvati was taking a bath with her handmaidens . . .'

Ajay moved his thick brows up and down mischievously and she gave him a playful slap on his arm.

'Naturally, Ganesha, who had been commanded not to let anyone in, barred Shiva's path with the stick. "Where are you going?" he asked. "No one can enter at this time without the permission of my mother." Shiva, now in a rage, asked Ganesha, "Do you know who I am, stupid one? I am none other than Shiva, the husband of Parvati. How dare you prevent me from entering my own house?" As he tried to force his way in, Ganesha struck him and a fierce battle ensued. Some say Ganesha single-handedly defeated entire armies of gods. Others say that it was a more private duel, just between father and son.

'In the end, Shiva prevailed by cutting off Ganesha's head. But when he saw Parvati, dumbstruck and grief-stricken, waves of affection and regret flooded Shiva. He asked his bull Nandi to bring him the head of an elephant, which he fixed on Ganesha's neck, bringing him back to life.' Here she remembered how little Ajay would trumpet around like an elephant, flap his hands like giant ears. 'Parvati looked on, her eyes full of tenderness. So, in a way, Shiva does eventually play a part in Ganesha's creation, you see? And from that point on, whenever Shiva went away, meditating or doing his dance of destruction on some part of earth, Parvati would spend her time dictating stories to Ganesha, who became a tireless scribe, the universe's first author. And at the end of it, she would kiss his broken tusk and stroke his broad, wrinkled forehead in appreciation.' Pooja's eyes, which had wandered across the room as she had narrated the story, returned to her son just as he polished off the meal. 'More?' She asked, pointing a manicured finger at his plate.

'No, no. No way,' he said, leaning back and patting his stomach.

'Maybe I should have extended the story.'

He laughed. 'No, really, Mom. I'm stuffed. I'm gonna' have to make up for this with another hour at the gym.'

'If you want to go, no need to worry about me, Ajay. I'll be fine.'

'Ah, it's alright. I'll just go tomorrow.'

'Really,' she said. 'Go. Go work out. I'm okay now.'

'You sure?' he said, studying her face intently.

'Very, very sure,' she replied, touching his.

'Okay, well, just an hour or so of cardio. Thanks, Mom.'

'I'll just clean up.' She pointed at his cellphone. 'It's probably going to explode if you don't turn it back on.'

Ajay rose to his feet, kissed her forehead. He sprinted up the stairs and disappeared into his room, where he changed into his gym clothes. She sat in her chair for a few minutes longer, culling a strange comfort in the sound of him moving through the now respiring house. Only a short time ago, she had sought solace from sounds of other peoples' lives but now her world had come alive again. She had bonded with her little Ajay again and he had wiped away her tears just as she had licked them off his cheeks when he was a baby, each tear a glistening, briny pearl.

Before leaving, he gave her another concerned look, the softness in him returning. She assured him that she was okay, reminded him not to mention it to his father. She cleared the table, loading the dishes into the dishwasher thinking of what he had said about her tears – 'It's only water.' She waited until she heard the sound of Ajay's red Mustang pull out of the driveway, and then, taking deep breaths, went up to their room and locked the door behind her, the gold bangles on her wrist clinking hauntingly in the air. *It's only water.*

Self-acceptance was a prerequisite to tolerance from others. Atif realized this early on when he moved to Los Angeles as a lonely teenager. Since God, in his malleability, was always used to justify oppression, Atif figured it was best to seek answers in the many works authored by Him.

Atif started with the Koran. Allah seemed contradictory and wily. Verse 4:16 said: 'If two men among you is guilty of lewdness, punish them both.' Yet in Verse 76:19 God promised: 'And round about them will serve boys of perpetual freshness: if thou seest them, thou wouldst think them scattered pearls.' So it was prohibited on earth, but Muslims could look forward to homosexuality in Paradise. The word of Allah made him more confused than he already was.

In a dusty book in the Eastern Studies section in his college library in Burbank, Atif found a story from the *Shiva Purana* in which Agni, the same fire-god that consecrated marriages, was summoned to swallow the scalding semen of the god Shiva so that the warrior-god Kartikeya could be born to slay a demon. The epic Hindu tale failed to mention why the all-powerful deity couldn't simply impregnate a woman or just take care of the nuisance himself.

So he ventured further, into testaments new and old, and found that the Old Testament vehemently condemned homosexuality, while Christ never even bothered to mention it, too busy making wine out of water when not walking on it. According to the Kabbalah it was a disease, much like chickenpox or leprosy, which could be cured. Only in Sufism and Hinduism did Atif find an unconditional acceptance of same-sex love, in its mythic tales and stirring poems, although he was aware that both Muslims and Hindus were notorious for their intolerance of it.

Legendary mystics like Jelaluddin Rumi and Farid ud-Din Attar had written evocatively about the love between two men – the ecstasy in their melding, the scorn and outrage it incited amongst the people, and the superhuman lengths to which such lovers went to keep their love alive. The tales of Shiva and Agni, of Shiva and Vishnu, Krishna and Arjuna, again validated Atif. He resented how believers ignored these stories or tried to homogenize them into some kind of convenient metaphor for loving God.

To Atif, there was nothing ambiguous about who was crying out for whom, whether the soul to God or the lover to the beloved. Rumi's verses were addressed to Shams, the wandering mystic who introduced him to Sufi mysticism and with whom he lived for several years, as others were to God Himself. No reason to confuse the two. It was people's inability to digest such relationships that compelled them to unnecessary interpretation. It seemed to Atif that in doing so, they had completely missed the point: that loving another person, regardless of his sex, was a way of loving God after all. The divine is neither man nor woman, neither good nor bad, so why should the heart make that distinction in loving?

More than ten years later, when he brought this up to Rahul, he received a mystified look, as if to say: who manufactured this fiction? I've never heard of any such thing. Atif, proud of his research, had presented him with books, some out of print, lovingly covered in clear Mylar dust jackets, to prove his point. Rahul groaned. 'Oh, Atif, all that ancient stuff, nobody reads it. The Gita, the Ramayana, the Mahabharata – well, okay, maybe not that last one – too much strife. Anyway, that's what they all read. All this other strange stuff, Puranas this and Puranas that, nobody cares about them.'

'You know what's so damn frustrating?' Atif countered. 'That you have one of the oldest, most progressive religions in the world. But all anyone ever wants to focus on is the same old sanctimonious crap.'

Rahul smiled. 'Isn't that how all religions are? People

want a standard, uncomplicated belief system, Atif. They're not trying to change the world or even accept it. They just want to feel right about how they think.'

This was tragic but true, thought Atif. *Ultimately, if you looked hard enough, you could always find something to support your claim. In the end there was no right or wrong. Only interpretation.*

Just as there weren't words enough in the world to help him justify his sexuality to his own parents, none of Rumi's yearnings or Allah's contradictory promises could help him here.

Standing naked against the sink while gently peeling Rahul's semen from his chest, he saw his father's face and thought, *so this is what you disowned me for, the right to love another man. You'd have preferred me dropping mine into the womb of an unsuspecting woman, my eyes shut to keep from seeing her face while thinking of another man.* Even after six years, it hurt him to think that in the eyes of his parents, his aberration had been so severe, so monstrous, that it had not warranted a proper conversation. He could not understand, no matter how hard he wrestled with it, how any relationship, most of all a paternal one, could be dissolved with so little resistance.

His mother's trembling face during their last cruelly brief conversation played in his mind and a chill spread over his body. Would he ever see them again? He put his arms around himself, closed his eyes to the tears. Anger and hurt bubbled within him and as his head fell forward, he felt himself weakening and wanting to call Mumbai so that he could hear his mother's voice. But he knew he was not welcome any more, that even that rare chat with her could only take place when his father wasn't around.

It had all started with Hiten Khanna who had come from Mumbai to study business at USC. The son of wealthy parents who owned a textile manufacturing company, Hiten came from a different social class and knew Atif only distantly back home. He came armed with the confidence and money that Atif lacked. Spoiled and condescending, they were nothing alike, yet in a strange country, surrounded by the biases of another culture, they had forged a convenient friendship. Equipped with the fake ID cards Hiten had secured for them, they even went to their first gay club in West Hollywood together.

Hiten burned quickly. Spending his entire tuition on partying, drugs and blonde, blue-eyed escorts, he eventually dropped out of college. His parents cut off his allowance and Hiten found it beneath him to find a regular job to support his lifestyle. So he returned to Mumbai to flaunt his sexuality and hang out with connected, closeted gays in Bollywood and the fashion industry. It was nothing new. Hiten's parents blamed Atif for 'making him gay'. Atif knew Hiten's parents had to find a culprit because those who loved someone found it easier to impute his vices to others, preferably someone unrelated so that it didn't seem remotely atavistic.

Talk spread like wildfire. Everywhere the Khannas went they were either questioned about their scandalous son, now a staple of the 'Page Three' culture, or found the need to proffer an explanation, and Atif became the culprit. 'That Rahman boy, he's the one! He's responsible for infecting our poor little son,' Sheila Khanna dispensed promptly from the vault of tears she carried around. 'He made him gay. But God is just and will take care of that wretched Muslim boy when the time is right. Pray for our Hiten, won't you? Please pray for Hiten. Oh, those Muslims!'

Atif received a phone call in the middle of the night.

'Ask him! Ask him if this disgusting thing is true!' his father hollered in the background. 'Only Allah knows where your son got this from! Ask him!'

'Atif, beta, what is all this we are hearing? It's all lies, *nah? Kehdo yeh sab jhoot hai.*'

At this point, it would have been easy for Atif to deny the whole thing. To sling the blame back at the Khannas and reassure his parents of his intention to marry, give them grandchildren. They were too far away to verify the truth. Even if they were suspicious, his vehement denial was expected and welcomed. The benefit of living at such a distance from your family, after all, was that you could maintain a lifestyle of choice while keeping their illusions alive. He already knew that he was never going back and in time, if he had not secured his rights, would join the millions of illegals who had become the fabric of California. By now he had tampered with his Social Security card, whiting out the 'Not Permitted for Employment' above the crested logo of the red bird in flight and making copies which he had used to get a job. Why should he break hearts only to unburden himself?

But when Atif opened his mouth to allay their fears, to accuse the Khannas of spreading malicious lies, the words got stuck in his throat. He realized at that moment, just like the time when he had fallen short of money and had been unable to ask them for more, that he had outgrown that phase. Something in him had evolved so that acquiescing to such things made him feel shameful, no matter what the consequences. Slowly, he was becoming a man.

'Beta? Are you there? Say something, please.'

'Ma,' he said slowly, 'would it be so wrong if I was?'

She was silent and he could hear only her shaky breath. He could see her. Around his father, Atif's mother had always looked extinguished, her eyes nervous, her colour changed, her openness gone. Pretending she hadn't heard him, she pressed on like before. 'Allah help them,' she cried. 'They are rich so they think they can treat us this way. But money doesn't make them right. They are vicious, vicious liars. I know you are not like that, beta. You are not like that boy.'

'But Ma, I am,' he said.

'Yes, yes, I know they are lying. Leave them alone, who cares? Let them say whatever they want. Allah will show them. We don't have to . . .'

'Ma, please. Listen to me. What difference does it make? I'm still me. I'm still the same Atif.'

'Oh, I don't know why they would say such things.'

'Ma, listen!'

'I am listening. I am listening. What are you saying, beta?'

'I'm saying, Ma, that I had nothing to do with Hiten being that way. I didn't do anything to him. But I am that way, Ma. I don't want to lie any more, please. Not to you.'

Abdul Rahman snatched the phone away from Khadija's trembling hands. 'Deny it! Deny it now!' he roared.

'Papa, I . . .' Atif broke down. For a few seconds, the gap between them, of continents and emotions, filled up with Atif's sobbing. They could feel the land mass between them increase, pushing them further apart. 'I don't want to lie to you, Papa.'

'Enough. Enough you've said. You shame us,' he said. 'This is why we struggled to send you over there? So you could turn into a sinner, rub our noses in the dirt? Better we are dead – dead – than to hear this. Better you had died than to become like this.'

Atif wept, unable to utter a word. Seeing his father's hurt, bitter face in his mind's eye, the same father who had carried him on his aching back through the crowds at Jama Masjid, who had tutored him sternly in Islam, helped him fly a kite on the roof of their building and recite the Koran, he began to doubt whether he had done the right thing. Perhaps he should have spared them from it. Lied.

But deep inside, he knew he had been right. Isn't that what we owed those we loved? The truth?

There was so much more Atif wanted to say – things that may have helped his parents understand, which may have shifted the blame somewhere else, but he knew that this would not change anything. It would only create more pain. His parents were like the branches of a tree, still ignorant of the decaying roots.

'You are dead for us,' his father said as Khadija wailed. 'Don't ever call here again. Forget you have a mother and father. Unless you can change, unless you can repent in front of Allah, do not bother to come back.'

For what seemed like an eternity, he had sat in a corner on the floor, letting the tears wash through him. When his head began to pound and he grew short of breath, he began to call several of his friends, all of whom, as luck would have it, were unavailable and not responding even to their cellphones. He tried to convince himself that his father's anger would abate in time; that in a matter of days, his mother would call and even though his father would hesitate to come on the phone, a kind of tentative peace would be reached. It would never happen.

It was at that moment, more than seven years ago, that the neighbour he knew only from their shared wall, appeared at his door to find out if he'd be interested in buying a plush, red velvet sofa she owned. Nona Nguyen had stared at Atif's devastated appearance for a few seconds while he politely declined the sale and then said, 'Well, that's too bad because I'm feeling really generous right now and I want to give someone a really good deal,' and then, without pause, 'I'm sorry, but did somebody die or something?'

Atif sputtered into tears again, at which point Nona marched into his apartment without being invited in, and let him unburden himself while she listened patiently.

Then she treated him to a steak and chicken combo at a local sizzler. She had coupons.

'Family should be unconditional, I know, but, you know, it doesn't always work that way,' she said between mouthfuls of steak soaked in sauce. 'I mean, the very fact that they didn't get to pick you makes them feel screwed if they got stuck with a rotten apple. But friends, now that's a different story, you know what I mean? We choose our friends, and continue to be with them knowing well and good what they're about, how they piss us off, how they add to our lives. So sometimes they become more family than any blood relative, know what I mean?'

It was clear to Atif that Nona Nguyen had also dealt with her own demons and had decided to substitute a group of close friends for her parents. He wanted to say something stupid and insensitive like, 'But you don't know my parents. They're different. They love me,' but he clamped up, realizing that his situation bore witness to the error of his logic. Instead he said, 'Your parents are here. At least you see them, talk to them.'

'Yeah, twice a year,' she grunted, looking away. 'Thanksgiving and Christmas. I'm telling you, those holidays were invented so we could be punished on an annual basis.' She began peppering her steak excessively. 'Actually, I think my father just wanted a son. My brother's the apple of his eye.' Then she quickly changed the subject, pointing at a couple of attractive men who had just walked in.

Slowly, Atif grew accustomed to his exile. The pain, which was sharp and exacting, became dull and submerged by time. The hateful words of his father, the pleas of his powerless mother, all turned into distant echoes, much like the memories of their love for him. But every once in a while, out of nowhere, a dream, a smell, an expression he caught in someone else's face, the breadth of space left by Rahul's untimely departure, would remind him of them and the urge to pick up the phone would seize him. This now was one of those moments. As his mind filtered all sorts of assurances – *yes, yes, they must have forgiven you by now, they can't possibly stay angry with you after all these years* – he had to remind himself that they had not called him.

I'm not going to do this, he said to himself like a mantra. *I'm not going to do this. I'm not going to do this. I'm not going to do this. I don't need you. I don't need any of you any more. I have him now. He is everything to me.* And he shook his head determinedly, taking deep breaths, squeezing his eyes shut, banishing them as they had banished him.

On the day Rahul met Atif, the skies wept.

Los Angeles, a desert camouflaged by the indiscernible shift of seasons, canopies of swaying, imported palm trees, and constant blue waters finally heaved a sigh of relief. The earth had burned year-long, allowing Angelenos to bake on beaches and amble the promenades in their designer tees and Havaianas, but now, as the rain fell torrentially, the earth avenged its deprivation, paralysing freeways, emptying out car washes and sending everyone to their television sets for up-to-date forecasts.

But Rahul loved the rain, how it quenched the fiery heat of the city; he liked how it dampened the pace, suspended plans and managed to take him out of himself. He knew that soon, everything in the city's complexion would change for the better: all that was ash and arid would turn green and fecund, naked branches that forked skywards like protesting arms would eventually rustle with growth and vistas that had remained hidden from sight even as the sky had been a confused blue would suddenly appear, snowcapped mountains carving themselves into the sky.

That night, as the rain pelted his windshield, he drove home to Pooja, the set of books lying in the passenger seat of his car, Atif's business card beating against his chest. After he had purchased the books, Atif had scribbled something on the store's card and instead of dropping it into the bag, handed it directly to Rahul, gestures pregnant with expectation.

As the single wiper sloshed from side to side, offering intermittent glimpses of clarity into a sea of blinking red lights along San Vicente Boulevard, the radio reported yet another fallout in the peace talks in the Middle East, and Rahul felt himself drift from his surroundings. Even as his eyes carefully monitored the distance from the car in front of him, they were unable to erase Atif.

He changed radio stations, feigned interest in the stores and restaurants that lined the boulevard, but kept coming back to Atif. He beheld again the gentleness of Atif's demeanour, the planes and curves that formed his face, the kindness in his eyes and the pain that lurked behind them. Though he couldn't make sense of it, Rahul couldn't deny that something powerful had transpired. He wondered if perhaps he was not the only one affected. He had experienced, much to his surprise, an inner expansion, a kind of restlessness, a youthful longing after something just beyond his reach; a feeling so vivid, so dormant, that he wanted to stop driving so he could grasp it better, and in the process, end the nervous churning in his belly.

Rahul thought back to the brief sexual encounter with a schoolmate named Hanif in Kenya, lifetimes ago. He had written this off as a rite of passage, something that all young boys went through in a culture where sex with a woman was not readily available. He grew agitated now, wondering if it meant much more.

That evening, the celebration started with Pooja cutting into a pale yellow Dulce de Leche cake adorned with a lavender floral design that Ajay had picked up from Sweet Lady Jane on Melrose. Pooja carved out hulking slices of the caramel dessert for her son and husband, a small wedge for herself. Rahul and Ajay both took turns feeding her a piece of cake as she mock-remonstrated and blushed from the attention. Rahul presented her with the set of books artfully wrapped in lapis blue agate marbled paper, gold ribbon and bow. He placed it in her lap and she marvelled at the gift-wrapping before gently pulling on the tails of the oversized bow.

'Oh, just tear it, Mom! It's not like you're gonna' use it again,' said Ajay.

But Pooja took her time, smiling, rolling up the ribbon carefully and placing it aside with the bow, peeling off the flaps one by one, revealing the set as if it were an ancient codex whispering secrets. With every gesture that Pooja used to open her present, Rahul saw pieces of Atif assemble in his mind; when she lifted up the book, he could see Atif as clearly as if he were standing in the room with them. His heart felt heavy with an emotion he could neither contain nor identify and which left him sighing. Rahul leaned over and kissed his wife on the forehead, expelling the phantom presence.

Then Rahul took an elated Pooja and reluctant Ajay to a Bollywood show featuring some of the hottest new film stars and playback singers at the Pasadena Civic Auditorium. The rain, which Pooja romantically referred to as Ganga descending into Shiva's locks, gave no sign of ceasing, but having purchased the special 'VVIP' seats for the show, and knowing how much she had been looking forward to it, they stuck to the plan, even though she obligingly suggested they stay in. During the show, when a popular new female artiste hailed as the next Lata

Mangeshkar took to the stage and performed a medley of sentimental *filmi* songs, Pooja held Rahul's hand on the armrest.

But Rahul, though corporeally present with his wife and son, his ears flooded with melodies and applause, his eyes accosted with the colourful lights and stage spectacle, was, unbeknownst to any of them, and to his own consternation, holding Atif in his arms.

During intermission, a disgruntled Ajay, who couldn't understand how after a solid two hours of the show there was still another half to follow, found some solace in his cellphone and eager American girlfriends who sympathized with his entrapment. The rain also took a break; people swarmed out of the hall and into the cold night for air, cigarettes, food and calls.

Rahul and Pooja drank hot chai and snacked on doughy samosas, which he remarked with a tender smile, were comparatively inedible to hers. She became coquettish and said: 'Samosas you appreciate, but what about the one that makes the samosas?' to which he put his arm around her and gave her a kiss on the forehead, inches away from her bindi.

Startled when her name was called out in high pitch, they turned to find Sonali Patel aggressively weaving through the crowd, throwing nettled glances at the women and seductive smiles at their lascivious husbands. '*Ei*, Pooja, there you are! I've been looking all over for you,' she called out, waving to them excitedly. 'I'm coming. You stay right there.'

'Smile,' Rahul said, 'it's too late to run.'

Sonali was wearing an opulent parrot-green sari bordered in gold and was decked out in blinding jewellery. On her wrist dangled an impracticably small purse studded with rhinestones. Her short hair had been freshly coloured to an impossible jet black and crowned her caked and recently pulled face in great contrast.

Behind her trailed a gaggle of her much younger girlfriends, carrying on raucously with their mélange of gossip, gasps and giggles. 'Ei! Be careful!' she flitted around, ready to give someone two tight slaps. 'Make sure you don't step on my sari!' They shrunk back momentarily but continued to follow her timidly as she switched back into an elated expression for the Kapoors.

'Did you see the show? *Hai hai!* Did you see? Did you see how vulgar that Suman Shetty looked? She doesn't even look like a film star.' Sonali didn't pause for breath. 'Oh, and what a terrible dancer. You know, I hear she's quite a boozer. She almost fell down on the stage. Did you see that? Oh, probably not. My seats are so close that I can see everything!' She made it sound like a terrible disadvantage and screwed her face up into a nauseated expression.

Sonali shot a look at her friends who instantly responded with vehement approvals: 'Yes, yes, she was definitely drunk. Most definitely.'

'Oh-ho, but that Karan Singh. *Hai me marjava!* Nobody can measure up to him. So-o-o handsome!' She shook her head and fanned herself with a diamond-bedecked hand.

Wedged between the front of Sonali's teeth was what looked like a dark patch of cilantro, probably from the snacks she had just devoured. Nobody said anything about it. When Rahul and a nervous Pooja exchanged a glance and laughed, Sonali grew delighted, thinking they were appreciating her humour.

Ajay appeared, pocketing his cellphone, and Sonali's gang grew visibly coquettish. To Pooja's annoyance, even Sonali started batting her eyes. 'Oh, hello, Ajay. What a surprise!' she cooed.

'Hey, Sonali aunty. Always a pleasure.'

'Aunty? *Yeh* aunty, aunty *kya hai?* Oh! Why must you call me that?' she said with an indulgent tone of reproach.

Ajay almost pointed to his own teeth to alert Sonali but Rahul threw him a sharp look.

'Soni! Just call me Soni! How many times do I have to say it? You must stop with this aunty-banty nonsense! Soni's not really that old, you know.'

'True,' said Rahul. 'What's a few decades? *Achar* has a long shelf life.'

The disciples gasped audibly. Sonali shot Rahul a look and then proceeded to make light of his comment with forced laughter. 'Your father gets so much pleasure out of troubling me. Sanjay was the same way, always teasing me and annoying me, but deep inside, there was nothing but love in my husband's poor, weak heart. Poor Sanju,' she acted sad, blinking back invisible tears. 'Oh, how I miss him. But you know, that reminds me, the promoter – he was such a good friend of Sanjay's. He's promised to take me backstage so that Karan Singh can meet me, so, you know, I can't just stay here and idle away. We must go now,' she announced to her party. 'But Pooja, I will call you tomorrow and fill you in on my rendezvous with Karan.'

Sonali smiled at Ajay, half a tooth obscured, and Ajay winked at her. She ignored Rahul and walked away with her minions, all of whom had to tear their gaze away from a grinning Ajay.

'Why must you be so rude to her?'

'Oh, Poo,' groaned Rahul. 'You know you can't stand her either.'

'She's just lonely.'

'Lonely? With that flock she herds around everywhere?'

Ajay was looking in their direction, rubbing his chin. 'Maybe I could provide some distraction.'

Pooja slapped his arm playfully. *'Besharam!'*

'I'm just trying to help, Mom. Although I'm convinced it's really Papa she's got the hots for,' he said, nudging his father.

The house lights flickered and people began to shuffle back into the auditorium. Ajay groaned and Pooja said, 'Come on, now. Can't you do this much for your Ma?'

'I swear. This is for your birthday, your Diwali, everything in one shot, Mom.'

She tucked a wisp of hair behind her ear, revealing the mole on her lobe that Rahul found cute. She then intertwined her left arm into her son's and her right arm into her husband's and with a smile that made her look radiant, walked back in with the two most important men in her life, protected, never happier.

And for a while, Rahul seemed to return to his life, comforted by the presence of his wife and son, but somewhere during the second half of the show, he felt the snake of restlessness uncoiling inside him again and excused himself to go to the bathroom. As he edged his way out through the row of miffed fans dodging this way and that so they wouldn't lose sight of their beloved stars even for a second, an otherwise benevolent-looking grandmother-type with a bindi the size of a quarter grumbled in Gujarati: '*O-ho-ho!* Does this one have to do toilet right now? Now I can't see anything! My evening is ruined!'

He stepped outside, gulping the night air into his lungs as if he had been underwater. The cold winter air on his face, Rahul looked up at a sky devoid of stars but sensed them there anyway. A veiled moon looked down at him impassively. There wasn't a soul in sight, as if the auditorium was a giant vacuum that had sucked everyone into its sack.

Taking deep breaths, he asked himself with a little more

courage: *why can't I get him out of my mind? Can I really be feeling* this *strongly for another man? Why now? How do I stop it?* The answers, like a face appearing from under a sheet of ice, filled him with panic. But his body followed a different rhythm, defying his fear, and he lifted out the business card from his breast pocket, noted the perfectly executed letters that slanted to the right, a tendency he remembered from somewhere symbolized a sense of pessimism in the writer, as if leaning from the sheer weight of life itself.

It was then, after the third time Rahul had looked at Atif Rahman's name, that he turned the card over, read the numbers written down on the back, one for his home and another for his cell, and again he felt the roiling sensation in the pit of his stomach.

His other hand gripped the cellphone in his pocket. The urge to see him again, to hear his voice, filled Rahul with an alien vernacular of pain – burning and freezing simultaneously, throbbing, liquefying, electric. *I must be going crazy,* he thought, loosening his grip on the phone, a grenade relinquished. *I must fight this. Keep it under, where nobody can see. Even to think of it is to give it life, bring it to the surface.*

What he needed was cover, more insulation from such feelings.

He pictured his wife and son sitting inside the auditorium, wondering where he must be, and dredging himself out from the marsh of emotion, he walked back in.

A few days later, when Atif came home to the blinking red light of three hang-ups on his answering machine, he wondered about the caller. It amazed him that after years of futilely bartered telephone numbers and email addresses, the heart could still dare to hope, as if a last breath, some atom of life, might still be left to reanimate a future.

Nona Nguyen, who had overstayed her visit and was still holding on to the roll of toilet paper she had come for, planted herself cross-legged on his sofa and sympathized. 'Fucking telemarketers, man. They're relentless.'

He pressed the 'play' button again, hoping that somehow a breath, some voice, anything that could confirm his suspicion, had been captured by his automated substitute. But there was nothing except the notification of three blocked calls on the caller ID. He was momentarily reminded of the painful, feckless period in which he had waited for his parents to call. Every ring, every missed call, had become them. Until the day that something in him hardened and he stopped waiting. Now it was Rahul.

He turned around to find Nona lost, still holding on to the double roll like a consolation prize, her eyes on the floor, her thoughts a million miles away. He knew at once that she was disappointed over the latest blind date and needed to talk. *Different playing fields, but maybe we're not so different after all,* he thought.

'Some chai?' he asked, moving to the kitchen.

'Oh, God no,' she said. 'Your chai keeps me up all night!'

He pulled out a jar of loose black tea, a container of powdered spice, some brown sugar and a new can of evaporated milk.

'Oh, what the hell,' he heard her say. 'If you're making some, why not? I'll stay for a cup.'

As he punctured the can of milk, he felt the urge to tell her about Rahul building up in him, constricting his chest. But he resisted, knowing on some level how ridiculous it would sound, how unexceptional. So he remained silent, continued the ritual of making chai. He couldn't be sure if it had been Rahul calling so he imagined it so, prayed that he would try to call him again. He tried to conjure Rahul's face in his mind, knowing with some frustration, that it was only the faces he tried desperately to remember that his mind had a cruel tendency of wiping away.

By the time Sonali Patel finally landed an appointment with Dr Goldstein, she was significantly agitated but managed to act obsequious as the tiny pricks of transformative poison were fed into her furrowed brows and crow's feet.

She felt that she would have been perfectly justified if, after the coveted 'derm' had ministered the increased dosage she had pleaded for, she had turned the syringe on him and jabbed him a few times in his ample buttocks for having made her wait so long before coming back in. She was still miffed about his refusal to minister the new Intense Pulsed Light treatment she had read about. 'Mrs Patel, you must understand, IPL is just not suitable for your skin type,' he had tried to explain. 'Coloured skin is too sensitive for it.' She hated the way he called it 'coloured skin' like she was some *kalu,* a customer service operator in Mumbai who was only suitable for tubes of mercury-laden skin-bleaching ointments.

The trick to appearing ageless, Sonali knew, was in being in a state of constant restoration, in never being caught in the startling periods in-between when the crinkles and lines came back and you caught your reflection in a mirror. Dr Goldstein, preoccupied with his celebrity following, all of which she followed in the various fashion magazines, had become increasingly elusive to her. But now she felt rescued from the ravages of time at least for a few months and this mitigated the anger she had lugged in with her. Now if she could only find a way to make him see her more frequently and agree to minister the treatment he seemed determined to save for his *gora* patients so that she could look more like the Hollywood icons deified on the walls of the medical spa.

After he had pricked her sufficiently, Dr Goldstein handed her an ice pack and asked with notable discomfort, 'Mrs Patel, you are Hindu, are you not?' to which Sonali looked at him strangely and nodded with some hesitation, wondering if this too could be used to keep her from receiving some kind of treatment.

He seemed agitated, and started asking lots of questions about Hinduism – the tenets, customs, traditions – and Sonali grew irritated again. She preferred to be thought of as a sophisticate, someone who was above cast or creed. Personally, she had no need for religion and while she had never gone out of her way to repudiate it, she cared nothing to discuss it. God had never been there for Sonali or her loved ones and she had little patience for people who romanticized life with religion, like her neighbour Pooja.

But then it occurred to her that maybe Dr Goldstein was interested in converting and she became visibly excited, her mind filling with visions of becoming a kind of mentor to the coveted doctor. It was the latest trend after all. Gullible Americans couldn't get enough of yoga and meditation and self-help books, so if Deepak Chopra could do it for Demi Moore and Madonna with all his hocus-pocus about the Upanishads and quantum theories, why couldn't she do it for the dermatologist to the stars?

'Dr Goldstein – Mark,' she said, feeling suddenly entitled. 'You know, it would be an absolute pleasure for me to do this. Sonali can teach you all you need to know, even take you to temple.'

'Oh, no, no, no!' Dr Goldstein said, even more distressed, wringing his hands. 'That really won't be necessary. I'm concerned, Mrs Patel –'

'Soni, please.'

'Yes, thank you, Sonali. I'm concerned about my son, you see. Greg calls himself Ramesh or something and well, he's been utterly brainwashed, become obsessed with your culture. Please don't take this the wrong way. I have the greatest respect for it. It's just that he's got it into his head to go to India and lead this life and . . .'

Sonali was deflated again. Now she was being made to feel responsible for his son's affliction. As he droned on, she looked at the framed picture of the young boy on Dr Goldstein's desk, scanning the unexceptional face. To her, he looked no different from the average American kid, the kind she saw around her neighbourhood, creating a ruckus with his skateboard.

'. . . And we're wondering what can be done to break this spell. I mean, is this what your faith, what Hinduism teaches, Mrs Patel? To resent privilege? Give everything up and move to some ashram? I mean, I know you're not like that.'

Suddenly she sat up, smiled catlike. 'Maybe what Greg needs is to spend some time with real Hindus. Not those Hare Krishna types,' she said, wrinkling her nose. 'People like myself who know the faith from within, for what it really is, Mark, not the export version, you know? Let him see it as being ordinary instead of exotic. You know, Mark, Sonali would be more than happy to talk to him. Knock some sense into his head.' And in return she envisioned herself waltzing in without appointments, getting higher dosages of the treatment-du-jour, maybe even being considered a part of the Goldstein family. Surely, helping to avert such personal disasters afforded one the charter of kin.

Sonali had no recollection of Pooja's involvement with The Banyan, that her golden goose actually drove up to their block at least once every week to pick up deliveries from her neighbour. She had actually hollered at him once for parking in her driveway. Instead, she made a mental note of the places where Dr Goldstein mentioned his misled son spent time so that she could execute a seemingly accidental meeting – The Banyan on Montana Avenue, a Hare Krishna temple in Culver City and the spirituality section of some obscure bookstore called Elton's.

'Now, Mark, about the IPL . . .' she started to say.

From where he stood behind the counter at closing time on Sunday, Atif could hear the roar of thunder. In his wing at Elton's, now vacated of customers, he looked up at the impassive ceiling but could see the sky beyond it, a concrete slab of gray. His fingers played tentatively on his lips, touching the scar, a gesture he had seen his mother make so many times and which now, and what seemed like centuries later, had become a part of his trait. This, he had learned, was how we killed those whom we were unable to possess. We absorbed them.

Unlike the spoiled Angelenos chafing at the slightest change of weather, Atif liked almost everything about winter and instead of growing depressed at the oncoming holidays, he welcomed the season's inherent romance, when sun and shade gave way to rain and mist and prolonged days surrendered to early twilight. Every year he crowned a corner of his balcony with the plastic battery-operated jack-o'-lantern and stocked up on variety packets of miniature chocolates for the trick-or-treaters. When October went, he carried home a Lilliputian Christmas tree with colourful lights from the local supermarket and gorged on spiked egg-nog while watching gospel TV specials. Over the years, he had taught himself to be self-sufficient, to live soulfully through his books and music and HBO so that his world had expanded into realms that didn't require much human interaction.

What was changing in him now? Why, suddenly, was he craving the warmth of another body at the end of his monotonous days, for the memories of someone to keep him occupied in the spaces in between?

Rahul. Rahul. Rahul. The name played off his lips like warm, honeyed bread. How could anyone want someone this much, with so little justification? Where was sanity, commonsense, rationale – all the things that kept us from bounding off a cliff and crashing to the ground?

Have I learned nothing from the past – that the world of the imagination is dangerous territory, better left uncharted?

Its dark, beguiling corners may fuel fantasies and art but left you stranded and lost in the end. To repeat mistakes, to fall for those that couldn't – wouldn't – reciprocate, to continue marching through roads that have previously misled you, is that testament to man's capacity for hope or a sign of his inner despair?

Atif picked up the leather pouch containing the day's cash deposit, threw it into the crinkled brown paper bag in which he had brought his sandwich, and, after arming the alarm, promptly turned off the lights and exited the bookstore. *This is a trip I can't afford,* he thought, steeling himself. The entry ramp is always there, beckoning, beguiling, but the ride is unpredictable, always a gamble, likely to get you trapped.

In the courtyard, with key in hand, he paused for a moment so he would be unnoticed by the employees of the other shops who would insist he join them for a round of drinks at the English pub down the street. He could hear Becca telling the others that she was done with 'him' and that this time she had summoned the courage to erase the bastard's number off her cellphone so she wouldn't be tempted to call him. He smiled to himself. He knew better. When you needed it badly enough, someone always had the number.

After they had ambled on, Atif walked out onto the street and coiled his red wool muffler snugly around his neck, the deposit bag safe in the pocket of his leather car coat. It was then that Atif noticed someone standing across the street on the centre divider, under the large fanning tree. He paused.

Rahul raised his hand, gave Atif a slow, abbreviated wave.

He could scarcely believe his eyes; he breathed in deeply. It was enough just to see Rahul – standing there in his dark wool overcoat, windblown hair, his tie hanging loosely around his neck, the evening stubble on his face – and to know that for once in his life, he hadn't imagined the whole thing, that someone was reciprocating, that the countless hours of willing Rahul to appear might just have worked, to bring Atif to the verge of grateful tears.

For what seemed like a long time but perhaps was only seconds, they stood rooted.

When Atif finally went towards him, a huge flock of pigeons took sudden flight, screening them from each other momentarily, settling on the periphery of the bookstore's roof like guards. He reached the curb and waited for the cars to grant him passage, his ears catching the medley of avian gurgles and swishing cars. He swayed back and forth lightly, his feet balancing on the edge of the curb. Beneath him could have been inches from concrete or the infinite plunge of a chasm. It made no difference.

He walked across, each step closing the gulf between

them. And even though the ground beneath him must have been solid, he felt its plates shift and shuffle. When he stood against Rahul on the moist green grass, he felt as if his body was surrendering to vertigo, falling into him. He looked into Rahul's eyes, determined not to let his nervousness and emotions undermine him. *I must look what I desire in the eye,* he told himself. *To appear deserving, worthy of what I want.*

Rahul looked down at his feet, as if making sure that he was still subject to gravity. Something in him was untangling – something that he knew he would never be able to wind up again.

'I'm sorry,' Rahul said facetiously, reciprocating Atif's deep, determined gaze. 'I was nowhere in the neighbourhood.'

From the outside, Blue was an inconspicuous jazz bar on Fourth Street in Santa Monica, flanked by a guitar shop specializing in acoustic and folk instruments on one side and a furniture upholsterer on the other. During the week it was frequented by happy-hour locals from surrounding retail stores and undiscovered musicians who, still eluded by mainstream recognition and record deals, took their art seriously and with a sense of tragedy.

Atif had noticed it many times on the way to the beach or the promenade and imagined it as a smoky, sensual joint where the likes of Billie Holiday would have crooned or Raymond Chandler might have found his noir over gin martinis. It was the first place that came to his mind when Rahul suggested they go somewhere for a drink.

There was little conversation as Rahul drove them over. Neither felt the pressure for it. The lulls that made most people uncomfortable and which they tried so desperately to fill up with the clutter of words – perhaps because they knew that words were less dangerous than silence, much less telling – did not bother them.

A blue neon sign beckoned them through a tiny wooden door. Inside it was so dark that it took them a moment to adjust their eyes to the room. Then, gradually, the room opened itself up and they saw a long wooden bar that stretched back endlessly along the spine. On their right were deep, tooled, red leather booths and tables running parallel to the bar, illuminated by votive candles ensconced in red glass globes. Chet Baker, John Coltrane and Ella Fitzgerald lined the walls as if they had been there once. A stage at the end of the room, now visible, was set up with music equipment. Terrence Blanchard's smoky rendition of 'Detour Ahead' began playing on the jukebox.

From behind the bar gleaming with yards of bottles, an older bartender waved them in, indicating they could sit anywhere they liked. They took the second circular booth from the door and settled in across from each other. Atif got up again and took off his coat and muffler and Rahul, smiling, did the same. They threw their coats on the seat in a mound between them.

'Nice place,' said Rahul, his fingers tapping lightly on the table.

'Best dive bar in town.'

'You come here a lot?'

'Would "yes" make me easy?'

Rahul stiffened up.

'My first time,' Atif said. 'Wanted to try something new.'

Rahul managed half a smile. He clasped his hands together and began to look around the room, nodding his head in a kind of evasive way. Atif recognized the shift. He had seen it before in men who started having second thoughts, became suddenly uncomfortable with the possibilities. The band on Rahul's finger glinted incontestably from the light of the candle and qualms raced through Atif.

The bartender appeared and set down a tray of peanuts. After some hesitation, Rahul ordered a Johnnie Walker Black Label with a single rock of ice. Atif asked for a dry vodka martini with three olives, causing Rahul to raise his eyebrows. 'Not shaken,' Atif said to the waiter. 'We'll save that travesty for Bond.' He looked back at Rahul. 'It's been a hard one,' he said, not specifying whether he meant just the day or life itself.

Rahul felt sympathetic, guessing that Atif probably worked long hours and made little more than minimum wage. The furrows between his eyes and the dark circles around them, while not diminishing his handsomeness, gave Atif a weary look even in the dim light. Rahul wanted to ask so much – about where he came from, about his family, age, the scar on his lip, everything – as if this would somehow explain his attraction to the boy. But he knew that such inquiries elicited personal disclosure as well so he postponed them.

Atif found an easier way, sensing their acquaintance would have to begin with their initial point of contact, and asked about the cookbooks. Rahul smiled nervously, trying to keep Pooja out of the conversation for as long as it was possible. 'I hope they paid you a commission on it. The last time I needed a bank loan to buy books, I was in college.'

'Graphic Arts,' he said, pointing to himself.

'Finance. Not as exciting.' Rahul talked about his MBA, how a close Persian friend who chain-smoked Marlboros and was addicted to Starbucks had got him his first banking job as a loan officer more than a decade ago. The years had fleeted by with escalating goals, tedious spreadsheets, interminable meetings and hustling clients away from the competition – all that between countering the threat of lay-offs and adjusting to a new corporate culture between bank mergers. Now Rahul was the branch manager of a hundred-million-dollar facility in Westchester, which was seeing a rebirth thanks to developers like Howard Drollinger.

It should have been a success story but Rahul sounded bored, bitter and lonely. It was as if he had been tricked into living someone else's life.

The cocktails arrived. Atif lifted the martini off the table and his lips approached the meniscus without taking his eyes off Rahul. He took the first sip, felt almost immediately at ease, his body warming up, recognizing an old friend. Rahul sipped his Johnnie Walker, winced at the metallic bite, the golden strands of fire in his throat. He stirred his drink vigorously with the red plastic stirrer, hoping to dilute it, while the rock of ice clanged away. He looked at it with disdain, as if at an old foe. 'I don't drink any more.'

And I haven't felt more normal, thought Atif. *A martini in my hand, jazz in my ears, you in my eyes.*

Atif told him about his life. Of his family back in Mumbai with whom he hadn't spoken in umpteen years, his job at Elton's, his freelancing in journalism. What he didn't say was how he had kept his job for over five years now, not just because he liked being surrounded by books, but also because he was petrified of applying for another job with his illegal status. By then he had finished his drink and only a solitary olive nestled in the valley of his glass.

The band returned and struck up 'Watch What Happens'. A couple got up and started dancing to the side of the tables. They looked tipsy and enamoured with each other. Atif looked at them and smiled. The woman, probably in her fifties, had a mane of silver hair and was draped in a dark shawl. Every now and then she lost her balance, spinning in the arms of the younger man, and giggled like a teenager as she nestled in his shoulder. Silence came and went between Atif and Rahul as they sat across from each other, drinking, exchanging glances, watching the couple, smiling awkwardly at times and still waiting for something. *That must be it,* thought Rahul, *the source of this attraction is that we are both, in our own different ways, exiles.*

'Were you surprised?' Rahul asked.

'Not surprised.'

'Then what?'

'Afraid.'

'Afraid?'

'Afraid,' Atif said, smiling sadly, his eyes shifting from Rahul's intense gaze, his fingers rubbing the beads of condensation on his depleted glass. 'Afraid that you wouldn't show up and then nothing would've changed.' Their eyes met. 'Afraid that you would show up and there would be reason to hope things will.'

By the time they walked back out in the cold night, the streets were deserted. Atif could feel Rahul's gaze upon him, as tangible as a touch, and promptly averted when Atif looked back at him. He could feel the familiar tingling of intoxication in his legs. This was the moment at which, had he been the old Atif, carousing with his pack at a club, he would have induced the high further by chasing down a hefty shot or two so that, just a few minutes later, he would enter an amnesic zone, the shocking details of which would have to be related to him by a friend the day after.

I wish I could do that shot right now, he thought as they headed for Rahul's car parked across the street. *Something to make me bolder, to take consequence away.*

They got into the Mercedes and Rahul hesitated starting it up, his fingers poised over the keys in the ignition.

Quickly, without a single word and barely a glance, their bodies came together and they started to kiss, awkwardly at first, then hungrily. Rahul leaned over, sinking Atif back into the black leather seat, holding his face tight in his hands. It was one of those moments when it became impossible to remember whose lips had found whose, who had made the first move, a moment which, in recollection, would lack transition, the seconds leading up to it forever shrouded.

Suddenly, Rahul pulled back, wiping his mouth with his hand. 'I'm sorry . . . I don't know what I'm doing here.' His body constricted and Rahul leaned over the steering wheel, unable to look at Atif.

Atif turned away from him and looked out of the window, brokenhearted. If they were to pursue this, there would be many obstacles. Regret, Atif knew, could not be one of them. In the distance, he could see a man was pushing a supermarket cart, loaded with his belongings, searching for a warm alcove between the shiny patina of a spa and designer boutique.

'Please, just take me back,' he said, his eyes on the lone vagrant.

Rahul started the car and they drove back to Elton's.

This time the silence was deafening.

On the short but desolate drive home on San Vicente Boulevard, lined with expensive homes, coral trees, and peppered even at this time of night with joggers, Atif's first impulse surprised him – to plug in a cassette of romantic Bollywood duets and visualize Rahul and himself together. The face that had eluded him for the past week was now so freshly imprinted on his mind that he could fuel any Bollywood-esque fantasy. They could unfurl on a bed of marigolds, run to each other, arms wide open, across tulip fields, or embrace on snow-capped mountains to a melody of triumphant love. *Good beginnings can end in disasters,* he thought. *So why can't the opposite be true?*

But he resisted. Fantasies may allow you to skip the degradation, the hopelessness of the situation for the time being, but ultimately nothing had really changed. Instead he reached out for *Sajda* in the glove compartment, a collection of poignant ghazals by Lata Mangeshkar and Jagjit Singh, but then, realizing this would only lure him into a swamp of despair, pulled back his hand. The key, he knew, was to find equilibrium between the states of hope and despair.

Even in the silence, there was nothing he could do to keep his last moments with Rahul from playing in his mind – Rahul unable to look at him and apologizing in Elton's deserted parking lot; Atif, despite reeling from the rejection and fighting the urge to touch him, saying, 'Look, there's no need for this. Thanks for the drink.'

Something within Atif was welling up like a great big tide. He began speeding. If he could only get to his apartment before it erupted. Surrounded by the comfort of his books, music, the serene Buddha statue, potted plants, even Nona's incessant yakking from next door, everything would be okay. You can't mourn what you've never had, he told himself. It was never yours to lose.

At the door he found Anaïs, the neighbour's kitten, waiting for him as she often did late at night. She mewed upon seeing him and curled around his leg. He picked her up, settled down on the staircase. She splayed herself out over his lap, her paws clawing the air as he rubbed her gray coat.

'Well, at least I have you,' he said, 'but then even you don't really belong to me, do you?'

Anaïs belonged to Phyllis, an American teenager living in the complex across the way, and it was not unusual to find the feline during one of her many unsupervised forays, lurking behind the communal dumpster, terrorizing even dogs. By the time Anaïs hunched up in attack mode and growled menacingly, the poor canine, sometimes twice her size, would be scampering behind his bewildered, embarrassed owner.

To ensure that Anaïs returned home to her second-storey apartment overlooking the alleyway where she carried out her acts of terrorism, Phyllis had requested all neighbours not to let the kitten into their homes. Atif and Phyllis had never met, but Nona, who detested cats, had conveyed the message for her. 'She doesn't want you spoiling it. Don't get too attached.'

He played with Anaïs for some time, letting the animal's unconditional love soothe his pain, then he walked her down to the alley, hung around for a couple of minutes, and when she was looking away and least suspecting it, ran back up the staircase. Anaïs sprinted behind him but wasn't fast enough. The deception saddened him every time because he knew the cat would wait for a little while on the other side of the shut door, brushing up against it.

He went to the answering machine. One message. He could barely breathe. When he pressed the button, a telemarketer pitched him the virtues of refinancing his home. Atif hit a button, erased him.

Why did it always have to be so immediate with him? he wondered. One chance meeting, a simple glance, and there he went – ready to throw his life away, beating heart in open hands, fantasies freed from congested vaults. Why couldn't it be gradual, restrained, Victorian? Like Gaskell or Austen? He smiled wryly. Because he wasn't Miss Matty or Emma. No, he was Indian. And not the kind of Indian that aspired to be like the refined yet repressed characters he so liked to read about but in whose lives there was never any room for people of his kind or colour.

He was an Indian throbbing with blood and mud; one who believed love should be riotous, unbridled, passionate. Love had always struck him like a bolt of lightning, leaving him a bit scorched in the end. Subtle nuances and complexities may be the stuff of Western literary classics, but for him, the stories of Anarkali and Salim, of Laila and Majnooh, of Shah Mahmoud and his slave Ayaz were the standard; where thrones were abdicated, heads prostrated on the bascule, timeless monuments erected to immortalize love. He saw love as epic.

Atif carried out his nightly ritual – flossing, brushing, and washing his face and feet. With one foot propped in the sink, tepid water gushing over it, a towel slung over his shoulder, he looked in the mirror and noticed how sallow his complexion looked. As he raised a hand up to his face, he saw the glinting band again, as if on his own finger. It was better this way, he thought. That the episode with Rahul Kapoor was over, quick and reasonably clean. They will never see each other again. Then, in just a matter of days, his mind would play that merciful trick, blotting out Rahul's face from his mind, one feature at a time. Time is the perfect balm.

He couldn't have been further from the truth.

After Rahul pulled up in his garage, he emptied a canister of green mint Tic Tacs in the palm of his hand and chewed them vigorously, his eyes moistening.

The drug had been ingested. He could feel his heart pounding in his chest, his body tingling all over, every nerve ending alive. Images of him and Atif, their bodies entwined, tongues forging deep into each other's mouths, flashed through his mind. The silence assumed a sound and he could watch the air move around him, smell the musk of their contact. Something that had lain undetected, dormant, prodded outward from within, cracking his shell.

He knew what was waiting for him inside the dimly lit house. Pooja always left the kitchen light on for him and there, on the table bare but for a single place setting, he would find a covered plate of food that he would pick through just to please her. It was not what he hungered for. If Ajay was at home, he would be locked up in his room as boys his age, hankering for privacy, were known to be; Pooja always retired by nine-thirty.

He opened the car door and stuck out his hand, poured some bottled water over it and then patted his face, neck, lips with it. He went into the house and ignoring the covered plate on the table, headed straight up to their bedroom. In the night light she always left on for him, he could see her reclining figure under the down comforter she liked to use even in the peak of summer, her head of thick black hair neatly tied into a bun. She was sleeping on her side, her back to him, snoring lightly. He stood over her for some time, hearing their discordant breathing – how out of sync – while trying to supplant the boy with her.

It would be one of the last times he would touch her.

Atif normally awoke by six a.m., after which he prepared breakfast leisurely – an egg fried in butter, sourdough toast (always bakery-bought), French-pressed, dark roast coffee. He relished this while watching the quirky team on *Good Day LA* on KTTV, preferring Jillian's boisterousness,

Dorothy's tabloid banter, and Steve's ineffectual attempts at giving the news some credence to other morbid newscasts. As a rule, he never read the whole newspaper, keeping the disasters of the world at bay, only indulging in the Calendar section of the *Los Angeles Times* to search the Arts listings and read about celebrities and restaurant reviews.

After that, he spent about an hour on one of the three books he was reading or, if he had been granted the assignment, he'd work on a book review for *WEHO*, a complimentary local gay fortnightly. Because he freelanced from home, the editorial staff rarely saw him and they communicated mostly through emails. Over time, they came to know him as the 'cute reviewer who likes to cover books nobody wants to read' but which lent the magazine some intellectualism. His selections, while not limited to academic books, had included such studious ones as *Homoerotics in Hollywood Film, The Essential Gay Mystics,* and whenever possible, any Eastern-themed book, like *Same Sex Love in India,* a new interpretation of the *Kama Sutra,* or tomes on Indian interiors and Islamic architecture.

When he had first begun writing for an upscale, glossy gay monthly, his articles titled 'Herbal Anti-depressants' and 'The Perfect Martini' had stood out like warts amongst 'How to be a Perfect Bottom' and 'Steps to Seduce the Straight Jock.' In time, he had amassed enough tear sheets, carefully cropping out of the adjacent lube bottles and porn ads, waived the pittance the glossy paid, and found another home at *WEHO* where he could write what he was passionate about. Atif started his days with books and communed with them all day long at work. At night, he again turned to them, looking forward to that moment when his eyes felt leaded, words on the page performed a gavotte, and he surrendered to sleep.

On nights he couldn't sleep – when the fast, hot Santa

Ana winds stoked wildfires and made it hard to breathe, or in spring, when pollen joined the invisible quantum dance and incited his allergies – he adopted a practice of lying on his back and taking exactly nine deep, full breaths through his deviated septum, coaxing his breathing into a manageable pattern, the air moving in and out of his lungs, his heartbeat pacified.

This had made him wonder if a tranquil disposition, that admirable Zen-like quality in some people, came not because they were more spiritually tuned-in, but because they had been blessed with the right bone structure, a clear passage for breath. Breathing fully and effortlessly, something he had always had difficulty with, was after all the kernel of any meditative ritual. Nature then had hard-wired him for anxiety.

The night Atif and Rahul first kissed, he jousted with the cast of his life. There was the cavalcade of lovers, some from as far back as his confused, closeted adolescence in Mumbai; Becca, miscast as his enraged employer, sacking him for his carelessness, blaming him for her perilous love life; and his parents, passing his forged social security card back and forth disapprovingly, running their finger over the thick white skin of correction fluid and wondering if they should turn him in.

The morning after, Atif broke his ritual for the first time in as long as he could remember. He couldn't muster an appetite and skipped breakfast, procrastinated on the writing, rushed to work earlier than normal. He needed to be around people, even if he didn't want to confide in them.

Rahul was haunting Atif's apartment and had destroyed his solitude.

For the first time in as long as Rahul could remember, he was terrified.

It wasn't just that he couldn't understand his mind, but that even his body felt different now, alive, like a teenager's – confused, excited, guilty. He went through the motions of the day in a narcoticized state of desire, pretending to be part of the world spinning around him; but as hard as he tried, it was as if a veil had fallen over him so that when he looked at others – things, places – he saw only Atif.

At the bank, he stared at files begging for management approvals, initialling them mindlessly, as if thousands and even millions of dollars weren't hanging in the balance. He swallowed cupfuls of sugar-loaded black coffee in the break room, which only fuelled his restlessness; he paced around the air-conditioned branch making perfunctory conversation with his staff yet hearing little of what they said, and he took a two-hour lunch during which he walked endlessly, as if trying to escape the unrelenting opera of his mind.

All day he shook his legs under his desk, trying to deal with clients negotiating rate bumps on large Certificates of Deposit or demanding overdraft fee reversals despite having carelessly issued checks on insufficient balances, and he could think only about Atif, granting them the gratification he so desperately sought. Everything was eclipsed by Atif.

Another day he endured an appointment with the controller of a major airline on Century Boulevard, amazing himself by sitting through the entire conversation, nodding his head, offering neutral expressions, and grasping absolutely nothing of what was being said about liquidity requirements, no-hold policies and priority service. At a meeting later that afternoon, Rahul sat in a room crowded with other managers as a district manager droned interminably about the institution's market share, and how to best compete with others with a better distribution, the projected slides flashing at Rahul. All of it the concern of an alien race, nothing to do with him.

He was everywhere but there, even in the past, that foreboding realm that he could only access moments at a time before feeling singed. Atif had pried the doors open, doors that he had spent a whole lifetime barricading. He sat in a dimly lit room full of obsequious suits and pie charts but in his mind he saw the crystalline waters of the Indian Ocean dotted with dhows; instead of the stale cologne and perspiration, he smelled the beach's salty air; talk of new sales campaigns and incentive plans warbled and turned into the rustle of palm trees – the sound of beads in a silver tray – as they craned over the seaweed-strewn beaches of Mombasa. Slowly, he stopped chewing the gum in his mouth and tasted early morning breakfasts of *mahambri* and *bharazi,* creamy beans liberally dusted with cayenne and salt and eaten with sweet, fried bread.

He saw the cricket field of Aga Khan High on a torpidly hot day, the foreboding old baobab tree rumoured to house spirits rooted in the middle of it. He tasted the fruit of this ancient tree, broken down from its pod, cooked and dyed in sugary red syrup. As he grasped the bat with its familiar smell of linseed oil and leaned into it, the roomful of suits transmuted into an elated crowd anticipating his hit. In the throngs he saw Hanif again, the one who was never found. Hanif with the pained expression, longing for him, and Rahul averted his gaze, embarrassed, ashamed. He found that his parents and sister were also there, safe and hale, cheering him on to glory. But then the sun accreted, surged, its flames inflaming everything. Harrowing cries. Bodies alight, whirling like spindles of fire.

Rahul convulsed, drew a sharp breath, jolted back.

People started to look but quickly turned their attention back to the motivational speech on household acquisitions, punctuating the presentation with an endorsing laugh track. The manager sitting on his left, a balding, hefty Latino from Pasadena, sympathetically offered him a stick of chewing gum. He felt the impulse to flee from the room but he sat very still, dabbed the beads of perspiration from his forehead with his handkerchief and retuned to the presentation, more lost than ever as new charts flew up. The district manager was attempting some humour about the banking industry now, prophesying that at the rate of mergers, one day they would all be working for the same bank, hopefully theirs, and this drew more gratuitous laughter from the obsequious ass-kissers.

You are all dispensable, he thought, looking around the room. *Don't you see it? Replaceable. Ants in the colony of commerce.*

He had hurt Pooja last night. Instead of making love to her, he had cast himself upon her like a punishment, in a way he had never done before. She had recoiled from him, unable to recognize the man who had come to her and who, even when she remonstrated out of sheer pain, had continued to drive himself into her until he had fallen upon her like some heavy animal, unsure if he'd ever be able to rise again.

In the morning, they said nothing to each other about what had happened and although she made breakfast for him – golden brown *aloo* parathas and south Indian egg *ekuri* – just as she had for the almost twenty years of their life together, she would not look him in the eye. Shame rose in him and he had wanted to explain, to touch her with the tenderness that had been lacking the night before, to apologize, but he did not understand his own heart and averting his own gaze from her, left for work.

For the first time Rahul understood something

quintessential about the nature of addiction. In the end addiction was not so much about externalities, about seeking something transcendental or outside of you. Rather, it was about reaching fractal interiorities that had been blockaded. He had seen Atif, tasted him, and in doing so, he recognized something more than he had bargained for. Something no longer obscured by a marriage, offspring and career.

Himself.

A week had passed but Atif thought of Rahul constantly. He kept seeing Rahul, tall and masculine in that immaculately cut suit and the five o'clock shadow on his handsome face, standing on the other side of the counter, giving him that lingering look, wordlessly reaching out to him, asking to be understood and then, just as quickly, letting his gaze fall, as if he had said too much, revealed something. It had been so long since Atif had desired someone, so long since someone had looked at him, actually looked at him, that he felt as if Rahul's eyes had polished years of tarnish and grime off him.

Atif prayed that they would meet again and at one point had even called directory assistance in his desperation, unsure of what he would do if he actually tracked down Rahul's number. Seventeen Rahul Kapoors existed in the Westside. He was grateful and crushed simultaneously.

He was scheduled to work the late shift on a weekday, which meant he had to help close the bookstore at ten o'clock and drop off the daily deposit in the bank's night vault on his way home. It was about an hour before closing time when the phone rang. Atif was standing next to Becca, who was fretting that her boyfriend had not called her as he had promised to. The caller hung up and she became visibly perturbed, convinced it was he who was trying to make amends. When the phone rang again, less than a minute later, Atif picked it up while she loomed over him expectantly.

'May I speak with Atif, please?'

That voice. Atif's heart leapt in his ribcage. 'Hi, it's me.'

'I'm sorry,' he said, assuming Atif already knew who it was. 'I tried your cellphone but it –'

'I know. No reception here.'

'You probably can't talk right now . . .'

Becca's hands were practically on the phone, ready to wrestle it away from him. Atif shook his head to indicate it wasn't for her. She slumped back. 'Can I call you right back?'

Rahul gave him his cellphone number.

Without bothering to explain, Atif ran out onto the patio and tried to find a secluded corner from where he could use his cellphone. No bars. He waved the phone around in the air frantically but the little gadget refused to grant permission. He walked to the other end where a gay couple was seated on the bench, flipping through a book. The younger of the two smiled at Atif sympathetically as he continued to shake his cellphone and pace around like an agitated animal, and said 'Cellphones, I swear,' and Atif politely smiled back. He wanted to hurl the phone across the street but told himself to calm down, to breathe, breathe, breathe.

Suddenly, as if by a little miracle, he noticed a payphone located across the street, outside an elegant Italian restaurant, past the centre divider where they had met. He made a dash for it, thankful for the lunch change jingling in his pocket. At the centre divider, he waited for the heavier eastbound traffic under the large fanning tree and felt elated at the memory of their meeting. When he got the chance, he sprinted across as fast as his legs would carry him and panting, seized the phone and fed it with a quarter.

It rang interminably. He tried to calm himself, his heart still racing, every trill drawing Rahul further away from him. Maybe he wouldn't be there, had changed his mind. His hand closed around the impotent cellphone in his pocket and he fought the urge to smash it against the wall. But then Rahul's voice poured into his ears, salve on a wound.

'Can we meet?' Rahul said.

'Yes, but not here. My place,' he said. 'I can be there in half an hour.'

Now that the boy who had haunted him unceasingly stood barely inches away, Rahul's body trembled. 'God, I'm shaking,' he said, a hundred hunched fears and desires uncoiling. Everything he had pushed down for so long came loose now, in a rush, intoxicating, dizzying.

'There's nothing to be afraid of.'

'All the way here,' he said, 'I kept asking myself what I was doing. Something breaking. Dying.'

Atif touched his arm. 'Yet you've never felt more alive.'

They went to each other not like strangers but like lovers who, after an interminably long and thirsty separation, were merging again, rediscovering each other.

They sank to the ground, their bodies gnarled together. Words unnecessary. Their bodies expressed what language could not, with a hunger devoid of grace. When an animal rends his prey seeking sustenance, he lacks the finesse, the elegance of his normal gait and powerful pursuit. This is how they were. Rahul responded with the voracity of his kisses and with hands that clawed and tore at Atif. Sometimes their bodies locked in impossible configurations, their limbs intertwined, but always they bore each other's weight, supplying nourishment to each other.

When Rahul finally entered him, Atif called out his name over and over again with such abandon and yearning that it sounded like the invocation of a man possessed. Rahul pressed his hand over Atif's mouth, trying to lose himself, shirking recognition. He continued to drive himself further into Atif's body, a man struggling to shake himself free of his own skeleton.

When they lay on the floor next to each other by the side of the bed, all they could hear was the sound of their breathing and from somewhere out there, a distant aria clashing with the laugh track from someone else's television. Light streamed in through the window from the lamp outside and could have easily been mistaken for moonlight. The heady scent of tuberoses wafted in from the living room.

In the silence between them, in Rahul's gentle caresses, Atif sought hope; now that the first hurdle had been overcome, now that Rahul had come this far and hadn't taken flight in a surge of regret or shame, he would come back for more. Atif raised Rahul's large hand into the shaft of light and placed his palm against it. The hand of a child against his father's. Pearly light glowed around the silhouette of long fingers, the band on Rahul's finger glinting dully. Atif circled his fingers around it, unsure if he was trying to block it out or recognize its significance. Sensing this, Rahul's hand closed in around Atif's, pulling them down.

'I've always felt great love for her. But never great passion.'

Atif looked at him. It was not just the face of someone who could betray a lifelong wife, a wife who could after decades be so easily deceived, but the face of someone who had outlived something much more unspeakable.

Rahul's face began trembling and suddenly, as if a wave that he had no control over was washing over him, he heaved into tears. Atif drew him into his arms, kissed him tenderly, the way his mother had when he'd been little – on his forehead, the curls of his lashes, on the strong aquiline nose and fleshy lips – and conveyed in gesture instead of words that he would be there for him if Rahul would only let him.

In the morning, Rahul hoped to evade Pooja. He woke earlier than usual, careful not to wake her as he lifted himself out of their bed and prepared for work. But by the time he had emerged from the shower and walked into the kitchen, she had already washed up in the kitchen sink, as she sometimes did despite the extra bathroom, and was laying out stacks of thick parathas and eggs on the table. Z-TV played mutely on the television set and Bollywood heart-throb Vivek Oberoi was twirling his on-screen love interest against a multitude of extras, also gyrating to the ghosted soundtrack.

She poured him a cup of steaming chai and glanced at the screen. 'He's so talented. Can't believe it's the same boy from *Company*,' she said.

'Put the volume up. I don't mind,' he said and took his seat at the head of the table.

She returned to the kitchen. 'Yesterday you worked very late.'

He unfolded the *Los Angeles Times*, which she had also

placed on the table before him, and tried to occupy himself with the collapse of the tenuous Middle East peace. Hundreds tortured, displaced, killed. And though he cared, he could not bring himself this morning to empathize with anything; he could only think of the war within him. 'You know how it is,' he said simply as if this explained everything and mitigated all that upset the equilibrium of a marriage.

She reappeared with a jar of spicy pickled mangos, stirring the pungent, swampy concoction with a teaspoon and placed it next to his untouched plate. 'Eat first. It will go cold. The war will still be going on after you've eaten your eggs.'

'Hmm.' He looked up at her, smiled, conceded. At least Ajay wouldn't be up for another hour and he wouldn't have to pretend. If she sensed something different about him that morning, he would be the last to know. She fed him, fussed over him, gabbed about Sonali's latest antic, touched him on the shoulder as she hovered over him, and life continued as if nothing had happened.

There was so much he could do, so many possibilities. He could grab her by the wrist, sit her down next to him, tell her, 'Pooja, listen, I was with someone yesterday. I was with another man.' He could tell her that it wouldn't happen again. Or that he couldn't stop himself from thinking about the boy. He could just get up, the food she had so lovingly prepared untouched, say nothing, leave her wondering, flummoxed.

Despite himself, Rahul felt resentful that she was making this so easy for him. He dug his fork into the cumin-speckled pillows of egg and vegetables and she settled next to him, wedging fist under chin, watching him partake of her love adoringly.

It was so easy to just continue as if nothing had happened.

Book Two

As the clouds scatter, her tears flow
as night deepens, her sighs increase
Like a bird in flight, her laughter vanishes
Lightning strikes and robs her of her sleep
Like a bird, she cries 'Piu! Piu!'
Waves of fierce heat rise up within her.
Listen, says Kesav, this is her condition:
There is no fire, but her limbs are burning.

– Radha's Lament for Krishna
Granthavali

I must go
in spite of my kisses,
my passionate embraces,
he keeps repeating
that he must go.
He goes half a step
and then he turns back
with anguished eyes,
gazing at my face.

– Chandidasa
14th century

IT WAS DARK by the time Atif got home. Becca had pulled a no-show but Atif had been grateful for the extra work that kept him from his solitude, the thoughts of Rahul.

He entered the quiet, warm apartment, illuminated only by the powdery light of the security lamp filtering in through the sheer curtains. He had forgotten to turn the thermostat off in the morning and the heater thundered back on, its roar never failing to surprise him. Having slept restlessly the night before, he felt drained today.

In the dark, he walked over to the answering machine, checking it out of habit, expecting no messages. Nobody called any more. Telemarketers and occasionally Nuru, trying to rope him into another drug-fuelled circuit party at The Mayan or some renovated hip spot.

Many of Atif's close friends had disappeared altogether. As they had grown into their late twenties, the loves of their lives had miraculously materialized out of nowhere, rescuing them from a future of crippling solitude and unreasonably high expectations; like his friend Enrique, whom the gods of the Internet had rewarded by materializing Steven from the void. Within mere weeks they had all but moved in – baking cookies, catching up on entire seasons of *Sex and the City*, planning international trips to the Amazon and Europe, spending time with other couples, fantasizing about home purchases.

'But seriously, Enrique. Are you in love with this guy?' Atif asked and he got, 'Well, I do love him.' Or there was that incredulous look, as if Atif had refused to grow up.

As time went by, Enrique called less and calls were returned less punctually until one day, not at all. Some months later, Atif had run into the blissful couple in the Halloween throngs on Santa Monica Boulevard. Enrique's awkwardness and Steven's coldness confirmed to Atif that he'd been sold out as the friend who once seeded doubts in Enrique's mind, daring to question their love.

Atif refused to make the compromises that would allow him to accept just any man who came along. *I'm not picky, just specific.* The model boyfriend may look good on paper, armour buffed and strapping, but if he didn't make your heart sing, weaken your knees with a feverish jolt of desire, set off butterflies in the stomach, what good was it? Just a lot of tin and clangour. Atif was convinced that friends like Enrique had eventually settled, capitulated. Now they had no time for friends, especially the ones they had known when they were single. They were required to be home – to cook dinner, look after the dog, play house, invite other couples over – and even having dinner or catching a movie with an old friend was suddenly a betrayal to the relationship.

Atif had always hoped that if love didn't come, at least the friendships would endure, that in the end they would grow old together so that they could look each other in the eyes and say, 'It's okay that we didn't find "the one". I know you at least. Over all these years we've remained. We've seen so many things happen. I still love you.' That's what he searched for in friendships, the common thread running through them all. They would age together, watch each other become wiser, stronger, and when they saw each other's frailties, they would prop each other up. But ultimately, most had been too terrified of being alone.

The answering machine came alive with Nuru. 'Girlfriend, where you are these days? You get kidnapped by UFO or what?' he said in his thick accent, laughing delightedly at his own humour. 'You know, I not calling any more, okay, bitch, because you don't call back no more. So what is this, your problem? Listen, you have to come to Red Eye this weekend. And no to worry, I treat. Okay, *habibi*, call me,' and he rattled off his number three times just in case.

The son of wealthy Kuwaiti parents, Nuru spent his family fortune on circuit parties and designer drugs as freely as the free-flowing oil that had produced it. In many ways, he reminded Atif of Hiten Khanna. Nuru loved to wear dazzling Versace shirts unbuttoned down to his navel to reveal a forest of chest hair against which he always wore gold chains and pendants. The backlash of 9/11 had done nothing to dampen his enthusiasm for the country or curb his flamboyance. Whenever asked about his so-called marketing major, Nuru liked to flash a smile as bright as his conspicuous Dolce and Gabbana belt buckle, prop his buttocks out and say, 'Yeah, baby, here is market. Come, you want juicy watermelon? I give you halal meat too, habibi.'

Of all his friends, Nuru was the one Atif had the least in common with, and the only one who bothered to stay in touch. Nuru was always generous with his money, supplying rounds of ecstasy and an assortment of powdery bumps from brightly coloured bullets to fuel the party. Atif, never a regular in this scene, had made it clear that he was not into it. But, perhaps owing to his privileged background, Nuru was never one to be discouraged or to take anything too seriously. He still called occasionally, sounding mildly wounded as if they had been in touch only last week, and hoping he could sway Atif into an eight-hour marathon of carousing. No chance.

Atif emptied his pockets of the loose change on the writing desk and stripped down to nothing, tossing his clothes carelessly around him. Naked, he went to the kitchen and from the freezer he retrieved a tin that used to contain rose-flavoured pastilles but now held a thatch of marijuana, and from the cutlery drawer he took out some rolling paper. He placed everything on the coffee table, pressed some buttons on the remote control and let the honeyed voice of Abida Parvin pour into the room. He had a formidable collection of CDs and was especially fond of the ghazals of which the Sufi singer was a legend.

Abida deliquesced in Faiz's poetry while Atif closed his eyes, swivelled his tired neck, hunched his aching shoulders and allowed her melody to soothe him. Even though he knew that Abida Parvin and his Zainab Aunty were two different people, when he listened to her ghazals, he liked to think that it was in fact his long-lost aunt that was singing them, that she was also there somewhere, quietly validating his taste, savouring them with him from a corner of the room.

Sham-e-firaque ab na pooch
Aayee aur aa ke tal gayee

Pray don't ask me of my evening of waiting
How it came and went and how.

He settled into an easy chair from across the entertainment centre and rolled himself a tight, plump joint, working expertly in the dark. He heard his neighbour's footsteps across the ceiling, the floorboards creaking. Abida soared:

Bazme khayal me tere husn ki shamma jal gayee
Dard ka chaand bujh gaya hijr ki raat dhal gayee

Enveloped by thoughts of your beauty, the evening passed
A night of pain ended, the hours of waiting passed.

He lit the joint and drew in its rich, aromatic fumes and as the smoke filled his lungs he felt the looseness of his body, pure emancipation, levitation. He sank back in the chair and emitted whorls of smoke, watching them dance up in arabesques in the shaft of light cutting through him, and felt the day with its taxing thoughts seep gently out of him and dissipate in the atmosphere.

Listening to the yearning in her voice and in the lyrics, he wondered how long had it been since someone had held him all night – bodies tossing and turning, adjusting but always staying in contact, an arm thrown over his waist, a head leaning against his back, hot breath against his skin. He thought of Rahul, wondered what it must be like to find him there in the morning.

He took a deep drag and decided it had been much too long. Too long since he had been held. Much too long since he had smoked. At times like this, the marijuana allowed him rein in his ricocheting thoughts. To quiet down the noise a little, prevent a mental collision. He could take one memory, one thought at a time, and after inspecting it momentarily, vaporize it.

Abida's twisting alaps, tablas, lamenting sarangi and the cannabis fused together to help Atif escape in a way his expired visas never could. He drifted back to Mumbai: the throng of people, rickshaws, taxis and cattle locking and moving intermittently through the streets, barely a hair's breadth from each other. God, he never thought he would miss it so much. He hadn't even considered how he'd never be able to go back after overstaying his student visas.

Now he truly understood what it meant to be lost. In his new country, Atif technically didn't exist. He was but one of a myriad of people in hiding; a fake social security number, pending eventual unearthing and castigation. Sure, he had learned to call this his home, but could someone truly be at home in a country that wasn't his own? Where the colour of his skin, for better or worse, automatically exacted questions about what exotic languages he spoke or whether he knew how to make good curry?

He knew other Indians, born and educated here, with American passports, the vernacular dripping off their tongues and limbs effortlessly like honey, and their only bond with the motherland being the cinema and nouvelle cuisine Indian lounges that were all in vogue these days; they proudly dubbed themselves 'desis', but could even they truly feel at home here? Like they would there?

Maybe it was easier if you didn't know any better. But once an Indian has lived in India, smelled its dung fires, been slapped by its pandemonium and assaulted by its colours, once you've seen that the maimed infant begging for coins and the rich gold-bedecked madam in the cool cab have the same caramel skin, could you ever truly blend in anywhere else? When you knew what it was like never having to hear someone tell you to go back where you came from, because that would be ludicrous, wouldn't it – this is where your kind began and this is where, with the land, they would perish one day – could you still feel like anything but an outcast, temporarily sanctioned?

He remembered the smell, of *bombil* fish drying on stilts in the open, the dank perfume of the Arabian Sea mingling with exhaust smoke and sewage and sandalwood, and he felt a dull ache of nostalgia. One day he would go back. Not to see his family or the friends he grew up with, but to course through the same spaces, eat the foods, take in the heady smell and pollution of the city. What it would be like to amble through the food stalls of Chowpatty beach again and eat pani puri and *sitafad* ice cream and sit on the gritty brown sand and watch the fiery red Mumbai sun dip into the sea?

A man never forgets where he is born, the streets he played in, the foods he ate – both those forbidden and which he enjoyed, and the ones prescribed and which he still carries some disdain for. These things stay with him always, mental tattoos, glowing. At the end of his life, these are the visions that regale him as he prepares to say goodbye to the world of mortal senses: the sweet, milky flesh of custard apples, the heady fragrance of the attar of roses, the first time he looked into those eyes and fell in love.

Atif smoked some more, Abida continued to lull him and in time, he fell asleep in the chair, his thoughts skipping from one rail to another, like a train determined to move but uncertain of its destination.

Back in Mumbai, when Atif had been about ten, they had lived in Byculla, once a prosperous and elegant suburb with grand British and Parsi houses, the home of the Byculla Club, one of Mumbai's first residential clubs. After the Byculla railway station was completed, and the first mills were already polluting its clear air, a plague finally drove the British and richer Parsis to the more fashionable Malabar Hill, and Byculla became the lower-middle-class enclave mostly of Muslims, with its charming air of genteel decay, which Atif came to know as a young boy.

Their apartment was in one of two chipping five-storey buildings slapped up against each other, drying laundry flapping from the balconies like sails in the wind. The rooms were dirty, unfinished and worn, but Atif's mother had done her best to cover the unsightly parts with plants and tapestries, one of which was a gigantic depiction of the Ka'aba in Mecca. Their neighbours, the Vaids, had been a fairly traditional Hindu family and Atif went to school with their youngest son Kamal.

Atif tried as hard as he could to spend as much time with Kamal, whether they were exuberantly flying kites from the rooftops or studying. Both families innocently joked it away by calling them brothers separated at birth in an ode to the formula frequently used in Bollywood cinema. *'Ek bana Musalman, doosra bana Hindu. Chalo, een dono par hi chhod dete hai sab logo ka jhagra mitana,'* joked Atif's father. 'Let's leave it up to these two to solve the feud between Hindus and Muslims.'

Kamal's mother, Mrs Vaid, was a heavy-set, highly strung housewife well versed in the mystical art of numerology. One late afternoon, Mrs Vaid pulled out a freshly sharpened pencil and a pad of graph paper. Planting herself on the floor between Kamal and Atif, she began her Pythagorean evaluation of Atif's full name. If he was going to be spending so much time around her son and their family, she might as well decipher what kind of a destiny the numbers had in mind for him.

'Each letter,' she explained, deftly allocating numerical values, 'has a vibration. See? 'A' has a one, 'T' has a four, 'I' is a five . . .' and she went on this way until she had reduced his entire name to a single potent numeral.

Even then, Atif had known there was something forbidden about the 'super science', as she called it. Palmistry, graphology, physiognomy, numerology – all these were pagan to Islam and strictly forbidden in his household. He had seen his father get worked up and passionately decry them whenever someone had suggested this to find out if a financial crisis would come to pass or a new opportunity might be on the horizon.

'But . . . but,' Atif blubbered, 'Papa says it's a sin to do this –'

'O-pho! Trouble with you people is you just love making things overly hard for yourselves! This is God's way of letting you in on a little bit of inside information through sums. See, if He didn't want you to know, would it exist? Hunh?'

Atif knew better than to argue.

'*Arre, dekha?* See how accurate this is? You are a number one!' she proclaimed, circling the number on her pad with a flourish.

Kamal and Atif looked at each other and started laughing.

'*Ey-yey!* This isn't laughing matter. See, according to this, beta, you are a very, very headstrong boy. Number one, they are very strong people, very successful. But you are also very stubborn. Very selfish. You must think of others, not always what you want,' she scolded. Atif swallowed and looked at Kamal. He didn't have the heart to tell Mrs Vaid her analysis couldn't be further from the truth. He was always being picked on at school, was confused about what he wanted, reflexively conceded to others, especially Kamal, and his mother always told him that he should be a little stronger, otherwise the world would gallop on his back.

'You must be more like my Kamal. He's a number two. So sensitive, so selfless.' She swatted him on the head and he yelped. 'Stupid thing's always being taken advantage of by everyone!'

In his dreams, Atif sometimes went back to that afternoon. Mrs Vaid looked the same as she had that torpid monsoon afternoon in August, nearly twenty years ago. Even Kamal was there, grinning mischievously, sprawled out on the floor in the white cotton shirt and khaki shorts that comprised the school uniform. Kamal dug his nose thoroughly and then, inspecting his find on his index finger, ingested it before Mrs Vaid could catch him.

Atif pleaded with Mrs Vaid to read the numbers again. He told her that although he'd spent a few years living it up, he had involved himself in all sorts of meaningless situations and relationships, and had ended up the classic underachiever, increasingly withdrawn and disillusioned. But Mrs Vaid, prone to passionate outbursts when her beliefs, most of all her divination methods, were under attack, didn't even turn around to look at him from the kitchen sink. Her hair was matted with sweat and tied in a bun around the nape of her neck. The dampness under her arms looked like large blots of ink on the blouse under her sari. She continued making *srikhand* to celebrate the birth of Krishna on Gokulashtami, whisking the sugar and saffron into the sour curds with concentration.

'Just you wait,' she said. 'The numbers are never wrong.'

Indian cinema churns out close to a thousand films each year to whet the prodigious appetite of the masses wishing to escape their mundane lives. Much of this comes from Bollywood. Atif, like the crores of Indians, knew this magical realm well. They had all been steeped in it since birth, as if in strongly brewed chai, and would remain forever charged and drunk by its potent flavours.

Over time, he had seen the gods of the celluloid pantheon change roles and rank – from the tall and charismatic Amitabh Bachhan to the ultra-sensitive, dimpled and impishly mischievous Shah Rukh Khan – but the plot remained invariably loyal. Poor boy meets girl, they fall in love, endure family opposition, and in the end, struggle through with their love intact. There were other tried and true formulas as well – siblings separated at birth and ending up on opposite sides of the law, heart-throb sacrificing himself at the altar of incurable cancer and bequeathing his *mehbooba* to his best friend who has secretly loved her from the start – but they all found a convenient way to accommodate serenades on snowcapped mountains where the suffering lovers looked impossibly ethereal, and big fight sequences ensued in which the ailing hero assumed Herculean powers and kicked a whole pack of villain asses. If you were especially lucky, there would be the wet sari sequence in which the heroine felt the irresistible urge to jump into waterfalls for a bath and burst out into song while still expecting privacy.

Atif's earliest memories included his visits to the cinema and of re-enacting the pivotal scenes and dance numbers of Bollywood. Sometimes Kamal and he would assume roles from the latest film Atif had seen, with Atif always playing the part of the damsel. On the rare occasion Kamal would object: '*Aiy! Aiy!* Why you are always Hema Malini? *Humko bhi dance karne ko ataa hai!*'

Atif would hook his hands on his hips, *tsk,* and say, 'That part is more difficult, *yaar*, and you haven't even seen the picture. And please! I'm playing Rekha not that Hema-Bema!'

Atif wasn't interested in the suave choreography of the male leads, the comparatively reined-in emotions, the mysterious frowns, the stretch-your-arms-out-wide and then run-your-fingers-through-your-hair move. He rejoiced in the expansive, seductive moves of the actress – the undulating shoulders, hip thrusts, trance-like spins and then, after still managing to fall on the ground like a cat on its paws, the breathless over-the-shoulder glances.

Once, his mother had caught him enacting Geeta Dutt's '*Babuji dheere chalna*' on the portable record player which Atif was forbidden from touching when his father was at home. Although the song was from the 1950s film *Aar Paar* and he had never seen it, the seductive allure of the voice and melody had been enough to dictate his femme fatale moves. His mother, standing in the corridor, had covered her mouth and laughed. Embarrassed, Atif had jumped into bed and rolled himself up in the sheet that had served, at various points of the performance, as his long silken hair and the folds of a glamorous dress. But then suddenly, from between the folds of cotton, Atif saw the mirth drain from her face. It was replaced with nervousness and perturbation, as if a grave realization had dawned upon her. She had returned to making parathas in the kitchen. Even later that day, when his mother had massaged Atif's scalp with dark and fragrant Amla hair oil, as was a daily ritual for them, she had said nothing other than, 'You'll thank me when you're older and have a head full of hair!'

They had known instinctively that there was something taboo about what had happened and that his father had better not find out. It was the first time that he had sensed that there was something wrong with what had come naturally to him.

Because money was always a bit scarce in the Rahman household, going to the movies was not always a priority. As the owner of a clothing store in the bustling shopping district of Bandra, Abdul Rahman's income was dependent on the vagaries of retail and his days filled with the stress of competing with neighbouring boutiques with similar merchandise and street kiosks willing to sell for much less. Unless it was a guaranteed blockbuster with his favourite Dev Anand or Khadija's favourite, Rajesh Khanna, most of the time an outing on Juhu Chowpatty beach sufficed.

This is where 'Chacha' became indispensable.

Mahmood Rahman or 'Chacha', as Atif called his paternal uncle, was a robust, well-built man inflicted with a pockmarked face from a near-fatal case of chickenpox as an infant. Having no children of his own and a failed marriage – his wife of two years, Zainab, had mysteriously run off – Chacha was much more indulgent with his film-crazed nephew and happy to take him to the theatres where they could enjoy the latest boon from the Bollywood gods.

'Why don't you two spend some "honeymoon time"?' He would tell Atif's parents. '*Arre, akhir hamara bhi beta hain*. He's my son, too. Don't I have the right to spoil him a little?'

Compared to his older brother, Chacha had done considerably well, selling refurbished refrigerators from a store in Fort. Whenever times got especially tough for Abdul, Chacha generously offered to help out, but Abdul was too proud to accept any kind of help even from his brother. As the elder of the two, Abdul felt that it should have been he that was assisting his brother and setting an example. Only twice had Abdul made an exception and approached his baby brother for money – for bills when Atif was born and owing to the difficult delivery, Khadija had been retained for a longer period, and another time when Abdul had got into an accident and his already ailing Bajaj had to be replaced with a new scooter.

Even then Chacha had generously insisted on a reliable used car, but Abdul had said, 'Remember, Mahmood, in Mumbai there are only two kinds of people who have cars – those who sit in the back and have the money and those who drive them around and have none.' Abdul Rahman hadn't been fortunate enough to belong to the first class and considered it beneath his dignity to serve in the second.

Sometimes Chacha let Atif bring Kamal along to the film and these outings became more special. Atif puffed up with immense pride for having such a well-to-do uncle. *Kasme Vaade, Trishul, Don,* Atif relished all these hits with his generous Chacha at the Nandi or Gaity in Bandra. It was a well-known fact that the hero in these films,

Amitabh Bachchan, who was married to the actress Jaya Bhaduri, was having an extramarital affair with his leading lady, the southern siren Rekha. The public ravenously ate it all up, delighting in the scandals of their celluloid deities. Like the gods of the Hindu pantheon who indulged in all sorts of conduct that would be deemed inappropriate and even sinful in mortals, their headlining love affair was validation that real life indeed was and could be as bizarre and magical as the films they flocked to see when escaping their dull existence.

During the interval, Atif also got to choose between popcorn and masala chips and share a Coke with his Chacha. In the bustle of the canteen, where the ratchet of people talking, clanging trays and chomping away loudly reached a crescendo like that at Victoria Terminus, little Atif was given the freedom and some rupees to squeeze his way through the throng of people demanding service at the faux marble counter, and secure the tasty snacks.

They had just seen Amitabh Bachchan's new super-hit film *Muqaddar Ka Sikandar* and although it was already nightfall, as a special treat, Chacha was taking them to Juhu Chowpatty for some ice cream. It was to be their little secret. The motorized rickshaw found its way through the multitudes of the city, weaving through yellow and black taxis, BEST double-decker buses, trucks requesting HORN PLEASE OK, vacant strollers and relentless beggars.

The end of such an outing always depressed Atif but at least there was one more stop today. He wished he could stay on with Chacha and never have to go back to his disciplinarian father and nervous mother. As the motor rickshaw zigzagged like a buzzing bee between the unceasing flurry of men, motors and animals, Chacha slunk away into a deep silence and Atif wondered if he too was sad and that maybe that was why he had decided on this excursion.

Atif sat next to his Chacha, bumped by the choppy ride, cradling images from the film like a newborn. In the film, Rekha, who had become Atif's screen goddess, played the stunning prostitute Zohrabai who ends up giving her life for Sikandar, played by her real-life lover, Amitabh Bachchan. Their doomed love affair, laced with songs that became instant classics – especially *'Salaam-e-ishq meri jaan'*, – made an indelible impression on Atif's young heart. Their simmering chemistry and passionate performances convinced Atif, as it had audiences all over, that the two of them belonged together, on and off screen, society be damned. In his little mind Atif could see that this was the only way to love. Recklessly and without rules.

He was sure to play the scenes out with Kamal later on, especially the part when Zohrabai was dying in Sikandar's arms, bidding him a tearful goodbye. He was regretful that Kamal couldn't be there so he could play Sikandar's role more authentically. No matter, all Kamal had to do was cradle him in his arms and regret his misplacement of affection for so long. It was Atif who would have the tough part – gasping for air as he delivered the heart-wrenching dialogues. Would the soundtrack cassette include dialogues? He wondered. How much easier that would make it. Chacha would surely buy it for him.

When the rickshaw came grudgingly to a halt, street urchins and beggars, sometimes entire families, equipped with karmic promises and reminders of the virtues of altruism, closed in on them for alms. Years later, in another part of the world, where the smell of rot would be replaced by the weight of smog, Atif would balk at the cold steeling, the rigid indifference that the city had adopted towards the surrounding poverty. But for now, Atif sat next to his Chacha, more treats waiting for him at the beach, and a lollipop clutched tightly to his breast.

When an old, dark woman in a soiled sari cradling an infant with his big, haunting eyes persisted on getting some coins, Chacha shooed her away. Normally he just plain ignored them. '*Arre, kai ko tang karti hai? Mana kardiya na? Chal, patli gulli pakad!* Get lost!'

The woman scampered away to the next car before the lights turned and another opportunity would be lost. The little boy in her arms looked back at Atif, who suddenly felt the urge to surrender his lollipop to him. Too late.

When the rickshaw came to a blinding halt to avoid a swerving cyclist, who in turn was clearing out of the way of an ox, Chacha, like all Mumbaikars who were accustomed to this hazardous kind of driving, lost his temper. '*Arre, akal ka dushman, gadi zara dekh ke chalao!*'

Was it Aunty Zainab that Chacha was upset about? Atif wondered. Maybe the powerful film had resuscitated dormant emotions in him. Who wouldn't melt against the fiery passion of Zohrabai and Sikandar? Atif couldn't remember much about Aunty Zainab. She was a like a figure in a fog. The only thing he could recall was that she had waist-long hair and had once brought him a tin of Cadbury hazelnut chocolates when she had visited with Chacha. He had heard her name being mentioned in the hushed *guss-puss* of his mother and the gossiping neighbours when they congregated in his kitchen in the afternoon.

Of these, Darya '*Durbin*', dubbed such because of the binocular-eyes with which she kept surveillance over the comings and goings of the entire neighbourhood from her third-storey flat in the next building, had been the most vocal and mysterious. Darya Durbin was a tough, shrewd old woman, small and frail only in appearance. The cataracts in her eyes did nothing to compromise what she absorbed with manic dedication. She was a Parsi, famous for etching out a safe strip between the perennially rioting

Hindu and Muslim, East and West, Indian and English. The Parsis typically clustered together as if by forming their own little nexus they could forget the city that their homes were actually domiciled in. But her deceased husband had gambled all their money away and their grown-up son only provided a paltry stipend from his luxurious Apollo Bunder apartment. So she was no longer able to live in Khusrao Baug or other Parsi colonies. Whenever this realization came upon her, she fell into a black mood and she heaved and groaned like a sick woman. When she vented out her problems, Darya Durbin expected others to wear suitably mournful faces and to fall into loud exclamations of pity at her sufferings. The rest of the time, Darya Durbin, having fallen upon hard times, now found twisted solace in the misfortune of others.

'Far be it from me to say anything mean about anyone, what is the benefit to me anyway?' she always began with a few perfunctory *tsks*. 'But from the very, very beginning I just knew that that Zainab was up to no good. Something, don't ask me what, told me.' A heavy sigh. 'Some shameless women, *tsk, tsk, tsk,* they have only one thing on their mind! And what can you expect? After all, these days they are reading all those *firangi* magazines, no? And they are filling their heads only with all these strange ideas. A little bit of plumbing problem, and *whoosh!* off they go! *Faata-fat!*' Darya's bitterness curved her lips downwards like a bent spoon.

'*Chee! Chee!* What besharam things you are saying, Daryabai! Arre, how do we know anything about their problems?' Khadija jumped to her brother-in-law's defence.

'Arre, *deekra*, I know such women. Just look na, at that *daakan* who has put a spell on my poor Sorab.' Darya dabbed her eyes even though there were no visible signs of moistening. 'God knows what she's thrown in my poor son's food. Something was fishy as a pomfret. I knew from the very beginning but would he listen? No! It was all 'Firoza this and Firoza that'. Stupid woman also started to rearrange our whole place, did you know that? Went on and on about some Sheng fui, Feng fui, who knows what? Hunh! The stupid cow doesn't even know that all this we already have in the Vaastu Shastra. Don't need some *angrezi*s to tell us about such things!'

'O-pho! That is not angrezi,' Mrs Vaid corrected, stifling a laugh. 'Feng Shui, it is Chinese, Daryabai.'

'Chinese-finese, we don't need them!' she barked and Mrs Vaid almost jumped back, frightened.

The way Darya Durbin squinted her eyes with concentration and gnashed her dentures in silence for the next few seconds, it was obvious she was picturing Firoza flung into the Tower of Silence so that the vultures could have their way with her long before her death. Then, she could toss roasted peanuts into her mouth while sitting on a bench at Hanging Gardens, and watch with delight the vultures in the distance, circling the tower where in less than forty minutes they would have picked her to the bone. Truly, there is no justice in this world!

'*Kabhi aankhen dekhi hain?* Have you seen her eyes?' Mrs Vaid chortled. 'She was breastfed on carrot juice. We don't call her durbin for nothing! Arre, once she opens her eyes, forget the window, she can see through every man's lungi in town.'

Atif couldn't understand why Aunty Zainab would have left over something as trivial as a plumbing problem in their house. Why couldn't someone have been called to fix things before they got this out of hand? He wondered what Zainab must have looked like. Must be like Rekha. Why, even the names sounded alike. Zohrabai and Zainab. Yes, all beautiful women looked like Rekha. And they always knew when to exit and leave their men devastated.

Some, like Aunty Zainab, thundered out of the front door because the faucet wasn't working, and others slipped out of life itself, like Zohrabai in the film, as a way to take up permanent residence in the hearts of their lovers. Women who stayed on, who lingered long after the poetic lines had been delivered and the mundane set in, became inevitably dowdy and plain; the lacklustre girl-next-door types, who never got to sing the wah-wah-eliciting torch songs or dance the pulsating *mujra*. Like Amitabh's real-life wife, Jaya Bhaduri. Or his own plain mother.

When they disembarked the rickshaw at Juhu Chowpatty, Atif and Chacha headed straight for the ice cream stand where Atif asked for a sitafad kulfi and Chacha got some coconut juice and bhelpuri. They walked along the gritty sand of the beach, the brackish waters of the Arabian Sea on one side and the crowds on another. Away from the donkey rides, dancing monkeys, acrobats and romancing couples, they found a secluded spot, where they could sit facing the ocean. Chacha, still somewhat lugubrious, had already discarded the bhelpuri tray and coconut, but Atif continued lapping away at his ice cream.

'You are enjoying yourself, na?' he asked, scratching his cheek with the stained, elongated nail of his little finger.

'Yes, Chacha. Best film! Very good ice cream!' he said, shaking his little head from side to side.

'Yes, yes, *ekdum* solid! And Rekha, ekdum *jhakaas!* I will be buying you the cassette, too. So fond of music you are.' He slapped the back of Atif's head playfully. 'Rekha is staying around here only, you know?' As one of Mumbai's posh localities, Juhu domiciled many of the famous film stars' bungalows and it wasn't unusual to find crowds gathered outside the gated properties, hoping to catch glimpses of their celluloid gods.

Atif grew delighted. He could already feel the cassette

in his hand, hear the soundtrack in his mind. And he didn't even have to ask for it! This had worked out easier than he had imagined. He licked the remnants of the ice cream, tossed the depleted stick on the sand and leaned over Chacha's knee to kiss him on the cheek and thank him.

Chacha laughed, revealing paan-stained teeth. 'You are a good boy. Very good boy. Now you do something special for Chacha?'

Atif nodded eagerly. 'Hanh, Chacha. Should I kiss the other cheek?'

Chacha surveyed the surroundings carefully and then began to undo the drawstrings to his cotton pants. When he leaned back on the sand and pulled them down to his thighs, he revealed his limp cock resting on a dark thatch of hair. *'Idhar aa,'* he said, reaching out for Atif. *'Arre, kai ko gabhrata hai? Aja. Dekh, Chacha ko bahut dard hota hai, na?'* he said. 'Touch it a little bit to make the pain go away.'

Something within Atif made him hesitate, step back. Chacha beckoned with his large hand impatiently. *'O-pho! Kaha na, idhar aane ko.* Why you are scared, *henh?* You don't want Chacha to feel better?'

Atif gnawed his fingers, feeling something was inherently wrong.

'Phir? Chal, chal, jaldi kar. Hurry up now. You want Chacha to buy you cassette, na?'

Atif would forever remember the salty smell of the sea, its distinct fishy odour mingling with the smell of garam masala and sweat emitting from Chacha's pores. At first it had made him retch but in time – over the almost two years that they had repeated this after hours in the dark theatre during which Chacha also managed to fondle him as if out of paternal affection – Atif grew accustomed to it and, innocent to the forbidden nature of their relationship, even began to crave his uncle.

Then one day, without any explanation, Aunty Zainab returned.

Chacha, like the emasculated man everyone accused him of being behind his back, took her back in without a word and with open arms. Chacha and Atif stopped going to the films together because Chacha was now spending time with her and Atif began to despise the woman who had ripped the fabric of their relationship. Every once in a while when Chacha visited, he would toss Atif the cassette to a film he would now never get to see. This only exacerbated his pain. He longed for afternoons at the cinema with Chacha, to be touched, to relieve Chacha of the pain in the sand dunes at the beach while Chacha's eyes surveyed the surroundings and his hands pushed Atif down into the mustiness between his legs. No longer would he remonstrate or show any reluctance before giving in. If only he could have another opportunity to be needed again.

Broken-hearted, Atif even took the matches from the primus stove in the kitchen and set the latest cassette ablaze by the hills of garbage outside as morose dogs mewled around, then watched it melt and curl like a howling face through his own teary eyes, cursing Zainab under his breath.

Then he met her.

Atif was devastated that this woman – who had the temerity to walk out on Chacha and then waltz back in like a *rani* and usurp everything that he had built with Chacha – looked nothing like Rekha.

As if it wasn't enough that Zainab had, by her very reappearance, sabotaged Atif's place with Chacha, she now began to spend time over at the Rahman residence. Chacha would either drop her off on his way to work as if it were a detention centre, or she would take a rickshaw over from their apartment nearby and spend the day helping Khadija with household chores.

Although close to his mother's age, Zainab looked much older. She had a round, swollen face crowned by a shock of curly and prematurely greying hair, arthritic legs and a strangely masculine demeanour. Her clothes were drab and like her face, cheated of colour. She seemed to say, 'This is not the life I wanted and I'm not going to do a damn thing to disguise it with exuberance just to spare your feelings.' But underneath it all, there was also an unmistakable sadness about her and most of the time, when Zainab didn't let out her husky laugh, she was quiet, lost, as if in another world that had continued without her and where she wished she could still be.

And all Atif could think was, *This? This is what Chacha was mourning for? But surely this can't be her! She looks nothing like Rekha! She looks like a man.*

At first, Atif tried never to look at her and when hard pressed, kept his responses to her to a minimum. But he could sense how wounded she was and he found his alienation strategy tough to follow. It was as if something within her had died and she had resigned herself to a state of inner mourning, never speaking a word of it because that would do no good, nor would it change anything. Besides, it looked like nobody wanted to talk about it anyway.

Before this, Zainab was rumoured to have been boisterous and bubbling with laughter. In a city like Mumbai, where cultural iconography was freely borrowed for allegorical use, she was the rebellious Ganga that had been cast down from the heavens as punishment for her irreverence, to be trapped in the locks of Shiva's hair for eternity.

During Atif's holidays from school, he remembered that whenever Zainab was over she would bring along a plastic bag full of cassettes, most of them without shells and quite worn out from use. The ghazals of Meer, Kabir, Ghalib, Daagh – it was Zainab who first introduced Atif to these. Like wine, it was a taste he would acquire over time. 'Just for a little while,' she would suggest to Atif's mother, holding her fingers bunched up. 'Then we can go back to that filmi music.'

'O-pho, Zainab. But what is the point of hearing this kind of heartbreaking music and hurting yourself?' Khadija would say. 'Deliberately why inflict pain?'

And the sinewy voices of the filmi playback singers would be put aside so that the more classical voices of Mehdi Hassan, Munni Begum, and Zainab's favourite, the queen of mystical singing, Abida Parvin, could infuse the air with melancholia. At such moments, Atif would see the life come back in Zainab's face as she stopped stirring the bubbling pot of lamb curry or folding the linen to cock her head to the side and raise her hand in the air as she felt the music, ignoring the spying of Darya Durbin who hoped to catch a glimpse of something gossip-worthy transpiring in the house from her second-storey window. So not only did Zainab Aunty admire Abida Parvin but, Atif decided, she also resembled her, and it was easy to think that it was because of this that Zainab related to her music so much.

Jab se tu ne mujhe deevana bana rakhaa hai
Sang har shakhs ne haathon mein uthaa rakhaa hai

Since you've bewitched me
Stones have appeared in the hands of men

Pattharon, aaj mere sir pe baraste kyun ho?
Mein ne tum ko bhi kabhi apnaa khudaa rakha hai

O cruel stones! Why do you rain down upon me?
At one time, I even worshipped you as my God

Pejaa aiyaam ki talkhi ko bhi hans kai 'Nasir'
Gham ko sehnai mein bhi kudrat ne mazaa rakha hai

O' Nasir, imbibe the sorrow of these forlorn days with laughter
Nature has blessed even grief with a certain pleasure

Zainab was late one morning and Atif's mother had dashed off to the butcher for cuts of halal meat. He seized the opportunity to plug in Chacha's latest guilt offering of the *Silsila* soundtrack and used his mother's most diaphanous chunni to complete his transformation. After he had drawn the curtains, censuring Darya Durbin's view of the bedroom, he twirled against the mirror lip-synching the female parts of '*Dekha ek khwab*'. He didn't hear the car pull up or the front door open.

From where she stood at the door frame, Zainab had watched him for at least a full minute in his full Bollywood regalia before he caught her reflection in the mirror and froze, the chunni falling to the floor in a puddle.

They considered each other momentarily. Then Zainab went to the portable cassette player that was by the side of the door and pushed a button to stop the music. Slowly she walked over to Atif and knelt down by him with some difficulty because of the pain in her joints. She picked up the chunni and draped it around Atif's head, throwing the end of it around his neck and over his shoulder beautifully. She rubbed some of the paint off her lips and then ran her finger around his lips. She tucked her hand under his chin and raised his face so that she could look him in the eyes. One corner of her mouth turned up into a slight smile. She seemed to be saying, *Brace up, dear boy. If this is the path you'll be walking, you're going to need all the strength you can muster.*

'Aunty doesn't like to miss any part of a show. Shall we start from the beginning? You want I play Amitabh?'

Where she seemed to suffer around others her own age, Zainab came alive with Atif. The soft sighs evaporated and were replaced by the uproarious laughter that had been consigned to her past and rumour. And where it had been Chacha that Atif had depended on for his excursions to the cinema, it was Zainab who now became his partner to the Gaiety Cinema. She was only too happy to escape from the daily gossiping in Khadija's kitchen.

'*Bak, bak, bak, bak,*' she said. 'All day they go on. Like bleating goats they are. Just sitting around and spreading malicious gossip about others! One day it's going to bite them in their fat buttocks!'

Atif's feelings about having to relinquish Chacha to his aunt underwent a metamorphosis. After the afternoon she discovered him in front of the mirror, they formed a bond, and his resentment melted like an ice-*gola* in the sweltering Mumbai sun. Better to lose to someone like Aunty Zainab, who didn't make him feel wrong for dancing with his mother's chunni and went as far as to participate whenever they could steal a private session at home. Better Aunty Zainab with her coral pink hairpin and flat leather chappals than some man-eating siren who would have used his little belly as a cushion for the spike of her heels.

Aunty Zainab was different from every adult person in his life. She noticed him in a more meaningful way than the polite, cutesy way of adults. Beneath her lacklustre appearance, there was vibrancy, an undeniable strength that only Atif was privy to. Unlike Chacha who, despite his formidable build, had stood a little distance away from the near-rioting in the canteen during intervals, Zainab clasped his hand like she was preparing him for bigger battles, and charged right into the crowd with gusto that made even Atif nervous.

She bellowed out to vendors: '*Arre, chulo bhai, jaldi karo! Philum shuru hone wala hai! Popcorn ke liye kya saari raat yaha guzarni paregi?*' 'Hurry up, brother. The film is starting. Will I have to spend the whole night here just to get some popcorn?'

When the lights went down again and Bollywood lifted them from the disappointments of their own world, Atif noticed that his aunt would pull out a little silver flask from the pocket of her billowing pants and without missing a beat or taking her eyes of the screen, discreetly pour some of its contents into the chilled bottle of Limca lodged between her legs.

He sensed that Zainab had made an enormous compromise by returning. She had, for reasons unknown, snuffed out whatever dreams had emboldened her to leave in the first place and had capitulated to what was expected of her. The only clue to this other life she had sacrificed – the one nobody ever spoke about, as if by refusing to acknowledge it, it would erase itself – was a photograph that she had shown him.

They were sitting at a curb, the Gateway of India behind them, the two sister Taj Hotels in front of them. People were milling around them – hawkers selling maps and postcards, tourists trying to evade them and take pictures, families and friends enjoying the sunset, and on the street, bullock carts and taxis and cars jousting for the right of way. He was telling her about his best friend Kamal over the relentless pandemonium of car horns and voices, how hurt he was because Kamal was now spending more time with other friends. Girls.

Unlike the purses that Atif's mother or the other women

Atif knew carried, Zainab pulled out a wallet much like the one his father and Chacha owned. In its plastic holder was a faded colour photograph of Zainab standing next to a dark, pretty, much younger-looking woman. He looked up at Zainab expectantly.

'You know this is who? This is *my* best friend, Kanta,' she said. 'Pretty, na?'

Kanta was no Rekha either. But somehow he sensed that this validation was important to his aunt and nodded. He took the weathered brown wallet in his hands and ran his finger over the picture but because the dust was trapped beneath the plastic, he could not wipe it away and it remained time-worn, irrecoverable. Kanta was wearing the pink coral hairpin that Zainab now wore. On Kanta it looked much better, more fitting because unlike Zainab, she wore make-up and the pink of the hairpin matched her lipstick. She had long plaited hair and was smiling brightly, the white teeth in dazzling contrast to her dark southern skin. When he gave the wallet back to his aunt, she closed it gently like a sacred prayer book and tucked it into her side pocket. She took a deep but shaky breath. She looked into the cloudless blue sky, her hand patting the wallet involuntarily, as if trying to pace something, either the souls preserved within the plastic or her own weak heart.

Atif sensed that at that moment, Aunty Zainab might have wanted to cry, so he put his hand over hers.

When Atif was eighteen and leaving Bombay for America, knowing on some subconscious level that he would never return, family and friends gathered around the taxi that was going to take him, his father and Chacha to the airport.

Of all the people there, including his mother, Darya Durbin wept most hysterically. 'What am I to do now!' she wailed, knocking fists to forehead. 'Another son I am losing and even that in this old age! Have I not suffered enough already? America steals everything from us!' Then she spat in the mud, narrowly missing Khadija's feet.

Atif hugged his teary-eyed mother who asked him to write regularly, call every so often. He promised he would eat properly and take good care of himself. His excitement overrode any sadness he felt until he saw Aunty Zainab, who had dyed her hair for the very first time to a shocking jet-black and stood mutely by his mother, her eyes brimming with tears. He noticed that the dye had stained her skin around the temples. He put his arms around her, held her there for a long time. Not one to succumb to perfumes, Aunty Zainab had made an exception and applied some rose attar, and he could smell it commingled with the peroxide as they clung to each other.

By now, Darya Durbin had spread out the front of her sari like a beggar. 'How much more? How much more will you take?' she demanded, looking up at invisible gods.

Atif knew that while everyone would miss him, all their lives would return to normal in a matter of time. His father and Chacha would boast and fantasize about his son's new-found American life, his mother would pour all her affection and nurturing into her father, and Kamal, now a well-built young man who had also come to the party to wish him luck, would occupy himself with yet another smitten girl. Aunty Zainab would be left all alone.

He wanted to say, *I don't know why you came back, I'll never understand it, but I'm so glad you did, Zainab Aunty.*

She kissed him on both cheeks. 'Go now. Go and live for us all.'

Even after Atif had been forbidden from calling home, he did so in the hopes of catching his mother when his father was away at work. Once he had been surprised when his father had answered. He had quickly hung up, his heart pounding. It was only later that Atif realized that his father had been home because it was Eid-ul-Fitr and that he himself hadn't fasted in years.

As the years passed by, his phone calls ceased and his need for family also faded. His family seemed to exist in another realm and the consolation for this came as the end of his intense need for them. He called occasionally – on his mother's birthday, when a song reminded him of her – but in time, he began to resist even this. He had hoped to speak to Zainab as well, but he was told she had stopped visiting them almost completely. After he left, she had plummeted into depression. 'And after that very terrible fight you had with your father, she won't speak to either one of us!' his mother said agitatedly. 'Imagine! As if I had anything to do with it! Is she *pagal?* Crazy woman refuses to speak with anybody. She just roams around all day and doesn't tell anybody what she's doing. I know you two were very close but Allah-*kassam*, her *khopri* is not straight! Never was! '

Then, finally, at the age of fifty-three, Zainab had gone and done it again.

Vanished.

Pooja shut the door behind her and faced the standing full-length oval mirror in the bedroom. Her home, silent now that Ajay had sprinted off with his friends, became a charter house again, a place where belongings lay everywhere but nobody but herself seemed to reside any more. Without the pandemonium of TV, or a soundtrack of music, you could hear the ghosts, their phantom sounds marking past moments of shared laughter.

She began to unwind her sari, keeping her eyes on her reflection. Folds of chiffon fell without protest on the carpeted floor, a pond of gold paisleys in an ocean of saffron. She continued to shed endless yards of it, thinking of Draupadi, whose honour Krishna had defended when her five husbands, the Pandava brothers, had gambled her away to their Machiavellian half-brothers. She unhooked her blouse, stepped out of her petticoat and stood naked with only the gold bangles on her slender wrist, the voluptuous earrings dangling against the velvety mane of her black hair, the almost glowing bindi on her forehead.

She stepped closer to the mirror and looked at herself, drawing her uncertain hand over her skin. Her flesh broke out in little goose pimples. By all accounts, she was still a beautiful woman, able to turn heads wherever she went. She should have seen that her skin was still smooth and soft. The few wrinkles that traced through her tea-coloured skin were more like beautiful rills racing across a sea strand, the curves in her body like sensual dunes in which to lie.

But she could see none of this. Instead she saw Rahul's rejection, how time had carried out its careless dalliance with her body. She saw the brackets etched permanently around her full mouth, no longer just an indention from the smiles she had reserved for Rahul. She saw – not the ampleness of her breasts or the tamarind in her nipples – but their weight and slump. She ran her hand over her belly, no longer the taut landscape of a young girl but that of a mother, soft and fleshy. *Is that when it stopped?* She wondered. *Did he stop wanting me, looking at me the same way after I gave him his son? Or did it begin before that, after the nightmare back home?*

She summoned more strength and let her fingers traverse further, into the thatch of hair where she wanted him again, recalling the last time he had come to her, angry, gruelling, back-breaking. Yes, she would take him any way he would come to her, especially if he was suffering. He was her husband, her lord, and the years had done nothing to dissipate her desire for him. After all this time, she still burned for Rahul.

All her life, someone had needed her. For a while it had been Rahul, during those nightmarish days that they had struggled to forget and which they never spoke about. Then Ajay had tugged at her with all the need of a growing child, and while Rahul had drifted from her – more meetings, client appointments, longer hours at the bank – this had given her gravity. Suddenly, she was left without purpose.

While she had tried, as any self-respecting Indian woman would, to let her husband initiate their love-making, to be there for the taking and not to take, she simmered with desire for him and the passing years, instead of quelling her desire, only seemed to encourage it like a consistently fanned fire. Pooja remembered how in *Bhagavata Purana*, it was said that when Krishna's beloved Gopis danced with him on the moonlit banks of the Yamuna, they assumed the outward form of all his masculine qualities. Even though by nature they were not the lovers but the object of their lord's love, the women became so aroused that they changed into men.

Her fingers dug into her, in the moist and primordial regions of her being, alien even to herself. Her body began quivering, her eyes filled up. Somewhere she could hear a dog barking, children playing. Pooja closed her eyes, let her head fall back and she saw Rahul more than twenty years ago, like in a dilapidated film, dressed in white, walking across a cricket field to her, his eyes boring holes into her skin.

She summoned her husband, her Shyam, her personal god but as hard as she tried, he began to dissolve into a faceless lover, the celluloid spooling in her mind plagued with dust and scratches.

Home embraced Pooja. It cost a lot more to dial direct but the convenience and ease shocked her. Savita Bhatt sounded tired, the age creeping into her voice, and this depressed her. 'Ma, are you alright? You don't sound okay.'

'Yes, yes, we are all fine, *beti*. Don't worry about us.'

'You are sure, na? Nothing wrong?'

'So, how is he? And my little grandson how is he also?'

'Not so little any more, Ma.'

'And Rahul?'

'Okay. He's okay,' she said, smiling but only to camouflage her sadness. 'Busy, very busy. I'll send some new pictures.'

'Hanh, hanh, but that's what you always say, na? "I'm sending photos, I'm sending photos" but where are they? You are sure you have the right address? You must be posting them to the moon because so far, we have not received anything. So long it has been since we have seen you,' she clucked her tongue. 'What, do you think we have no feelings?'

Pooja smiled at the sudden emotional vigour in her mother's voice, even if out of hurt. 'Promise. I'm sending next week only,' she said. 'You know, Ajay, he has this new camera. It's digital and it takes such good photos. You can actually see the pictures then and there, fata-fat, right after you take them and, if you don't like any, you can erase, just cancel them also.'

'Hanh, hanh, don't cancel-bancel anything! Just send!'

'And Papa?'

'He is here. Where else? Sitting outside in the verandah, cracking his finger joints. Papa is fine too, not to worry. Always eating my head everyday with his same old *bhashans*. Only now you are not here so I have to listen to everything, na?' She laughed. 'Day and night there is something he must lecture about. Should have become minister or something. Just his legs are hurting, bas. Arthritis,' then, without warning, she switched to reminiscing about just the two of them. 'Beti, you remember our time together? Remember when you used to insist I sing, '*Jaago Mohan pyaare*' for your Krishna? How you wouldn't stop eating my head until we brought the little one into the temple?' Even as a grown-up man, Krishna was best remembered by some as the mischievous little butter-thief of Vrindavan. The first statue they had installed in the puja room had been of cherubic Krishna caught red-handed with butter. At least this, Savita had reasoned, had been before the god's more amorous phase.

Pooja smiled sadly. She could see herself sitting in front of the dressing table again, under her mother's watchful eye, applying the bindi to her forehead, and hear them singing in the puja room. She felt the tears rising again but was thankful that she had already cried earlier, emptying herself out, so that now she was able to control herself a bit more easily. So much she wanted to say. That she was tired, lonely, homesick. At what point do daughters become mothers, the roles reversed, so that it's no longer easy to admit your weaknesses for fear of worrying those who once took care of you?

'And you, beti? How are you?' Savita asked.

'You should see the demand for the kaju barfis, Ma. Your recipe. Such a hit they are with my customers.'

'Barfis are good, I already know. But how are you?'

She gave a short laugh. 'What's wrong with me? I'm fine, just fine. Look, what about coming for a little holiday? We can send tickets for you and Papa.'

Savita did not answer immediately because she could already sense everything in her daughter's voice and she did not ask why they couldn't come and visit. She knew better. 'Oh, Pooja, we are much too old now,' she said. 'Sometimes I think it is better that you are here, you know. Lately, things, they are . . . so bad here,' she said, clucking away with her tongue. 'And, *Hai Ram!* Everything is so expensive! There, you are at least safe. Your friend, that Rukhsana, you remember her, the one that cried every minute? Only God knows what has become of her. After marrying that boy Sajid, you know the one you all went to school with? That very quiet, nice boy? Well, he is going with some other woman now. She has left him now but I don't think she is ever going to be okay, you know, up there. But, you know, she doesn't cry any more. Bas, just like that. Can you believe it? She doesn't cry. Now that it makes sense too, she has run dry!'

'I miss you. I miss everything,' Pooja said, her voice quivering so that her hand went to her chest.

'Beti,' Savita Bhatt started carefully. 'We also miss you. Be strong.'

Pooja's tears spilled over. She could feel her mother's arms around her, smell her comforting perfume, and again her life in Los Angeles felt like an exile instead of the promising future it had once seemed.

Suddenly, her father's voice came through. 'Your Krishna is still here,' he said. 'Fluting away in the puja room! Now, when are you coming home to save us from his deafening music, *henh?*'

Pooja smiled. The arthritis had not dampened his fire. She tried to explain that her place was with her husband

and child, that they needed her and she couldn't just get up and leave for a holiday; but all the time her eyes rested on the bare dining room table across from her while she craved to be back home, subjected to his endless lectures.

'And listen,' her father added as a final enticement. 'I won't even insist you eat any beef curry.'

Whenever Pooja had delicately remonstrated on the slaughter of the sacred beast at the dinner table back home, her father would declare, 'Arre, that is all hogwash.' Savita Bhatt would continue laying out the food, cooked by Munao, the house servant they had reluctantly agreed to share with the Hajis family next door, and trying to ignore both obstinate husband and daughter. 'Hindus, they have always eaten meat. Where this bullshit about raising cows to your head has come from, only your God knows!' Then he would spoon voluminous quantities of the *kheema* masala – ground beef curry accented with green peas – onto his plate with extra vigour, as if to underscore his point.

'Hari, please, come on now. Let it go,' Savita said. 'I have already made something for her, na? Some tasty kingfish and roti.' She looked at her daughter with adoration. 'Okay, Pooja?'

Pooja nodded eagerly, relieved that she had been rescued from the peculiar and somewhat savage gastronomical habits of her incensed father.

'Where does she get this from?' Hari said. 'Where does she get this from, I ask? You and I are not like this! Even her grandparents ate meat!'

Savita refrained from pointing out that Pooja's maternal grandparents did not and rarely did she, and even then only to appease him.

'People are starving in this world and she's giving me lectures on cow conservation! Where do you think your shoes come from, henh? Tree bark? Where is it written that we are not supposed to eat meat?' And then unfailingly, his theory on what he considered the pragmatic rather than religious reasons for the observance would follow: 'Do you know that there are temples in India where meat is also distributed as part of prasad?' Of course, Hari neglected to specify the whereabouts of the mysterious temples where meat was being offered.

But thirteen-year-old Pooja couldn't care less. The fact that her beloved Lord Krishna, known also as Gopala, Govinda, and Gorakshaka (all meaning protector of cows) was often depicted with a cow in *murti*s and paintings supplied further proof of its sacredness, and the incumbent role of the devotee to uphold Lord Krishna's bulwark.

Of course, there was no stopping Hari Bhatt when he was on a rant; the veteran high school teacher in him, the one popularly feared by his overwhelmed students, took over. Between mouthfuls of roti and spiced meat, he explained how the Hindu scriptures did not specifically prohibit the killing or consuming of cows, that the cow was undoubtedly highly regarded, almost like a pet, but it was the beast's ability to provide milk and till the land, not some Vedic mumbo-jumbo, that had secured its place in the home and not on the plate.

'Do *gopalan* and not *gopujan!*' Raise cows, don't worship cows! Hari declared, freely plagiarizing his hero Veer Savarkar, the famous revolutionary and progressive mind. '*Aa che neh badhui Krishna na kaam chhe!*' This is all Krishna's fault!

Even here Pooja was different from her parents. While Hari Bhatt had observed a respectful yet detached relationship with the gods – occasionally pulled into puja and compulsory sociability during religious celebrations by the craftiness only a wife could muster – he prided himself in his ability to rise above religious orthodoxy. He was not above blaming the gods for their double standards, Krishna for his promiscuous dalliances and the resident Lord Rama, the object of Savita Bhatt's worship, for being the most misogynistic and pompous of them all.

Mortals and near-sacred national heroes also were not beyond Hari Bhatt's reproach. He was proud to harbour what he claimed were still revolutionary ideas, calling most Indians buffoons who couldn't think for themselves and steeped in Bollywood and corruption. 'Hunh! So much for the Mahatma! Did you know that even Gandhi, for all his concerns about fairness and reformation, was a firm believer that people should continue in their hereditarily ordained professions? For him Hinduism was all about remaining in your station: a cobbler must remain a cobbler, a sweeper a sweeper. So why shouldn't the imperialists stay as such? They were born to loot the world! True? True?'

Pooja ignored her father's ranting, just as Savita Bhatt tried to, and remained pacified, her eyes fixed on carefully wrapping chunks of fish, the bones of which had already been extracted by her mother, in her buttered wheat roti and parcelling them into her mouth. But just when she thought it was over, her father would get riled up again, ideas mushrooming in his head. 'Do you know that fish is sacred for Christians? Do you? And even *they* don't have a problem eating it!'

But in her mind she saw the blue god Krishna, smiling approvingly at her as his lips were poised upon his reed to play the music that had hypnotized the Gopis of Brindavan.

Years ago, when precocious Pooja demanded Krishna's inclusion in the puja room, Savita Bhatt protested ineluctably: 'Oh, Pooja, but why Krishna?' And Hari Bhatt articulated what his wife couldn't but with a sly smile, delighting in Pooja's subversiveness: 'O-ho! Krishna, that flirt, that philanderer . . .'

But Pooja's eyes widened and the corners of her mouth tightened in anger. As if gods were to be judged by human standards! Even as a teenager, the choice had always been simple for Pooja: Shiva was too fierce and destructive; Rama was too righteous and like her father, she could never abide by his intractable treatment of his wife Sita, banishing her though she was pure and innocent, letting her endure a trial by fire and eventually get swallowed up by the earth to uphold his infallibility. Whenever Pooja or Hari brought this up, they sent Savita fleeing in the opposite direction, her ears plugged. 'Ram! Ram! I don't want to hear this! Stop at once!'

Only Krishna, with his playfulness and myriad humanistic nuances, would do. As a child and butter-thief, Krishna's impishness delighted mischievous children; as an adolescent, his aggressive behaviour, rife with sexual overtones, appealed to the romantic Gopi in every girl; and ultimately, as the lover, there was again no equal to Krishna who, doffing aside puritan ideals, pursued each of his affairs with equal vigour and passion.

Pooja smiled at the memory now.

This was the structure of their relationship: they met twice a week, always at Atif's apartment and almost never on the weekends since there was no bank business to be conducted then and Rahul couldn't come up with an excuse to be away for too long.

The weekends grew the loneliest for Atif. He paced Santa Monica's Third Street Promenade, surrounded by couples holding hands and watching the street entertainers with their balancing acts and dance performances, shopping along the endless row of boutiques, sharing pretzels and Starbucks' drinks and doing all the mundane, romantic things that formed a relationship.

The place that he felt most comfortable, around people he perceived were most like him, was in the bookstores where solitude was appropriate. Here certain people staked out their regular places with a heap of books and magazines, and perched like birds around the window sill of the store or in one of the many sitting areas, nearly turning the store into a library.

Sometimes, when even Nona wasn't available – either because she had latched on to yet another promising date from the Internet or composing one of her magnum opus emails to someone she was hoping to meet or drop – he ventured into a late night movie by himself and almost always felt consoled after losing himself in the drama unfolding on the screen and a tub of popcorn he didn't have to share.

When Rahul was available, they would override his reluctance and step out to Roosterfish in Venice. While this neighbourhood bar with its juke box, jeans-and-T-shirt-clad locals, down-to-earth vibe had never been Atif's hangout (his pack had always preferred the trendier, attitudinized spots in West Hollywood), he was thankful now that at least here he didn't know anybody, that there would be no explaining to do. 'Rahul, I promise you, it's nothing like what you're thinking,' Atif had to convince him. 'This is just a regular little dive – so much like Blue – without any attitude or pretence. You know, just regular people.' Rahul would invariably pound a couple of vodka shots to summon the necessary courage.

While they kept to themselves most of the time, they managed to befriend Carl Berman, a retired photographer in his late sixties who had been featured in many high profile magazines like *Harpers* and *British Vogue* and who had enough anecdotes to keep them all entertained while he sipped his Manhattans.

'You can be horse-ugly. But use the right lighting, strokes of paint, and suddenly you have the face of an angel,' he said. 'Nothing is as it seems. All just shadows and light.'

Even in the closest of couples, sometimes there is a need to reach outwards and connect with other people together, as if by doing so, the relationship gains perspective and breadth that allows it to form more fully. Carl Berman became the perfect, occasional acquaintance, asking few questions about their relationship, having seen enough of the world to know that secrets existed and were better left in the dark. And they were thankful that in some small way, by involving him, their little world had expanded, that they had brought their relationship out into the dim light of a local watering hole.

When they stepped out, Atif was able to show off, no matter the limitations, like when he stood between Rahul's legs as Rahul sat on the bar stool with his hand ever-so-lightly on the small of Atif's back or when Atif leaned back against the bar knowing Rahul's arm was thrown around him. At such moments, unbeknownst to Rahul, who was engrossed in Carl Berman's fascinating stories, or his generous offer to lend them his place in Palm Springs, or his enthusiastic recommendation for The Nest in Ojai, Atif surveyed the room subtly and found guilty pleasure in being observed in the company of the man he loved. *Yes, I have someone. Here he is. Come, bear witness.*

Rahul let himself in with his set of Atif's keys and caught the answering machine having to record Nona Nguyen's profuse apology.

'Oh, Atisha! I'm so sorry, honey. Will you forgive me? I know you must be thinking, "What kind of a friend am I?" Shit! I completely forgot yesterday was your birthday. But you know what, sweetie? I'd love to take you out for dinner or . . .'

Rahul made himself comfortable by pouring himself a glass of Cabernet and settling into the reclining easy chair where he sometimes caught a little nap while waiting for Atif to return from Elton's. Nona continued for a couple of minutes more, rattling down a list of options for a belated celebration, and the answering machine, set to its full volume, grew clangorous and Rahul wished he could just intercept it to shut her up. Wouldn't it make more sense to call back and negotiate all this in person?

Rahul had bumped into her only a few times; when he was coming into the apartment and she happened to be leaving hers, when he was going home and Nona was lugging her garbage to the dumpster, and the time she had shown up unexpectedly at Atif's, who had kept the conversation clipped so as to not encourage her to stay. All three times – and at least once, through her formidable spectacles – Nona had stared at him with the subtlety of a nautch girl eyeing wads of currency. Nona's inquisitiveness and meddlesome nature reminded him of Sonali and in both cases, he made his disdain apparent with his lack of niceties.

By the time Atif walked in, Rahul was savouring his second glass of wine listening to Abida. 'When were you going to tell me?'

'What? That I used wine and Abida to put a spell on you?' He dropped a large Elton's paper bag on the floor, threw his weathered leather jacket aside and placed a bunch of tuberoses wrapped in newspaper on the coffee table. Wisps of its intoxicating perfume suffused the room.

'More books?' he asked, jerking his head at the paper bag.

'They're my only solace.'

'I thought I was your only solace.'

'You drive me in search of it,' Atif mocked. He came closer to Rahul and eyed the half-bottle of wine standing by the chair. 'Is that a good idea?'

'Not too bad. Apparently California wines have come a long way.'

Atif gave him a look of disbelief.

'Oh, it can be explained,' he said, swatting the air. 'I'm supposed to be wining and dining clients.'

'Instead you're whining about something I didn't tell you.' Atif straddled Rahul, who put the glass down, enveloped Atif in his arms. 'Even now, I come home wanting to see you so much, I'm half afraid it won't happen.'

'Careful now. Wasn't it you who said, "The universe picks up on these things?"'

'Yes, especially the negative,' he said, rolling his eyes. 'It seems to have a penchant for it.'

'Then banish the thought.'

'Clean as a slate.'

Rahul kissed him tenderly on the forehead. 'And how old did we turn yesterday?'

'Oh, God. How did you find out?'

'Connie Chung next door,' he said, nodding at the answering machine blinking away.

Atif slapped him playfully on the chin. 'Racist.'

'And you're avoiding the question,' Rahul said, fingering the scar on Atif's lip.

'Old. The big three-oh.'

'God, now I'm depressed,' Rahul groaned and tried to reach for his glass, but Atif stopped him, taking his hand and bringing it to his lips.

'Why? Need someone younger?' Atif adjusted himself in between Rahul's legs. He felt Rahul's hardness against his own, raised a brow. 'Already? Trust me, mister, you have nothing to be worried about.' The smell of Rahul's cologne, its notes of bergamot, vetiver and woods mingling with his sweat, made him ravenous. He unbuttoned Rahul's shirt and began gnawing at the mat of salt and pepper on his chest.

'You really should have told me. Why didn't you tell me? We should do something.'

'We are . . . we are . . .'

'Something special. Seriously.'

'Oh, this is very special.' He began unbelting Rahul's pants as his mouth hungrily traversed Rahul's body and tasted the salt of his skin.

'Come on, really, Atif, I want us to do something. Let's go out and celebrate.'

'What, now?'

'Tomorrow.'

Atif stopped, looked up at him. 'But tomorrow's Saturday.'

'I know.'

'And . . .'

'I'll think of something,' he said. 'Don't worry.'

Atif looked at him with incredulity. An ancient instinct warned him to be careful. When, after an interminable period of deprivation, something you want so desperately is offered without solicitation, you should be suspicious. Could he dare to hope, after six months of fantasizing, of seeing Rahul only on weekday evenings, spending every weekend alone and trying not to feel sorry for himself, to see his lover in bright sunshine?

'And work? My work, I mean.'

'When was the last time you took a sick day, hunh?'

Atif shrugged.

'Then it's set.'

'You're sure?' he knotted his brows, his finger suddenly darting on Rahul's chest, afraid to rest.

'Yeah, I'm sure. Dinner, shopping, a movie, let's just stay out of the Rooster Fish.'

Atif's eyes filmed with tears even as they lit up. 'Stay in, make love, catch a siesta . . .'

'Anything.'

They kissed deeply. Rahul's stubble grazed Atif's cheeks and they prickled, but he mashed his face against Rahul's, welcoming the discomfort, a reminder for the next day. They heard Anaïs mewling at the door.

'She knows you're in here,' Rahul said, wrinkling his nose.

'They can sense these things. But she's not going to steal me away from you, the silly pussy.'

They laughed. Atif clasped Rahul's hand and noticed the band of discolouration where he normally wore his wedding ring. He felt the pillows of Rahul's finger joints and said, 'You don't have to do this any more, you know.'

Rahul looked at him.

'I don't need this or some ceremony or a certificate to validate what we are.'

'I know,' Rahul smiled. 'We go way back.'

In many Hindu stories, even the most impossible marriages, those relationships that were inexplicable for their intensity and attachment, their suddenness and unconventionality, were attributed to possibility of rebirth. Atif caught Rahul's allusion to this and tears sprang to his eyes. 'You're going to make me cry, aren't you?'

They tipped onto the floor so that Rahul was on top of Atif and shed their clothes like old skins. They made love with tenderness and hunger, so that time and gravity wound themselves around them, losing their log and weight.

When Atif lay on his stomach on the carpeted floor, his body covered with a film of sweat, his limbs stretched, his body exerted to the point of sweet exhaustion, he reached out for the bottle of Cabernet within arm's reach and drank from it, rivulets running sensuously down the corners of his mouth. Rahul lay next to him, leaning on one arm, smiling down at him. He plucked out a starry bloom of tuberose from the bouquet on the table next to them, and crushing it in his hands so that it released its rousing perfume, rubbed it down the valley of Atif's slender back, creating an intoxicating medley of oil and sweat, the perfume of their love-making.

Later, they lay in bed together, their bodies woven in the heat. In the rare moment when the sheer curtain floated up and the air kissed their moist skin, they sighed almost in unison. Rahul had his hands knitted behind his head and Atif rested his face in the cavity of Rahul's chest, his fingers playing with the mat of hair.

They heard the tenant upstairs shuffling across the ceiling, the floorboards groaning. The toilet flushed and then his footsteps retraced back across and ended with the creaking of bedsprings. Outside, the world raged on – an older couple, embittered by the familiarity of a shared life, squabbled over what TV channel to watch, a child at play fell and wailed in pain as his mother tried frantically to calm him, still less than a block away a man sat by the curb, cocooning himself in the comfort of cheap whiskey that he swigged from a brown paper bag outside the liquor store. But inside this room, Atif and Rahul lay in a state of temporary grace, disconnected from the dramas of the outside world, their minds free to revisit cherished memories and to create new ones.

Atif hummed a tune that sounded vaguely familiar to Rahul and he looked at him.

'I don't remember there being too many lovey-dovey moments between my parents,' Atif said. 'But I do remember this one time.'

'Just one time?' Rahul laughed. 'Sounds blissful.'

'Well, it wasn't a regular love-fest but I have no doubt they cared about each other,' he said. It occurred to him that he was referring to them in the past tense, as if they were dead. 'My dad's favourite actor was Dev Anand.'

'Dev Anand?' Rahul asked and began imitating the actor's youthful, gestural style of acting.

'Yeah. The Gregory Peck of India they called him, didn't they?'

'They still do,' Rahul snorted. 'What is he? Eighty? Ninety? And still going strong! You know, there was a time when he was responsible for some of the most significant pictures – *Taxi Driver, C.I.D., Hum Dono, Guide.* Of course, all this was way before your time.'

'I've seen some of them. But that one song in *Guide* –'

'Let me guess. "*Aaj phir jeene ki tamanna hain*"'?

'No, no, not that one. It was – "*Tere mere sapne ab ek rang . . .*", know it?'

'Of course,' Rahul said and began to sing it:

Tere mere sapne ab ek rang hain
Jahan bhi le jaye rahen
Hum sang hain

Our dreams are now in the same colour
Wherever the road may lead
I am with you.

'That's the one! It was my mother's favourite.' A classic of Indian cinema, the song was penned by Shailendra and sung by the late legendary playback singer Mohammed Rafi about a fated love affair that surmounts all, as bona fide Bollywood love stories always did. 'My mother, she played this little 45 to death,' he continued. 'You know the little ones, with the angel sitting oh, so seductively, on the vinyl, a plume for a pen. Well, anyway, one day she found it all warped in the sun so you could no longer play it. She even tried to press down on the needle when it was playing but it was just impossible to keep it on course. Dev Anand sounded like he was –'

'Mohammed Rafi, you mean.'

'It was Dev Anand on screen!' Atif said, petulant. 'Well, you know what I mean. Anyway, Dev Anand or Rafi sounded like he was on some kind of bad acid trip or something. She was literally in tears, over a record, can you imagine?'

'Couldn't she just get another one?'

'Oh, but that's not the point,' he said. 'Anyway, that day my father went to her in the kitchen while she was cooking this lamb *yakhni* with whole black peppers. I can still smell it. She was wearing this deep yellow salwar-kameez. I don't think they knew I was back from our neighbour's. And I heard him tell her, "*Arre, record ki kya zarurat hain? Main hoon na.* Come, I'll sing for you." And he scooped her into his arms and sang to her, in an astonishingly good voice, so tenderly. She blushed, giggled, just ate it all up even as she tried to act coy.' He looked at Rahul wistfully. 'I'd never seen her like that . . . so young, so alive.'

Rahul took him in his arms and began singing in a melodious baritone and Atif, moved to the verge of tears, joined in with fragments:

Tere mere dil ka, taiy thaa ek din milna
Jaise bahaar aane par
Taiy hain phool ka khilna
O mere jeewan saathi

Laakh manaa le duniya
Saath na yeh chootega
Aake mere haathon me
Haath na ye chootega

Our hearts were destined to meet
Just as the coming of a season
Heralds the blossoming of flowers
O my companion for life

Let the world try
Our bond will never break
Now that your hand is in mine
I will never let it go

But sometimes, right before Rahul had to leave, Atif found that he had lost him. Already taciturn by nature, he withdrew further inward and although physically present, he would appear worlds away, tormented. Atif, sharing the pain of separation, of the knowledge that the man he loved would bed down with someone else, tried at first to ignore Rahul's dejection, but ended up asking.

'I don't know how to do this. This going back and forth, one life to another,' he said. 'It's too hard.'

'But I thought you were happy here, with me.'

'I am. But then I have to go back. All this, it becomes a dream. I don't know who I am, which one is real.'

He didn't know that there were nights in Rahul's life when he awoke as if he had been fighting with forces for hours, just struggling and exhausted. And although for a while he felt relieved, because when he awoke he appeared physically unscathed, Rahul knew that the wounds ran deeper, invisible to the eye, and that they would come again.

Atif pulled him close into his arms, stroked his hair. At such moments, witnessing Rahul's suffering and at a loss for words, he wondered if he was supposed to hold on to him tighter or just let him go.

Back within the walls of a life prescribed by centuries of tradition, Rahul now sat in the darkness of the kitchen. It was past midnight and all that could be heard was the intermittent groan of the old refrigerator and the unusually loud ticking of a burnished gold clock above the stove.

He sat by the covered thalis of food that Pooja had left for him even though she had known he had dinner plans. It was like an offering she felt compelled to make at some altar – afraid of breaking from ritual and half-expecting he would still be hungry upon returning. The steel plate glinted from the distant light in the living room.

He didn't bother to discover what she had made. Whatever it was, he knew with indifference, would be tasty, prepared with the utmost precision. She was so reliable, beyond reproach, exhaustively impeccable. It was impossible for her to even botch a meal once in a while. How does one measure up to such a woman? Infallibility eventually grew oppressive, reminding the recipients that they could never be as pious or truly deserving of such devotion.

Rahul surveyed the room as if for the first time. Wisdom dictates that you should cultivate a sense of self intrinsically instead of from possessions but in reality who could extricate himself from his belongings? He thought of his mother with some difficulty, saw her smiling face, stroking his young face as her glass bangles clinked, and telling him in the words of the greatest sages that the world around us was just maya and that one must learn to live in the world without becoming of the world. Then he saw his boisterous father in the signature safari suits he wore, clutching a heavy crystal glass of his umpteenth peg of whiskey and ice, intercepting: '*Aare, iski baton me mat anaa*. Don't listen to her. She doesn't remember any maya-*baya* when she's draining the bank account to buy more jewellery at Premchand's.' His heart felt heavy in his chest and he dissolved the image in a deep sigh. Never had two people been more unlike one another and never had he known a more loving, suitably balanced pair.

We brand ourselves on our walls, onto the furniture, in pictures, in the dust and air of rooms, thought Rahul. *A little energy is deposited into everything we touch and everywhere we delve. Everything material becomes evidence of experience, an extension of who we are.*

The microwave and the yards of crockery reminded him of the time Pooja and he went to Sears as she was setting up her catering business; of the bank's Christmas party where Pooja, trapped into compulsory sociability, had been introduced to his customer, Charlie Ackerman, with whom Pooja had so much in common that in no time they had moved on from Hinduism to her agreeing to test out a catering arrangement for him. Who would have known a chance meeting would lead to all this for her? He could still see her excitedly introducing Charlie to him and how skeptical he had been about the whole affair.

'Arre, Poo, he's probably drunk or something,' he had told her later as they drove home. 'You know how people get a party. Let's just wait and see.'

Pooja had felt chafed by his remark but went on to agree with him as she always did: 'Yes, I suppose you're right. I shouldn't get so excited about such things, no? It does seem a little strange. And besides, what do I know about this catering-fatering? But, my God, he does seem to know a lot about our culture!'

'Hanh, hanh, but this is the classic problem. About their own culture they know nothing but with other peoples' culture they're Einsteins.'

But Charlie had turned out to be more than some inebriated gora paying lip service to their enterprise over too much bourbon. And it had been so much simpler than they had anticipated. Provided Pooja only made baked goods for The Banyan (keeping the curries and more elaborate fare more discreet and on a private basis), the law didn't require that she apply for a licence or have a separate kitchen, only that the ingredients be kept separately. Rahul had helped her apply for the insurance and Charlie had also helped to set up a little workspace in the back of The Banyan where she could label the food, although she always accomplished all this at home.

His eyes continued surveying and paused at a family picture on the wall. It recalled not just the Diwali festival of several years ago – Pooja so much younger, breathtakingly beautiful, and Ajay, pudgier and full of laughter instead of the brooding teenager he had become – but also the painstaking frame selection process at some store on Lincoln Boulevard (she had wanted the matting to match the powder blue colour of his shirt). Even the VCR, an old Panasonic flashing its digitized clock, silently screaming its disconnect with real time, recalled the frustration of figuring out the programmer and the hundreds of Bollywood films they'd seen on it. Take away these walls, the inanimate objects within them and who do we become?

He heard footsteps coming down the stairs and he looked up to see Ajay entering the kitchen wearing only his flannel pajama bottoms.

'Papa?'

'Hey, Ajay,' Rahul said, suddenly aware his eyes had filled up and wiping them deftly before they gave him away. 'What are you doing up?'

'Why are you sitting here in the dark?'

'I don't know. Just walked in. Come, sit,' he said, slouched uncharacteristically. He pushed a chair out with his leg. 'Just, please leave the lights off, will you?'

Ajay hesitated momentarily, thinking it a strange request to keep them engulfed in darkness, and sat across from his father.

'Can't sleep?' Rahul asked, suddenly reminded of the nights Ajay kept them up wailing as a baby. Such powerful lungs, they used to joke. Maybe he would grow up to be a qawwali singer. He had never had the chance to attend to his son's fierce cries as an infant; Pooja had leapt out of bed like a soldier on a battlefield to minister to him. Now he wished she had let him. Or that he had insisted. He longed to cradle the little baby that fitted on his forearm, circling his little fingers around his own. 'Everything okay?'

Ajay looked away, shrugged.

'Well?'

He looked back at his father, eyes gleaming in the dark. 'What's going on with Mom?'

Rahul tensed up. 'What do you mean?'

Ajay paused, not as much for effect as to permit his father to acknowledge his culpability. But when Rahul remained perplexed, he sighed, impatient.

'Ajay, I don't know what you're talking about. What is it? What's wrong with her?' he asked, leaning forward and touching his shoulder. 'Is she unwell?'

Ajay sniffed, grimaced. 'Are you – you're drunk!' He said incredulously, pulling back.

'No, I'm not drunk,' he laughed nervously, sitting back. 'What kind of a thing is that to say?'

'I can smell it!'

'Not that I have to answer to you but it was, you know, a couple of glasses of wine with some clients, that's all.'

'But you don't drink.'

He sighed, too tired to engage in this. 'Well, I do now. Is that okay with you?' Even in the dark, he could see that his son was disgusted but instead of becoming concerned, he found this mildly amusing considering Ajay had developed quite a reputation for being a rebel himself.

Ajay got up almost furiously, the chair grating across the linoleum, and Rahul strained back in surprise. Without another word, Ajay went to the refrigerator and searched for a tub of double fudge chocolate ice cream in the freezer, the only indulgence he allowed himself. His mind was racing. Suddenly it all made sense to him and it made him feel ill. His father's absences, the drunken breath, his mother's devastation. Earlier, the sight of his mother's breakdown, the tears and hurt on her face, had transfixed him, but now he grew enraged at his father.

Rahul meanwhile appraised his son, now a tall and attractive young man. Even though in his youth Rahul had had more than his fair share of attention, something that had continued to a considerable degree as he had aged, it was as if Ajay, blessed further with his mother's genes and his obsession with fitness, had reached a kind of pinnacle of physical beauty. He watched his son's strong, expansive back with its well-defined musculature, his strong arms and the peculiar scar. He saw the smooth skin of his waxed chest glistening from the pearly light of the refrigerator.

In his son's youthful bearing he was reminded suddenly of Atif and this brought about a stirring within him, the inappropriateness of which immediately made him cringe. That he could even feel such thing while looking at his son, that all of these emotions could reside in him simultaneously like feuding spirits inhabiting a house, appalled him. Perhaps it was better that he had been distanced from his son. His own confusion he could live with, but to besmirch his son in any way, he could not endure. Although he turned his eyes away from him, Ajay caught his stare, reading guilt into it.

'Is this why Mom was crying?'

'Crying? She was crying?' Rahul's heart skipped a beat. In that fraction of a second, he wondered if she had found out, saw Pooja's anguished face.

Ajay plunked down the tub of ice cream on the counter

and looked his father dead in the eye. 'Are you cheating on her?'

'What?' Rahul felt the room fall away from him so that it seemed like Ajay and he were floating in atmosphere.

'You heard me, Dad,' he said, defiant. 'Are you screwing around?'

'What the hell are you talking about, Ajay?'

'It's a simple question.'

Rahul rose to his feet, reminding himself to take a deep breath so he could steady himself. *No, this couldn't be. How the hell could she possibly have found out? Had someone seen them? Had she found something?* Then something within him kicked in, an actor inhabiting a role, believing its truth. 'You're being ridiculous.'

'Really? It's past midnight, you're plastered, Mom's been crying –'

'Hey! Hey! Hey!' he held up his hand forbiddingly. 'Last time I checked, I was still your father, okay, and I don't remember being on any kind of curfew.'

'Okay, so just come clean.'

'Come clean!' Rahul flared up. 'Do I need to remind you who the hell you're talking to?'

'Maybe you should,' Ajay said, 'because you know what? You sure as hell aren't around enough for me to remember that.'

For the first time Rahul thought he was going to hit his son, uncertain if it was the truth in Ajay's words and his corresponding guilt, or his son's audacity that incensed him. Rahul, always slow to provocation, now stepped up to his son who was nearly his height. 'That's enough from you,' he said, his voice an ominous hiss. 'I want you to stop this *bakwas* before you upset your mother.' He began to walk away.

'You don't give a shit about her,' Ajay cried. 'If you did she wouldn't be in this state. I want to know who's more important to you than Mom, why you're fucking bailing out on us.'

He stopped in his tracks and slowly turned around. Ajay's words cut through him like blades not because of the accusation but because of the pain that resonated in his broken voice, something Rahul had never heard before. He looked upon his son's face, could see the glassiness in his eyes. It crushed Rahul to see Ajay this way and the anger sieved away. They had always been at a distance, like comrades on a battlefield, passengers on the same ferry, not as much father and son but offshoots of the same branch. Their relationship shared none of the intimacy Rahul had shared with his own father and it was not a gap Rahul had been happy with but one that he had accepted as a defect in his own personality. He never wanted Ajay to think that he didn't care.

'I'm not going to let you do this to her,' Ajay said, shaking with rage.

'Rahul?' Pooja's voice called from upstairs. '*Su thaye chhe?*'

Placing a finger to his lips, Rahul signalled to his son that they should keep this between them and Ajay complied with his silence. 'Nothing, Pooja,' he said over his shoulder. 'Sorry we woke you up. Everything's okay, *jaan*. Just go back to sleep. I'll be up shortly.'

They both felt her lingering on the banister, wondering if she would come down. She didn't. Rahul walked up to his son. He had always known of the power that his wife had on Ajay, that impenetrable bond from which Rahul himself had felt excluded and which, at one point, had made him feel resentful. But to see his son this way, gripped by such fury and hurt, gave him new insight into the depth of Ajay's devotion to his mother, and this both surprised and concerned him.

'Is that what you really think?' he asked tenderly, his

voice lowered to a whisper. 'That I would abandon you? My own family? *Bevakuf*, you, your Mum, you're my life. I could never, ever be without you. There is no other woman. None. Get it?' And somehow, making this about another *woman* gave Rahul conviction.

But Ajay looked at his father, unbelieving.

'I swear on Pooja,' he said then put his hand over Ajay's head. 'Upon you.'

Slowly, Ajay nodded. He wiped his eyes with the back of his hand, feeling awkward. Rahul cupped his son's face in his hands, wanting more than anything in the world to hold him close, to protect him. That's also when Rahul noticed the crescents of purple and black around Ajay's right eye, unnoticeable in the dark until now. 'What happened to you?'

'Oh, it's nothing,' he said, waving it off with his hand.

Rahul turned on the kitchen lights, came back to him. 'Who were you fighting with? Has your mother seen this? Maybe this is why she –'

'It's got nothing to do with this,' he remonstrated quickly, some of his anger springing back, and turned away from his father.

'Come here, let me take a look at it.' He went to the freezer where he ejected ice cubes from a plastic blue tray. He balled them up in a paper towel and brought the compress to Ajay's eye.

'Mom already did this,' he said, squinting from the pain.

'Yeah, yeah, fine. Now it's your father's turn.'

They stood in the kitchen for a few moments and the intimacy of the moment wasn't lost on either one of them. Rahul couldn't remember the last time he had been there for Ajay. Attending to him now felt like long-awaited recompense. The young man in front of him, while unable to fit into his arm, be lifted in the air or swung around, became his little boy again.

'How did this happen? Fighting over some girl or something?'

Ajay hesitated. Rahul paused, looked at him insistently.

'Some guy,' Ajay grunted. 'He came on to me. I know, can you believe that shit?'

Rahul froze, his hand suspended inches away from the bruise.

'Look, seriously, I don't want to talk about it,' Ajay said, embarrassed, pulling his father's hand back to his eye. 'Don't stop now, Dad, that feels good. Anyway, don't worry, he's going to think twice before pulling that shit again.'

Rahul withdrew, breaking away from his son's grasp, the ice pack now heavy.

'Dad?'

Rahul turned away, dumped the ice pack into the sink. 'It's been a long day, Ajay. I'm tired, really tired. Drunk, as you said,' he managed a conciliatory smile but was unable to look at his son. He began to walk out of the kitchen.

'Dad, you alright?'

Rahul paused, nodded, but didn't turn around to meet his eyes.

'Sure?'

'Yeah . . .'

Ajay walked up to him. He put his hand on Rahul's shoulder and faced him. 'Look, I thought that since Mom's been, you know, down and all, maybe this weekend we could all spend some time together. We could take her to Little India or something. Catch one of those silly Bollywood movies, do some shopping. Spend some of your hard-earned cash.'

Rahul nodded, extruded another tenuous smile.

'Cool,' Ajay said and hugged his father as if reclaiming something. For a few moments, Rahul held his son, felt the hard musculature of his flesh and blood, but then something within him contracted, hid, and he released Ajay. Without another word, Rahul turned around and climbed the staircase up to where Pooja waited, the ground undulating beneath his feet.

It's not that Ajay was embarrassed of his heritage but that he simply could not relate to being Indian. It was as if a fanatically devoted mother and an atheist father had left him lost somewhere in the middle so that he found it easier to get his answers from somewhere else, in a mythology and culture that belonged to neither one of them.

Unlike his parents who, while not having lived in India or having even spoken of their past in Africa, had managed to preserve at least some of the Indic, like an infant brought across the oceans, he was born in America, in the bosom of what the world still perceived as a bastion of freedom. He took this freedom for granted, never feeling like an outsider. He saw himself as one of the rightfully fitting, colourful threads in the tapestry of Los Angeles where Latinos, Asians, Jews, African Americans all weaved into each other with just the occasional tangle.

At school and in his social interactions, Ajay had little patience for Indians of his generation who droned on interminably about prejudice and threw around words like 'displacement' and 'diaspora' to somehow explain their own lack of adaptability and social ineptitude. He never felt compelled to find others under the united political identity of a 'desi' just because someone's family hailed from India or Pakistan or Bangladesh. Who cares? There was a reason their families had left that world behind and come to America, so why now were they so determined to find a way back? Ajay welcomed the erasure of such markers, felt comfortable in the loss of identity through integration. He found, due in part to his exceedingly good looks and powerful presence, that he could fit into diverse circles. Most of his friends were non-Indians and he almost always dated the white girls who frequently mistook him for Mexican or Spanish. He was fine with that also. He spoke near-perfect Spanish.

Like so many American-born Indians, he felt more comfortable with English than Hindi or Gujarati; he found more affinity with R&B and rap than filmi music, with Hollywood than Bollywood; he chose Tupac over Lata Mangeshkar and Facebook over desiclub.com. A girl he had once dated told him that one dreams in the language of one's soul. Ajay had never heard a word of his mother's Gujarati or his father's Hindi in his dreams.

He was familiar with the pantheon of mythic gods and goddesses, even had a favourite or two, but unlike his mother could never make the leap into thinking that a blue-skinned flutist actually had lived in Vrindavan and continued even today to tune in to their problems from some heavenly abode as soon as the incense was lit and cymbals came clashing; or that Shiva, after neglecting Parvati, who had once immolated herself to uphold his dignity and reincarnated just to be with him again, had returned from hundreds of years in meditation just to behead his own son and then to bring him back to life with the head of an elephant! In this way, he was more like his father who at one time in his life must have believed in a higher power, but had since decided to pass on the romanticism of religion that his mother more than compensated for, as if she also had to appease the gods for their irreverence.

Tonight Pooja would invoke rain, beseech the half-human, half-snake *naga*s, guardians of rain upon whom Vishnu slept and dreamt up the entire universe, under whose hood the Buddha meditated protectively, to end the drought in their marriage.

Emboldened by Ajay's fight at the gym, she was realizing more and more that they had paid an exceedingly heavy price for living in this country with its strange mores and liberties. She was not one to adopt the attitude of other immigrants who bemoaned the alienation of a new world, as if in doing so they somehow maintained a loyalty to the past they had abandoned. But hard as she tried, there was no denying that she was losing her son and her husband. She was wondering more and more if they might have been better off in Kenya.

But from the countless hopefuls, they had been the ones to win the US visa lottery. After Rahul's family had been wiped out, there had been even less reason to stay in the country in which they had been born but which no longer wanted them. She had stood by him and together they had renounced Kenya. She had followed, obedient, unquestioning, just like Draupadi had followed the Pandavas, like Sita had followed Ram into exile.

Tonight she must swallow her pride and end the stalemate. Take matters into her own hands, turn the game on its head, anti-chess, and pluck them out from the paralysis of their relationship. She stretched out on the expansive bed. Sleep came but without its expected succour, holding her in an unsteady embrace. Savita Bhatt laid out de-boned fish with rotis for little Pooja while Hari, peering disapprovingly at Pooja over a copy of *The Standard*, waited for a generous helping of beef kheema. Bells rang in the distance and Pooja, drawn by the cry of a reed flute, got up and ran in that direction.

Savita Bhatt called after her daughter, '*Arre, kya jaye chhe?* Pooja! Eat your food!'

Pooja floated into the puja room, her feet barely touching the ground, hypnotized by the relentless melody. Incense burned all around as if a cloud had descended into the white marble room. But there was something different about this room. An entire wall was missing, opening it up to the talcum-white beach of the north coast. It was autumn and moonlight poured down celestially, illuminating the sand. The ocean was like a bed of dazzling jewels. There Pooja saw him, under a palm tree, with one leg over a piece of driftwood and the reed poised at his lips. Others came too, like in a trance, forgetting families, wisdom, belongings. They all wanted to be touched by him, to be dissolved into him. Pooja's heart leapt with joy. This was reality. Everything else had been a dream. How could she ever have doubted it? She hastened and falling to his feet, clung to him tightly, so tightly that he would recognize his favourite, so that others would not take him away from her.

Only after he had pulled her face up by the chin, smiled at her reassuringly, did she relax her grasp on his ankles. He began playing the flute again. She rose and hovered like a bee around a blue lotus craning out from the swamps of life. The melody ascended and she twirled around him, clapping when her arms swooped up and met over her head and then again when she bent forward and clapped below her knees. And although everyone around her joined in the dance, rejoicing, transforming the once inert shore into a dizzying pool of helixes, she felt that she had him all to herself, just as they all must have.

But then she heard the commotion. They were calling her back. Voices from her dream, trying to reclaim her. And she struggled not to look back, to listen, but they got louder and louder, more demanding, and the spell began to break like the silken threads of a web thoughtlessly demolished by probing fingers. Slowly she stopped moving.

The music died. She looked over her shoulder and saw her parents and next to them, a strong, young man with whom she felt an affinity, yet whom she was blocked from recognizing. They were angry, demanding that she come back but she shook her head, refusing to leave. And that boy, how could she know and yet not know him? Confusion.

When she turned away from them and looked back at him, her beloved, she was gripped with horror. Rahul stood motionless, his reed limp in his hand. The rich blue was draining from his face, quickly moving down the barrel of his body, leaving behind chalk as it bled into the white sand like blood. She thought she would die, and cried for her parents and the young boy to go away, to stop their commotion, but even as her mouth moved, nothing came out of it and the air seemed to amplify their protest. There was nothing she could do as they destroyed him. Others around her, equally grief-stricken, looked at her with accusing eyes. It was all her fault that this was happening.

Her hands clawed at her face and she wailed out without a voice. She threw herself at his feet, seeing the last of his indigo run out from him, as if the sand was sucking it, and was now soaked with ink. *Stop them! Stop them! Don't take him away from me!* But it was already too late. Slowly, the chalk crumbled, hunks of it falling off like lath and plaster off a building, and his magnificent body collapsed into the sand under her grasping hands.

That's when she awoke, drenched in sweat, and realized that the shouting was coming from downstairs. But even after she had rushed out in her confusion, even after she'd been reassured that everything was okay and returned to bed, she was unable to coax the comfort of sleep.

Normally when Rahul entered the room, Pooja, fully aware of his entry, pretended to be asleep. Lying on her left side, her back to the door, she grew completely still and concentrated on deep, slow breaths. She was never entirely sure why she did this any more since he never seemed to demand anything of her. Perhaps it was because it made things easier. Now, turning around, she looked up at him, and even in the darkness, as his figure neared the bed upon which he laid down his suit coat, he looked beaten and taxed.

'*Janu?*' she said tenderly, not having used the endearment in as long as she could remember.

He sat by the edge of the bed, creasing the jacket beneath him.

'Everything's okay, isn't it?' She thought she saw him nod, and the fact that he didn't utter a word confirmed that it wasn't.

The light coming in from the hallway silhouetted his handsome profile with the strong jaw line and straight nose. But Rahul looked like he was in a state of suspension, as if a bullet had pierced his heart and he was moments away from keeling over.

'Rahul?' She moved her foot across the bed and touched his back, the little bells on her silver anklet chiming lightly. Still he was unable to speak.

Sitting up, she reached out for the lamp on the side of the bed. Without turning to look at her, his hand struck out and he caught her by the wrist, pulling her arm down, halting the light. She touched his shoulder, thinking this must be about their son's brawl. But still his reaction seemed a little excessive. This wasn't the first time Ajay had been disruptive and in the past, Rahul had always been infuriatingly nonchalant. 'He's a boy, Poo. What, you think you gave birth to a girl? Boys get into trouble. That's what boys do.'

Why then was he taking this so severely? What was different about this particular incident that it crushed him like this?

She sensed a mixed blessing in his state. Earlier she had resolved to end the distance between them, to rekindle some intimacy, no matter how hard or awkward. He seemed needy and despondent now and this made it somewhat easier for her to do what she must. With one swift wave, she pushed the copy of *India Currents* she had been reading off the bed and it rustled to the floor like a wounded bird. Her slender arms enveloped him and she kissed the stubble on his cheek, noticing its silver glinting like filaments of light.

What was it about the people you loved, she wondered. Just a hint of pain on their faces and everything was forgiven, every slight erased. How young they had been when they first met. She rested her head on his shoulder as she had when they had sat above the sun-baked ruins of Fort Jesus and looked out at the Indian Ocean. For a brief moment they returned to their past. She saw him, dressed in white, bringing her roasted maize pressed with chillies and lime. Again she shared sweet coconut juice through a straw with him and then watched him scrape the hunks of white meat from its inner core for her to relish. She remembered his tenderness on their wedding night. Her eyes welled up.

He clasped the arms that had enveloped him and when he looked over at her, she noticed the glistening in his eyes too. Their foreheads touched. She kissed him, encountered the alcohol on his breath but hesitated only momentarily. His scent filled her with an emotion that went far beyond lust or desire. It was the memory of her youth, of her innocence. A whole life thrummed in the notes of his aroma.

When her lips searched him out again, he moved his face away, his body straining away from her. Despite the fortitude she had amassed up to this point, she felt embarrassed at her brazenness, but was not ready to give up. In that evanescent moment when a woman can transform from wife to mother, she pulled him back into her arms with some persistence, this time placing her hand maternally on the back of his head.

He capitulated, falling into her with the need of a child seeking protection. She had seen him this way before, when he had lost his family, and had hoped never to see him so broken again. Although she had long ceased to be the wife he had circled the fires with and in whom he found sexual pleasure, in that moment she became much more. She was the sister he had bullied and played with; she was the mother who had raised him, whom he had looked up at from the folds of her sari and whom he would always search for no matter how old he grew.

We're lost, Pooja thought, tasting the salt of tears and holding on to him with all her might. *Unable to go back and struggling to stay. We belong nowhere now. Perhaps not even to each other.*

After a lifetime apart, she found Rahul enveloped in her arms, felt his face against the softness of her breasts, watched his stony disposition crumble, found the tears like precious, silver drops of dew on his eyes. She took it to mean that he had returned to her.

By the time the sun had begun its ritual ascent in the morning sky, Pooja was already at the feet of the divine couple to pay obeisance and offer gratitude. She placed two small wooden platforms on the floor, sitting on one of them and placing the instruments of her worship on the other: a clay lamp, a small bronze bell, a silver bowl half full of distilled water and a tray of dried fruits and nuts. From a little brass holder, incense fanned out like a peacock's tail and tendrils of sandalwood smoke danced up to the figurines of Radha and Krishna, smiling down at her with their pink cheeks and rosebud lips from the altar she had made in a corner of the kitchen. Radha, Krishna. This is how they were to be acknowledged always, with her name before his. When Krishna had left Vrindavan, he had promised Radha that no matter where he resided physically, she would always dwell in his heart, and pledged with her that her name would always precede his.

She removed their silk outfits – Krishna's golden robes, Radha's crimson sari – and placed the statues in a silver thali of rosewater with three basil leaves. Slowly, she bathed them with the love and care of a mother for her infant, patted them dry with a plush cotton towel, re-dressed them and returned them to their throne. She dipped her finger in a canister of dark-red powder and applied it to their foreheads, leaving tilaks that looked like small open wounds.

Even as she ardently observed the ritual, something within Pooja danced euphorically. She remembered, when in the beginning stages of their courtship, Rahul had joked with her with the mischievous twinkle in his eyes. 'Your Krishna had so many gopis and he got away with it. Why can't I have many girlfriends and get away with it too?'

'If you can lift a mountain with your little finger, if you can turn the poison that was offered to Meera into nectar, if you can dance on a thousand-fanged cobra like Krishna, you too can have a million gopis like him and see if I care,' she had said, snorting and tossing her head back.

Smiling to herself, she lit the lamp and its flickering glow made the gods come alive. Ringing the bell with her left hand, she picked up the tray with her right and moved the burning diya around the gods, not in a perfect circle but something more irregular, as if she were delineating a presence that she saw before her adoring eyes. She began her slokas:

Om jaya Jagadisha Hare
Swami jaya Jagadisha Hare
Bhakta jano ke sankat
Kshan mein dur kare
Om jaya Jagadisha Hare

Deenabandhu dukhaharta
Thakur tum mere
Apne hath badhao, apni sharan lagao
Dwar para tere
Om jaya Jagadisha Hare

Glory be to thy name
The Sovereign of the Universe
With thy grace
The evils of the worshipper vanish instantaneously

Friend of the meek, Annihilator of evils
Thou art my master
Grant thy grace and take me into your fold
I pray knocking at your temple door

Pooja scooped some of the bathwater into the palm of her hand and drank it. Then she ran her wet palms over her head for blessing, touching the wreath of jasmine at the back of her head. She ate some of the prasad – raisins, almonds, sweet halwa – and warmed her hands over the flame of the dancing diya. When she pressed her fingers to her eyelids, she thanked the gods for their benevolence, felt in her heart that finally everything would turn out okay, that she had been fortified with patience. After all, if it's a miracle you're waiting for, you must also know how to wait.

A whole world can begin and end in one day, sometimes taking pitiably little to make it happen. On the morning of their planned day together, Atif awoke elated, as if his world had been created anew. Every sense was heightened from the anticipation of what lay ahead. He had pictured them at the Promenade, lunching in a sun-dappled patio shaded by a large umbrella, later cocooned in his apartment, making love endlessly, followed by a languorous siesta with complete disregard for the clock. But with each passing hour, his heart grew heavier.

Neither of them had fixed a time for their rendezvous – Rahul still unsure as to how he was going to explain his absence to Pooja, and Atif, too grateful to negotiate such mundane details. Rahul was coming to spend the day with him, had assured him that he would work it out somehow, and this had been enough for Atif. But when he didn't hear anything by midday, Atif grew despondent. At first he resisted, wanting desperately to show more confidence in Rahul, but later he acquiesced and called his mobile number, his heart fluttering like a caged bird. But the call went straight into voice mail, depriving him of even the hope that could be extracted from a single ring.

Two o'clock. He consoled himself: *Rahul's getting a late start. It's the weekend. Surely he has to spend some time with them before making his escape. He can't simply run out and come here the moment he wakes up. Arrangements have to be made, excuses offered; delays were inevitable. Why didn't I ask him what time? God, we should have set a time. Fuck.*

His mobile in tow, Atif made a dash for the neighbourhood supermarket to keep occupied while keeping his spirits high. *Something about immigrants and supermarkets,* he thought. He could never get enough of the sheer variety, or get over the abundance. He could stock up on weekly groceries, treat himself to a butter pound cake, obtain quarters for the laundry waiting in the closet hamper, grab bottles of Gewurztraminer now that Rahul allowed himself to drink when they were together. Sooner or later the phone would ring. He would feel foolish for tormenting himself so needlessly.

He walked the three blocks to a Pavilions market, the phone gripped his hand, not willing to compromise the reception by pocketing it. All six bars were essential to his survival now. The florist outside the supermarket, where he customarily stopped to select flowers or just admire the artistic bouquets, did nothing for him this time. The effusive colours, even the thought of their fragrance, made his anticipation surge, his stomach turn. So this is how beauty turns ugly, how balm becomes poison.

He walked through the aisles in a daze, throwing items into his cart mechanically, able to think of nothing else but the call that wouldn't come. When he checked out, he forgot to ask for the quarters and almost left groceries behind until the bagger ran after him. In his mind, there was only the beseeching for divine intervention: God, please make him call. Make him pick up the phone. Please. Please. Please. Where is he? He heard the chatter of shoppers, the wailing of an infant, the blare of horns, the babel of life, but the skies didn't open, the phone didn't ring.

Back at the apartment, Atif opened up a can of chunk tuna and searched for Anaïs. He stood in the alley facing up to her second-storey home and made silly tutting noises, risking the owner's irritation, but nothing appeared at the grilled window, so he left the open can by the dumpster, expecting that she would find it.

Rahul's absence assumed menacing power over him. Flopping on his couch, powerless, his mind raced through darker, morbid routes while the groceries, still unpacked, lay scattered around him. Could something have happened to him? An accident? How would he know? Who would tell him? They shared no one in common. Days could go by without him finding out. Weeks. Longer. As all plausible possibilities exhausted themselves, his unlikely imaginings assumed a credibility of their own. Would he have to go into Rahul's office only to be met with a grief-stricken bank teller who would look around nervously before revealing the tragedy to him? Or would it be broken to him over the morning news by Jillian, who would make a departure from her light-hearted prater about fashion trends and pet adoptions to drive the freeway fatalities that Angelenos had grown jaded to nearer to home? Must make sure to discuss this with Rahul the next time, he noted mentally. There has to be some way, a contingency plan to ensure they were both informed if something were to happen.

Then he began to doubt his sanity, wondering if perhaps something had gone wrong between them, if some kind of quarrel had been expunged from his mind as he had slept in the night. But the memories of the night before filled his heart with only a heavy joy, one which, in Rahul's failure to show, was slowly beginning to crush him under the burden of the hopes it had inspired.

Hesitantly, he dialled Rahul's mobile phone again.

Nothing.

The walls moved inwards, choking the air out of the room. Atif fled towards the beach, wishing for the smell of home – of sun-dried duck and fish – that he knew he wouldn't find at the edge of the Pacific and the man he knew wouldn't be there.

'Maybe the silly boy's finally run off.'

Pooja packed the little plastic containers filled with

savouries neatly in the large delivery box on her kitchen counter. Arrows of sunlight streamed in through the window above the sink and fell upon her glinting gold bangles as her hands shifted around. The day had emerged impossibly beautiful, somewhere in the lower seventies, the kind of day that Los Angeles was envied for. She was thankful that it wasn't too hot because she knew how Rahul, unlike her, had such low tolerance for heat.

'*Tch,* what must have happened?' she said to Ajay, glancing at the circled date on the wall-mounted calendar of scenic photos from around the country.

Miffed, she looked now at the box waiting to be delivered. Each of the little cartons had been carefully sealed and labelled with details of the ingredients and approximate weight. As of her last few deliveries, she had included the latest item – cashew marzipan squares lined with silver foil, which, while not too popular with the calorie-conscious patrons of The Banyan, had become a big hit with the rest of the locals who now came in just to purchase the milky dessert. Of course she had eased up on the sugar to suit their taste.

'Oh, this isn't like Greg at all. I don't know where he is. Maybe he forgot. You know, now I'll have to deliver these to the store before we do anything,' she said, a bit irritated that this would have to happen on this day of all days.

'So why do you keep calling him that when he wants to be called something else?'

She looked at her son, sitting at the dining room table, ravenously spooning milk-drenched cereal into his mouth. 'Look at you. Like a raccoon you look!'

He winked at her with his black eye.

'What are you smiling at, *junglee?* I'm not giving you a compliment.' She looked at the covered plates sitting next to Ajay. 'O-pho! Your father's food is getting all cold. Is he still showering?'

Ajay had not seen his mother this energized in a long time. She buzzed around, doing everything at once, undoubtedly due to her excitement over their long overdue outing together. He felt proud to think that he had made it happen. She wore a deep violet salwar-kameez bordered with golden peacocks and sprinkled with paisleys, quite overdressed, but he said nothing. He felt a warmth in his heart from seeing her this happy. He vowed to himself to never let her sink into depression again.

'You didn't answer me, Mom. Why do you still call him Greg?'

'I don't know!' she said, a bit defensively, running packing tape across the flaps of the box. 'I don't call him that to his face. I mean, why does he insist otherwise? It's like calling a cat a dog. Do you look at a cat and call it a dog? It doesn't matter what you believe or what you worship but, you know, he looks a certain way. I feel kind of ridiculous calling him Parmesh just because he's garlanded himself with beads.'

'So you're stuck on outer appearances.'

'*Oho-ho*, and who made you a maharishi? In your case, you look hundred per cent like a goonda!' she said, shaking her finger at him, 'and that's exactly what you are.'

He waved his fist in the air and let out a couple of dog-calls, revelling in his mother's mock chiding.

'Maybe you should take me there,' she said. 'What do you think? Save some time while your father's getting ready.'

He shrugged. 'I don't mind.'

Just then his cellphone rang and she threw him a disapproving look. Ajay looked at it, hit a button, and silenced it. She shook her head. 'And I'm telling you, Ajay, if that cellphone of yours rings even one more time today, I'm warning you –'

'Okay, okay,' Ajay got up and held his phone out to her, its display still blinking urgently. 'Keep it.'

She waved her hand dismissively. 'As if I want to be your secretary.' She detected a strange, almost metallic smell coming from him and wrinkled her nose. 'Oh, Ajay, you really must use some deodorant! You have taken your shower?'

'What're you talking about? I don't smell!' he said, sniffing under his armpits.

'What happened to my little boy? Smelling of talcum powder and baby lotion.'

He grabbed her in his Herculean arms. She struggled to release herself but he held on tightly, laughing aloud. She gave him a playful slap on his cheek, her nose still wrinkled. He kissed it, the display of affection as special as it was rare in her grown-up son.

Parking around Montana Avenue was always a challenge. The pavements were bustling with shoppers in casual attire, wearing sandals and holding the perennial Starbucks cup while others ambled down to the Pacific Ocean, which beckoned from a few blocks down.

Pooja and Ajay were about to turn onto a side street when a black SUV suddenly swerved in front of them, cutting them off. Ajay slammed on the brakes, the car screeching to a halt. She let out a cry as the two of them were jerked forward sharply and then yanked back by their seat belts. Only the box of food, wedged against the back of Ajay's seat, sat snugly in its confinement.

'Motherfucker!' Ajay roared as the car raced away. He pulled over on the side of the street while Pooja stared at her son, astounded by his language.

'Are you okay, beta?' she asked, her concern overriding the need to reprimand.

But he was still shaking with rage and pounded his fist against the steering wheel so hard that she cringed, more frightened by his reaction than by what had caused it. She had only always seen the aftermath of his troublesome behaviour, like the black eye he had come home with the night before, but had never witnessed his violent side.

'Ajay, beta, calm down! Calm down! We're safe, no?'

He continued to glare into the distance, his eyes like burning coals, his face wrought menacingly at the speeding car. Upon feeling his mother's gentle hand on his shoulder, he held up his hands and began to take deep calming breaths but something in him, unyielding and conflagrant, refused to dissipate and he broke out again. 'Fuck!'

She shrank back, horrified. 'This much anger, Ajay? What is happening to you?'

'What? Did you see that car?' he shouted.

'But it happens. Why get this excited over it?'

She looked away from him with that patented hurt look, one that spoke volumes without employing a single word. A car pulled out from a loading zone a few spaces in front of them and he promptly parked against the yellow curb, around the corner from The Banyan. When he turned off the car, she was still looking away from him dejectedly.

Ajay groaned.

'Why? Why pick such fights?' she asked.

'But Mom –'

'No "but Mom!" How many times do I have to tell you to stay out of trouble? Yesterday you got beaten, tomorrow who knows what will happen? Maybe someone will have a gun.'

'I did not get beaten!'

'How much do you think your mother can endure? Last night, the same thing! Do you know what this is doing to me? Do you? Don't you know that in this country you say one thing wrong to someone and God knows what they might do. Why pick *panga* with these people?'

'Okay, I already said it, no? I'm sorry, okay?'

'What "sorry, sorry?" One of these days . . .' Her voice petered off and she became silent again, her head turned away from him. It was not just that he was growing up but that he was morphing into something she could no longer control or protect. It was this country. Yes, this country. If they had never come here, things might have been different, better. Every day this was becoming more and more apparent. Maybe Rahul would have cared to spend more time with them instead of at his bloody job. And Ajay would have had the love and nurturing of his maternal grandparents, too, a normal upbringing.

Her eyes welled up and suddenly the optimism she had felt before leaving home began to dissipate. A sigh escaped her lips and although she looked out of the window, she saw nothing, the cars melting into a mass of metal through the filter of her tears. Ajay laid his hand on hers. She pressed it and he came closer and put his head on her shoulder. She placed her lips on his thick black hair, kissed him, easily and affectionately, forgiving everything.

'You are my life. Don't you know this? If something should happen to you, I –,' she couldn't bear to think of it. 'Promise me you'll stop behaving this way, Ajay. For your Ma's sake.'

He nodded his head, still resting on her shoulder and allayed by her familiar perfume. 'Should I take it in for you?'

'No, no. You stay right here *chup-chap* and mind the car,' she said, disengaging. 'God only knows what else you'll get up to. This is a special day for us, for me, Ajay. Please, let's not do anything to ruin it, okay? I'll be right back.'

'But it's heavy, Mom.'

'I carried you, didn't I? And let me tell you, you weren't very light, *pahelwan*.'

As Pooja hauled the box from the back seat of the car, she noticed that her son drew the curious glances of a group of adolescent girls attracted by the coppery, muscled boy at the wheel of a luxury car, distracting him completely. How he lapped it up. She noted with disdain that none of them were Indian and her first instinct was to drop the box and shoo them away like a pack of stray cats. Nobody could be worthy of her son. But she let them enjoy the drama of youth that she herself had once participated in.

It wasn't until later, when Pooja had disappeared around the corner with the box wobbling in her struggling arms, the thick gold bangles cutting into the board, that the irony of her feelings about America struck her. More and more she was growing resentful of the country and turning into the very people she thought ungrateful and hypocritical. *It was so easy to be seduced by nostalgia, with the craving for something we were forced to leave behind,* she thought. *But if things had truly been any different back home, would they have come here in the first place?*

If he could only kill the relentless montage of their moments together, block his mind from manufacturing the dreadful possibilities explaining Rahul's absence, maybe Atif could have stopped the churning in the pit of his belly and the feeling like his heart was being constricted in his ribcage. But as he walked to the Pacific, bypassing the supermarket on Montana Avenue, he could not keep himself from drowning in gloom. He remembered why it had been so easy to stay uninvolved all these years, stay guarded, unavailable. His loneliness had returned, demanding crushing reparations for his giving in.

He was oblivious to the sanguine people around him – the joggers in their designer sports apparel, shoppers trotting conspicuous name-brand bags and popping in and out of boutiques, beach-and-mall-bound pedestrians and stroller-pushing couples, multi-tasking habitués checking emails from their laptops and getting their caffeine fix at pavement cafes, organic-obsessed shoppers with burlap and paper bags full of fresh produce from the farmers' market – all of it happening in a superimposed universe that he could see but not partake in. It was only when he saw the beautiful Indian woman dressed in stunning purple crouched in the middle of the street, gathering the spillage of little containers, that he managed to escape the grip of his thoughts momentarily.

An older, avuncular man was kneeling besides her, carefully placing the containers in the large box. 'Why didn't you just call? I would have come out.'

'Oh, it's ruined!' she cried. 'God, what a day this is turning into!'

'Not at all, love. Nothing's ruined,' he said in his clipped English.

Atif got nearer, watching her cluck away disapprovingly. 'So where is this boy today? It's not like him not to show up,' and then quickly, as if she could barely believe her own insensitivity, 'I mean, he is alright, is he not?'

'Oh, someone rear-ended the poor boy. Look, they're perfectly alright. Nothing's broken,' he assured her.

Atif picked up a single container that was in his path, noting that it was *chevda*, a spicy Gujarati trail mix containing rice, peanuts, raisins, cashews, fennel, curry leaf; it had been a staple at Kamal's home in Mumbai, enjoyed with a dollop of plain yogurt, a drizzle of fresh lime juice, some salt and accompanied by a cup of piping masala chai. It had been forever since he had tasted it and seeing the comfort food made him salivate. He resisted the urge to raise the box up to his nose and inhale its familiar spicy aroma, dive into its grainy turmeric dunes. He carried it over to the kneeling couple.

'That's what happens when these daft people are busy chattering away on their mobile phones instead of looking ahead,' the man was saying. 'And what's the use? The more time we save, the more of it we need.'

They both looked up at Atif as he handed the packet over. She thanked him, smiled with a mixture of embarrassment and gratitude. He caught the sharp scent of her attar, a mélange of musk and roses, and breathed in deeply, reflexively, momentarily transported to the folds of his mother's chiffon chunni.

'Would you like to keep it?' she asked.

'Thank you, no,' he said politely and walked away from the fragrance and taste of home.

On the dining room table, next to the plates of covered food, Rahul found the note Pooja had scribbled for him, indicating that she and Ajay would be right back. Behind him, on the widescreen TV, *Namaste America* was regaling the country with a current dose of Bollywood cinema and its host, Reshma Dordi, was fulfilling a request for a video of the industry's reigning king, Shah Rukh Khan. Grabbing the wireless and the cold steel cup of salted lassi, he went out into the back yard, through the frosted glass-panelled doors, where an abundant lemon tree produced the impossibly large fruit that Pooja used for *nimbu pani*.

He walked several feet to the other end of the patio, as far away from the intrusive presence of Sonali's neighbouring house. According to Pooja, after seeing some new racy Bollywood film, Sonali had grown obsessed with wind chimes, cramming her house with them to imitate the film's siren. Now even the slightest breeze set off a pandemonium that drove him insane.

Surrounded by intense white, orange and pink bougainvilleas, the kind that had been everywhere in Mombasa, he chugged down the salty cumin-infused lassi, feeling its milky coolness temporarily calming his inner turmoil. He looked at the lemon tree, heavy with offering. When Ajay was about six, they had caught him pissing on it and Pooja had joked, 'Just look at the size of these lemons! God knows what special fertilizer our little pahelwan has put.' When the gardener had suggested they uproot it, they had protested vehemently, asking him to work around the tree.

He placed the steel glass upon the abandoned outdoor grill. There had been a time when it had roared and spitted, when little Ajay had watched wondrously and dared him to make the flames dance higher and higher while Pooja admonished him about getting too close in her typical overprotective fashion.

He surveyed the sun-dappled patio, artfully decorated by her. Oversized wicker seats and chaises with colourful silk pillows, a stacked foam bed covered with a vibrant pink batik full of elephants invited lounging. A picturesque garden of calla lilies, eternally blooming roses, bougainvillea and jasmine formed a private, abandoned Eden. He leaned up against the lavender pergola, under a trellis dripping with scarlet trumpet vine, and wished he could remain calm. He craved a cigarette. Yearned for the balm of nicotine. He made a mental note to purchase a pack the next time he got the chance.

Above him a squirrel scuttled along the electrical wire against a palette of clear blue sky. When it noticed Rahul, the little creature froze, keeping perfect balance. They assessed each other momentarily and then it went off, apparently reassured of the lack of danger. Rahul looked at the phone in his hand. It was not that he was avoiding calling Atif but that after raising his hopes so high, Rahul didn't have the heart to crush him. At least that's what he told himself. His finger still poised upon the buttons that would connect him to where a part of him lived, he processed more of his feelings. How long could Atif and he go on this way? Was he willing to risk everything to be with Atif? What if this was some kind of warning, one last chance to avert a disaster? Then again, was it not too late already?

He remembered Ajay's words, saw his curled lip, and wondered if Atif could ever understand what he was going through as a father, if not as a husband.

That he couldn't live without his family, Rahul already knew.

Could he live without Atif?

Upon calling home, Atif found a message on the answering machine. All Rahul said was that he couldn't make it, that he would call him again later.

But why would Rahul call him at home instead of on his cellphone? To avoid talking with him?

Why couldn't he get away?

Why had he sounded so different – quick, vague, nervous?

Having heard his voice, Atif's desperation escalated and he imagined the most audacious scenarios. He should show up at Rahul's place, find out for himself what had happened, demand that Rahul keep his promise, threaten to reveal everything to his family unless they could be together. Was this love? Perhaps not, but in the grips of his fear of losing Rahul, suddenly no thought was irrational, unwarranted. It was as if some vital nerve of communication travelling from his head to his heart, the one responsible for ferrying logic, had been rent.

Warm breeze grazed Atif's face, now streaked with tears. He stood against the concrete railing of the park overlooking the Pacific, barely feeling his feet as pain coursed through him. The sun was burning against his back and sweat dampened his sheer cotton kurta. On his left the remodelled pier, thronged with people and loaded with amusements, stretched out grandly but like an incomplete bridge to nowhere. The Ferris wheel revolved languidly. Next to it, a canary yellow roller coaster coursed through its preordained path with serpentine grace.

A homeless woman trudged past Atif with a cart overflowing with dross. Atif saw her misapplied bright-pink lipstick and unruly Afro, and recognized her at once as Dottie, one of the first homeless people he had seen upon moving to LA. He had been shopping at the neighbourhood Vons when he had heard the checkers snickering about her. Right now she was embroiled in a ferocious argument with her demons.

'You better leave me alone, you hear me? Or I'm gonna' kick yo' ass!' she threatened, brandishing her fist in the air. People scurried away from her. Atif tried in vain to find some quiet in the pandemonium of life.

As an unspoken rule, he only ever called Rahul on his cellular. But after repeatedly being dumped into his voice mail, on which Rahul announced himself punctiliously as the bank manager, he found himself pressing the button that would connect him to that other realm to which he lost Rahul on a daily basis. His need had finally surpassed his pride.

When Rahul answered, he was struck silent for a moment,

stunned, as if he had, after a lifetime of trying, successfully infiltrated the afterlife and heard an evidencing voice, found proof of its existence. 'Rahul, you're all right . . .'

'Yes, I'm all right.'

And suddenly, the proof that nothing had harmed Rahul, that he was alive and breathing was enough to override any anger that Atif should have felt at that moment. Atif thanked God in his mind, breathed a sigh of relief. 'I had only two choices,' he said. 'To think that you're an asshole. Or that something terrible had happened to you. I prefer the former.'

'Atif, you're calling me at home.'

'Yeah, but what did you want me to do, Rahul?' he asked. 'I've tried calling you on your cell. Have you turned it off?'

'I'm sorry. I should've checked with them first. They'd already made some plans,' he said feebly. 'I can't do it.'

But Atif didn't care. If not today, then tomorrow. If not tomorrow, then whenever. As long as Rahul was still there, as long as they were still together, connected, it didn't matter and he could endure anything. But something gnawed in Atif, hinting at grave possibilities. Rahul was not just asking for a rain check, the timbre of something more than a postponement in his voice. He had made himself deliberately unreachable until now. Remorse, reluctance, impotence, doubt – they were all there, lumped together like a concrete block tied to the feet of a drowning man.

'You could at least call, Rahul. What's really going on?'

'I can't right now.'

'Why? What can't you do right now?'

'I knew it would be hard,' said Rahul. 'But this is . . . I'm not sure I can do this, Atif. You know my situation.'

'And I've dealt with it, haven't I?' Rahul was silent for only moments but in Atif's ears they stretched on for eons.

Then the wail of an ambulance sawing its way through Ocean Boulevard drowned everything. Although Atif barely glanced at it, he reflexively recited prayers as he did whenever he saw an ambulance, a police car, any augury of tragedy – *Ar-Raoof, Ar-Raoof, Ar-Raoof* (The Compassionate, The Compassionate, The Compassionate) – except this time, he wasn't sure if he was invoking one of the ninety-nine names of Allah for those out there or for himself. 'Rahul?'

'It's just not going to work out, Atif. I wish I could cut myself into two but . . .'

He tried to keep afloat, thought of that world from yesterday – one filled with hope and love and laughter. How can you lose all that? It was too precious, too real not to fight for, to hold on to. 'You know what? It's okay, we'll just make up for it next week,' he tried sounding jovial, to conquer fear with hope. 'Maybe we can go to that new restaurant that just opened, you know, the one at Shutters, the one I was telling you about? Or, of course, I can always cook and –'

'I need some time, Atif. Time to think.'

'Think? About what?' Nothing. And even though Atif knew that his persistence might push Rahul further away, he was unable to withstand the pain, to be left in abeyance. 'How much time? Rahul?'

'I don't know. I don't know . . .'

He gave a short, sharp laugh and it sounded as if someone had punched him in the stomach. So this was indefinite. He felt like his whole world was caving in. 'So this is *that* moment. Commonsense sets in. Suddenly you need a reason for us.'

'Atif, it's really not that simple.'

'Simple? Who ever said it was going to be simple? You think love is simple, Rahul?' he shouted. 'Is that what you wanted when you came to me, Rahul? Simplicity? And what do you want me to do while you think us away into nothingness?'

'I can't tell you what to do.'

'But you can. You can,' he cried. 'Don't you see? You can tell me to do anything and I will. Just . . . don't ask me to give you up.' If he could only see Rahul in person, look him in the eye, ask him what had happened to harden him, to draw the love out from him, everything could go back to the way it was. 'What happened? Talk to me, please.'

'I can't right now,' Rahul said, his voice breaking. 'I have to go, okay?'

'No! No, you can't go. You can't do this to me. I deserve an explanation, Rahul. Something. This is *me* you're talking to!' Just then he heard a woman's voice calling Rahul in the background. He froze. In all the time they had been together, he had never heard her voice, seen her picture, so Pooja had been a phantom presence. But now, for the first time, here she was, absolutely indubitable.

'Please,' he said, his voice lowered. 'I must go now but I'll call you later. I promise.'

'Rahul, I can't be without you,' he said. 'I won't.'

'Where am I going?' he asked wearily. 'Where can I go?'

Atif heaved with sobs. His anguish was so immense that he could barely hold himself up. He had promised that when the time came, he would let go without a struggle, without imposing any guilt-trips or emotional blackmail, but how could it happen like this, after such a special night? And how could he have known it would hurt this much, like someone rending his heart out?

All his life he had crammed his mind with the romanticism of the mystics – the likes of Rumi and his Shams, people from another time and place, who now lived only in the pages of books few even opened. But this wasn't Rumi's Konya, it was California. And the world had never fostered the soul-elevating yearnings of mystical love. Anybody could have told him how this was going to end. So many had.

'I'm scared, Rahul,' he said. 'And you know what the fucked-up thing is? You are the only one I can talk to.'

Over the balcony, just a few steps away from him, the cliff dived onto Pacific Coast Highway, teeming with speeding cars. Beyond it and over the strand of private beach houses, the sand was crowded with people, seemingly a thousand cocktail umbrellas flowering in the sun. Atif fixed his gaze on a pair of children frolicking with a large beach ball, the parents watching them from a distance.

What must his parents be doing right now? At this time, in Mumbai, while the city raged on, the sounds of traffic its faithful soundtrack, his parents must be soundly asleep in their beds. His father's snores would be filling the house and his mother would have wedged the pillow between her face and arm, almost as if trying to drown out her husband's sounds, his totalitarianism.

Do they think of me any more? he wondered. *If not with maudlin emotion then even with surprise, in passing, by chance? When they bit into the soft cheesy* mithais *that he loved so much and which his mother had sneaked out of the kitchen for him? On Fridays, when a new Bollywood film premiered at the Gaiety or a new hit soundtrack looped its catchy tunes on the TV, did they miss his irrepressibility? Did his mother miss massaging his head with the Amla oil he always protested about?*

Look, Ma, a full head of hair. You were right.

But why should I care? He thought, breathing in sharply. *I am dead for them. I have a father who, given the chance to do it over, would have snuffed me out at birth; a mother who strangled her maternal love to keep her marriage alive. I have a man who pours declarations of love into my ears, his seed in my bowels, yet wakes up next to a wife he has taken an oath to be with for his next seven lives. What do I have?*

The ocean didn't heave and chop like it did over the broad footpath and sea wall at Marine Drive. Even here gusts of wind carried its salt but the ocean appeared like a calm sheet, nature itself pretending to be something else in a city famous for its thesping and duplicity. He remembered reading somewhere that there was a reason why the ocean comforted us: because the smell of the ocean was the same primeval smell of woman. It was the smell of birth, of a life before life, that safe cocoon where we lay snug before we learned disappointment and hate and pain. Returning to the ocean then was like returning to the womb. Coming back home.

It would be so easy now. Just to let go, jump over, get it over with, to die. A leap and it would be all over, the pain, the humiliation, the rejection. He felt the breakneck dive, imagined the crushing of bones as he met with the tarmac, heard the commotion about him. The goading was loud and clear in his mind, that voice of defeat, the whimper of crushed self-esteem. But something in him stalled, a spark of hope still embedded within him, a distant, lost prayer finding him, enabling him one more breath pregnant with yearning.

Swerving through a puddle of creamy yellow daal, Rahul's fingers made hillocks of drenched basmati rice before parcelling them into his mouth. While hardly an act requiring concentration, Rahul looked so immersed in it that Pooja, seated across from him at the Ashoka Palace on Pioneer Boulevard, was certain her husband's mind was adrift. And now too, she longed to lay her hand on his chest and soothe his suffering, continuing to surprise herself as to how her feeling for him remained unabated. She watched him for a while, wondering if her focus would jolt him from his reverie, and willing him to look up at her. But when it was clear that he was beyond her psychic grasp, she reached out and, touching his hairy wrist, reclaimed him. '*Aiy*, where are you?'

He looked up as if he had been pulled out from slumber, shrugged, like it wasn't important. Ajay, making an exception in his diet, was already procuring another mountainous helping from the buffet table. 'I don't think they'll be offering any more buffets after this one's done,' Rahul said, throwing a look at Ajay. 'Owner starts sweating every time Ajay gets up for more food.' She laughed delightedly.

Even though the air conditioner could be heard toiling over the din of families gathered for brunch at the Little India eatery, and the windows were laminated with reflectors to keep the light out, the room felt hot and soporific. Nobody except for Rahul seemed to mind. They were all busy polishing off plates of spicy foods, pausing only to shake a reprimanding finger at their unruly children, gulp down cooling lassi, dab at the beads of sweat with their already turmeric-soiled napkins, or to chime in on some filmi song also competing for attention over the bass-burdened stereo.

Pooja looked up at her son as he approached the table with his black eye and two full plates, her joy more than apparent to Rahul. She had everything she ever wanted right there. Rahul knew that he too should be content with this; that this is where he belonged, with his wife and son, but something within him mourned. He had spent an entire lifetime in the shell shock of his disasters only to be jolted awake by Atif. Excising him now was like returning to death.

They first made a stop at The Patio, a bustling martini bar in West Hollywood where Atif had been a regular and which he hadn't been to in an eternity. Thanks to Nuru's connections, they didn't have to wait in the dauntingly long line of bristling queens lamenting on their cellphones, and practically waltzed past the startlingly handsome though superhumanly built straight bouncer. Nuru had depleted his supply of 'party petrol' as he liked to call his drugs, and was meeting his supplier, a closeted Italian guy whom he claimed to have serviced in the parking lot after paying him an extra fifty. 'Oh, they are only being the straight until they meeting Nuru.'

Still in a daze, Atif had allowed Nuru to convince him into going out because he couldn't bear the thought of being alone. After his talk with Rahul, he had found it impossible to stay in his apartment, every inch of it reminding him of some shared moment. It had taken him his whole life to learn how to be on his own and now suddenly he had been reduced to the worst kind of dependency, crawling for love.

They stood by one of the four crammed bars outside. As the music blared from the sound system and swarms of cocktail-armed men tirelessly squeezed their way through one another under the open sky, Atif found that the place hadn't changed much since the last time he had come here, even though the venue itself had been renovated and expanded. He found it hard to believe that at some point he had been able to relate to these people, and more dishearteningly, that he was back again.

What the hell am I doing here? What was I thinking, coming back to all this? He looked at Nuru, at all the others around him, either lost in their delusions or searching hungrily for fresh meat, and found it hard to imagine he could ever have felt a sense of belonging here. He beseeched God under his breath, craving Rahul; wondering what he must be doing, how it was possible for him to be doing anything at all when he, Atif, could barely breathe.

He could remember even further back, when The Patio had been a simple, unpretentious coffee bar, less than a tenth its present size and frequented mainly by students who sipped the coffee from fishbowl cups and laid out their homework instead of their phone numbers over the patio tables, before the oversized martini glasses and bleached smiles. Once the place had been remodelled, many of these under-age students had found themselves on the other side of the velvet rope, their backpacks getting heavier, unable to enter with their junior IDs and encouraged to hit some other forgotten java haunt down the street.

There were some of the old faces – their worn expectations undisguised by Botox or base foundation – and newer ones that had just taken over from those that had given up or found reprieve in someone or somewhere else. The dance, however, remained the same. He didn't miss it at all. The constant jostling for right of way, the balancing of cocktails in precarious oversized martini glasses freely spilling over one and all, the gossip, the lusting, the hook-ups and rejections.

One of the old-timers, Upul, a very dark Sri Lankan man of about forty, approached them as they waited. A perpetual smile on his face with bright teeth in startling contrast to his complexion, Upul was known to persist in teaching patrons phrases of Sinhalese whether or not they were interested. '*Karunakara* means "please". Say it!

Karunakara!' he would say. Or, 'Did you know the word 'rogue' is actually a Sinhalese word? The English stole it from us! It means big, savage elephant that lives by itself. What do you think?' Most people wished he could have been trampled by one rather than listening to him.

Upul appeared to be wasted but was clutching a full glass of Long Island Iced Tea, spilling little bits of it as he sashayed his way over, already smiling as hard as he possibly could without tearing his face. 'Oh, my God! Oh, my God!' His voice rang over the pandemonium. 'It's been forever! *Ayubowan*, my darlings!'

He bumped into a bystander, spilling more of the cocktail on the boy, and instead of apologizing, grew terribly agitated. 'Why don't you watch yourself? Why?' Upul demanded.

But before the boy had a chance to respond, Upul had taken off and with arms spread out, embraced Nuru. 'Hey, Miss Nuru! How you doing, girl? Oh, look who we have here. I know this girl too! Where you been?'

Atif shrugged, smiled.

Upul threw a look back at the drenched boy who was now being patted dry by one of his friends. They were looking at him furiously. 'Stupid queens! Don't know how to hold their alcohol!' Upul grumbled. 'So, what's going on, girl?'

'Well,' began Nuru, posing like a mannequin at his favourite department store, shoulder pulled back, hairy chest jutting out, eyes drooping to condescending slits and mouth pursed. 'Since last week, I've become a personal whore for Dolce & Gabbana, *m-kay?*' He spun around and then, stretching both arms out, clicked his fingers in self-validation.

Upul responded by cutting an arch in the air and clicked his fingers back approvingly. '*M-kay!*'

Around his neck Nuru dangled a massive tusk pendent

that gleamed against the matt of curly hair, and with which he liked to perform a curious clawing gesture. He did this now as Upul encouraged him, 'Go, Nuru! Go, Nuru! Go, Nuru!'

Typical dance music blared from the speakers around them but louder still, in Atif's mind, were the razor-sharp riffs of Abida Parvin, other ghazals, the sound of the sarod in his head, and the honeyed voices of Diana Krall, Randy Crawford. Together they gathered force within him, their melodies alternating back and forth in an aching medley, until he thought he would lose consciousness.

'You! You! You! You are not smiling! You must smile. Come on, smile!' Upul said, pointing at Atif.

Nuru nudged Atif back into the present. 'Smile!'

He obliged but although the corners of his mouth pulled upwards, his smile failed miserably. 'Oh, now that's not a real smile!' Upul said, handing his drink over to Nuru, who sneaked a generous sip of it. He pulled up at the corners of his own mouth, a rabid dog exposing his fangs. 'See? Now this, this is a smile!'

Normally indulging and tolerant, Atif grew irritated. 'You've gone a little crazy, haven't you?'

'Huh?'

'Crazy,' Atif twisted his finger at the temple and looked at him in such a way that it was obvious he wasn't trying to be funny. 'Mad. You've gone mad, haven't you?'

Nuru and Upul looked at each other, stunned at his bluntness, the lack of social Patio-etiquette.

'Oh, don't worry about her. She feeling different today,' Nuru offered as explanation. 'Forget it, yeah?'

'Oh! *C'est la vie!*' Upul shrugged. 'Whatever! I don't need no attitude from her tired tandoori-ass.' He snatched his drink from Nuru, did a couple of pirouettes to show his feathers hadn't been ruffled, and pranced away.

Nuru shook Atif by his shoulders. 'Hey! Hey! Hey!

Easy, girl. She is drunk. What is matter with you? Come on, you know that she doesn't have any harm, yeah?'

Atif looked away.

'Why can't you just have some fun? You used to love this place!'

'A long time ago, Nuru.'

'So what is wrong with it? What?' He looked around, apparently still impressed with the menagerie of men who were bathed salaciously in red lights. 'Is still better now.'

'It's proof that hell is finally full and the overflow has been sent to earth to hang out at The Patio.'

Nuru snorted and said nothing, perhaps because, as Atif suspected, he hadn't understood what had just been said. *God,* Atif thought, watching Upul weaving through the crowd and stirring the cocktail with his long, dark finger. *Life happens and we all go a little bit crazy on our own. Even solitude, while certainly a luxury, was eventually prone to madness. This is funny. I should laugh. I should really laugh. My being here of all places instead of with Rahul. Surrounded by all this desperation instead of his arms. All tragic situations are incredibly comedic if one has the benefit of the right perspective.*

But no matter how much he tried, he could not hoodwink himself into lightening the situation. 'Where the hell is this guy?' he asked impatiently. 'Maybe this wasn't such a good idea after all.'

'You are really having period today! We no ordering pizza here, you know! He gonna call me any time. Relax! Relax!' And then to Atif's irritation, Nuru launched into the 'Frankie goes to Hollywood' song with less-than-accurate lyrics. *Relax, you can do it. Why don't you just suck to it? Relax, you can do it. Do you want to come?*

And the parade continued with another one of Nuru's friends. This one, a tall, blonde investment banker in his early fifties but always claiming to be in his thirties, was loaded with gossip and some substance that had dilated his pupils to the size of dinner plates. 'She's gone crazy,' he dished on someone else, gesticulating generously. 'Completely cracked out. Too much Tina, girl. Oh, as if that god-awful rotten eggs smell isn't bad enough!'

'Really? Oh, poor girl!'

'She thinks everyone is spying on her!' the investment banker continued. 'She thinks her apartment is bugged. Bugged! Like anyone would be bothered with her tired ass. So she's pulling out all the sockets from her wall because she thinks there are devices planted all over the place. Can you believe that?'

'Oh! No wonder she not calling me. She probably is thinking I am like FBI or something. Somebody get her to rehab! I mean quick!'

'Her whole apartment is a fire hazard now. And that's not all, honey,' he continued. 'She bought this cute little puppy not too long ago and now, guess what?'

'Oh, don't tell me!' Nuru shrieked with mock horror, clutching his chest.

'Uh-huh. She thinks there's a camera or something planted in the poor dog, can you believe this? So she's come this short of sticking her finger up its ass and tearing it to pieces.'

'Too much of that reality TV.'

'Thank heavens she called one of our friends to come and take the little darling away before she bites into it. E-e-e-w! Druggie- druggie!'

What hypocrites! What in God's name made me think I could come back to this and feel better about anything? Atif thought, disgruntled. *I'll just take the damn taxi back, I don't care, but I have to get out of here.*

But then Nuru's cellphone went off. He checked the number and grew palpably excited and did his little signature dance, lifting one leg off the ground and shaking his shoulders from side to side like some harem girl confirming his ships had pulled in. He quickly exchanged air kisses with the investment banker and pulled Atif out of the bar. 'Come on, we have to go airport now.'

'Airport?'

Nuru's coded destination was across the street where, standing in the dark backside of the hamburger joint, next to a Harley, was a tall, thuggish guy in a leather jacket. As he took off his helmet, Atif saw that he had a hard, almost menacing look and that he was conspicuously out of place in the predominantly gay area. Approaching him, he felt instantly uncomfortable. The feeling, although without cause, invaded him so strongly that he fought the urge to flee.

'Hi, T,' Nuru drawled, batting his eyes like a lovelorn schoolgirl. He elicited barely a nod.

Nuru shook hands with the dealer and in the process dexterously made the barter. It was only when Nuru said, 'keep the rest' that the guy managed to crack a smile and nodded at them toughly.

When he had mounted his bike and ridden off after causing what seemed to Atif an unnecessary amount of ignition roaring, Atif looked at Nuru with alarm and said, 'Are you mad? What the hell are you doing with this guy?'

'What?'

'I don't know . . . this guy,' Atif said. 'He's so creepy. Don't you know any gay dealers?'

'Oh, he just big pussy, girl. Don't worry. Plus, you know, he's got the good stuff. Down there also,' Nuru laughed wickedly and did his dance with a smirk on his face. 'Big one, like torpedo, you know? So maybe he is not pussy after all, yeah?'

Atif shook his head.

Nuru brandished his loaded fist. 'Oh, honey! A little bit

of this and there is nobody you will not like. Come on, let's fly!'

An ocean of half-naked bodies swirled around them and Atif couldn't help but think that perhaps for some, this is what circling the Ka'aba must feel like. A sense of dissolving into the masses, destroying the identity of self to become a part of a larger conglomerate being. Some were lucky to find that feeling of corporeal melting, no matter how fleeting, with someone they loved; others could find it, at least for a few hours, dissolving under a giant glittering disco ball.

Once Nuru had tapped on the little green bullet and, placing it under Atif's nose without any fear of detection, let him sniff from it twice, the feeling began, or rather, ended. A numbness from everything that ailed Atif came gently over his body like a comforting blanket. Anything could happen now. People were known to have been thrown into the pits of hell or to find God. What a little cat tranquillizer could do.

It started with Atif feeling rubbery, as if his body was losing its structure; the thought of taking a single step became daunting. To do this, he would have to wade through what was slowly becoming a marsh of flesh and free-floating, loosely attached faces. Whenever his eyes met another's, the stare seemed to linger forever, like a romance scene in a film. As the wooziness invaded his body, he felt as if the vital stream of signals from his brain to his body was being excised. But at the same time, a strange sense of clarity and calm was replacing the cacophony of thoughts, giving his imagination freedom to soar.

All familiar objects became strange and new, as if he was a child again and discovering the world for the first time. His anxiety, fear, attitude, even the burden of hope began to evaporate from him and leave him vacant and free. Passages in his brain were being cleared and re-routed and he could feel nothing but indifference towards the reconstitution of his being. Around him, the bodies that were pounding away frenetically seemed to surrender to a gentle swaying. The music, once fast, hammering, deafening, slowed into a ballad, muted, as if coming from another room.

Nuru placed the bullet under his nose again. He took more of it, feeling the powder shoot up and drip into his throat. Now his spatial perspective began to change. The walls, once closing in, now stretched out so that the room opened up into the night sky itself. As he dangled on the edge between consciousness and oblivion, he could no longer speak, nor did he care to. It was as if he was preparing to say goodbye to the physical world and all tangible connection to his surroundings were being terminated. Opinions, analysis, judgement, attachment – all poisons of thinking were rolling off him like beads of sweat.

The music slowed to a crawl, as if the DJ had slapped down on the turntable. And then, only silence. A tear in the fabric of reality sucked Atif in and he found himself travelling with considerable speed through a dark pipe until, at the end of the journey, he stood facing an ocean of flashing yellow beacons. Atif watched the little bulbs with wonder, recognizing instantly that the people around him had turned into throbbing buds of energy. He perceived a presence, knew at once of its power. Shame washed over him.

I'm sorry. I'm so sorry, dear God, that I had to find you like this. That it has taken this for me to reach you. I love him but I will accept your will. I will not fight it. Let me crave only what you want me to have. Help me surrender whatever it is you do not desire for me to have.

The room swirled back into Atif's consciousness and there, standing across from him shirtless, in a strange, new body, stood an incarnation of Rahul, smiling. It was he and it wasn't he and some part of Atif knew and believed both of these, comfortable with the paradox. For how could he possibly be Rahul since he had begun multiplying himself infinitely? Five smiling Rahuls. Ten smiling Rahuls. A hundred smiling Rahuls. Thousands of him, everywhere, wherever his eyes fell. Even the lights above him, only a multitude of Rahuls smiling down at him.

Atif stood still, at peace and surrounded by the magnificent whorls of dance, and the multiplication accelerated infinitely, until there was nothing for him but a universe of smiling, dancing Rahuls.

He came home with the sun, breathing with such ease, the air moving in and out of him, that he felt almost light-headed. By the time Atif strolled by the roses blooming along the iron mesh fence dividing his complex from the neighbour's and scaled up the stairs to his apartment – a trek that he couldn't help thinking Rahul had made so many times – the sky was filled with light and the air was warm.

Taped to his door, he found a yellow note from Nona. He pulled it off and some of the dark green paint peeled off with it. She had got into an accident yet again: *Fuck, I've rear-ended another one! Can you believe it? Call me. Need a ride. XOXO. So this Asian definitely can't drive! N.* He took the time to fold the note neatly and went into his apartment, feeling neither urgency nor irritation. He heard the dismal beeping of his depleted cellphone, looked at the flashing battery icon and turned it off.

As he fell back in the bed in which Rahul and he had lain just days ago, his sleep was sporadic but peaceful. This time he was on his back and not on his side with his cheek gnashed and pulled back against the pillow so that he could breathe. Air moved in and out of him like a blessing. He heard the mundane soundtrack of life: kitchen utensils clanging as someone prepared breakfast, cars whooshing by on the street, garbled conversation, birds chirping. Even when he heard commotion from somewhere outside, he laid still, his arms by his side, his palms open. He could hold on to nothing. Not even a melody.

This is the place people aspire to reach in mediation, he thought. *A place where random thoughts came and went through your being, but instead of getting stuck in the swamp of contemplation, drifted away effortlessly. Where silence became the sweetest music and non-attachment was precious. Was it so wrong then to arrive here through a drug? Could anything that stopped the pain, eradicated judgement, filled you with such bliss and contentment be sinful?*

For hours he just coasted, seeking meaning in nothing and yet finding something of meaning in everything, no matter how ordinary. The texture in the ceiling, the almost indiscernible brushstrokes captured in the white walls, the subdued light filtering through the drapes, the jacquard embroidery resembling henna-painted hands on the curtains, the exquisite melody of silence – what more could one desire? Yes, this was the state where desires could spontaneously come true. His mind became that still, glassy pool, into which any intention could be dropped like a pebble. Ripples would be sent out into the universe to bring his desires to fruition, the thought, like the pebble, finding its destination in the fertile bed of fulfilment.

He was thankful the pain had dulled so that he could barely feel, but he also knew that if he didn't ask for what he wanted and lost this opportunity, life would become unbearable when the world returned. Once the anesthesia wore off, the pain would rebound, a jilted lover, determined to avenge its dismissal. Now was the moment. And if there was the remotest possibility that he could tap into that source where desires could be manifested, there was no choice. He must grasp it.

I am content now but I know it won't last. Here and now, in this moment, I am not afraid of tomorrow. But I know that when it comes, it will be unbearable; this peace will have abandoned me. It will break me into bits. So I must ask now, in the strange absence of yearning. I want to know what it's like to be with him in a way we haven't been. Together. Uninterrupted. Happy. No matter what the cost. No matter for how long. You see, I know I could have this with someone else but I could never feel for anyone the way I feel for him. So a little time with Rahul is worth all the time in the world with somebody else. A moment with him is a moment for eternity.

He closed his eyes, sending his prayer forth.

In asking for Rahul, Atif had asked for everything. In the womb of silence, his desire began its gestation. As he felt the breath enter and leave his body effortlessly, he knew one other thing. That granted wishes were not always the reward for goodness or worthiness. Sometimes the gods gave you precisely what you asked for but only as a means to punish you with eventual deprivation.

It was dusk by the time Atif stepped out onto the balcony and noticed the girls huddled around the metal fencing below with candles, wild flowers, incense and books. Phyllis, seated in the middle, rocked back and forth as she read from a book in her hands. Still in the faded blue kurta that he had slept in, Atif went down to them, the sleep deprivation and hunger now making him feel feverish. Phyllis looked up at him as he approached and said, 'Are you one of Anaïs's friends?'

'Yeah.' He noticed a photograph of the boisterous cat by the candle and flowers and began to fully realize the ceremonious nature of their gathering.

She extended her hand, 'I'm Phyllis.'

'Yes, I know,' he said, barely touching her hand.

Phyllis was in her twenties, had startling green eyes and a beautiful, trusting face framed by shoulder-length wheat-blonde hair. She moved aside to make space for him on the blue-and-black striped blanket they had spread out over the pavement and the girls shuffled to accommodate him too. 'Here, why don't you join us?' she patted the spot next to her.

He sank down next to her, Anaïs staring back at him from the photo taped to the fence with her wide, alert, gleaming, golden eyes. Bunches of rose and spears of lavender had been wreathed through the metal mesh, and an anthology of Anaïs Nin – who he now realized had inspired her christening – sat next to the gently flickering pink candle with an image of the Virgin Mother on the glass tube. The scent of the bromidic Nag Champa incense hung in the air.

Phyllis introduced the three other girls and he managed to smile weakly, not caring to remember any of the names. 'She crossed over yesterday. She got herself stuck,' she said. 'Right there.' She pointed to one of the openings in the fence. He imagined the cat's fragile neck caught in the wire, struggling, asphyxiating.

He couldn't help thinking that this was the very phrase that was used in the circuit clubs when describing someone who had binged on a cocktail of drugs and fallen into a K-hole or collapsed with an overdose of GHB. Crossing over. Last night, had they crossed over at the same time? Where had he been at the exact moment this had happened?

'One of our neighbours, Jim, he heard her but it was too late by the time he came down. Did you know her well?' she asked, smiling, clearly wanting to celebrate life more than to mourn its passing.

'Yeah,' he said and cleared his throat. 'She was like a little dog.'

The girls laughed approvingly. 'Yeah! Yeah, totally!' she said. 'She was like a little puppy.'

'I even saw her scare a dog once,' he shared, smiling. 'I couldn't believe it. The owner asked me, "Whose cat is this? I've never seen my dog so terrified!" And I told him it was mine.'

But in fact he had never claimed ownership of Anaïs and he wasn't quite sure why he had just lied. He could still see the uncharacteristically responsive kitten intersecting his path, throwing herself on her back and clawing in the air imploringly at him, rolling back up and doing it over and over again until he gave in to her at least for a few minutes and played with her, nuzzling her and rubbing her coat to the appreciative sound of husky purrs.

Phyllis gently placed her hand on his, understanding somehow. 'Thank you for loving her,' she said.

It became impossible for him not to believe that something much bigger, more irrevocable was happening now, as if the universe was systematically revoking everything he cared about or which had kept his life in some kind of equilibrium. As he looked at Anaïs's photo, the pools of her eyes glowing back at him, he knew that he should have cried but nothing came, his eyes remaining strangely dry.

By the end of his workday, his pain was so unbearable that all Atif wanted to do was curl up in bed and never rise again. Whether it was the aftermath of the drug or his delayed response to the losses he had suffered in the last two days – perhaps a lethal combination of both – his body verged on keeling over.

When in love, he thought, life was charged with an energy permeating everything so that one felt truly alive. Existence found its significance. Fulfilment reached a zenith. And despite all of life's accumulated cruelties, innocence returned miraculously – why else did lovers insist on making baby talk even at the risk of appearing ridiculous? But now that the love was gone, he felt sapped, as if the current that had kept him alive had been depleted. He couldn't bear to look at the centre divider across the bookstore, at that consecrated ground where Rahul had come for him.

Becca, always soaking in her own pain, focused on Atif for a change, forcing upon him cups of herbal tea that promised therapeutic benefit and expertly tending to customers while Atif slumped in a corner of the bookstore every chance he got. Even the bright-eyed white boy who took his post by the Eastern Studies shelf like clockwork, and whom Atif had humourously dubbed 'Gora Guru' failed to inspire or entertain him with his spiritual meanderings on life. This time, the boy had looked up at him with the same clear green eyes and saintly smile, and perhaps intuitively responding to Atif's pain, volunteered how he had escaped a potentially fatal car accident and the totalling of his car; then spoke on the merits of non-attachment so that he sounded like he would soon be embarking a space ship to some distant empyrean nebula with Deepak Chopra. And only now could Atif actually see how well-intentioned advice could come off sounding insensitive and condescending in the face of devastating pain.

What the hell could he possibly know about the kind of

life Atif had led? How could anyone dare suggest there was still something he had to glean from the rejections in his life?

It was just as well that the opulently dressed Indian woman whom Atif had spotted scrutinizing the store with her pencil-browed eyes over the last week or so, the one who never bought anything, hotfooted over to introduce herself to the 'Gora Guru' in the most forthright manner, completely ignoring Atif.

'Oh, my! What an impressive grasp you have on the subject! Forgive me, please, but I just could not help listening to all the remarkable things you were saying. Now how did a young boy like you get so much wisdom, *henh?* My name, it's Sonali Patel. You can call me Soni. And you? You are?' She extended a hand bedecked with dark gold bangles to the surprised boy. She completely overlooked Atif and he excused himself with a polite smile, feeling instantly distrustful of her.

He drove home reluctantly past spirited joggers on San Vincente Boulevard. All day he had struggled to escape the confines of the bookstore, yet now the thought of returning to the empty apartment petrified him. The only place that Atif wanted to be, he couldn't. In his desperation, Atif imagined showing up at Rahul's, calling him again, hoping he had changed his mind. But if his own parents hadn't reverted to acceptance, forgiveness, what expectation could he hope for from others?

We are told that we must learn pain so we shall know compassion, he thought. *So we may know His mercy, His forgiveness. But why must we learn it in the first place? Why should we have to feel anything other than happiness? Why must we have to find our way back to enlightenment? If we never asked to be born, to learn such lessons, and were simply thrust into the morass of life, why couldn't we have been born with those values inherent so that we wouldn't have to clamber through its harsh peaks only to learn lessons we never asked to learn in the first place?*

He would have begged for strength, for Rahul, for some kind of understanding, but by now the certitude he had experienced on the dance floor had vanished and was replaced by a hot wave of hate for the god that had orchestrated his perdition. There are others who are happier, he thought, those who have found love and have never had to observe any kind of penance for it. Providence came to them naturally, as if love in all its nuances – from parents, lovers, friends – was their natural birthright. Not all of them believed in the existence of a higher power. They had the right words; a necessary quota of restraint, an intelligence that could not be taught and which empowered them to draw love closer without soul-crushing sacrifices.

In contrast, I've prayed, he thought bitterly, *not with a salat or namaz, but with the sincerity of words that need no translation, a dialogue between friends, yet I am without love. Alone. Perhaps I don't have the right words, maybe too many of them and you've turned stone deaf, weary. So tell me, God, how would my life be any worse if I denied you now?*

When Atif reached his apartment, past the dried flowers and depleted candle by the fence, the door was a crack open. He stopped breathing. Upon stepping in, he found Rahul reclining on the leather easy chair, his arm crooked over his face as if asleep or trying to shut the light out from his eyes. He must have gasped because right then Rahul came to, looked up at him.

Atif dropped his satchel by the door, unsure if he could believe his eyes, unsure how to react. Rahul sat up. Taking an audible, laboured breath, Atif remained rooted to the spot, every pore in his body hungering for Rahul's skin. He leaned back against the wall, afraid his knees would buckle.

'I know I've hurt you,' Rahul said slowly. 'I hope you know that I've also hurt myself.'

Atif grunted, looked away from him, certain that Rahul could never fathom the depths of such pain. How else could one be capable of inflicting it? While Rahul had managed to function – eating, dressing, defecating, sleeping – without feeling the maniacal, blinding need to be with him, Atif had tasted a kind of annihilation. The last thing Rahul had said to him – about needing time, about not being able to see him – raced through Atif's mind and he turned his face away.

'Please, just hear me out,' Rahul said. 'Please . . .'

Atif slowly came into the room, still dimly illuminated by the day's receding light, and stood across from Rahul against the glass panes of the French window. He noticed that Rahul's face looked worn, deep lines scored his face. The room, once dancing with the sounds of their love-making and mirth and music, swelled again with deafening silence.

The conflict of desire and anger within him was so overwhelming that he could barely meet Rahul's eyes. Part of him yearned to throw himself into Rahul's arms, to never let him go, but even as his body seemed to lean forward, something restrained him. He felt the foolish urge to save Rahul from the encumbrance of his own words, from what he knew was difficult for him to express, and simply let Rahul's presence, his return, serve as a balm. But another part, still writhing from rejection, afraid that he may be forsaken again without warning, remained apprehensive, scorched.

He struggled to let Rahul finish what he had to say –

even if it was what he feared the most – but there was nothing he could do about the welling in his eyes. What made it worse was that he wasn't sure if he wanted to cry now from his own hurt or that which he sensed in Rahul.

'In so many ways,' said Rahul, 'I am in such awe of you. You know yourself so completely, unlike anyone I know. You know, it takes people a whole lifetime, maybe even a few, to figure out who they are – husband, father, son, brother. There was a time when I thought I knew. But for a long time, I . . .' he swallowed, his eyes dropped. 'I've made such a mess of everything.'

'But you've always been loved,' Atif said emphatically, feeling his own rejection as a son and now, as a lover. Whatever Rahul had done or not done, he was still needed not just by Atif, but also by his own family. He would never know what it was like to have a family that was alive and well but didn't want him. 'It isn't fair, that you should be loved so much. Why should you? Why should you be able to live while a little part of me dies every day?'

'I've been dead for a long time, Atif. Too afraid to look too hard or too deep. To feel too much.' As Rahul recounted the paralysis of his life, he continued without tears, detached, as if delving into the story of someone other than himself. 'Then you came along. So passionate. Unafraid. Open. With your books and your music and the sadness in your eyes – ,' his voice grew lighter, gentler, 'And suddenly, I felt like someone understood, you know? Recognized me.'

Atif's tears ran, his hand flew to his mouth. 'Yes, but you'll never understand what it's like to be me. To want someone so much, to want to see him so badly, you can hardly see yourself. Just constant, unending, like phantom pain. A missing leg that still hurts. You've led me to this. And my surrender to you, it's made this possible. All this time, I was safe. I'd made sure of it. Now,' he found it difficult to continue, 'now I'm back to where I was. You are everywhere . . . I'm nowhere.'

Rahul's remorseful gaze fell away from Atif and he sat hunched from the weight of his actions. Although he had never doubted how much Atif loved him, it was as if he had just recognized Atif's fragility, how much power he held over the boy's very existence. Slowly, he rose to his feet like one who had completed an infinitely exhausting journey and went to Atif. A slat of dying sunlight poured in from behind Atif and cut across them, siphoning them between darkness and light. He lifted Atif's chin, looked into his plaintive, bloodshot eyes. 'You are here,' Rahul said, touching his heart.

Atif clasped Rahul's hand tightly, held it close to him, against his thudding chest, as if in that grip they held a common heart. His tears unbounded, Atif cried now not only for the love that he knew Rahul felt for him, but also the love that he had lost, for his mother and father, all the rejections he had suffered up until now, and the realization that when at long last, love had arrived, it had been so that he would be able to neither claim nor keep it.

It would have sufficed to be cocooned in a local luxury hotel, but they managed to head north-west to the lush Ojai Valley, a little over an hour from Los Angeles and nestled at the edge of the Los Padres National Forest. Revered by the earliest settlers, the Chumash Indians, as a place of healing and mystical powers, the serene valley was often referred to by many spiritual seekers as 'The Nest.'

Atif remembered Carl Berman, over his many gin and

tonics at the Roosterfish, recommending The Nest, an intimate Spanish-styled landmark inn built in the 1940s over oak-covered land. He had made a mental note of it then and there, and now that the opportunity had arisen from their reconciliation, Atif had combed the property online and made all the arrangements for them. Although Atif had never been to Tuscany, from photos he'd seen, he thought that this was what it might look like.

They drove up in Rahul's car, the trunk packed with only an overnight change of clothes for Atif but a hefty suitcase for Rahul containing a freshly pressed Armani suit and tie, laptop, several bulky files, the accoutrements necessary to make it look like he was going on a business trip. In his satchel which lay on the backseat, Atif also carried a copy of Coleman Bark's version of Rumi's poetry, bottles of pink dragon-fruit-flavoured Vitamin water, bags of potato chips, unopened bottles of Gewurztraminer, a bar of imported chocolate-covered marzipan, his red rosary.

'I was thinking,' he said, fingering Rahul's knuckle as it rested on the gears, the platinum band from his finger removed and tucked away for the time being. 'Do you know what song they were playing when we had that first drink?'

'What drink?' Rahul asked, keeping his eyes on the road as the car began its descent into the valley.

'You know, the song, at the little bar in Santa Monica, that night.'

Rahul snorted funnily, 'What, now we have a song?'

'Detour Ahead. Billie Holiday,' Atif said, keeping his hand over Rahul's. 'Now that should have been a sign right there.'

Rahul gave him a look, unfamiliar with the song, so Atif began to sing it in a lazy, raspy voice, a bit out of tune:

Smooth road, clear day
But why am I the only one travellin' this way?

How strange the road to love should be so easy
Can't you see the detour ahead?

'Nothing else? Just that?'

'Not even the ring on the finger,' Atif said sardonically. 'Life was scoring the moment.'

After the initial talkativeness – the tempering of the weather, the demons that fuelled Billie Holiday's art, caused her addictions and penniless demise, the idea to invite Carl Berman for a drink back at the bar when they returned – they drove the rest of the way in contented silence, their hands webbed together for much of it even when their eyes were away from one another. The city slowly faded into carpets of lush green landscapes and little towns whose names meant nothing to them but which now, away from the city that made it difficult for them to be together, felt like little havens. Atif had printed out a map that now lay discarded on the floor next to his leather sandals, forgetting that the car came equipped with a navigation system, one that Rahul didn't even need to consult. This confidence in him, as he drove them, imbued Atif with the kind of assurance a child would derive from his father.

What he could not have seen is that by the time they had left the city limits, Rahul had started to feel displaced, his mind pulling back to his home, his chest filling up. He held on to Atif's hand but in his mind, he replayed the excuse to be away on a Branch Managers' retreat in Irvine, and realized that the awkwardness of a lie might have seeped through. Pooja had cleared the dinner table, looked at him strangely, more than ever convinced that this job was robbing them all of a quality life together. She let out a soft sigh as if to say: *When can we stop working so hard? We are getting old. Isn't it that time now when we can just reap from the years we have already toiled?* And somehow, as she had sat in the kitchen, her hands fluttering over the canisters of fragrant spices that had become her faithful legion of confidantes, she left him with the distinct feeling that he was yet again abandoning her.

For a while they were stuck behind a cargo truck and Rahul recognized the company name on its mud flaps, a shipping company in Westchester that he had solicited with one of his business bankers. He skirted around the truck, picked up speed as they left it behind. They passed an outlet mall, landscapes spotted with grazing cows, barns with rusted roofs, small communities of farm workers, groves of lemons, oranges and avocados. And as they streamed down the ribbon of tarmac, the cars dispersing with each mile, the skies cleared, mountains revealing themselves in all their majesty against wisps of puffy clouds flirting with the summits.

Eventually they turned down a long dirt road fanned by tall sycamore trees, stones crunching under the tyres, the aroma of orange blossoms, sage and dense forest permeating the air. Except for the inn's wooden sign, made by a local artisan, there was nothing to mark where they were going and at first there was no structure visible. Then they came to a clearing where they found six intimate, old mission-style bungalows with arched entrances and terracotta curved roofing nesting behind a low wall of ochre-coloured stones. In the centre was a fountain burbling crystalline water into a tiled basin, studded with coloured stones. A Labrador peeked out at them forlornly from the porch of the middle bungalow, his tail wagging in anticipatory delight as they pulled up next to a parked Saab and Atif thought of Anaïs with a sudden, sharp pain but said nothing.

No sooner had they turned the engine off than the dog bounded over to them and as if alerted by the excitement, a heavyset, tanned woman in a floral cotton sundress appeared from the cottage. She ambled over, calling after the dog and trying to calm him down, and introduced herself as Dottie Wharton. She swept the honeyed bangs away from her sparkling blue eyes and asked questions about their journey with genuineness, making Rahul feel uncomfortable, as if she were prying. He flashed her a smile and looked away, letting Atif make niceties. The dog darted around by their legs, seeking affection, and although Atif hesitated, Rahul reached down and gave him a good cuddle.

They were given the keys to their cottage after a quick sign-in process in the office where jars of scented candles slogged unnecessarily to create an atmosphere already prevalent in the surroundings. If Dottie Wharton, drenched in magnolia perfume, had been the least bit curious about her two male guests, she didn't show it. When she handed them copies of signed paperwork and a map of the town, Dottie also offered suggestions on how they could spend their time in what she proudly called 'the city of pink sunsets', although actually witnessing one was not on her list of things to do. They could go golfing, cycle over to the picturesque arcade downtown where dozens of shops, restaurants and spas awaited, go hiking. But all they could think of was banishing the outside world.

'So, welcome, Mr Ka-Poor' Dottie beamed with her hands tightly webbed together in anticipation as they slung the bags over their shoulders and prepared to leave through the screen door where the dog mewled away. 'Oh, I just know you and your son will have such a neat time here!'

Now, removed from a life that had to be choreographed to the ticking of minutes, they found themselves uninterrupted, in a self-contained bungalow that stood in for the home they would never share, the desperation of their love-making metamorphosed into an ease found only in couples who could take time for granted, feel the reassurance of the years ahead of them.

They stood at the foot of an expansive rustic brass bed, enclosed by ochre walls finished to an aged look, and could hear the narcotic melody of quietude. There was an abundance of windows opening up to private gardens and mountain vistas. Sunlight streamed into the room through the wrought-iron-grilled windows, etching trellis-like shadows onto to the polished wooden floor. The air was lightly perfumed with lavender potpourri, placed around in small earthenware jars around the room. Black and white photos depicting the inn before a fire razed it in the late 1950s hung on the walls.

This time, they regarded each other not with desperation, but like grateful survivors. They put aside their shields, removed their guards and breastplates, and looked at one another with tenderness and the exhaustion that comes from the end of a shared and infinitely demanding ordeal. Somewhere else, as the world clattered away, Atif and Rahul held each other in an embrace, comforted by the beating of their hearts, their solitudes slowly merging.

There is such an alchemy, Atif was reminded, *where two people can dissolve in each other, a closeness where tragedy and loneliness can, at least momentarily, be expunged, and every earthly cause that has driven us to trauma finds a cure.* This, Atif thought, savouring the taste of what he knew might be certain blasphemy, *is what religion tries to teach us and miserably fails in: abandonment. Here is my Islam. I have submitted completely to him – mind, body and soul – consequence be damned.* He knew now the meaning of the Sufi poems he had pored over, as if he had been given the key to their secret door, no longer shrunk down to just poems and love songs translated sometimes in a language in which there couldn't possibly be a word to describe the kind of fire he felt inside, but expanded infinitely like a sky within.

Standing there, it occurred to Rahul that although Pooja and he had spent a whole lifetime building a house, brick by brick, over a dungeon full of painful memories neither one of them could bear to confront, Atif was now reacquainting him with his past, to a part of himself he had been unable to accept. The thawing brought hope. And where there was hope, there was life.

Atif sensed Rahul's pain and looked up at him, cupping his face in his hands, feeling the stubble prickle his palms. 'I would have liked to age better than this,' said Rahul. 'Just to be more, give more, something of real meaning.'

But you have! Atif wanted to say. *Can't you see that?* He had created a son, of whom Atif knew nothing about, but was certain was a model child, the kind who would surely enter some coveted college and become the proverbial Indian engineer or doctor, anything other than a striving, tortured writer or underpaid bookseller. And he had not walked out on his wife.

Atif wanted to tell Rahul that he had brought happiness into his vacuous life, replaced the family that he had lost, given him, despite the shortcomings of their relationship, the chance to love.

But Atif said nothing, covering Rahul's face with kisses, knowing that there was nothing he could do or say that would make Rahul feel absolved about being there with him; that ultimately, the guilt of abandonment would always linger, no matter how small.

'This will sound banal, I know,' said Rahul. 'But I still want to say I'm sorry.'

'Well, you know love means never having to say . . .' and they both laughed at the reference to *Love Story*. Atif held Rahul's face and looked deeply into his still-brimming eyes. 'They say that life is about balance. That it trades one sorrow for one joy and so forth until it finds some kind of harmony. Well, I want none of it. I've never been as dead as I was when I was balanced. I don't want life to be contained. I want it unbound, inspired. Alive.'

After they made love, they held on to each other like children recognizing tactile sensation for the first time. No one came to disturb them and they had nowhere immediately to go. When Rahul slept, Atif would look at him, studying all the lines and contours of his face. After he had looked his fill, graphed Rahul's image in his mind, Atif would shut his eyes and still see the face; when he opened them again, he would see that Rahul was really there, the face just inches away from his, his breath warming Atif's neck.

Atif remembered Rumi and fell into sleep's comforting embrace, the words of another love, dancing in his mind:

I am happy tonight,
united with the friend.
Free from the pain of separation,
I whirl and dance with the beloved.
I tell my heart, 'Do not worry,
the key to morning I've thrown away.

Patterned moonlight poured into the room. Atif slept deeply, the strain gone from him, his face as clear as it must be when he felt completely safe. Every now and then he smiled, cajoled by some dream, and said words that meant nothing. Rahul should have slept soundly as well, allayed by the thought that both his worlds, at least momentarily, were spinning in perfect axes. He slipped out of bed and leaned up against the bedside window to look out into the night, the pearly light bathing him like celestial waters from above. Crickets and occasionally the lawn sprinkler thrummed over the silence, the world outwardly quiescent in the realm of the subconscious.

He had a sense of being here before. Could it have been a dream or a trick of his consciousness, a moment that had just happened, suddenly being remembered? He remembered reading somewhere that a sense of déjà vu was a validation of your destined path. Somehow, someone was showing you milestones to reassure you, to confirm that you were accurately following a predetermined course.

He remembered humid nights in another lifetime, the hours before sunrise over another ocean, the barrelling herald of ships at the port of call, carefree days of innocence. Pooja was his only enduring link to that memory and he began to think of her and Ajay now, feeling for the first time removed from them, wishing that he could have found a way not just to be corporeally present with them, but to be content also.

Why now was he missing the fragrance of her freshly washed hair, peonies and vanilla, when she gave him a hug or leaned over his shoulder at the table to lay down breakfast? He saw her sleeping alone, now, still sticking to her side of the bed, turned away from his side as if afraid to look at the vacancy there, lonely and wondering about him. He was connected to her in a way he wasn't when he was sleeping beside her, more there now than he had ever been.

But he also wished he could stay on here, the whole world dwindled into a murmurous quiet, swaddled in white cotton sheets with Atif, letting himself be held like an infant by a boy half his age, and not feel like a convict awaiting his sentence. So he remained somewhere in the middle, neither here nor there, too late to change anything, to have made other choices. *We are more than just the sum of our mistakes,* Rahul thought. *But that, sadly, doesn't make them any less costly.*

Rahul thought now of Hanif again, saw the boy's face as if he had seen him only yesterday and not more than thirty years ago, as it had been. He remembered that scorching afternoon in Fort Jesus, that brief and shameful moment of weakness when they had, as two young boys, found shade and privacy in the ruins of the still formidable Portuguese relic. He saw them frottaging against the rough, ancient walls resembling coral, tainted with moss and blood, and the two of them, who seldom spoke to one another in public, now slapped against each other with lust. Rahul saw his semen splatter against Hanif's white polyester school pants. He remembered the shame and alarm that overcame him, before he had zipped up and, deserting the frequently bullied, gentle Muslim boy, darted out of the sunken cove as the sounds of people encroaching had grown louder.

Because he hadn't actually been there to witness it, Rahul now imagined Hanif's casketed body, adorned with fragrant frangipanis, being lifted high above the heads of tall Muslim men, being carried to the community hearse and then to the burial site. 'He drowned, the poor boy, can you believe? Such an expert swimmer but he drowned!' he heard other students – the same ones who had reproached Hanif for his effeminacy – lament a few days later. Rahul had frozen then, thinking of how Hanif had reached out to him at school, only some days before the incident, trying to say something, and how Rahul had rebuked him, as if rejecting his own deed.

Atif's words came to him: 'Rumi's *Mathnawwi* begins with the flute crying out for the reed bed from which it was plucked. All Sufis – regardless of the religion one was born in, because one is ultimately a Sufi by heart – feel this homesickness. But there is also a kind of hope in this pain because essentially, we are all exiles, longing to return home.'

Strange tears prickled at his eyes. What if he didn't know where home was any more? The last time he had felt like he was at home was too long ago. He had been just a young man then and now he was older and suddenly he didn't know how the years, all at once bedraggling and rapid, had passed. Nothing remained of that home in Kenya but debris and ash, echoing howls in his mind. Would talking about it with Pooja, who had been there, made things any easier for him or for her? He decided that there had been no other choice. The events, so horrific and purely evil, had left him no choice but to be at a distance from himself, as if the life he had been leading up to that point, and the events that marked the end of its carefree blissfulness, had happened to somebody else, in a foreign language he could not speak.

Sensing Atif stir, he looked back at him, the slender arm stretched out across the vacant pillow, as if to feel reassured, even as he slept, that their togetherness was not just a dream. Lifting the sheets, Rahul climbed back into warmth, pulling himself closer into Atif, as if to shut out the rest of the world and thoughts of consequence that hung heavy in the night.

Many times in the night, each would wake up, their bodies intertwined, sweat matted between their skins, and sleepily they would wipe it away, change positions, always an arm harbouring, a leg flung across, some part of the body entwined, as if from the touch they were drawing life.

The light had risen as they'd been talking, still in bed, and the room was filled with a warm glow. It was only now that they began to realize that the room had dreamy goose down comforters but no TV set, a black rotary phone and old books that once belonged to someone else and had been left behind for others to find, but no locks on any of the doors. Everything felt different here, slower, more focused. Even their speech had slowed down and they had gained the gift of concentration. Thoughts came up and lingered in the air for full moments before they articulated themselves in words or dissipated like bubbles.

Atif turned to look at Rahul lying by his side, his chest rising and dipping with each breath, the pasture of hair converging into a serpentine trail that ran down Rahul's abdomen and dived under the sheets below his navel. Even the inches between them felt like too much distance, so he reached out and took Rahul's hand in his. *This,* he thought, *was what Rumi must have meant when he felt consumed by Shams; the yearning to merge with someone else, the dissolution of distance. And yet, even now, there was so much he didn't know about this man he loved. Would Rahul reveal himself now, away from the city and those who awaited him?*

Atif rolled over on top of Rahul, straddling him.

'Already?' Rahul laughed. 'I'm not that young any more.' Atif held Rahul's hands apart messianically, massaging the mounds on his palms. 'Ah, okay, keep that up . . . I think it might be working.'

'Rahul,' Atif began carefully, 'you never talk about your past.'

Rahul looked away, the smile fading.

'I just want to know more about you . . .'

Slowly, Rahul withdrew his hands. 'It's gone, Atif.'

'Look, really, I know how difficult it must be for you. My own past –'

'It's much more than that . . .' And then he said nothing more, his voice strangled, the words lost, signalling that this was as far as he was willing to go. The change in their surroundings made no difference in how much access he would provide. He had sealed all doors to his past and was standing guard over them. Diffidently, he sat up in bed. Atif slid down to Rahul's lap, keeping him pinned so that they were sitting up against each other, their chests barely touching. Atif looked down on Rahul's head where a few strands of silver penciled through his still-dark hair and the faint fragrance of citrus and mint from the remnants of his styling gel rose up. He reclaimed Rahul's arms that had fallen off to the side and circled them around his waist. He got the sense, as he often did, that the more he asked on this subject, the less he would get but it was too late to turn back now.

'Still, your parents, Kenya. You act as if – as if by not talking about it, it doesn't exist. You tell me about how you had to leave Kenya, leave everything behind, but there are gaps in your story, Rahul. The details,' he said, skimming his thumb across Rahul's lower lip as if coaxing the words out, 'they're missing.'

Rahul gave a short laugh and shook his head, unable to believe Atif was being this persistent. A tear trembled at the corner of his eye. 'I can't do this.' He started to bolt.

'I'm sorry,' Atif said, quickly wrapping his arms around Rahul and pulling him in. 'I'm sorry. Shhh. I just want to be there for you, that's all.' Atif felt Rahul's heart pounding, sensed the panic that had paralysed him. He wanted to avenge whatever had hurt him, to heal the wounds, but the enemy remained faceless. He clung on to Rahul, covering him with kisses.

'I wasn't there for them,' Rahul said finally, his face resting upon Atif's shoulder, looking past the walls of the room. 'That's all you need to know. I wasn't there.'

While Rahul showered, singing some old Bollywood song that Atif recognized, something about a beautiful journey on a beautiful day and of being afraid to lose oneself in it, he picked up the tanned leather wallet that Rahul had left on the dresser, and found them in a laminated sleeve between credit cards.

Pooja Kapoor was an astonishingly beautiful woman. Ajay was the inheritor of both his parents' good looks. Atif thought that she resembled a legendary Bollywood actress who, even in her forties, remained one of the most beautiful faces to have ever graced the screen. They appeared to be at a party, decked out, looking normal, enviable, like those perfect family pictures that could be used to sell insurance premiums and could be believed by the most sceptical and unromantic. Jealousy and admiration simmered within him.

After this, Pooja's face was grafted onto his consciousness and he felt the urge to go back to the picture again and again to search for some kind of flaw in her. But he resisted, seeing now the wisdom in not having done so in the past. Until now she had been a phantom, but now he had helped her to materialize. He grew apprehensive. By crossing the line, violating the terms of their relationship, opening the verboten box, had he opened up a portal, provided her access to their world?

It was the aroma of sweating onions, sizzling in a pan of ghee as they anticipated a mélange of spices and vegetables that drew an eager Sonali Patel to her neighbour's house that Sunday afternoon. How a little bit of Pooja's food and a glass of cold, sweet rose-water lassi would energize her for her important meeting, thought Sonali, smacking her lips as she made her trek across the well-manicured lawn. With her new Louis Vuitton handbag in tow and white, oversized Jackie-O sunglasses, Sonali was on her way to Elton's where she was meeting the junior Goldstein, poring over books on Hinduism to understand his own soul.

She never thought of herself as metaphysical or spiritual but understood the simple fact that Hinduism was indomitable precisely because it was open to interpretation, providing myriad variations on its impassioned tales. The gods, in the context of their oft-conflicting histories, became like plasticine dolls, mouldable to your brand of belief. Each god is multidimensional, each story multilayered, the message morally ambiguous.

People knew little about Sonali Patel, or what they thought they knew was inaccurate, and she liked to keep it that way. She would rather be respected than liked, feared than taken advantage of. No shrinking violet, Sonali took pride in being known as formidable, even if it meant being abrasive and intrusive.

For instance, what did any of them know about how, as a young girl, she had watched her hard-working though plain mother, Jaya Desai, being abused and beaten by her drunk, debauching father? From a lower-middle-class Mumbai family, her father, Ravinder Desai, a short, pudgy imp of a man, had worked as a lighting assistant in a Bollywood studio. He spent all day perched on precarious ladders, being barked at by temperamental film-makers as he made sure that even the mediocre looked ravishing when the lights were manipulated correctly.

This should have turned Ravinder Desai sour to the world of glamour but instead, like a deranged man who learns the exact opposite from his lessons, he returned home at night from the red light district drunk on the local brew *chakti,* inflamed that his wife looked more like the dark-skinned dhobi who cleaned the utensils and trailers at the studio than like the heroines that lit up the screen. This might have been somewhat bearable had Jaya's father been able to come up with a handsome dowry or had Jaya given him a son. Clearly Ravinder had felt cheated on both accounts, so he even blamed Jaya for her mother's death at childbirth. 'What a face you have come with! Poor woman took one look at you and breathed her last! Meanwhile, look how fat you have become! One day you will even eat me up!' And then, mystifyingly, it was he who would break down sobbing like a child over his misfortune while Jaya tried to comfort him.

Sonali's mother remained pained but demure, deprived but dutiful. She continued to cook and clean, to watch over Sonali and protect her from her father's drunken wrath in case it spilled over on her. Every morning she touched his feet like he was God, and all he could do was grunt and pick his paan-stained teeth with a toothpick. In the evenings, she waited with cooked meals and the futile prayer that he would come home sober, even if she could never expect that he would look at her with love and not be tainted by the heady perfume of whores. Her husband, Jaya Desai often found herself explaining to little Sonali, was a version of god. To serve him was her *kartavya*, her duty, and which god doesn't put his devotee to the test?

Then, one day, Jaya became deathly ill and began the steady decline into a bundle of bones. But even as fever inflamed her body and she took to cowering in a corner of the room, even as she carried on conversations with phantoms and deceased relatives, and her nondescript face began forming strange purple lesions, she refused to seek medical help. It was as if part of her was willing death on herself, the only way to find moksha.

She died alone. Nobody was with Jaya when she pulled the sheets high above her head, as if to hide from whatever was coming to get her – or could she have been inviting the darkness in? She didn't struggle for breath, just let go with a sigh. It was unfortunate that even her daughter, whom she had tried so hard to give the love she knew could not be expected from her father, had grown apathetic to her by then.

Sonali had begun resenting her mother. Powerless herself, she grew up to hate her mother's piety, her sense of duty, her impotency against fate. She began to blame her mother for submitting to her father's treatment, for her unceasing devotion even as she crouched under the fists befalling her. Towards the end, Sonali had even taken to treating her mother with cruelty, calling her names, shouting back at her at the smallest of things so that she was reduced to a mere servant in her own house, serving two masters instead of one.

When her mother finally passed away, Sonali was filled with grief and remorse. But she had also learned vital lessons first-hand: that beauty was a currency in itself and compensated for many personal shortcomings owing to our astonishing appetite for aesthetic perfection. Barring that, one must have wealth, which in so many ways could also secure beauty. Only the truly unfortunate were born into an absence of both.

Young Sonali also learned that gods did not exist, or if they did, they didn't care. Where was Laxmi, goddess of prosperity, when her grandfather had fallen short of a dowry and Jaya had been carted off like a hump to live with a tyrant who would never let her forget it? And where were the gods when Ravinder had lain with the prostitutes of Bhiwandi only to come home and beat Jaya limp so that Jaya was only grateful that like other brides she hadn't been doused in kerosene and set ablaze in a locked kitchen? What was Lord Krishna up to then? Still spooling out swathes of cotton to a distressed Draupadi?

After Jaya's death, Ravinder practically forgot that he had a daughter. He stayed out all night, even losing, at some point, the job he revered at the studio. Meanwhile, instead of feeling grief for having mistreated his wife, perhaps causing her death, he bereaved his own broken fate, cursing Jaya now for defecting on him and leaving him to fend for an unruly daughter who had inherited none of his own good looks and all of her mother's unsightliness.

So he was relieved when her maternal aunt took Sonali in when she was about the age her mother had been when they had married. Here, her snooty cousin Manisha never once let Sonali forget her burdensome position as an extra mouth to feed. But Sonali bit her tongue and got back at her in more surreptitious ways, like whisking globs of mucus into Manisha's pot of turmeric cream, then watching her cake the cream onto her face each night so she could obtain that treasured bridal glow.

Sonali attended Davar's College at Fountain where she learned typing and shorthand among other hopefuls, even some who clearly considered themselves better than the institution and those in it. She watched these girls more particularly, eyeing their luxurious manes of dark hair, their revealing, modern fashion, their painted filmi faces, and how they looked at others disdainfully from under the tips of their noses.

Then she met Sanjay Patel, quite by chance, and everything changed. A visiting NRI from America, Sanjay was a wiry, soft-spoken man with oily, slicked-back hair who had been sent to recruit other promising engineers and skilled workers from a country that was slowly becoming a gold mine for the West. No longer seen as just indentured labourers like in the eighteenth and nineteen centuries, this stream now consisted of doctors, engineers and scientists and Sanjay was sent as an emissary of the better life waiting for hard-working Indians in America.

Having lost both parents in a freak accident which had killed them on the spot when driving to visit Indian friends in San Jose, Sanjay, only twenty then, grew lonely without any siblings to share his grief with. By the time he was thirty, he had managed to build a lucrative career, almost as if to compensate for all the love he had been robbed of.

Someone or the other had invited Sanjay to a matinee of *Dil Apna Preet Parayi*, where Sonali was also present with the only rich friend she had at Davar's, a rather unpopular, overweight, dark-skinned girl called Rachna who made overt passes at any man she spotted. Rachna was known to plug her fingers straight into her mouth, let out a piercing whistle, and say things that made even grown-up men blush: '*Arre, jata hain tu kahan, Ranjhe? Teri Heer to idhar hai!*' Where are you going, Romeo? Your Juliet is waiting here for you.

As the lights dimmed and an orphaned Meena Kumari fell for Raj Kumar's Dr Sushil character, Sonali, for the very first time, found herself being looked at with desire by the man sitting one person down from her. She was suddenly glad she had worn her fitted parrot-green blouse with white flowers embroidered at the neckline, black pants, and had left her hair loose with just a emerald rhinestone pin on one side.

Separated from Sanjay only by a popcorn-chomping Rachna, who couldn't eat fast enough to finish the samosas she had stashed away under her seat and carelessly wiped her hands on her bright-yellow cotton dress every now and then, Sonali encouraged him with a smile in the dark room. He must have caught the glint of her teeth because right then he looked away and Sonali had wondered if, like a fool, she had smiled too hard and scared him away.

Halfway through the film, Rachna farted and then looked around angrily at others. But everyone knew it was Rachna, it was always Rachna, and one of their friends, a lanky outspoken guy called Salim said, '*Tch, tum bhi kya,*

Rachna . . .' and was greeted by a volley of blows from an indignant Rachna. 'How dare you! Salim, I say how dare you!' That's when Sonali looked over and saw Sanjay smiling directly at her.

It was after the film, its romantic melodies fresh in everyone's minds, and when Rachna had rushed to the bathroom, grasping her cramping stomach, that Sanjay picked up the courage to ask Sonali out. That was when she knew that truly there was someone out there for everyone. She didn't need Rachna's money. What good had it done Rachna, that uncouth cow? Someone had finally made her feel like those other women with the black manes, immaculately painted faces and pert noses. She considered her suitor right there and then. Sanjay didn't look like a strong man but he was financially sound. He was not good-looking but he seemed kind.

This man didn't think of her as plain or ugly, or it didn't look like he would ever dare raise a hand to her. From his wiry glasses, he could barely look at her without breaking into a smile and shyly averting his eyes. Unlike those who might imitate the relationships of their parents in a misguided attempt to correct past wrongs, she would trade up, let Sanjay be her ticket out of Mumbai, taking her a lot further than shorthand and typing ever would.

For their first date, she skipped classes and they went to the Prince of Wales Museum. Even though she was a Mumbaikar, she had never set foot in the museum and was impressed when they looked at the collection of miniature paintings and bas-reliefs from the nearby Elephanta Caves, and a worldly Sanjay commented on their history as if he had discovered the relics himself.

When they met again, she suggested Malabar Hill where they walked in the lazy afternoon through the Hanging Gardens, over acres of lush greenery laid out over a series of reservoirs that supplied water to the entire city. Here, as they walked past the topiary, she made the mistake of asking him about his work, something she was not terribly interested in, and Sanjay, a normally subdued person, became remarkably excited.

'The world is shrinking, Sonali,' he said, gesticulating in the air. 'They say the world is round but, no, wait, you'll see it's quite flat after all.'

She tried to pay attention but underneath it was all too complex and boring and she was only able to tune into it mildly, feigning interest because it was all coming from her future husband, her saviour in that charming broken Hindi.

'India is slowly becoming a major player in the world, Sonali,' he continued, his black eyes shining behind the glasses. 'You know, we are some of the most intelligent people in the world today. But look, they're all sitting around like *gobi*s in the market. You know why?'

Sonali gave an almost imperceptible grunt and Sanjay accepted this as a prompting. 'No infrastructure,' he said, shaking his head and clucking his tongue. 'But now, all sorts of advancements are being made. We're taking over the world, Sonali!'

Somewhere between Sanjay buying her a peacock feather from a little boy who spoke several foreign languages fluently, drinking in panoramic views of Mumbai and Chowpatty, and taking pictures in the 'Old Woman's Shoe', the walk turned into a nervous yet determined proposal from Sanjay. Of course she had already known her answer then – why, she had been praying for this – but still Sonali asked for some time to consider it. He was staying for six more weeks with Rachna's relatives, and she calculated correctly that she would have enough time to respond favourably, with dignity.

One afternoon, they shopped along the famous Colaba Causeway, along a strand of little stores and pavement stalls selling everything from shoes and handicrafts to clothing and trinkets. Sanjay spoilt her by buying her a pair of leather chappals and a lilac-coloured shawl of blossoming *mogra* flowers. He had acted like a typical foreigner, embarrassed of bargaining, and she had jumped in, advising him that not to do so was actually an insult to the merchants. They savoured chai and samosas at the Leopold Café, peppered with white travellers, the kind Sonali hoped she would be surrounded with one day.

Later at Juhu beach, Sonali and Sanjay enjoyed masala Cokes and *vadapav*. Sonali ate crudely and with relish and it was only when she noticed Sanjay looking at her, albeit with an adoring look in his eyes, that she stopped eating altogether, almost throwing her plate away. But here she also realized that for the first time in her life she felt comfortable enough to let her guard down in front of someone.

By the time they were being driven home in the taxi along Marine Drive, the strand of lights famously knows as the 'Queen's necklace' had come alive. She put her hand gently on his. 'If you want me, darling, we must leave together. I cannot wait for you to come back. It's not that I don't trust you to but that I don't know if I can bear to be separated,' she said, balling her fist at her heart, 'And there is also the matter of that Chaurasia boy.'

'What Chaurasia boy!'

'Oh,' she said, feigning turmoil. 'They've been trying to marry us . . .'

So Sonali Desai shed her name, her life, like soiled clothing, and preferring, unlike girls her own age, to opt for a simple civil ceremony instead of a pompous wedding, embraced the future with gusto. No mandaps, no Sanskrit-chanting priests, and no dowries, only a glittering diamond ring around her finger, first-class tickets to America, and the adoring eyes of a man who she knew would love her as much as her father had detested her mother.

'No lassi? None?' Sonali almost shrieked in Pooja's living room. 'Oh, but you always have some!'

'Rahul isn't around this weekend. He's really the one that drinks it,' Pooja said, relieved and secretly grateful for the spontaneous visit. Americans didn't believe in just dropping by unannounced; it violated too many of their notions about space and propriety. It was something she missed terribly about home. 'But don't worry, I can make some for you. Or what about some fresh nimbu pani instead?'

Sonali cleared her throat as if fearing a possible infection and frowned, knowing with some delight that the expression would not translate accurately in light of her latest jabs from Dr Goldstein. 'Hanh, hanh, okay, I'll try some. I don't want to be difficult. Bring it, bring it,' she said, flapping her hand in the air, displeased at having to resign herself to something other than her first choice. Her eyes darted around surreptitiously, trying to educe guarded secrets from the walls.

'Sit, sit. You'll like it,' Pooja said consolingly, as if to a child. 'I made it with some baking soda, you'll see,' she winked, letting her in on a secret.

Sonali plunked down on the sofa, crushing the decorative silk pillows and their resident strutting peacocks under her, and launched into a grievance about some precious handbag she had lost. Pooja went into the kitchen and, retrieving a full glass pitcher of nimbu pani from the refrigerator, poured some into a freshly washed highball glass, allowing one of the decorative lime slices to fall in over the bobbing ice. Over the sound of Sonali's litany, she considered just how desperate and lonely she must be to be able to extrude pleasure from her company. Strangely, it was only in Rahul's extended absence that she could allow herself to agree with his disapproval of their neighbour. The life she had woken up to resembled an empty house more than ever, her only formal protector gone on some impractical business assignment, her son spending the weekend with his best friend, and all of her still here. She quickly inspected the simmering pot and, lowering the flame some more so the flames barely licked its black underbelly, returned to the living room with the glass and a serviette, sweeping her thoughts of self-pity aside.

'. . . of course, you know, I'm glad I could get a completely new style but what really bothers me is just how immoral people can be. *Chors*! I believe people don't get away with such things, you know? It always comes back to them. Oh, and the nostalgic value I have for it!' she clicked her tongue wistfully, as if she had lost an heirloom.

Pooja handed over the glass to her and was about to ask what kind of nostalgia some designer handbag could possibly hold for her when Sonali suddenly switched topics, remembering something more vital to her existence, the famous monogram of her purse erased from her ticking mind temporarily. 'Away? Did you say Rahul is away for the weekend? Why? What for? Where did he go?'

'Business meetings,' Pooja answered and despite herself, felt as if she was fabricating this.

Sonali's left brow arched up suspiciously like an arrowhead. 'On the weekend?'

'Some kind of big conference or something.'

'The *whole* weekend?'

'O-pho!' Pooja sighed, exasperated, and moving the decorative pillow onto her lap, sat across from her. 'You know how these corporate things are. He's a vice president.'

'No,' Sonali said, shaking her head delicately and taking a quick sip of the nimbu pani. 'I don't know.'

'Well, how is it?' Pooja asked.

Sonali gave, though so lightly as to be almost

imperceptible, that upward toss of her head and downward twist of the mouth, to show her displeasure. 'It's okay,' she said, and she sipped some more.

'Well, anyway, it's all work, work, work. And it's all the way in Irvine. Who wants to go there? He asked me to go with him but what will I do there, sitting around in some hotel room while he's busy? Watch TV all day? No, no, better I stay here, in my home, and not get in the way.'

Sonali shrugged and gave her a look to indicate she was not entirely convinced. 'Uh – any bitings?'

Pooja almost sprang up to bring something – yellow sticks of *gathia*s, a mound of chevda, cocktail samosas that she could have easily microwaved – but something in her stalled. The implication in Sonali's demeanour, that there must be some deception at work, and the virulent talent she possessed for injecting such suspicion just by averting her eyes from you when you answered her, bristled Pooja. Suddenly she wanted her out of here. That she should feel this strongly about it – since by now, she felt she should have grown used to Sonali's antics – surprised her.

'Unfortunately, right now I don't have much of anything. Just threw out so much that had become stale. Anyway, I'd better get back to my orders.'

Sonali twisted her face. She sucked down the rest of the nimbu pani, placed the glass squarely on the coffee table, letting it form a ring of water at the base, and paused for a brief moment before looking up dreamily and saying, 'You know, Sanju couldn't stand to be away from me for a moment. He couldn't do without me at all. Even when he had to go somewhere, my God, you should have seen him, just begging me to go with him, such a child.' She shuddered, as if the memory had enveloped her with goosebumps. 'Ah, but that kind of love . . . where can you find that kind of love these days?'

Pooja felt the urge to seize her and throw her out but

she sat there, her hands folded neatly on her lap and did her best to ignore Sonali's insinuation. Instead she imagined Sonali's stupid bag torn to bits and lying in some filthy gutter.

'So how are your moods these days?'

'Moods? There's nothing wrong with my moods!' Pooja said. *Why did I ever confide in her?* she admonished herself, remembering that afternoon over chai and the damn *Cosmopolitan* magazine that Sonali used to diagnose all sorts of chemical imbalances in her.

Sonali shook her head and clicked her tongue, determined not to be dissuaded by the sudden denial. 'A man can't handle being overwhelmed by a woman's emotions. They can be so . . . fragile, you know?'

'Really, Sonali, where are you going with this?'

Sonali delivered her twisted, lopsided smile, the one that made her look like a snake that had swallowed up a juicy rat in one lavish slurp. 'Oh, Pooja. Men can build great monuments. Fight epic wars. They can do so much, but only, as they say, if the right woman is standing behind them. A strong woman,' she said, and her chest billowed out proudly. 'You have heard this, no? "Behind every great man, there is a great woman." They need us, you see, to be their pillars of strength. But they cannot deal with us showing them our need, our weakness, holding them accountable for our feelings. It drives them away.'

Pooja was used to her brand of sarcasm, her vulgar way of showing off, making others feel like they were at a disadvantage to her, so why now was she so affected by it? Was it because Rahul wasn't around to deride Sonali and she no longer needed to balance him? Or was it because she had sensed awkwardness in Rahul this time, something she couldn't put her finger on but felt as surely as her love for him?

She was standing before she even realized it, her body shaking. 'I really have to get back to work now, Sonali.'

'Of course, of course,' replied Sonali, unruffled and planting her sunglasses back on. 'One must keep busy. It's the only way to run away from your problems without hurting others more.'

Brunch at Lavender, overlooking a golf course spotted with oak trees. They were seated in a sun-dappled patio dotted with terracotta pots of lavender, under a sweeping canopy of wisteria blossoms. Atif opted for the shaded seat, typically avoiding the sun, the voice of his mother still ripe in his mind after all these years: 'Stay out of the sun! You want to turn dark like a rag?'

Platoons of liveried servers waltzed around the large open space, appearing out of nowhere to top up glasses with cucumber water from glass beakers, take orders and clear tables. Atif ordered mimosas for both of them even though Rahul had insisted only on water, part of him shutting down systematically as it rejoined the world outside of their private bungalow.

Surrounded by couples and at least two families with exceptionally well-behaved children, Atif couldn't help noticing that they were not only the sole male pair, but they were also the only non-white people. The only reminder of the outside world was the *Los Angeles Times*, which someone was holding up and reading. The front page screamed of yet another suicide bombing. An insurgent had detonated himself and taken six Israeli civilians with him at a café in Hebron. Here, the paper with its clamorous headline felt offensive and unsettling. Although both Rahul and Atif noticed its incongruence, neither one of them commented on it at first, preferring to ignore the disaster.

When something catastrophic happened to someone else, thought Atif, *there was always more than one emotion. The first was naturally sympathy, followed by feelings of karmic solecism, of being spared, and finally, the morbid fear that your good luck would also run out soon enough. Then one just became jaded to the problems of others and turning away from them became the only way to remain hopeful about your own life.*

While perusing the menu, Rahul noticed a suited, middle-aged Mexican man waiting outside of what appeared to be the manager's office across the patio. He immediately recognized the executive look. The way he stood, stoic and respectful, his hands held together as he waited anticipatorily, the large pager and cellphone holstered like a weapon on his belt, the starched shirt and nondescript tie, a large leather portfolio tucked under his arm, half unzipped, so that brochures and documents peeked out from the edges. He wanted to vomit.

'I think I'll tempt fate further, order the loin of pork,' Atif joked. 'This Muslim's ready to take his rebellion all the way.' He noticed Rahul's distraction. 'Rahul? You know him?'

'No, no. Just looks like . . .' he trailed off, turning back to him with a smile. 'Sure, go right ahead. It's maybe a little late to secure your place in paradise anyway.'

'Who cares about carousing with the beautiful houris, right?'

'At the rate these savages are going, there might not be much room up there.'

Atif glanced towards the newspaper and back at him. 'Savages?'

'Anyway, let's not talk about this.'

'Well, it's tragic for everyone involved.'

He looked up from the menu at Atif. 'You're not justifying their actions, are you?'

For a moment Atif was uncertain who he was defending in Rahul's eyes and decided it was better just to drop it. 'Oh, I don't even know why we're letting this interrupt our time,' Atif said, shutting the menu decisively. Their server appeared at the table like a genie, offering to tell them about the specials, but sensing he might have interrupted a serious discussion, he offered to come back in a few minutes

'No, no, go on,' Rahul said to him, still looking at Atif fixedly. The server rattled off some items, most of them creatively using lavender in one way or another. Once they had ordered and the server had ambled away, Rahul said, 'What did you mean by that?'

Atif sighed. 'It's war, Rahul. There are no clear sides.'

'You're hardly a fundamentalist!' He gave an incredulous laugh.

'Of course not. But I feel that all lives are important. I feel badly for all the deaths that are happening, not just some of them. Some lives don't count more than others, Rahul.'

'Yes, but there's a clear difference here. These are terrorists.'

'Others may think of them as freedom fighters.'

Rahul groaned.

'Oh, Rahul, we may all just be terrorists in the end,' he said, clearing his glass of water to the side and leaning forward. 'Nine-eleven. Fifteen of those nineteen hijackers came from Saudi Arabia. A fact. And you must also remember that in that country, for some fifty years or so, it's the US that has supported a very oppressive regime. And for what? Guaranteed oil. Isn't it arguable then, that all of us, people like you, who have failed to oppose this relationship, everyone who has supported this foreign policy, is also responsible for the oppression of those people? For helping keep those despots in power? For those poor people, we're the terrorists.'

'So, now what? Because our foreign policy is screwed up, we have to abide by suicide bombers who go around killing innocent people?'

'No, that's not what I'm saying. I'm not condoning it, God, no,' he said. 'I just think it's important to see things from another perspective. Suicide is wrong, period. But martyrdom, on the other hand, is heroic. One man's suicide bomber is another man's martyr, his freedom fighter, heroically seeking to liberate his people from oppression and occupation. See, when you look at it that way, what's the difference?'

'These guys go into supermarkets, Atif. Into cafes, buses, public places, blow themselves up and take mothers, fathers, children with them –'

'No difference!' Atif said, getting more vexed. 'Israeli troops who enter Palestinian villages also destroy houses and kill innocent people. So how's it any different? Sure, they're after suspected terrorists but some of those people may just be innocent civilians. Mothers and fathers and children die there too, Rahul. The only difference, if there is any, between the two is that one party is state-sanctioned and the others are acting on their own, clandestine agents who don't have either the infrastructure or the government backing to fight for what they believe in. But in the end, they're all resistance fighters trying to protect what they love.'

'Terrorism? An act of love?' Rahul balked.

'When you think of love, what do you think of?'

But Rahul was growing agitated. He had already got hold of a napkin, and unbeknownst to himself, had started tearing it to little bits. 'This is ridiculous!'

'No, indulge me, please. When you love somebody,

you'll do anything for him or her, right? There are no lengths to which you won't go to protect your loved ones. You'll even give up your own life because you can't live without them. Your very existence depends on them. If anyone harms them, threatens to destroy them, you will harm him too, and there will be no boundaries, moral or ethical,' he said emphatically, 'that you will not cross to protect what you love. Think of your son, your wife . . . me.'

Rahul stiffened.

'You must think about this kind of love when you think about those that are willing to give up their lives for their way of life to protect their mosques, their temples, their families. We are talking about old cultures here, Rahul. In this country, anything that's what, fifty years old, is branded historical? We are talking of civilizations that go back centuries, thousands of years. So, you see, in the end, that's what everyone's fighting for, isn't it? What they love. You must think about this kind of love when you hear about jihad and suicide bombers. Think about how you will do anything to protect those you love. There are no compromises when it comes to love and war.'

When silence fell between them, they heard the music of birds, normally drowned in the world they had come from. This was the kind of conversation Rahul could never have with Pooja and which he hungered for. It was the first time for many things, Rahul thought. The first time Rahul knew that Atif compulsively washed his feet before climbing into bed, an image that would stay with him forever; the first time they had been able to present themselves as a couple to the world, taste a public life; the first time they could understand each other outside the scope of their relationship.

It became increasingly clear to Atif that anything that challenged the status quo was a personal affront to Rahul, even if it was rebellion against a tyrannical regime.

Rahul had desecrated the napkin by now. Atif, in a gesture of peace, slipped out the napkin from under his own glass, and offered it to him. Rahul managed to smile. 'Your passion,' he said, 'is one of the things I like most about you. So, did you bring your checkered headdress with you?'

'A *kufiyyeh*? No, but if it turns you on, I can think of a million ways in which we can incorporate it the next time,' he smiled wickedly. 'You know what I find interesting?' he asked, tilting his head to one side. 'I come from a faith that considers it a sin to depict God in any kind of image. You will never find, in a mosque, or in a Muslim's home, any kind of painting of Allah, like that of Jesus or Ram or Krishna. Because we believe God's beyond human comprehension. So Allah becomes intimidating in a sense. He's beyond human traits, unreachable, never completely understood, and in a sense, there's purity there. Yet, strangely, Muslims have always been polygamous. And history shows, arguably, that the Islamic world has been notorious for homosexual relationships.

'And then you think about Hinduism: drama queens, all of them – waging war, changing sexes, cannibalistic, polygamous – I mean, how many wives did just Krishna alone have? Sixteen thousand?' he asked. 'And yet, who could be more repressed, more conservative, more monogamous than Hindus?'

'Oh, you think way too much,' Rahul laughed.

The food arrived and they indulged in it, but silence hung in the air. Rahul considered, as he rarely did, his own past, wondering if Atif could be right; whether guilt, victimization, even evil, were simply a matter of perspective; if ultimately, they were inconsequential in the *leela* of life. The world spun while nature wreaked havoc, wiping out entire villages, cities; human beings waged wars, while somewhere else, life ambled on in perfect harmony, barely affected.

Atif thought about his status as an illegal alien, of his social security card. He thought about the constant fear that assailed him, that at any moment, even the little he had could be expropriated because he wasn't born American. He considered how he had lost his freedom, or rather, sacrificed it, to remain not in Mumbai, the Middle East or some remote war-torn land, but in America, the iconic land of the free. The irony struck him as sharply as if he had been slapped.

By the time Sonali finally left, her condescending air intact, Pooja had almost finished cooking the *pau bhaaji*, when something overcame her and she tossed everything into the garbage, no longer hungry.

Rahul's absence began to cling to her more than she felt it had reason to. Then, needing simply to escape her own thoughts, she drove herself to the Santa Monica mall where she visited Williams Sonoma and perused a book on Indian cooking, picked up a Dutch oven and an assortment of sauces she knew she would probably never use. She paid with one of Rahul's credit cards and when the saleslady addressed her as Mrs Kapoor, she beamed, loving it when someone called her by her formal, marital name.

Then she drove to The Banyan, finding a parking spot in the back of the studio. On the rare occasion that she did make it to the studio, Charlie did his best to spoil her. Their relationship, somewhere safely outside the realm of romance, still involved a fair amount of innocuous flirtation, with Charlie making gallant gestures and paying compliments, and Pooja simply blushing from the attention. On her way in, she saw, perhaps for the very first time at The Banyan, a very pretty Indian girl with a blue yoga mat rolled up under her arm, heading into a class. Her body appeared lithe, her countenance confident, but Pooja could hear the loopy cadences and accompanying grimaces of teenage vernacular as she rattled on to her male companion about an upcoming audition. Pooja exchanged smiles with her and, like every other time she encountered another Indian, felt warmed.

Charlie's office was in complete disarray. The antiqued desk, incongruous with the modern glass and steel design of the studio, carried the weight of a clunky outdated computer. Paperwork cluttered the desk and even the walls, and the trash can was overflowing. In one corner, a sandstone sculpture of Ganesha, balancing on a mouse, was perched precariously atop a large shelf of spirituality books, bending the top plank with its weight, threatening to topple the dancing god from his now tentative throne after centuries of artful equilibrium. From where she sat, against a window that opened up to the serene meditation garden, Pooja could hear the calming water fountain. On the wall across from her, in the midst of the class schedules, post-its and articles of interest, was a framed quote that Pooja had seen many times before, but noticed as if for the first time:

'*And the day came when the risk to remain tight in a bud was more painful than the risk it took to blossom.*' – Anaïs Nin.

'So, I saw an Indian girl here,' Pooja mentioned to Charlie, pushing the quote out of her mind.

'Brilliant! We're finally legit!' he said with mock excitement. 'And did you immediately embrace, shower each other with kisses?'

'What do you think? Of course! We locked arms and danced around the studio. So sad you missed it.'.

'So should we sign you up for classes as well, love?'

'Oh, it's such hard work,' Pooja said, waving her hand dismissively.

'You know, somewhere under that casual comment, you have the answer to this conundrum,' he said, shaking his finger at her. 'Do you know what this swami once told me when I was at an ashram in Rishikesh? The reason why we were so attracted to yoga – hatha yoga that is – was because we had more *rajasic* temperaments.'

She looked at him defeated, as if to say that simply being Indian did not automatically mean one knew everything about such matters.

'Europeans and Americans have more energetic, intense constitutions, rajasic constitutions,' he explained. 'Indians are more *tamasic,* which is prone to more heaviness and inertia. You see, at the end of the day, rajasic personalities need to do something with all that excess energy; otherwise they'll go out of whack!' He made a gesture like he was swatting a fly. 'Yoga actually has this brilliant, calming effect, allowing people of such constitutions to become more calm, to use up that excess energy.'

'So, what are you saying, Charlie? That we Indians are lazy?' she threw him a look of mock anger.

'No, no!' he laughed, 'just that fewer Indians may be interested in the practice because they're already calmer. Both extremes are bloody toxic, love, neither one is good. It's finding that middle ground that's crucial. Now look at a lad like Greg, he's just careened off to the other side, completely missing that middle, don't you think? I hope you don't mind but I'll be cutting his hours a little bit. Perhaps I can pick up the deliveries once in a while.'

'That's not a problem. I can bring them myself. Ajay can help. God knows he needs something to keep him busy instead of running around . . .' she said, trailing off.

'The boy needs to go out and live it up a little,' he said about Greg, sensing a discussion about her son was out of the question. 'He needs to get some balance in his life! How long can you hide behind yoga and books?'

'Hiding behind – Oh, Charlie, sometimes you don't sound like a yogi at all!' she laughed.

'Let me tell you a little secret. Some of these people, they miss the whole point, using all this as an excuse to hide from the real world, from experiencing life. You know what they say; it's easy to find peace on a mountain. Try remaining calm on the 405 freeway. Now that's an accomplishment! Real spirituality, real practice comes from participating in life while maintaining your peace.'

She smiled. 'He's a good boy.'

'Well, yes, of course, but do you suppose it's healthy for him to shut the world out like this? A boy his age needs to create some raucousness, misbehave some, create some real anguish for his family.'

'Oh, I have a feeling his family's quite anguished just the way he is.'

'Yes,' his chuckle turned into robust laughter. 'Yes, I think you're quite right, love. The chap's got them wondering if their baby got switched at birth. Maybe the rightful Goldstein heir's somewhere up in the Himalayas. Besides, business is quite slow,' he said. 'Yoga studios are mushrooming all over the city now. Some of them are offering classes for free, some kind of donation, anything. Imagine that! There are limits even to altruism, don't you think?'

'Now, is that what the Buddha would say?' By saying this, she encouraged him in a conversation, even though her mind was beginning to drift away, conjuring Rahul's face. She had always been this way, letting others express themselves until they felt lighter, finding it easier to listen than to speak. But so many times she wasn't there and they never knew the difference, only needing to express themselves in the company of others, rather than needing to be understood or advised.

'Most people forget that the Buddha lived a full life

before he attained nirvana,' Charlie scoffed. 'What, do you think he was born enlightened? Before he parked himself under that *bodhi* tree one fine day, relinquishing the material world, he had already lived a full life, loved a famous courtesan of his time, even fathered a child, learnt what it was to be disappointed by the world and those you loved. You see, that journey that led him from Lumbini to that very pivotal moment in Bodhgaya, where he attained enlightenment is, according to me, the most crucial part of his story. But people just want to focus on him sitting cross-legged under some tree!'

Charlie dipped a fennel tea bag into a cup of steaming water and scowled at it, apparently displeased at the strength of its brew, but then, as was typical of him, he quickly recovered and braved a sip without waiting for it to cool down.

'Then again, maybe the boy's all right,' he said, completely contradicting himself, watching the steam dance up from his cup in whorls. 'Maybe he's exactly the kind of hero our world needs nowadays. He's said "no" to the system.'

'Heroes save the world.'

'The world within,' he smiled. 'What about that world? To be able to resist what the world insists you must have or be like, to divert from the programme, to have glimpsed the subconscious and to make that leap determinedly, you know, following your bliss, whatever it may be, wherever it may lead, that, love, is also heroic, don't you think?'

She slowly nodded, never having considered this. To Pooja, the heroic were always those who put others before themselves. But now, listening to Charlie, an old adage came back to her, about how despite his best intentions, a hungry man cannot feed others without eventually resenting them.

'A person who is informed by his true calling, his

passion, even if it takes him away from the life prescribed to him by his birth and standing, now that, *that* is a hero!'

'Oh, you'd better make up your mind, Charlie,' she said, exhausted. 'You can't seem to take a side. It's like watching a whole debate team in one person!'

'A true Gemini,' he laughed. 'Still trying to find my middle, love. Still trying to find that middle.'

He noticed her perturbation as she sat across from him, now lost in some thought that was pulling down at the corners of her painted mouth, and looking out of the window at the large flapping leaf of the banana plant in the garden. Even in her distracted, pained state, she glowed, as if a light was emanating from behind her, perhaps from her very suffering, and Charlie was reminded of saints like Meera, for whom their pain became a source of sublimity. It was as if some pain had granted her a luminous beatitude.

'You all right, love?'

'Yes, yes,' she said, much too quickly, and rose to her feet. Her eyes fell on a half-eaten piece of cashew marzipan on the side of Charlie's messy desk and although she didn't comment on it, she smiled, rewarded.

'Let me get you some tea, something,' he suggested.

'No, no, really. I have to get home now,' she said, glancing at her wristwatch, then realizing, yet again, that once she got there, there would be nothing to do and nobody to talk to or tend to.

A class had just adjourned and they could hear the shuffle of students leaving the studio. He smiled warmly. 'It sure is nice to see you, Pooja. I wish you would come by more often, really. It may even help with the business, what with clients seeing *pukka* Indians around here,' he laughed. 'Give the place some legitimacy, you know?'

She came closer to him. 'Tch, don't worry about this place. Spirituality tends to go through phases too. Once summer's gone and they can't go to the beach any more, they'll be here in record numbers. It's going to be fine, just wait and see.'

Charlie didn't tell her that summer was in fact the busiest time for the studio and chose instead to look deeply into her eyes, which he noticed were always moist, as if on the verge of tears. 'Yes, but are you?' he asked.

She looked at him, his question catching her off guard.

'Are you fine?'

She wished desperately to spill out her fears but some part of her, perhaps the one that had been groomed by her emotionally fortified mother, felt ridiculous for wanting to do so. *I am not going to let that witch poison my mind,* she thought to herself, still standing so close to her caring friend. *Sonali's whole life is built on causing destruction! Rahul is completely right about her. She is best avoided altogether. Soon he will be home, tired from the conference and weighed down by his suitcase and clunky binders, which I will expediently put away, and everything will feel normal again.*

She nodded reassuringly at Charlie but hurried out of the studio, weaving through the scantily clad students with their yoga mats, water bottles and towels hoping that she could get far away before the snakes of doubt uncoiled in her mind again.

As they cut across the mountains to rejoin the lives they had temporarily abandoned, Atif and Rahul were swallowed in the clotted freeway of cars juddering towards the basin of city lights. The air became brown, dense, thick. Now, they were anchored down, the open skies and space gone, the music of birds and the rustle of leaves drowned by the babel of life. Looking at the choking procession they were joining, Atif plummeted into depression, ready to cry. How can one deal with this hell after so much happiness? How does one not help but feel banished from grace?

He felt the churn of apprehension in his belly, the kind of gravitational pull that occupies one right before a disaster. He had never been in the least bit psychic but if there had been a moment when he could have sensed doom, this was it. There were, after all, moments in everyone's life when an uncanny clairvoyance invaded, and for just an evanescent moment, the future was hinted at, like the dimming of lights before the final plunge of an electrical failure.

'I wish we could stay like this forever,' he said, not looking at Rahul.

Rahul put his hand over Atif's and gave it an understanding squeeze. 'Sooner or later we have to get back to the real world.'

'I wish you would tell me something else. That nothing will change. That *this* is the real world.'

When they were off the freeway, Rahul still drove slowly, as if to keep their parting at a distance, and as their world slipped into the past, he took Atif's hand and held it tightly. Atif was transported to a memory in his childhood, that of the warmth of his father's fingers from which he ate a little hillock of daal-drenched rice as they sat cross-legged on the kitchen floor, Atif holding his little rotund belly, saying, 'Bas, Papa, enough. Enough, Papa . . .'

'Arre, if you don't eat, how will you grow up, hunh? Eat! Eat! And I will tell you about the angels,' Abdul Rahman coaxed him. 'There is Jibreel, he brings the messages from Allah to the prophets. And you know the Alkatabah, they do all the recording and they are always with you, always recording whatever you are doing and saying, sitting on your shoulders, here and here. And there is Meekaaeel, and this angel is in charge of the rain and all the rivers and all the sea and he is also in charge of forming the babies in the womb, making sure they get all their provisions. And then Israfeel –' and here Atif shook his little head vehemently at the mention of the angel of death. 'Hanh, you are frightened now, hunh?' his father would laugh, parcelling more food into his mouth. 'Come on, eat!'

With Rahul's hand clasped in his, he wondered now, looking out of the window, whether his father had ever blamed Meekaaeel for the way he had turned out.

When they were finally parked close to Atif's Mazda, by a wall at the end of the parking lot of Elton's, Rahul was still holding his hand and rubbing the back of it gently with his thumb. Now he put his arm around Atif and drew him close to him and Atif rested his head on his shoulder, trying to smile so they could part pleasantly, reminding himself to be strong and grateful, so that Rahul wouldn't think once again that it was best for Atif if they separated.

The world never felt so despairing as when you've had the chance to hold it in your hands, Atif thought.

Feeling his sadness, Rahul lifted Atif's face by the chin, noticed the glistening in his eyes, and gave him the same ritual of kisses that Atif always did – first on his eyes and then on his lips, holding them to his for many seconds.

The Sonali that showed up at Pooja's door on Monday afternoon was a remarkably different woman. Instead of speaking in that exaggerated way of hers, where she sucked in her breath, spoke through a clenched mouth, and delivered carefully selected words aimed at elevating herself, demoting others, or doing both, Sonali was palpably nervous.

They sat in the living room, not a drink or savoury in sight, and the words had tumbled out of Sonali's mouth, a scrabbled, almost incoherent litany. 'I'm so sorry, Pooja . . . I saw them . . . in the parking lot . . . I couldn't believe my eyes . . . It was Rahul . . . there was this boy with him . . . they were, oh, God, Pooja, they were kissing . . . *kissing,* Pooja . . . Oh, God, I'm so sorry.' All Pooja could think was, *Why is she speaking this way?* And she felt disappointed in Sonali's sudden lack of poise. It was as if the powerful words had transported Pooja outside of her body, allowing her a little bit of time before the full impact destroyed her.

Dimly, she was aware of the gardener and his son outside carrying on a conversation in Spanish, then the sound of the lawnmower. She began to realize that this was also the first time she had heard Sonali apologize for anything. Now that Sonali had regurgitated the crushing news, she kept doing it over and over again, as if to provide the cushion of apology, lessen the blow. She felt embarrassed for Sonali and looked at her strangely.

Sonali, having investigated the matter, went on. 'He works at the bookstore, at Elton's, you know, in Brentwood. Some Indian boy called Atif or something. Oh, God, Pooja, what are you going to do?'

A boy? What does she mean 'a boy'? She must mean a woman. A boy? For just a brief moment, when the words finally reached her, as if through a thick wall, so much congealed that she felt as if the room had started spinning around her, and she had to grasp the armrest of the sofa she was sitting on. *No, this couldn't be. This is some kind of sick joke. Sonali has finally gone completely, stark, raving crazy . . .*

But then she gave a short laugh, and suddenly got up. 'You don't know what you're talking about, Sonali. How dare you come in here with this . . . this filth? You're talking about my husband!' Pooja glared down at her, her body convulsing with rage. 'Do you know how long I've been married to Rahul? Hunh? We've been married twenty-one years. Twenty-one years, Sonali! There's nothing about him that you can tell me that I don't already know.'

Sonali looked up at her with pity, alarming Pooja even more. She began to say something but Pooja cut her off. 'Don't come around here any more, Sonali. Please, you just go . . .'

Pooja walked to the door and held it open for Sonali, who got up, but without haste and miraculously still maintaining a pained look of sympathy on her face even as she was being thrown out.

After she had closed the door behind her, Pooja returned to the kitchen, and for what seemed like a long time continued to prepare dinner mechanically, as if nothing had happened. Sonali's words came in and out of her consciousness and she felt suddenly as if language had lost its meaning or something in the circuitry of her mind had gone terribly wrong so that she knew there was something she had to react to but was unable to respond.

For hours after Sonali left, Pooja wrestled with her thoughts, but like Kaliya, the serpent king that Krishna danced upon, each time she severed one head off with a reaffirming thought or a memory – of their courtship, their years together, the birth of their son – another head reared up, hissing at her. By the time Rahul returned from work, early for a change, she had managed, at least temporarily, to convince herself that none of it was true.

She watched Rahul stretch out languorously over the sofa as she brought him a steaming cup of masala chai and a stick of Walker's butter cookie. She reminded herself that this was the man she loved more than life itself and suddenly she had the wild urge to fall at his feet, cover them with kisses. Rahul drank his tea quickly, leaving behind just a sip out of habit. He went up to their room and when he returned, in sweats and a T-shirt, so strong and masculine, Pooja observed him, trying to detect if there was anything different about him.

He settled back on the sofa and as he talked with their son about starting college under an undeclared major, she watched him, infused with pride. Suddenly, she wanted to laugh at the ludicrousness of it all. *Look at him! Look at him!* she said to herself. *There is nothing about him that is odd or resembles the kind of depravity that Sonali was accusing him of. Why would she say such things? How does she dare!*

She knew about those kinds of men. They were effeminate, imitating women's gestures, painting their faces. They didn't marry women, father children. They were either scorned or sympathized with, always met with an extreme response, unable to earn societal indifference. They were not like Rahul who was looked up to, admired by everyone.

As father and son moved the discussion over to the dinner table where she laid out the meal she had prepared before Sonali's inauspicious visit, she thought, *This is just what Sonali is trying to destroy, something she doesn't have. She has never liked Rahul, always been jealous of us. She is a lonely, bitter woman and I will not let her spew her venom into my life.* Suddenly, she became unnaturally elated again and joined their discussion enthusiastically. 'Hanh, hanh, you can manage all the rap star artist and *altu-faltu* bands you want, but you still need to be a businessman for that,' she chimed in concernedly. 'Look at your father, look, he didn't get to where he is by becoming something undeclared. You can take a business major, then you can do whatever you want to do.'

Ajay made a propitiatory sound, a tongue-click followed by a half-sigh. 'I know, I know –'

'Hanh, hanh, everything you know.'

'Look, all I'm saying is, I need some time to decide what I want to do and there's lots of people who don't declare their . . .'

A boy, she had said. He was kissing a boy, thought Pooja. *But kissing him how? What kind of a kiss? Was it just a kiss, a little peck, the way he would have kissed Ajay? Just saying goodbye? Or really kissing? But did men, friends, kiss at all?* Pooja brought a jug of nimbu pani to the table and filled up their glasses, still milling around, unable to sit down, the thoughts driving her into a frenzy. *Maybe she just misunderstood what she saw. It's so typical of Sonali to blow things out of proportion, to sensationalize everything. Maybe it was just a friend he had bumped into, someone he works with at the bank, and they were saying goodbye and they must have hugged, just an innocent goodbye, and now that horrible woman, with her poisonous mind, is convoluting the whole thing!*

'Sit down already,' Rahul said, pulling the heavy teak chair out for her. 'We have everything now.'

Pooja squeezed his shoulder. 'Just Ajay's chicken, a minute please,' she said, disappearing into the kitchen and father and son resumed their conversation. Bent over the microwave oven, she watched the lightly seasoned slabs of chicken breast rotating on the plate. *But what was he doing at the bookstore? Oh, why don't I just ask him? So, maybe he was just buying a book, something to do with work, maybe another cookbook for me, a surprise, and if I ask him, I'm going to ruin it!* From the window behind her, Pooja heard raucous laughter coming from Sonali's kitchen. She shrank with horror, assuming that Sonali was broadcasting this malicious lie over her network of gossipers. Pooja turned around but when she looked out of the window, she saw that Sonali's kitchen was engulfed in darkness and indeed it looked as though nobody was home. *Oh, God, I'm losing my mind,* she thought. *What's happening to me? Do I actually believe this? Why am I giving it so much credence?*

'Everything okay, Poo?' Rahul asked, suddenly standing right next to her.

She looked away from him, feeling the urge to cry. 'Yes, I'm coming.'

He reached out and tucked a wisp of her hair behind the ear, revealing the mole on her lobe. He touched it with his finger sensually. It was the lightest touch yet she felt it go through her like an electric current, charged with all the things he meant to her. 'You okay?'

She threw her arms around the strong girth of his waist and rested her head against his chest, seeking desperately to banish her thoughts. She knew what it was she must do and it terrified her. *I can't go there,* she thought. *I will not go there. I don't want to know anything about this boy. He doesn't exist. What if my suspicion, my question, brings him to life? And the lie becomes the truth?*

'Poo?'

She shook her head against him, as much to her thoughts as to his inquiry, closing her eyes tightly shut, reminding herself that this was her husband, her Rahul, and that she knew him perhaps even better than he knew himself. 'I'm just glad you're home.'

They heard Ajay groan. 'Are we eating tonight or what?'

'Come now, let's sit down. Let's eat.'

Rahul enveloped her in his arms, feeling a pang of guilt shoot through him. Although he said nothing more, he kissed her reassuringly on the top of her head, just inches away from the parting in her hair, from that trail of red vermillion that bound them for lifetimes to come.

Pooja went to bed, desperate to end the day and the thoughts with it. Rahul stayed downstairs for what seemed like hours with Ajay. Everything seemed so perfect now, her husband and son filling the house with their chatter, that she wished she could have found a way to go on with life as if the conversation with Sonali had never taken place.

Lying on her side, she watched the moon in the arms of the old jacaranda tree outside the window and invoked Krishna over and over again under her breath. *If only it were another woman,* she thought. *Even then I might have been able to do something, to come to terms with the fact that at a certain point a man just needed, wanted, a new body. But another man? How can it be another man? What does it mean?*

What worried her most was that she knew Rahul had never been the sort to be dominated by his lust. Other men, yes, Pooja had known the sort. But what had drawn her to him in the first place was the pure, discreet complexion of his affection. Rahul was not, and never had been, a womanizer, someone who sought to reinvent himself through new conquests. What had changed in him now?

When Rahul finally tiptoed in, it was already the darkest part of the night. He lay down lightly beside her and put a hand on her arm as they both pretended to sleep. But this time, she didn't respond, keeping still, letting his hand stay there, and not knowing what to do because her mind was already thinking of the times when he might no longer be there.

Room to room she went, clutching a risible variation of tea purchased out of sheer nervousness from the coffee shop. An imbalanced, cloying blend of black tea, Indian spices and milk, she hated to think that this was what most Americans thought of as the ritualistic elixir Indians found indispensable to their lives.

Pooja saw no one who resembled a young Indian boy there, only yards of books in a store swaying to a jazz soundtrack and tranquilly empty at that time of morning.

She seemed to recall that Elton's was the same shop from which Rahul had bought her the gargantuan cookbook that she had wanted for her birthday and this thought, instead of cheering her up, only made her feel more depressed. Had this boy sold the book to Rahul? Is that when they first met? Who started it?

She thought of asking someone for him. Maybe it was his day off and he wasn't there. Or maybe he was working in the back somewhere and they would just call him out. But maybe he didn't even exist and the salesperson would look at her strangely and she could put this whole fiasco behind her. But what if he did? What would she say? Would she have the courage to ask him if he knew her husband?

She finished surveying the last of the three creatively organized wings, then crossed the sunlit courtyard to go in and out of rooms crowded with books, and there was still no sign of this boy. She began to feel increasingly ridiculous for letting Sonali compel her to such indignity. She didn't want to inquire about him, finding the entire thing preposterous. So, knowing well enough that just a cursory inspection of the shop neither proved nor dispelled his existence, she felt grateful to God for having been spared. Pooja felt the sudden urge to buy Rahul something – a new tie, the Crabtree & Evelyn lavender shower gel that he liked to use, a leather portfolio, something – as if this would somehow compensate for mistrusting him.

As she was preparing to leave the Hemingway wing, housing mostly literary fiction, Pooja was approached by a bizarre-looking young American girl dressed entirely in black and covered with tattoos, who asked if she could be of assistance. *Didn't this poor girl have any parents,* Pooja wondered, *someone who could tell her how ridiculous she looked, teach her how to dress?*

'Oh, yes, actually, I'm looking for someone. Do you happen to know – ,' but then suddenly she clamped up. 'Well, you know what, it's okay. Thank you so much, I will just look around.'

The salesgirl shrugged, handed her a bookmark promoting some new novel and left. Pooja turned around and had barely begun to walk away when she heard the girl's voice: 'Atif, hon, I'm *sooo* starving! Can I just take my lunch now, if you don't mind?'

She stopped dead in her tracks. She heard his voice, deep and sonorous: 'Yeah, yeah, no problem. Actually, you know what, are you going to Vons? Can you pick me up a sandwich, too?'

Pooja turned around very slowly. Standing across the room from her, behind a glass-topped counter, was an Indian boy, plucking out bills from his leather wallet, ordering lunch. He handed the money over to the girl and she left the room with the same bored expression.

That's when their eyes met and they froze, a current passing between them.

There are moments, Pooja knew, in which the agency of words came after intuition, when a simple glance was able to convey the whole soul of a person. This was how they looked at each other. The way in which the boy's expression suddenly changed, the smile overshadowed by deep remorse, his eyes downcast, told Pooja that he recognized who she was.

And when Atif saw her anguished face, her world turned upside down, the picture he had seen in Rahul's wallet came alive. He knew too, that he had, in this naked moment, confirmed everything that Pooja Kapoor needed to know about them.

Pooja fled from the bookstore, tears blinding her eyes. She would never be able to recall getting to the parked car or driving away from the bookstore. Her heart was thumping so violently that she thought it might explode in her ribcage. *Dear God, what did I do to cause this? Where did I fail him? How did I drive him away? What has come over him?* Her mind swarmed with images of the boy's face, that regretful look on it, of Rahul and him kissing, their mouths gnashed against one another's, erasing her completely from existence. At one point, she even failed to notice that the traffic lights had changed, and it wasn't until an irate driver behind her honked furiously that she was startled out of her feelings. When he drove up next to her, he rolled down his window and barked expletives but she kept her eyes on the road, the pain inside her too huge to be affected by anything in her surroundings.

Upon reaching home, she was thankful that Ajay wouldn't be there to witness her state of mind. How would she explain this to their son? What could she say? She needed time to sort this out on her own before she could face anyone. Ashamed of how she must look, she tried to slink past the gardener, who stopped the lawnmower to greet her, perhaps expecting that she would attempt a conversation about the flowers in her broken Spanish as she normally did. This time, however, she only gave a curt wave as she disappeared into the house. Once she had locked the world outside, she sank into the sofa where only the day before she had received the blow from Sonali. What she wouldn't give now to reverse that day, to have avoided that woman altogether and not have heard any of it!

At first, she did everything she could to keep from breaking down, coaxing herself to explore the idea further, to ignore intuition for once and seek some tangibility instead. So what if the boy had looked at her strangely?

That proved nothing! After all, she had also stood in the middle of the store and looked at him just the same. How was he supposed to look back at some strange Indian woman looking at him accusingly? How could she doubt the man she had loved her whole life based on a single look exchanged between two complete strangers? How could she question her whole marriage because of someone like Sonali anyway?

But then, tossed around by her thoughts, finding solace in neither direction, Pooja treaded into murkier waters. Had he done this sort of thing before? Then how come she couldn't remember him behaving strangely? Why hadn't she noticed it? Didn't such men act a certain way? Is this why he never wanted to touch her? Had he always been – wanted to be – with other men?

She walked into the kitchen and leaned against the sink, afraid that she would throw up from the vivid images of Rahul and the boy churning in her mind. She drew the curtain to the window above the sink facing out to Sonali's house, trying to calm down but, now that she had seen the boy's face, it became impossible and a murderous rage gripped her so that all she could think of was how she wanted the boy gone.

What kind of a woman am I? she recriminated, burying her tear-stained face in her hands. *Dear Lord, what have I done to drive him to this? All this must be my fault. I've carefully built this sanitary life without sex, throwing myself into your worship, always craving Rahul but contending with just his platonic company. And now I've driven him away, to another man.* This thought, suddenly absurd, made her burst into laughter, the whole situation feeling like it was happening to somebody else. The weight, just momentarily, lifted. But then, just as quickly, she saw them together again in a car, kissing, and her laughter morphed into a sharp cry. If only she could talk to someone, someone who could steer her straight, tell her how to think, help her to get a handle on the thoughts running amok with her.

Brashly, she considered calling her mother, suddenly growing excited at the possibility of being able to unburden herself, but then she quickly realized the folly of such action. *Do I really want them to know this? Is there still a chance I could be wrong?* She could have just waited for Rahul to come home at the end of the day and then to confront him, but panic seized her. With each passing moment that she hadn't reached Rahul, she felt he was mutating into a stranger. So Pooja called the bank where Rahul's talkative assistant Amelia greeted her. Amelia launched excitedly into a conversation about when they would be seeing her next as Pooja tried desperately to get connected to him. 'Please,' she said, 'I really need to speak to Rahul.'

'And you know that dessert you sent that last time?' Amelia carried on. 'Oh, my God, oh, my God, oh, my God! It was so good! I don't want to sound greedy but you know what? Do you think you could send some more? You know, the really creamy, sweet . . .'

'Please! I need to speak to him now!'

'Oh, okay,' Amelia said, deflated. 'But Mrs Kapoor, he isn't here right now. I can tell him you called or you can try him on the cell . . .'

Pooja felt as if the whole world would come to an end in a matter of seconds. She must talk to him right away. But where could he be? With the boy? She realized that she had just come from the bookstore so the boy must still be there. Rahul was probably out on a business call. But then she wondered if there could be others, other men, and she felt as if she was going to pass out. She practically hung up on Amelia and tried Rahul immediately on his cellular, but the call went directly to his voice mail, not even ringing once, and she hung up, sliding against the wall to the ground, disheartened, silenced.

If Pooja had felt lonely before, now she felt like she was the only person on the planet, as if, were she to walk out onto the street, she would find not another soul. She wandered in a daze to the little altar in the kitchen and prostrated herself at the feet of Radha and Krishna, wishing this was all just a bad dream that she had awoken from, or that she could escape into some parallel universe where life was being lived as she had known it in her ignorance.

In that moment, when her imploring eyes looked up at the benevolent faces of the divine couple, blissfully plaited together in a love that had inspired thousands of poems and ecstatic ragas, another scrim dropped and Pooja's stomach lurched. She confronted, as if for the very first time, the irrefutable fact that the deities to whom she had prayed for the preservation of her marriage were themselves unfaithful, philanderers married to other people – Radha to the King of Mewar, Krishna to Rukmini.

Day after day, and in the moment of her crisis, she had petitioned a couple who had disregarded their vows and turned forbidden passion into a criterion for nothing less than perfect love.

At first Rahul had laughed with disbelief, thinking Atif was playing a prank, but as he had provided more details – about five eight, the deep purple salwar-kameez, the thick mane of black hair swept over to one shoulder, the large expressive eyes, the undeniably beautiful face – Pooja materialized in his mind. And then there were the three missed calls from her on his cellphone and Amelia's miffed message about her calling and sounding upset.

When Rahul walked into their home, he knew just from the way that Pooja stole her eyes from him even as she laid out the chai on the table, and from the heaviness that hung in the air like a thousand muffled screams, that the truth had been unleashed upon her.

'You're home,' she said simply, not a trace of joy in her voice. After more than two decades of being married, should one expect excitement when a husband comes home early from work? But then that was just Pooja, thought Rahul. And after all the years that she had nurtured the same zeal, he had finally stolen it from her.

In that very moment, along with the pain that invaded him, came also a curious relief that he hadn't anticipated, as if a heavy burden had been lifted. Now he could stop hiding. He quietly took his seat at the head of the table.

'How was the office?' she asked, still busying herself with arranging the table, her voice noticeably stroked by a tremor. She flitted in and out of the kitchen for little things. Then Rahul saw it, a decorative bookmark from Elton's that had slipped under the table and was lying just a few feet away from where he was sitting. He bent down, picked it up.

He didn't answer her, finding the response pointless now, and she didn't persist, letting the stillness hang in the air, an answer in itself. He knew where the conversation needed to go, away from the niceties. He felt his body shaking involuntarily from anticipation, a man unable to tear his eyes away from the spectacle of his own disaster. Beads of perspiration covered his forehead even though the room was pleasantly cool. He wished that she would, at least this once, abandon her decorum, unleash the agony in her heart. At that moment, he was prepared to deal with anything but her composure and the infinite suspension of their showdown.

Pooja had just laid a plate of fragrant, freshly fried potato fritters next to his chai, when he reached out behind him and clasped her by the wrist to keep her from disappearing into the kitchen.

Careful, careful, she urged herself. *Control yourself. Otherwise your heart may leap out of your body through your mouth in a shattering wail. Better just keep moving for a while. Don't stop. Move. Move.*

She struggled, not with the coyness of when he once caught her desirously but with the terror of confrontation, and twisting her wrist free from his grasp, her gold bangles chiming, she fled to the kitchen. Leaning her face against the refrigerator, she felt the steel cool her forehead as tears filtered through her lashes. Shame unlike any she had experienced assailed her and she wished that the earth would swallow her up: anything to keep from confronting him. Humiliation choked her so that she could say nothing and tears rolled down her cheeks but strangely, even as her heart heaved with pain, this humiliation seemed to exacerbate her passion for him.

'Pooja?'

She covered her face with both her hands, shaking her head like a frightened child, still refusing to look at him. She needed all the composure and strength that her mother had instilled in her, but it was nowhere to be found.

'Pooja?'

Reluctantly, she turned around to look at him. In that glimpse, she saw in his hands the bookmark from the store. She quickly turned away again, her back to him, feeling her heart in her throat. 'Please,' she said, her voice trembling, praying on the inside. 'I don't know how to do this . . .'

She felt him standing there, both of them feeling like fugitives who had run from the truth for too long. Pooja drank the air deeply, wiped her eyes with the end of her purple chunni, and went straight to the sink where she started to vigorously wash the greasy Crockpot with a sponge. She would not make a scene. She would not let them dishonour themselves in this way despite what he had done. She would remain strong, elegant, magnanimous.

'Your chai is getting cold,' she said, sniffling. 'These bhajias are very spicy, I'm warning you, just the way you like them. Then if you have heartburn or anything, just make sure you have some *sat-isab-gol* and you'll be fine.'

'Poo,' he said, the urgency apparent in his voice.

'You know where it is. In the closet over there.'

He grew silent but remained there unswervingly.

Then, as hard as she tried to suppress it, and perhaps because he had called her that name, the term of endearment that went as far back to when they had first met, something rose from the pit of her belly, a dark, toxic bubble, rumbling its way up to her throat until it erupted into heaving sobs. Pooja threw the Crockpot against the porcelain sink, its clangour shaking the air violently.

'Oh, Rahul . . . oh, Rahul,' she broke down, her face in her hands. 'How can this be happening? Oh, God, I don't know how to deal with this. I just don't know . . .'

He wanted to hold her, to say something, but realized the futility of trying. Overcome with embarrassment, he did nothing except clench his fist, crumple the bookmark and leave it on the counter beside him. 'Ajay? Is he . . .'

She shook her head to indicate he was out. She gulped more air, wiped her eyes with the back of her wet hands, streaking the mascara in the process, and grabbed hold of the pot. Hot water ran and as clouds of suds began to form, she scrubbed the kadai relentlessly. All the time she kept repeating to herself, *I must find a way. I must. I can do this. We've been through worse, yes, we've been through much, much worse.*

It came to her now, an epiphany, that she was perfectly willing, perhaps even able, never to confront what she now knew to be the truth, to just go on living as if nothing had happened to defile what she had accepted as a faithful if imperfect marriage. After all, had they not already built an entire life around denial, pretending the past didn't exist, moving halfway around the world to siphon away ugly and painful memories? Why should this be any different? They would dig deeper, bury this in the same grave.

'Well, never mind,' she said, finally, her voice strained by emotion. 'We'll just forget about this. We'll just move on, you know, just put it behind us.' She continued sloughing away under the scalding water, her bangles clinking away frantically. 'No need to talk about this. No need. No need.' But then she turned around and saw his hesitation. 'My God!' she gasped. 'Why aren't you saying anything?'

'Pooja, I . . .' he tried to sound confident but the words came out as a squeak. He could see the toil on her face, the dark circles around her eyes, her skin sallow, and could barely face her.

'Aren't you even going to try and deny this?' she asked.

He still couldn't bring himself to say anything. He wished he could lie to her, it would be so easy to just deny it all, and she would probably even welcome the deception, but nothing came out of his mouth and the silence served as his truth, his admission that after all the years of running, here was something they wouldn't be able to escape. There was nothing they could do now to camouflage this with the routine of their lives and the charade of marriage. No matter how hard they tried, she would always see the transgressor in his eyes and his love for her, however real, would always carry the taint of larceny.

'Then what are you – are you going to do this again?'

'It's not that simple any more, Pooja.'

'Not that simple?' she asked incredulously. 'Why? What's not simple?'

'This,' he said, struggling for the right words. 'I just don't know if I can make any promises.'

Pooja turned the faucet off, letting his words sink into her. She faced him, the amber of her eyes shinning like a lake between the heavy fringes of her black lashes. 'You don't know if you can make any promises? To me?'

His face fell.

'What kind of a man are you? Answer me!' she cried. 'I've given you everything. Everything. What more is left, tell me? I made a promise to you, remember? For you, I gave up my home, my family. Bas, just left them there, so that I could give you a home. And now you can't make any promises? How about just keeping the ones you've already made?'

Rahul cracked open and tears swept down his face. The worlds Pooja had moved to be with him, everything she had sacrificed to take care of him, his inability to even be a faithful husband to her, to resist the beckoning of his desires, made him feel wretched and helpless.

'Oh, no, you're not going to do this to me. Not this time, you bastard,' she said. 'After everything we've been through, now you want me to go through this? This? How do you think your son is going to feel, hunh? When he finds out his father is a . . .' she couldn't bring herself to say the words, wasn't sure if she knew the right ones.

He stared at her, mortified, never in a million years believing she would be capable of something like this, even in the most excruciating pain.

'I never wanted it to be this way,' he said, meekly.

'But it *is* this way and it's all your fault! What did you expect? Oh, God, Rahul, what were you thinking?' she cried, shaking her hands so that droplets of water flew up to his face.

'I don't know. I don't know . . .' he said, wondering how he could ever have thought it would turn out differently.

'Don't lie to me!' she shouted, her face contorted with pain. 'You do know! You always know! Always there's that moment, when you can decide not to do it, when you can stop yourself from throwing everything away. When was that moment for you, Rahul? When?'

He shook his head. How could he explain to her the moment? How could a lifetime of self-deception be truncated in a single moment? How could he explain his attraction to another man and his betrayal of the woman who had placed him above everything?

'Don't you love me any more?' she asked.

'Oh, Poo. I never stopped,' he said, his voice cracking, the tears running freely.

'But it's just not enough? For me, you've been my whole existence. And now, now what do I do?' she asked. 'When did it start?'

He looked at her, palms held open as if to say, what difference will that make?

'I want to know,' she persisted. 'How long . . . how many . . .'

'A few months . . . Six months. He's the only one. Pooja, I don't want to lose you.'

The remaining colour drained from her face. 'Six months?' she said in a whisper. And then she laughed, a cruel, mocking ring to her laughter. 'Then what do you want? You want us all to live together? One big, happy family? You want to bring that boy here? To share our bed?'

'No . . .'

'Then? You want to do it in front of your wife and son?'

'Pooja, please,' he said, reaching out to touch her.

She shrank away from him. 'Oh, God, Rahul, do you know what this is putting me through? You of all people, how can you do this? You know that when a woman marries, her husband becomes her god. She's raised to think that in everything he does, everything he says, *everything*, there's a god. His word, it's divine. His deeds are divine. But this, what you have done . . .' she heaved a cry, 'Where's the god in it?' And then her face hardened, a thought so harsh and irrevocable crossing her. 'It would've been better if they'd taken me too.'

He looked at her wildly, as if he were mad himself or thought her mad. 'My God, how can you . . .' But he was unable to finish, stupefied.

'Yes, it should've been me. At least then I wouldn't have had to go through this. I would have been violated but by strangers. Not you. Not my own husband.'

'Pooja,' he said, advancing cautiously towards her. 'I don't know what's happened. I never wanted to hurt you. Please believe me. It's something I've carried with me for so long, always, and now, suddenly, suddenly I just don't know how to stop . . .'

By the time she realized it, Pooja's hand had already swung across Rahul's face, halting his speech. She gasped, her hand flying to her mouth, and she stood paralysed between his words and the abject terror of the action they had provoked. But there was no shock on his face, nothing other than the anguish of the condemned.

'I'm so sorry,' he said. 'I'll just . . .'

He turned around and walked away and she stood rooted, waiting for something else to happen, for guidance, intervention, deliverance. But the earth did not open up, nor did the heavens, and there was not a saviour in sight, neither man nor god.

Something horrible could happen to him. Maybe the boy would die tomorrow. While crossing the teeming boulevard, he could be struck by a speeding car, tossed up in the air like a rag doll, his body mangled up, bloody like her heart.

Then they would both be free of him. Go back to pretending that it had never happened. That such a person had never existed and, in time, they would treat the whole episode like an unpleasant dream. In the beginning, while he suffered, she would be there for him, yet again, like she had been all his life – hiding him, shielding him, nurturing him – and he would need her again because she was the only one who had lived in his shame, the only one who could love him despite it. Yes, she would restore him to himself one more time. Neither by word nor by deed would she make a reference to his tendency and the shame it had brought on them, and in time, they would continue the ritual of aging together, that ritual which was the rightful dividend of every marriage.

He left the same night. As he silently packed a little bag in their room, she waited outside on the patio, listening to the wind chimes eulogize their marriage. Several times she felt terror-stricken and wanted to rush up to him, to weep in his arms, to shake the madness out from him, to implore him not to leave her, but she remained frozen, powerless like someone watching death seep the life out of a loved one, waves of sadness and anger crashing together within her. And after he was gone, she remained in the vast, cold bed, prayers tumbling out of her mouth in anger and desperation. There were dreams, both violent – where she saw the boy's body cleaved by metal and fire – and redemptive – in which Rahul, dissolving in remorseful tears, fell at her feet and they recommenced their life together.

When she went down at around six in the wintry morning, a scarlet-coloured Kashmiri shawl thrown around her feverish shoulders, she found the note that he had left for her on the dining room table. The note read in Rahul's slanting, exquisite handwriting – *I'll call you later* – and it had his cellphone number as if she didn't have this already.

It all sounded so casual, so palliating that for a moment she experienced a sense of relief, as if he was in fact coming back at the end of the day, no matter how late. But then she wondered if Rahul had gone straight to this boy, in some fantastic, chimerical abode where she didn't exist, and the pain stabbed at her again. She shivered, rubbed the tops of her arms, goose-pimpled with the cold emanating from within her.

In the hours before Ajay would rise and – she was afraid – inquire about his father, she showered, derived energy from a strong brew of Assam chai and performed her puja at the altar of Radha and Krishna. Grief had proliferated throughout her body like a cancer and her hands quivered as she performed the ritual she now observed with some bitterness. She tried hard to surrender to the familiar comfort of faith, reminding herself that even the staunchest – perhaps especially the staunchest – were tested to superhuman levels, but the rationalization felt brittle, and the frozen, blushed countenances of the gods provided little solace.

She longed to hear something now, audible words of advice, compassion, something from the stone simulacrums rather than having to make it up herself as she crouched at their feet, looking up at them, plumes of perfumed smoke dancing up majestically. She accepted that she lived in a time devoid of tangible miracles, but as tears pooled in her eyes yet again, Pooja wished for nothing less than a miracle, pure and unadulterated by commonsense or logic. Only then, perhaps, would her pain end. Through divine intervention. The tragedy of worship, she knew, was that the almighty could do anything except express himself in a base, human voice, and that was what the beseecher needed the most in times of crisis.

You can go through ten avatars to save your loved ones, to make sure the earth continues to spin on its axis. What do I have to do to hear one word from your lips? She cried silently.

By the time Ajay ambled downstairs in his flannel shorts, rubbing the sleep from his eyes, she had managed to pull herself together. Now more than ever, she needed to keep herself occupied, action being an antidote to thought, but finding nothing that needed tending to – the last order for The Banyan had been delivered just a couple of days ago and there were no other orders to fill – she sat at the bare teak dining room table and leafed through an old copy of *India Currents*. She tried to look engrossed in an article about the outsourcing of so many US jobs to India. She studied the black-and-white photograph of a room full of Indian men and women strapped to their headsets somewhere in Delhi appearing rapt in servicing Americans. They no longer had to leave their countries to spoor opportunities in a new, alien world. Instead opportunity had jumped on the bandwidth and globetrotted to them instead. In its own personally recondite way, this validated her feelings that America was no longer a land of opportunity; those who had found a way to resist its lure had, ultimately, turned out ahead.

To invite more distraction, she brought the TV set alive with the remote control. An unscheduled episode of Oprah, on how to get a handle on credit card bills, bounded upon the screen. Women were confessing unashamedly to vulgar levels of squandering as the audience oohed and aahed away. She imagined herself being on such a candid show, crying her heart out in front of millions of people about a sinning husband, and was convinced that nobody could beat Americans at turning dirty laundry into framed canvasses.

'So, what's up with Dad? Didn't see him last night,' Ajay said, pulling out the accoutrements of a fruit smoothie from the refrigerator and placing them next to the shining metallic blender in the kitchen that Pooja would later clean. 'Is he out of town again?'

She looked up from her magazine, directing her gaze at the TV set. How must he have spent the night? Would he have slept soundly while her world had turned upside down? Or would he have called that boy over, relieved to have found a way out?

Now a heavy-set Caucasian woman was crying profusely on the TV, her face flushed red, and a suited woman with very short, cropped hair, who appeared to be an advisor of some sort was intently talking her through her reasons for her recklessness. *Maybe,* thought Pooja, *it would be easier just to tell Ajay right now. He is going to find out sooner or later.*

'Yes, yes, you are the observant one now, aren't you?'

'Jeez! Just asking.'

'Suddenly you are all worried about us when half the time you are not here yourself.'

'Oh, not that again!' he groaned, filling up the beaker.

She rose and walked into the sunlit kitchen past her son. She walked through its long space, feeling the phantoms of the night before. It was only now that it occurred to her that while Rahul and she had been sparring, she hadn't cared much whether Sonali had been able to hear or see them from across the way. Suddenly she regretted the way she had treated Sonali, considering the unpleasant responsibility she had taken upon herself to reveal everything. She could feel Ajay's eyes on her and she tried to guard hers away from him. From a cabinet she lifted out the oversized tub of protein powder she knew he would need for his shake and silently placed it next to him on the counter.

'Thanks,' he said, keeping his eyes on her. His head was reeling with thoughts because he could sense the palpable change in his mother's demeanour. For as long as he could remember, there had been nothing remotely extraordinary or exciting about his parents. While his friends at school had endured domestic upheavals through trial separations and messy divorces, he had not witnessed a single spat between them. They had been the quintessential Indian immigrant parents – hard-working, faithful, loyal to the skies of their citizenry, ultimately committed to growing old together and seeing their children settled to repeat the same cycle. His father was a banker and his mother a homemaker, for Christ's sake, how much more conventional could things get?

She was definitely hiding something from him and now the thought that maybe he was right all along, that his father was indeed not only betraying his mother, but lying to him also, both crushed and inflamed him.

'So, is everything okay?' he asked, his finger poised on the blender's button.

She glanced at him.

'Dad, I mean. He didn't mention . . .'

'Just for a few days, he will be gone, nothing to worry about.'

He pressed the button, a whizzing sound filling the room. Pooja took her seat at the table once again, reducing the volume on the TV but allowing the anguished, spendthrift women to stay on. Muted, she could now see their mouths move but was able to fill in the words and personalize their grievances: *My husband is cheating on me! My husband of twenty-one years has fallen to the most shameful of perversions. My husband, for whom I have given up everything, has given me up for another man. Everything is wrong. I want to die.*

I can explain a few nights, Pooja thought, *but what will I do about all the nights after that? He is not coming back and Ajay will ask questions.* Then anger seized Pooja: *Why do I have to do this alone? Once again, I'm supposed to be the strong one. When is it my turn to be rescued from all this? And who will do it?* She looked at Ajay who, even as the blender churned away at full speed, was looking intently at her, as if expecting something. There was no place to hide. Rahul had already taken the easy way out.

'Come,' she said to him and pointed at Rahul's chair to the left of her, at the head of the table. 'Let's talk.'

He made out her words over the noise and immediately his face fell. He silenced the blender with the push of a button and approached the table, reflecting the pain on his mother's face with some of his own. As he stood by the chair, almost afraid to sit, Pooja looked up at her lithe, sculpted son, beholding him with the kind of prohibited, primordial lust that was a complex part of all maternal devotion. She saw in him Rahul and herself fused together, the best of them, a kind of physical perfection that was irrefutable – not the projection of maternal bias but pure aesthetic appreciation. And although she saw Rahul in Ajay – in his deep eyes, the strong jaw – Pooja preferred to think that she had created him independently of Rahul, as if his seed had meant nothing in the end and that he had been given to her by the gods as a reward for the sacrifices she had made when leaving Kenya. She wanted to protect him from all this now, to keep the world in which he had grown up intact, but she was powerless to do so without Rahul.

She felt sorry for him and was able to understand why he had turned out to be so different. Ajay had been deprived, through no fault of his own, of a proper upbringing. Together, they had deprived him of his own birthright – a history, a past, the truth – all locked away in a box that Pooja hid in her closet. There were no black-and-white photographs of the generations past where he could detect resemblances, no grandparents on whose laps he could be coddled while being treated to godly myths and heroic ancestral stories, and there were no siblings (even though Rahul and she had tried) to cure the isolation of an only child. Ajay had not been brought up in a country where most people – especially his friends – looked like him and spoke his language. He was an outsider, even more so than Rahul and she had been as Asians in Kenya.

How could they now be surprised if, in the end, he had chosen to abandon these values, to defy tradition? Perhaps if there was any advantage to Ajay's acclimation to the West, his American way of thinking, it would be that his notions of a relationship would be different from that of his parents and grandparents, she thought. It would make a separation between his parents conceivable, although painful.

'Sit, please, darling,' she said.

'Did I do something?' he suddenly asked, sensing now that there must be more behind his father's absence, that perhaps they had had a disagreement over him.

She gave a short, unexpected laugh. 'No! Of course not. No, darling. Sit here,' she said and leaned over to push the chair out, but he quickly helped her with this, sitting gingerly in his father's chair and rubbing his hands together anxiously. She tried to smile gently and said, 'You know, beta, when people have been married for as long as your father and I have, things happen, you know?' She began tentatively. But his stare was resistant, hard, as unyielding as she had ever seen it and she suddenly wished she hadn't attempted to do this by herself, or at least not just yet. Pooja felt nervous, was afraid that something in him would combust. 'Your father and I, we are taking some time to think about things, you know, it's nothing for you to be worried about or anything. Nothing serious, we still love you very much . . .'

He grunted.

'There is no reason for you to be worried, darling.'

'Who is she?' he asked.

She looked at him, confused, then caught his meaning. 'No one! There's no one, Ajay. It isn't anything like that.'

'You're lying to me –'

'No, no, I'm not. I told you,' she persisted. 'We just need some time. Who said anything about . . . another person?'

'Isn't that the reason you were crying?' he said, pointing at the couch. 'You found out something, you must have! And now you're lying. Just to protect him. I can't believe this shit!'

Yes, go, confront him! Make him see what he is putting us through, that bastard! He should feel ashamed of what he is doing to us. He has dishonored me, you, all of us. Maybe you can bring him back. 'Ajay, please . . .' she was unable to summon the words and put her hand on his instead. Although she meant for her grasp to be firm, reassuring, her hand was trembling.

'I'm not going to let this happen,' he said, yanking his hand away, jumping up.

'Ajay, please, won't you listen to me? It's not at all what you're thinking, I'm telling you.' *No, it's much worse, much worse.*

'Where the hell is he? I'd like to talk to him myself.' He reached out for the phone lying on the side of the dining room table but she grabbed his hand again.

'Please, for my sake, don't!' she begged, rising to her feet. 'He'll be gone for a couple of days but you can talk to him when he gets back. I just wish you wouldn't act this way, Ajay. Oh, God, why did I have to say anything?'

Seeing her distress, Ajay tempered himself. 'Mom. Just tell the truth, okay?'

'But I am, beta. Everything's going to work out.' He looked at her sceptically, waiting for her face to betray her but she remained resolute, forcing a smile through voices screaming in her head. He squeezed her hand, trying to imbue her with strength. 'I'm fine, don't you worry. Your father and I love you very much, nothing changes that. And that's the truth.'

'Yeah but don't you love each other any more?'

'Until the day we die,' she said, choking down the tears.

They had never been confidants but when Pooja, unable to sustain her grief, had called Charlie, he had responded like a concerned parent and asked her to come right away. In many ways, he reminded Pooja of her own father, perhaps because both shared such a prodigious appetite for knowledge and had volumes to say about practically anything under the sun.

When she walked into The Banyan in the middle of the afternoon, devastation was etched upon her face and Charlie grew agitated with concern upon seeing her so unhinged. He immediately asked Magda to ensure they were left undisturbed and shepherded her through the students traipsing around classes and into the back office where he closed the door behind them. Pooja took the chair by the window, which was already beginning to feel like her regular seat, but even here the soothing sounds of the burbling fountain and chirping birds failed her. Everything that was comforting and beautiful was happening in a world outside of hers. Her own pain was so deep, so expansive, that it cocooned her, the trappings of solace just a distant reverberation in another realm. Pooja noticed again the Anaïs Nin quote framed on Charlie's wall and she tightened her fists. *Don't want to blossom,* she thought. *Just want things to remain the same, to go back to the way they were.*

'So, how about some tea, love?' he asked. She shook her head but he insisted, 'Yes, yes, some tea. Let's fetch you some tea. With lemon? Or some honey?'

She shrugged, disinterested, and Charlie disappeared from the office. She sat in silence, looking out at the white statues committed to grace in their various asanas in the lush greenery. On a concrete bench under a shading tree, her eyes found a young couple picking at a muffin and talking intimately, shafts of sunlight veining through the branches and casting a warm, divine aureole over them. She smiled ruefully. Were such moments behind her now? Lost forever?

Charlie returned with a steaming cup of fennel tea and a large wrapped oatmeal cookie, which he laid on an ornately inlaid wooden stool beside her. 'Got it from Kashmir, that one,' he said of the furniture, trying to ease the tension. She managed a weak smile. He stood across from her, leaning against his messy desk, and waited for her to say something.

'So, is Magda your daughter?' she asked, taking him by surprise and still looking out at the blissful couple in the garden.

'Magda?' he laughed. 'No, no, love. But she very well could be, don't you think? She *is* The Banyan, runs the whole bloody place. Makes me wonder what I'm hanging around here for. Why do you ask?'

Pooja shrugged, 'I don't know, a certain resemblance, I just thought . . .' her voice trailed off. 'Have you never been married, Charlie?'

'No,' he chuckled. When she looked at him, and before she could ask why, he punctuated it simply with, 'She said "no".'

'My husband . . .'

'Yes?'

She glanced away from him momentarily, feeling her throat seize up.

'Rahul?'

'You know another one?' she managed to joke. 'You

know, I love the way you pronounce his name. Perfectly, Charlie, not like others.'

'Ah, you mean like other goras?' he laughed self-deprecatingly. 'Ra-hool, Ray-haul! Dear God, I can only imagine all the bloody variations!'

She laughed with him, then just as quickly her face solidified again, the smile waning, a look of distance shadowing it.

'Haven't seen that chap since that first time when I met you both at the bank party. Ah, you cut such a handsome pair, Pooja. How's he doing?'

She turned aside and continued gazing out of the window, but this time she wasn't looking at anything in particular. 'You know, Rahul is the only man I've ever loved,' she said. 'The kind of love that makes us abandon our life's plans, all other obligations. It's crazy – love, marriage. You give your whole life, your entire being, all your happiness over to another human being, trusting completely. I've loved him this way, down to the very last nerve ending.' When she turned to look back at Charlie, her eyes had filled up.

'That's the only way, is it not?'

'But you don't realize the peril of such love, not until it's too late. You see, mediocre marriages, and I've known some of those couples, they are not in this kind of danger, perhaps because the expectations are lower, I don't know. But the good ones, the ones you have invested so completely in, those are the ones that damage you the most,' She gave an uncharacteristically bitter laugh. 'All those years of feeling secure, grounded in love, in faith, all of that, just gone one day. Gone. It turns out that in the end, the stronger you feel, the more fragile you become. Everything comes unhinged so easily, so quickly.'

Charlie was stunned at such candour in the woman whom he always saw as being especially private. He drew closer to her. 'Love is never pure, nor constant, Pooja. Ups and downs, that's what's normal, love. We grow dissatisfied with one another and pull apart and then, if we hang in there, and if we are bloody lucky, the affection returns and we sort of pull together again, don't you think?' He paused. 'Pooja, has he done something?'

Unable to speak, Pooja grimaced and covered her mouth with her hand, the tears coming again.

'Pooja?'

'He's having an affair, Charlie,' she said, her voice strained to a whisper.

He touched her shoulder. 'I'm so sorry, love,' he said. 'How are you holding up? Oh, that's a bloody stupid question.'

'I don't know,' she said, shaking her head and gnawing at her fingers like a frightened little child. 'I don't think I can live through this, Charlie.'

He knelt down beside her. 'Is it serious? Maybe ... maybe ... it's just a phase?' he asked hopefully.

'Oh, God, Charlie,' she said. 'It's so much worse ...'

'Worse? Pooja?'

She tried to speak but the words were stuck within her. She thought again about Rahul and the boy, saw their naked bodies locked together, and the words swelled upwards from her chest in one enormous wave. She clamped her mouth shut with one hand, looked around frantically and, noticing Charlie's private bathroom, rushed past him and into it. There, crouched over the toilet bowl, she retched. Charlie rushed in behind her and he too got down on the floor next to her, bracketing her with his arm.

'Oh, God!' she cried. 'I'm so sorry. What have I done?'

'It's okay. It's okay. Please, don't worry about it, love,' he said, handing her the yards of toilet paper he ripped from the dispenser.

'No, no, it's not okay,' she remonstrated, flustered and

frantically swabbing the toilet seat. 'I'm so sorry, Charlie. Please, you must give me a moment. I'll just clean this up.'

'Pooja, oh, my dear, it's nothing!' he insisted, taking her hands in his. 'Please don't worry about it.'

But she broke away from his grasp, quickly slapping her hand on the flush button, disposing the bile, as if by doing so she could pretend no one had seen it.

'Pooja, it's all right, really.' In his effort to raise her, Charlie pulled her into his arms. She could smell his cologne. It smelled old, paternal, like vetiver, lavender and vanilla all mixed together. She ruptured into tears, hiding her face in his chest, consumed by shame and remorse, but not without at least some relief. They stayed this way for some time and when, at last, she raised her head and looked at him, she said, 'I'm so ashamed, Charlie. I'm so ashamed.'

'Why? You haven't done anything.'

'But I must have . . . I must have caused this.'

'Oh, Pooja, Pooja,' he sighed, taking her face in his hands and looking deeply into her eyes. 'You can't blame yourself for this, love. It's not your fault he's seeing her.' She started to tell him but then she heaved into sobs again and he took her back into his arms. 'There, there. There, there,' he patted her on the back. 'It's going to be all right. He's just going through some phase, I'm sure of it.'

'No,' she said, disengaging. 'No, it's not. It's . . . another man.'

Charlie started to say something but was struck silent.

'How can this be happening?' she asked, confounded. 'He was never that way, Charlie. Never! I don't know what has come over him.'

He ran his fingers over her tear-stained cheeks. 'Dear girl,' he said, suddenly noticing how warm she was. 'You're burning up.' Charlie helped to raise her to her feet and silently they went back into the office where she sat down by his desk, her head hanging low.

'The tea – no, one moment,' he said and from somewhere behind his desk, he retrieved a small plastic bottle of mineral water and a container of pills, a couple of which he shook onto his palm and handed over to her. He also placed a box of tissues by her. 'Apis,' he said to allay her fear when she looked at the little pearls in the palm of her hand. 'Completely homeopathic. They'll help, trust me, love –' but then he hesitated, suddenly unsure if consuming ground-up bees was against her Hindu sensibility. But by then she had already thrown them back into her mouth and chugged down the water unceremoniously. She plucked a few sheets of the tissue and dabbed at her face, regaining some of her composure. Her kohl had begun to run and left a streak on one of her cheeks.

'Sometimes,' she said. 'I feel like it's all happening to someone else, not to me. And then, I just want to laugh, a relief comes over me, like what was I thinking, you know? It was all just a hallucination, nothing else. But then it all comes back and –' she took more swallows of water. 'Do you know what *birha* is?'

At first the question seemed so out of context to Charlie that he was momentarily confused, but then he said, 'Yes, yes, of course. The anxieties and pangs of separation from your beloved.'

She nodded. 'It's necessary to cultivate love in separation, just as Radha did for Krishna or the gopis that he danced with . . .' but then she winced and started shaking her head, as if trying to stop the onslaught of another spasm of pain.

'Whatever happens, Pooja, you must know that you can't blame yourself for something like this. Such things,' he said, coming around the desk to be near her, and choosing his words cautiously, 'such things are seldom instigated by, or a reaction to what someone's done. Sexuality is deeply rooted, Pooja, so congenital. Nothing a wife did could drive a man to want another man.'

'It's wrong,' she said. 'It's not natural, Charlie, not for us!'

'Pooja, really. You mustn't worry about it on the basis of religion. I don't know of any religion that is more, well, progressive, inclusive about such matters than Hinduism.'

'But we don't have such things, Charlie. I should know,' she protested, slapping her chest.

'You have followed, you have read but . . . Oh, Pooja, let's not get into all that,' he said, waving his hand dismissively. 'The important thing here is that he's being unfaithful to you. Let's leave the gods to their own personal dramas.'

'I need to talk to him again. I must make him see,' she said frantically. 'This sickness . . . Maybe we can talk to someone. Maybe there is some kind of cure.'

'Not that it makes your situation any less painful,' he said gently. 'But these things, they're connate. They've existed from the beginning of time. That's why I don't think it's anything you've caused. And do you know what I find especially ironic? It's that a Hindu of all people can be so shocked by such matters. I mean, it's so prevalent in the culture, Pooja, in all your mythologies, sacred texts, all that imagery . . .' But then he noticed that she wasn't listening at all. He had lost her to the vortex of her thoughts again. Charlie abandoned his discourse at once. He knelt down beside her, took her hands in his and when she slowly looked back up at him, he said almost longingly, 'Just tell me how I can help.'

She threw her head back at the ceiling, a deep sigh escaping her lips. 'I wish I could understand. I don't know how to stop this pain,' she said. 'For the first time in my life, I don't know how to help him.'

'Then for now,' he said, squeezing her hands, 'we shall simply have to start by focusing on you, Pooja.'

But from the look on her face, childlike, puzzled, it was

clear that she had no concept of self-preservation, of what it meant to exist without being subsumed in another.

The house, empty again as it usually was in the middle of the afternoon, rang with silence. Instinctively, Pooja closed the bedroom door behind her. She got on the floor and opened the bottom drawer of the dresser in her closet, billowing with old undergarments scented by a sachet of magnolia fragrance beads. Even though she couldn't remember the last time she had done this, her hands dug deep into the clothes until her fingers felt a small, rectangular tin box resting where she had left it years ago. Slowly she lifted the tin, lightly rusted on the edges, up and into the light. The Cadbury's chocolates had been long depleted, the room inhabited now by the proof of several lives.

Her hands were trembling as she placed it gently on the carpeted floor and prepared to open it. *How strange,* she thought, *that in the end, this was all that remained of entire lifetimes, of a whole era, of love, something that could be neatly encompassed in a loaf-sized box that once used to hold hazelnut chocolates in little paper trays.* After looking at the shut door one more time, Pooja pushed the lid open. It gave no hesitation and snapped open like it had just exhaled. Photographs, letters, keepsakes, looked back up at her like long-forsaken paramours reaching for reconciliation. There was also a neatly folded, white cotton handkerchief with 'RK' embroidered in red, and there were faint, brown stains on it. Pooja lifted it to her and smelled it, hoping for a fragrance of the past.

She picked out a fading photograph and they were all there – Rahul's sister, Kiran, with her expectant smile and striking resemblance to him, and both his parents – the gregarious Ravi Kapoor in a checkered safari suit and the impeccable Suchitra Kapoor in a turquoise printed sari, and next to them, with Ravi's arm extending all the way around her back, Pooja in one of Kiran's saris, young and blissful besides her in-laws. They were standing on the verandah of the Kapoor household in Mombasa, against a trellis of abundant bougainvillea, and though she couldn't see it clearly from the old photograph, she sensed the Indian Ocean roaring over the balcony behind them as it broke over the coral reef on the island. It had been at the end of the Ram Navami celebration of Lord Ram's birthday when the family celebrated with temple offerings and feasts at home. For eight days there had been daily recitals of the Ramayana recounting Lord Ram's banishment and exile into the forest, the abduction of his wife Sita by the demon Ravana, and upon her returning, the cruel trial by fire through which she proves her purity.

Pooja heard them again now – Kiran's delicious, full-bodied laughter as she teased Pooja mercilessly about her brother, Ravi Kapoor calling her his 'little apsara' and the regal Suchitra Kapoor rolling her eyes at both father and daughter and trying through disapproving grunts to maintain some dignity as they were immortalized by Rahul's camera.

She ran her finger longingly over them. A single teardrop fell upon the photograph and one by one they rebounded from it, coming alive.

Book Three

Even God cannot change the past.

– Agathon (447–401 BC)

Kenya 1982

The Vedic astrologer looked unusually concerned.

He squirmed, grimaced and punctuated all to himself as he sat, cross-legged on the ornate, plush sofa of the Kapoor household that Sunday, even as the cool breeze bounded off the mangrove-bordered Tudor Creek and wafted through the open doors of the exquisite bungalow on Rassini Road. With bits of fritters trapped in his robust moustache, he stared raptly with spectacled eyes at the colourful diagrams that the self-amused Ravi Kapoor thought resembled a carrom board and into which his regal wife, Suchitra, devoted to the cosmic science, put all her faith.

This age-old science introduced by holy men and blessed by the Almighty, Suchitra reminded her husband constantly, was what had ensured their family's prosperity for generations in Kenya. They had consulted it for matchmaking for the marriages of their daughter Kiran and son Rahul, as well as their own marriage years ago. That nobody, including the famous astrologer, had foreseen their present financial turmoil was never brought up, Suchitra avoiding any taint to his reputation and Ravi wracked with too much guilt.

In the sunken living room that afternoon, extravagantly decorated with artifacts both Indian and African, sat the agitated Rajanbhai in his signature cream Kwanda suit, Ravi Kapoor with his constant companion – a heavy crystal glass of scotch on boulders of ice – Suchitra dressed impeccably in a red floral sari and the large tika on her forehead, and George Matiba, a highly educated Kikuyu native who had gone to primary school with Ravi Kapoor and now helped manage the Kapoors' Coastal Commercial College on Salim Road in Mombasa.

In the 1980s, this was still quite unusual. Asians, as they had conveniently been dubbed after the independence of India and Pakistan, did not mingle so intimately or freely with Africans and invite them over for tea. But to Ravi Kapoor, George Matiba was more like a cousin than Mwangi, their live-in Kikuyu servant. George had grown so familiar with the Kapoors that he called Suchitra 'bhabhi' and she did her best to respond with as much cordiality as a respectable Asian woman could demonstrate to a guest in her house, even if he was an African.

That afternoon, when Ravi had shown up at home with George in tow, expecting a home-made meal after beers and billiards at the Mombasa Sports Club, Suchitra had chafed at his forgetfulness. But first, like a good Indian host, she welcomed George into their home and instructed Mwangi to bring him a pilsner glass of Tusker. Then she goosed her husband into their bedroom where she slapped her own head disdainfully and said, 'Hai Ram! What is wrong with you? What is *he* doing here today? You know Rajanbhai is coming. Even the children, I made sure they were out.'

'O-pho, Suchitra! There are no secrets with George. *Bwana,* he's like family.'

'Family? He's African, Ravi, not Indian. Just as we are Indian, not African! When will you get that through your khopri? To them Africa is for Africans. That's all they know, bas! You are the only one, trying to be United Nations to everyone!'

While her husband lived in a make-believe utopian world, Suchitra felt that she had a better grasp on reality.

True, Africans could see that Asians tended to live separately, shop separately, and almost never married outside of their own groups – all things that reinforced their racism – but what they didn't see was that the Asians themselves were hardly homogenous. They were steeped in identities of caste, religion and language, which regulated relationships within their own community as well, so race, no matter where they settled, would always restrict relations outside of their race.

Now Suchitra, trying to appear unruffled over an African's presence at this most private and sacred of times, replenished Rajanbhai's teacup a third time while he pondered the movement and positioning of the stars. Rajanbhai had been summoned by her because of the financial slump that Ravi's gambling had landed them in. Unable to repay any debts, they were now considering the sale of the college which, they exaggerated, had been erected almost as far back as when the first Kapoors had set foot on Kenyan soil.

Suchitra's only consolation was that they had already married off both their children with great pomp and pageantry. Their daughter Kiran had been wed to Prashant Jhaveri, the only son of a wealthy jeweller family. And only three months ago, their older son, Rahul, had been married to Kiran's best friend, the respected daughter of a retired schoolteacher, Pooja Patel.

'So, Rajanbhai?' Ravi asked impertinently. 'Tell us, tell us, are the planets dancing in our favour or should we make the music a little bit louder?'

Suchitra glared at her husband. Such disrespect and even that in front of an outsider! 'But why are you dancing on his head? Let him concentrate, okay! *Maaf karna,* Rajanbhai.'

Ravi cleared his throat as George raised a brow at Suchitra's totalitarianism and suppressed a chuckle.

'*Koi baat nahin.* No problem, no problem, there's no problem, Suchitraben,' said the astrologer, now assuming his meditative composure. 'I am ready now . . .' but then he looked at George, who was seated on the left, and then to Suchitra.

'Oh. It's okay, Rajanbhai, really. *Yeh hamare ghar ke hai,*' Suchitra said, giving him a pleasant smile and then repeating in English for her guest's benefit. 'George is family. Please, please, feel free.'

Rajanbhai hesitated a little, thrust into an unconscionable position by the strange intimacies of the Kapoors. His face looked as if he had detected a strange, unpleasant odour. Then he shook his head, coming to some kind of inner compromise and began, 'Relief will come, all debts will be gone, okay, everything gone. No, see, there is something else which is troubling.' He scratched one of his sideburns and kicked up a light dust of dandruff. He stared at his empty plate beseechingly but everybody was so engrossed in his predictions that no one noticed. Then Suchitra caught it and called out to Mwangi urgently.

Within a minute, Mwangi scrambled into the living room in khaki shorts and a dull white shirt. He carried a plate heaped with freshly fried fritters and placed it reverently in front of the now palpably excited astrologer. Some of the oil from an errant bhajia dripped onto the wooden table, setting Suchitra off.

'*Aieee! Wewe na fanya nini? Panguza hapo haraka!* What are you doing? Wipe this at once!' Suchitra screeched, a little too late to remember that George, a fellow Kikuyu, was also seated right there. There was a moment of discomfort, and only the fan whirring above them and the trilling of birds was heard. But then George reached out for a bhajia (much to the dismay of Rajanbhai) and diffused the situation.

Once Mwangi had mopped up the table with the rag he

constantly carried over his shoulder and disappeared into the kitchen, everyone went back to the sun and the moon and the stars.

'Rajanbhai!' Suchitra urged him on. 'Go on, will you please?'

'Yes, yes,' he said, energized by replenished savouries glistening in oil. He then adopted a frown for his elaboration. 'You see, when Mars, Saturn, Dragon Head and Sun – all are hard planets – when they are not in their proper positions, there is trouble also. I see an end to your financial worries but we should all be worried. There will be events that will affect people, people in high positions, politicians, whole country, Suchitraben.'

'Arre, but we will get the money, no? The sale will go through?' Ravi inquired.

'Yes, yes, Ravibhai. Debts will be gone, *chokas!* Debts will be gone.'

Here George tentatively stepped in, mildly concerned. 'These planets, the bad position they are in, can you tell me what exactly is going to happen and when?'

Rajanbhai looked up at him, indignant. But then, diverting his gaze to Suchitra as if she had posed the question, he said, 'Terrible, terrible things can happen but I can't say exactly what. I am not God. That only Ishwar knows! The period from now until 23 August, this is the most critical. Can you not wait a little, Ravibhai?'

Ravi hmphed, slapped his thighs. 'Wait? You think opportunities are lined up at the door? We have a buyer and we must act now before he changes his mind.'

But the astrologer shook his head, his reservations unshakable.

'Can we do anything, Rajanbhai? Must be something, no?' she asked.

'Well, Suchitraben,' he said, stuffing his mouth with another fritter, fingers glossy with grease. 'Of course, you know I can do special meditation for you. And some yantras, now those can always help,' he said, referring to special talismans.

Suchitra focused intensely on Rajanbhai. 'Yes, yes, anything, Rajanbhai, anything that you can do!' she implored. Then she looked at Ravi sternly and jerked her head, instructing him to dole out some of the rapidly dwindling cash, while Mwangi was summoned from the kitchen yet one more time to replenish one thing or another.

Unlike his wife, it was not easy for Ravi Kapoor to accept his position as the perpetual weed in the soil of Kenya even though he had been born there like his father. As a child, he had been propped onto the lap of his frail grandfather and heard first-hand the heroic stories of how the Asians had come to Kenya, how they had helped build the country with their own sweat and blood.

He remembered as if it was only yesterday how emotional his grandfather got whenever describing the beguiling invitation that had made him seek his fortune in a strange, distant new land. 'Always I will remember when I saw that poster from the British,' Rajat Kapoor said with that characteristic affirmative roll of the head from side to side. 'Beautiful arched gates opening to a land so beautiful and vast, *wah!* Come, build the Uganda Railway! "The Gateway to British East Africa". I had just lost my employment at Mr Chandra's pharmacy. So, I took, you know, my permit, three hundred rupees, which by the way my father loaned me, and then I came to Kenya.'

In the three-tiered hierarchy prescribed by the British colonials in Kenya, industrious Indians like the Kapoors had been brought from as far away as the then United Provinces, Bihar and Madras Presidency as indentured servants to build the British East Africa Railway in the late 1800s. Rumour had it that the names of Indian workers, Ravi's grandfather included, could still be found etched in Devanagari script on the rails they helped lay down, at a time during which one Indian was killed every four miles by the infamous man-eating lions of Tsavo as the mechanical snake made its way from Mombasa to Kampala.

In time, they had gone on to become shop owners, hoteliers, commercial farmers and export merchants; some moved to the capital city of Nairobi, and the Asians slowly rose to the middle rung. Many of them had been young, poor labourers from middle castes, or peasants released from land debts in their agrarian villages, and they already had the experience of building railways back in India. Although beneath the white settlers who, through fraudulent freehold sales with native Kikuyus grabbed the fertile 'White Highlands', Indians remained nevertheless above the embittered Africans, who now felt trodden upon by two races, each a few shades lighter.

Ravi could not deny that they all lived in a segregated society. He resented that generations had come and gone and yet the Indians were always seen as the '*wahindis*', brown-skinned settlers who had prospered and overstayed their welcome. But unlike his wife, he also accepted that this racism was reinforced by the Asians and he did everything in his power to bring equality to his relationships with his fellow Kenyans.

Whenever someone like George Matiba brought up this observation over ice-cold Tuskers, Ravi would explain with some annoyance, 'We Indians are no less exclusionary than all of you! How are we any different from all the other ethnic elites that have lived in Kenya? Why are you not looking at the Kalenjin of President Moi? The Kikuyu of Jomo Kenyatta?' he asked, referring to the two presidents' tribes duelling for political dominance in a one-party state. 'Plus, where would Kenya's independence be without the Asians?'

Although over time Indians simply came to be seen as the exploiters of Kenya, Ravi felt it was important to remind Kenyans that by 1914, the East African Indians, inspired by the anti-colonial resistance in India, had already formed the East African Indian Congress. They had not only demanded equal rights and compensation for Indians' service in World War I, but also defended African interests before Africans won direct representation. His father had been one of those men. 'So bloody hell, why should we feel like second-class citizens? I am Kenyan first, Indian second.'

To which George, shaking his head and laughing, said, 'Yes, be that as it may, *bwana,* you still keep yourselves apart from us. Do you want us in your homes? Your temples? Not unless we work there!'

'You know, George, we, Kenyan Asians, are just like those German Jews. We have a complex, rich culture. No matter where we go, we have to keep India alive in us. Without it, of what use can we be to ourselves or the country we adopt? But because we have been unable to depend on those British bastards or this government for protection, we had no choice but to become self-reliant. Built our own organizations. Organizations, mind you, which your people have come to use and also depend on. But forget about all that. Look at you and me. We are the new Kenya, no? There is India within us, but I am still, first and foremost, a proud Kenyan, *bwana!* This,' he said, pointing emphatically at the ground, 'this is my home. I was born here. We have been here for generations.'

'Ah, yes. You talk of generations but you forget, my

friend, that your ancestors displaced people who had been on the same land for thousands of years.'

Apart from knowing that their ancestors had been brought to work on the railways, Ravi Kapoor knew little else about why they had settled in Mombasa; he assumed that unlike others who had ventured further inland, the Kapoors had just decided to remain on the coast because they had prospered satisfactorily.

Kisiwa ya Mvita, as Mombasa was called in Swahili, meaning the 'Island of War,' had a recorded history that stretched back two thousand years. It was first mentioned in the *Periplus of the Erythraean Sea*, a guide to the Indian Ocean written by Diogenes, a Greek in the first century AD and also by Ptolemy in the century after. The tropical paradise built on a coralline island had a history drenched in blood. Once, Mombasa had been the base of Arab trade in slaves and ivory and the place where the invading Portuguese had built the monumental Fort Jesus, which looked out at the Indian Ocean over which its conquerors had arrived. It was then taken over by the sultanate of Oman and again by the sultan of Zanzibar who presented it to the British, making it the principal seaport of British East Africa, until finally in 1963 it was ceded to the newly independent state of Kenya.

Some, including Ravi Kapoor, liked to think that the now idyllic island, swirling with Arabs, Indians and Europeans, in a country that was home to more than forty-three ethnic groups, had left its bloodstains on the psyche of its people so that even long after its turbulent history they continued to live under the psychic shadow of anticipated conflict.

As the perspiring African squatting under the towering baobab tree squeezed lemon juice on the freshly fried cassava crisps and then dusted them with cayenne pepper and salt, Rahul watched Pooja bite her lower lip with anticipation. At least a dozen other Asians – dressed in their Sunday best of colourful saris and tailored Kaunda suits and humming along to one of the many Indian melodies emanating from the stereos of more than two miles of parked cars – milled around them for the crisps, the roasted maize and cassava, and the water from the coconuts that had been hacked off from palm trees more than eighty feet high by the Africans now serving them.

Mama Ngina Road, or Lighthouse, as the scenic gateway into the port of Mombasa along the Indian Ocean was popularly known, was bustling with the music, chatter and laughter of nearly the entire Asian community of Mombasa. A Sunday ritual, at around three o'clock, cars freshly washed by the house servant would start filing up along the edge of the deep cliff fringed with benches, lush foliage, street vendors and age-old, graffiti-afflicted viewing towers to secure the best spots. People were known to get immensely territorial about their parking and one could depend on finding someone just by visiting a particular section along the stretch where they were known to park.

'*Ai,* Harshadbhai, *kem chho?* Ai, Yusuf! How are you, *bwana?*' Greetings could be heard from across the street as heads popped out of the windows of cars sailing along the stretch languorously.

But there was always one unpopular spot that most Asians avoided. Even if you came late in the evening before the sun went down, and Lighthouse was packed with a procession of cars driving up and down endlessly at barely ten miles an hour, you could still find at least some space around Florida nightclub, the hangout for local prostitutes frequented by young Asian boys under the cloak of night, long after the cars crammed with entire families had packed up and gone home.

Pooja held a newspaper cone full of spicy crisps in her hand, and Rahul held a cut coconut in his, as they walked away from the vendor and the shadow of the baobab tree, towards the edge of the ocean. The wind blew upon their faces as softly as silk, providing some relief from the heat of the sun, and Pooja leaned her head against Rahul's shoulder as she stood by his side, the pandemonium of the families behind them. As they faced the Indian Ocean together, they held on to their thoughts, domed in a private silence.

She would have liked to think she knew precisely what he was thinking about but she would never truly know. Was he looking down at the dhow sailing past them? The two young African boys precariously descending the jagged edges of the cliff against a canvas of rushing waves? Of America? It was always this way between them, a space to be filled even when their bodies were spliced together. This must be the way it was between all men and women. She thought about her own parents, the respectable distance between them which made it awkward for Savita Patel to even speak her husband's name in the presence of others. Pooja didn't want it to be that way between Rahul and her. She felt that in time, when they were in America together, by the time she would give him a child, their marriage would be more intimate than those they knew.

It was a gulf she would invest the rest of her life trying to bridge.

Some friends who had gone to the same school at Aga Khan Ken-Sec ambled by. '*Eiy, eiy,* love birds! What you are doing there? *Khulam-khula pyar?*' a rambunctious Muslim named Riyaz called out. The other two hooted and launched spiritedly into the film song about love on public display. She glanced back and smiled at them coyly, enjoying the attention. Rahul looked over his shoulder, shouted, 'Khulam-khula I'll come over there and give you a few knocks, you rascals.'

'Arre, bhabhi,' Riyaz cried in mock fear, calling Pooja his sister-in-law. 'Look, how this one is threatening us like Dara Singh!'

'Don't provoke him, *bwana*, or he'll come chasing after us with his cricket bat, *bwana!*' said another.

In the distance, Kiran and Prashant had joined up with the Jhaveris who, despite repeated warnings about appearing too opulent in public, were bedecked in gold as if walking billboards for their jewellery store. 'Is this any kind of time to show people Laxmi's blessings? You know how dangerous these people have become!' was the common admonition.

'Arre! As if we are going to live under such threats all our lives! Let them come, let them come, *subutu*, we'll see what they dare to do!' the haughty Paryus Jhaveri always retorted.

Their freshly washed white Peugeot parked under a fragrant frangipani tree, the family was helping themselves to some of the spicy appetizers – *kachodi*s and pack-potatoes – that their well-trained African cook had prepared and which Prashant's parents had laid out over the hood of the car as Hindi music blared out from it.

Every so often Kiran called out insistently to Pooja, beckon for her and Rahul to join her but Pooja would motion to give them a few more minutes, lingering with Rahul as they faced the ocean. By now, Pooja and Rahul's courtship had evolved through the last two years of high school. Pooja would never forget the sight of Rahul, cutting a dashing figure in his ducks, striding to the crease, or fielding in a slip, his thick dark hair ruffled in the wind as he played for the local gymkhana. She felt she had known him all his life, long before they had spoken a word. As Kiran's best friend, she had always heard about Rahul, through the typical sibling griping about how he was always the favourite, was given more freedom – and so what if he's a boy? – but also about how protective and nurturing he was towards his little sister. The mere mention of him had made her heart beat faster.

She had seen him, at chai or dinner at the Kapoors' house, and randomly at parties thrown by mutual friends, and although Rahul had always been friendly, there was a distance that, instead of quelling her passion for him, only fuelled it, as if because of that space, they shared a more intimate understanding. A private connection. She had known, even as other boys milled around her for attention, that she would one day marry the abstract though winsome Rahul Kapoor.

Then it happened, at a party thrown by the local gymkhana to celebrate the victory of Rahul's cricket team over the visiting Nairobi team at the Ski Club, just blocks away from the Kapoor residence. Kiran, already tuned into Pooja's feelings for Rahul despite her coquettish denials, had taken her there, making sure that they were both dressed fashionably. Pooja wore a custom-made parrot-green dress and precariously clip-clopped away on Kiran's stilettos all the way down the stairs hewn out of the rocks and to the outdoor dance floor facing the moonlit creek as American disco music buoyed everyone into dance, drink and smoke.

Rahul, surrounded by his raucous teammates and the girls vying for his attention, hardly seemed to notice her. It wasn't until after Rahul threw down one too many whiskey-sodas and accidentally crashed into her as he was playfully tussling with his teammate, that he turned around to look at Pooja and saw her horror as the icy cocktail dribbled down her astonished face and onto the silk dress she had worn with just him in mind. 'You bevakuf! What have you done?' Kiran hollered at her brother as a tearful

Pooja fled up the stairs as if the clock had struck midnight. 'What are you just bloody standing here for? Go! Go after her!'

He soared up the precarious steps, his athletic legs carrying him speedily and reliably, and caught her before she had climbed up to street level. He grabbed her by the arm and said, 'Please, Pooja, please, just stop. I'm sorry. Ek minute, bas!'

'I'm not going back down there!' she cried petulantly, still wet and refusing to look at him as he stood a step below her. But she didn't pull her arm away from him either, aware that she had never felt more alive than in that moment when he was touching her and that she'd never had a stronger wish to die from embarrassment. He handed her a folded white handkerchief, inscribed with his initials *RK* and she blotted her face and neck with it, stealing glances at his handsome face.

'Well then, if you don't mind I'll just go back myself,' he said in jest and turned around to leave.

'What!' she cried.

He turned back around, laughing. 'Or I could just go up with you?'

'You do what you want!' she huffed, her tears threatening to spill over her rouged cheeks.

She continued the ascent up the carved stairs and he followed her, holding her by the wrist until they got to the street, dimly lit, and in contrast to the mirth and music that was fading into the distance. The street was jammed with parked cars yet deserted of people and he said, 'Look, we can't stay out here. It isn't safe, you know. Should we go sit in the car maybe? I have the keys to Riyaz's . . .'

'What? You're scared?' she said.

He grinned at her, relishing the unexpected spark of defiance. His look travelled from her head to her toe and back up again, and it was so penetrating that it made her feel suddenly overwhelmed by desire, so that she could only look away. He took her by the wrist and wordlessly led her to his friend's car.

After his apologies, they spent two hours together in his friend's car talking about cricket and Rahul's plans to go abroad and start his own business in America, and only rarely did Pooja share anything about herself. When he asked about her, she proffered details about how she wanted to teach, as her father did, because she enjoyed children, and then she brought their conversation right back to him, as if to establish that in loving him, she was willing to yield her plans to whatever his ambition dictated. It must have worked because it was at that moment, in a stranger's yellow Datsun, that Rahul stopped mid-sentence, as if losing his train of thought to something more compelling, and leaned into her and kissed her.

Now, years later, the memory of that night imprinted in Pooja's mind, they stood together, married, ready not just for a life together but also for a new world. Just before they had got married, Rahul had applied for the US visa lottery, which welcomed residents from underrepresented countries like Kenya. Shortly after their honeymoon, which unlike most Asian Kenyans, Rahul and Pooja had spent not somewhere in London or Canada but on a safari in the Laikipia plains, they had received the news that Rahul had won. Everybody, especially their parents, had considered this the fortunate augury of their blessed union.

Ravi Kapoor's gambling debts had landed the family in troubled times. Rahul felt that the future now lay in America where, like his predecessors who had sailed the oceans to reach Kenya, he would now chart his way to another world where new fortunes could be made.

Much later on, Suchitra and Ravi were alone again in their room. Suchitra was putting away the little gold jewellery that they hadn't sold to a local jeweller who had been entreated into complete confidence so that the Jhaveris wouldn't find out. Ravi was lying back in bed with his arms behind his head, watching her, when he said, 'You really must be more careful, Suchitra. You know, we don't live in the olden days any more. This is a new Kenya and we just can't go on talking to them this way.' He was referring to the incident with Mwangi.

Already crumbling under the humiliations of the financial strain brought about by her husband, of the usurpation of their secure futures at the gambling tables of the casino, she erupted as she rarely did. 'Yes, yes, you know it all, don't you? Why then don't you go and gamble some more? Or better yet, why don't you just run for president of Kenya? After all, you are African, aren't you? But do you know what? You can think whatever you want but to them, you are always going to be a money-grubbing *Muhindi*, bas, you understand?'

'O-pho, Suchitra, I am only saying –'

'You are saying what? Nothing! Nothing you are saying!' she shouted, tears in her eyes. 'What are you thinking that now you are the *Mzee* or something? After everything we have done for this country, do you need me to remind you of what happened to my uncle?' She was referring to the time shortly after independence when, in the wake of misguided nationalism, it was not unusual for a young African to walk into an Asian's shop with a letter from some city official and intimidate him out of his own business. Suchitra's maternal uncle, who owned an auto-parts store on Nairobi's River Road, had met such a fate and rather than be deported, had given up the business he had nurtured most of his adult life. But then, heartbroken, he had moved back with his family to Mumbai where starting a new life proved daunting. A few years later he hanged himself.

Ravi sat up in bed. 'Oh, Suchitra, that was a long time ago. This is a different age.'

She glared at him. '*Hainh?* There is nothing different! If anything, this is a worse time than before. Now they actually think they can do everything themselves! What do they need us for?'

'Why must you say this? We fought for this country too, Suchitra. It is as much ours as it is theirs. Arre, we must not forget our fathers, people like Makhan Singh and Pio Gama Pinto who spent years in detention for Kenya's freedom. And . . . and those Patels, who was it? Ambu Patel? Lila Patel? They almost gave their lives for the release of Kenyatta . . .'

'But why are you giving *me* this lesson in history?' Suchitra asked, getting more incited, raising her hand at him emphatically. 'And why do you think any of it matters to anyone any more? We are like unwanted guests in their country, can't you see that? Look! Look at all those poor people in Uganda. When that *rakshas* Idi Amin threw them out, what, did he even say, "Thank you, come again sometime, thank you for building and fighting for our country?" No, he just threw them out, overnight, just like that! Fast, don't even worry about taking your *potla-bistra*s, just get out, go back to where you came from! But no, you want to give me history lessons . . . oh!' she cried and it all being too much for her to bear, slumped down on the edge of the bed as tears gushed from her eyes.

Ravi hauled his arthritic self out of bed and came around and kneeled diffidently by her side, taking her hands in his. 'I know, I know –'

'What do you know?'

'All this,' he said. 'All this, it is my fault, Suchitra, I know. But, I am so bloody lucky to have you, no? Things will get better now, you just wait and see, I promise. No more history and no more *jugar!* We will start a new life.'

'Yes, yes, why not?' she snapped, flipping up her hand as if she was volunteering for a campaign. 'I'm only sixteen years of age. I have my whole life ahead of me!'

The Kapoors, including Kiran, travelled to Nairobi so that the sale of the Coastal Commercial College could be finalized with Alnoor Samji, an eccentric and wealthy old Khoja friend who had moved back to the capital several years ago and now owned Sadolin, the largest paint manufacturing company in Kenya. Ravi would continue to run the college for a respectable salary (which Suchitra would have to safeguard from the roulette tables and especially the private card parties).

Also, because Rahul and Pooja were emigrating to America soon, there was no way of knowing when they'd all be together again, they decided to make a family getaway out of it. While they might still have managed to travel by Kenya Airways – and Ravi, in his extravagant fashion insisted that they all do – it was decided by Suchitra, with an eye on the shaky financial situation, to either drive or ride the train to Nairobi.

In the end, Pooja's sentimental suggestion won out. They would drive so that about a hundred miles outside of Nairobi they could pay their respects at Makindu, the legendary Sikh gurdwara, and hope to procure the blessings that the family needed so badly. After all, it was rumoured that whatever one asked for at this shrine was granted as long as you came with a clean heart and cloaked in humility. Makindu had a legendary reputation and a special place in the hearts of all Kenyans.

During the building of the railway, Makindu became an important service point on the railway's advance from Mombasa. Sikhs, Hindus and Muslims gathered together in the evenings to sing the praises of God under a tree, where the current temple was erected in 1926. Since then, weary travellers stopped by for a night or two on their journeys to and from Nairobi and Mombasa, always finding a hot meal waiting for them without the slightest discrimination against their race or colour.

Because Rahul was committed to a send-off party thrown by his buddies from the local gymkhana that Friday, he would follow them later and drive down in the family's second car, a modest Honda that was also going to be sold off eventually now that he was emigrating and Kiran had joined her well-to-do in-laws who flaunted an unthinkable three luxury cars.

On their journey, the Kapoors would stay with their eccentric friends, the Samjis of Sadolin fame, whose second home was located in the Ngara area. Although the Kapoors would have preferred to stay in a modest hotel or at least in a more upscale area, like Parklands for instance, they obliged for fear of offending their sometimes bizarre hosts and jeopardizing the main purpose of their visit.

Even in Mombasa, they had all heard about the latest Samji scandal involving, of all things, colour. They had painted their palatial four-bedroom house in the upscale Muthaiga area a startling shade of yellow so that passers-by gawked and joked that God had blessed them by pissing on it. Farida Samji had also been known to create infamy by taking her pet dogs, Kiki and Bubbles, everywhere she went, including the Jamat Khanna, an Ismaili mosque at Parklands. A maid was kept on guard by the mosque's shoe stall, minding not only the expensive, imported high-heels, but also the indulged, hyperactive canines that barked disruptively all through the evening prayers as devotees entreated God with closed eyes and supinated hands. But nobody in their right minds complained, at least not to their faces, for the Samjis were also the generous donators of hefty English chocolate bars for all the members of the community during their celebratory occasions or majlises.

When Suchitra first heard about their incumbent visit with the Samjis, all she could do was slap her head and groan, 'I don't know which one is worse, not selling the college or meeting those crazy Khoja friends of yours!' To which Ravi had replied with the patience of a parent with a child, 'Yes, Suchitra, but when you are rich, you can afford to be eccentric,' then muttered under his breath as he turned his back to her, 'I married you, didn't I?'

As the gleaming white Mercedes cut across the infinite heart of Kenya, along the historic Mombasa–Nairobi highway, an ebullient and robustly competitive game of *Antakshari* swelled up in the car. In a flash, each player had to come up with a song starting with the same letter that ended the previous song.

Kiran was the unrivalled champion, plucking out ghazals, filmi songs and religious *geet*s as if from an invisible archive in the sky. Even their Arab driver Salim, caught between Suchitra's scolding that he was going much too fast and the abetting nudges from Ravi next to him, joined in excitedly; although Salim's knowledge of Bollywood music was limited and he kept plugging '*Mera joota hai Japani, yeh patloon Hindustani*' even when the previous song didn't end with an 'M'.

Occasionally, the car would have to slow down or come to a complete standstill on the tarmac to let a troop of baboons cross the road, or to see majestic giraffes dipping over dwarfed, flat-topped acacia trees and Grevy's Zebras with their voluptuous carriages and large ribbon-like ears.

When Kiran promptly framed the family of monkeys prancing in front of them with her Nikon camera, cooing at the baby clinging on to her mother's grey coat, Suchitra, alarmed that the gadget would attract the beasts and encourage them to spring onto the car, struck her forehead with the flat of her hand and shouted, 'Haven't you seen a monkey before?'

'O-pho, Suchitra, let her take a photo, okay?' Ravi tried.

'What photo, photo? Next she'll want to get out of the car and play cards with them!'

When they continued their trek, Suchitra, who couldn't come up with yet another song starting with the letter 'K', claimed it wasn't her turn. Salim tried again in vain to sing the legendary Raj Kapoor song, hoping he would get the chance to belt out at least a few verses and show off his acclimation to the Asian culture. By the time it was Pooja's turn, the panorama outside her window, in all its primordial beauty, had claimed her and she was gone from them.

The coast, a city of salt, is ancient, blisteringly hot, flaking, a lattice of lanes, mosques, cramped old houses and kiosks, lost in its own maze of time. Nairobi, its antithetical capital, is a city of flowers perched atop the highlands, with cooler air, volcanic red earth, rife with Western-style sophistication and the idiosyncrasies of metropolis, like a city fulminating from a desecrated womb.

But it is in between these two states, in the sprawling plains mottled with sunlight streaming through clouds, thought Pooja, *that Kenya actually breathes, where her arcana reveals itself. In the vast plains where the air blows unhindered across the land, and the scenery – a mixture of grasslands, scrub, forest, still water, stark and grim mountains, dust – grows so monotonous and sprawling that she actually comes alive.*

As her eyes adjusted to the land's infinity, its elusive horizons, she had to wonder if the feeling inside her meant that she was melding with nature or if she was just missing Rahul and the silence in their togetherness. She had felt no particular attachment to the land her eyes were drinking in now, at least not to this virgin, unsullied part of Kenya, but she couldn't help wondering now what it was going to be like to have to give up all this and move to a strange land, profuse with opportunity but divested of family.

Her head leaning against the window, her eyes drifting over the savannah, she continued to drift until Kiran slapped her hand, startling her. 'Your turn! Arre, where are you lost? Oho-ho! You're missing Rahul?' she teased, bursting into delicious peals of laughter.

Suchitra leaned forward to smile at a blushing Pooja, who was sitting next to Kiran. 'You will be spending the rest of your lives together, I'm telling you, you'll become sick of each other,' and here she threw a look at Ravi. 'So you can enjoy some time with us now, no, beti? Hai, Bhagwan, we'll miss you so much! I don't know what I'll do!' and the tears sprang to her eyes instantly.

Pooja reached over Kiran and squeezed her mother-in-law's wrist, feeling the gold bangles around them. 'It's going to be okay. I don't know what came over me, sorry. It was nothing. Just thinking . . .'

'It was nothing? Arre, I caught you! Nothing?' Kiran started pinching and tickling her as Pooja bubbled in her seat. 'Really? Come here, I'm going to show you nothing – come here, sali!'

'Kiran! You stop behaving like a little girl!' Suchitra said. 'You are a married woman now, do I have to remind you? And why aren't you missing your Prashant even a little bit, hunh? Might not be such a bad idea not to look *this* excited about leaving him at home!'

'Arre, Ma, one Laila in the car is enough,' she said, likening her sister-in-law to the Juliet of India.

Pooja pretended to be angry and gave Kiran a playful slap, but in fact she could not help smiling and blushing, and thinking that, yes, theirs was truly a love story.

They decided not to stop at Makindu after all, forgoing the blessings for expediency and just slowing down outside it as a mark of respect.

The Samjis' live-in African maid, Mariam, had grown visibly excited upon receiving the Kapoors. Bored of looking after an empty house now that the Samjis lived almost exclusively in Muthaiga and spent most of their time at its country club, Mariam had started to fear her dispensability. Demanding guests who would need tending to and require the Indian cooking she had become such an expert in were a boon and filled her with a sense of security.

Mariam, now in her forties, lived in the same gravelled compound, in a modest servants' quarter located next to the warehousing garage at the farthest end of the grand house. She had grown accustomed to the smell of paint and thinners, and though the house remained empty most of the time, she felt no compulsion to take advantage of its availability, preferring to spend time in her little dwelling. A couple of stray mewling cats sauntered around it, apparently safe for the moment from the Samjis' pampered dogs. Mariam was kept company by servants from the neighbouring houses, also belonging to wealthy Asians. Most of the other servants envied her leisurely lifestyle if not her dwelling and called her 'Mariam Malkia' meaning 'Mariam the Queen,' to which she would say, 'What kind of a queen stays isolated from her family and only gets to see them one time in a month?' Whether she was referring to the Samjis or her actual family – two teenaged sons and a much older, frail husband – living in the Kangemi slums on the outskirts of Nairobi, nobody knew for sure or cared enough to inquire.

Many of her friends had asked Mariam why, if she missed her family so much, she didn't moved back to Kangemi where a small textile factory had been started by a rehabilitation centre to help women gain financial independence. But Mariam, having already worked for the Samjis for over ten years, said, 'And who will take care of them? Don't you know they are like my children? Mohammad and Bashir, and even that old husband of mine, can take care of himself. But the Samjis,' and here she shook her head in mock disdain, 'When they stay here, that Mama Farida can't even find her own pair of shoes without me!'

Dressed especially for the occasion in a bright yellow and red tie-died *khanga* dress but with an incongruous brown cardigan thrown over it to protect her from Nairobi's biting chill, Mariam sprang into action as soon as the car pulled up into the driveway. At the very first opportunity, she attempted to pick up all four suitcases that Salim had hauled out of the trunk and it looked like she was going to keel over in her rubber Bata shoes and land on her turbaned head.

At once Pooja tried to help but Suchitra pulled her back by the arm, 'Let her do it. It's her job, beti. Salim! Quickly, help the poor woman before she kills herself and creates more problems for us!'

The four-bedroom house in Ngara carried a distinct smell of turpentine. An outside garage had been converted into storage for cans of paint and related appurtenances, as if on stand-by for any sudden artistic inspirations the Samjis might have. Suchitra winkled her nose. 'What is this petrol smell? Oh, I already feel like I'm going to vomit!'

'Oh, only turpentine, Mama, no need to worry,' Mariam quickly explained, still trying to grapple with the bags and resistant to any help from Salim. 'You know, a pussycat knocked over one of the cans this morning and I have tried so hard to make the smell go away!'

Inside, the weary Kapoors found a house cluttered with the trappings of confused wealth. Ornate gold-leaf furniture and antique Louis XV reproductions combated with the Oriental motif of shoji room dividers placed indiscriminately around the living room, sumi-e paintings with goddesses and fire-breathing dragons on the wall, and a solid wooden Tibetan table dwarfed under a massive, blinding chandelier. But somehow, in all this chaos, the Samjis had managed to find a prominent place above the unused fireplace for an oversized picture of their smiling religious leader, the Aga Khan, in an enormous gilded frame. The intent may have been to create an appreciation for world cultures, or to act as a testament to their travels, but it looked as if world's cultures had come and regurgitated right in the middle of the their living room.

As the rest of the Kapoors stood frozen amongst the tumultuous décor, Suchitra clucked away with distaste. 'Chee! Chee! Just look at this! I'm telling you, all that money and still no class!'

'Ma!' Kiran nudged her mother, motioning towards the maid who was squeezing past them with two of their enormous bags.

'So? So what? As if we have to worry about that one!' she said, letting the maid pass through. *Since when did one have to mind their tongues in front of servants and maids?* thought Suchitra, now annoyed. They were invisible. And even if they were to say anything, as if their word would mean anything! Even if the servants were believed, the Samjis would no sooner brand the African maid a troublemaker and fire her for her insolence than take offence with their guests. And so her clucking continued, undisturbed by the presence of loyal servants.

After Mariam had pacified them with cardamom- and ginger-laden chai and samosas, Pooja's in-laws retired for a nap in the late afternoon. They occupied the master bedroom, filled with more of the global souvenirs the Samjis had collected, the most garish being an imposing Aphrodite bathing on the bedside. Even Kiran, the typically hyperactive Gemini she was proud to be called, surrendered in a less opulent room to the narcotic exhaustion of the long drive and the sharp change in temperature. 'Sell it so we can all go home!' Suchitra said before passing out.

Suchitra's snoring trumpeted in the air and Pooja, amazed at the indecorousness, walked out into the backyard, the chill biting through her dress. In the beginning, she had been unable to stop comparing Suchitra to her own mother, finding the Kapoor matriarch astonishingly audacious in everything she did, including how she treated her husband. Where Savita Patel's strength came from her being emotionally restrained and verbally economical, Suchitra Kapoor enforced herself passionately, initially demonstrating some struggle with her emotions but inevitably giving in to expressing herself rather grandly.

In time, Pooja had learned to adjust to her mother-in-law's temperament and found some redeeming qualities in her assertiveness. First, Suchitra cared for and accepted her daughter-in-law almost as her own daughter and secondly, Pooja discovered that there was indeed some benefit in allowing emotion to unfurl in the moment. Unlike her own mother and even herself, who clung to emotions until they leaded the soul, Suchitra unburdened herself whenever she felt like it and just minutes after that, her wrath would dissipate. In this respect, she could clearly see that Kiran had taken after her mother where Rahul, soft-spoken and gentle, was more like his father.

Draping her sari tightly around herself, she walked over the gravelled compound, looking up at the cloudy Nairobi sky. She yearned for the bright, scorching sun of Mombasa and its blanketing hot air, and for Rahul, who was still there. She had tried to call him but he hadn't been home and because the Kapoor house servant had been given the weekend off so that he could go and visit his family, she had been unable to leave a message. She had noticed the little blinking machine in the Samjis' living room, a 'message machine' Mariam had called it (except she had pronounced it 'massage') and wondered if, when they moved to America, they too would have one like it.

Suddenly she became aware of the squawking of a hen and when she turned around in the direction of the servants' quarters, she saw that Mariam was supervising a young African man squatting on the ground. He was dexterously slaughtering the bird with an ominous knife, its blade glinting in the sun. Pooja flinched and froze. Mariam looked up and smiled, not in the least bit alarmed, knowing only too well how wealthy Asians had prodigious, carnivorous appetites but were too weak to witness or minister the gruesome sacrifice that delivered meat to their tables.

'Mama, did you need anything?' Mariam asked.

Pooja shook her head and cringed as blood started gushing out from the severed neck of the bird, its wings still flapping around wildly even as its little head lay severed from it on the ground, the beak crying silently.

'Mama, go! You go back inside. I shall come and see you in a little while.' Then some of the blood sprayed out over Mariam's leg and she jumped back, yelping, 'Eh, Njoroge! Watch it, man!'

But Njoroge, unruffled by the bloodshed, was whooping it up and laughing as he thrust the body of the bird into an aluminum pan full of boiling water in which he could skin it. Mariam slapped him playfully on his head, their flirtation undisguised.

The arrival of the Samjis was heralded by the incessant barking of dogs. Before they entered their home, the two Pomeranians, Kiki and Bubbles, dashed in like the true masters of the house, and pounced upon the peacefully slumbering Suchitra and Ravi, nearly inducing a heart attack.

Suchitra jumped up in bed, screaming hysterically, one hand clutching at her heart. Ravi jumped out of bed altogether and, shocked at the dogs' ferocity, plastered himself meekly against the wall. Kiki and Bubbles gamboled around the bed, two coffee-coloured fur balls wreaking havoc until their tall and commanding mistress charged into the room.

'Kiki! Bubbles! Get off the bed at once!' Farida Samji ordered, and by some miracle borne of loyalty, the little beasts leapt off the bed and with salivating tongues and wagging tails awaited their master's next command. 'Silly darlings.'

Having just returned from a game of tennis at the Muthaiga Country Club, Farida Samji was dressed in a white tank top and panelled skirt and was holding a racquet almost threateningly in her hands. She smiled apologetically at her terrorized house guests, whom she was meeting for the first time. 'Hello, I'm Farida Samji. You can call me Falu,' she introduced herself. 'Tsk, tsk, tsk! So sorry about all this but really, they don't mean any harm. They are so loving, aren't you, Kiki? Bubbles? Wait and see. They are just so-o-o excited to see you! It means that they really, really love you! Really!'

A dishevelled Suchitra, still struggling to catch her breath, and Ravi, who now peeled himself off the wall, were still too stunned to speak. Neither could wipe the alarm off their faces.

Farida Samji was remarkably tall, toned and wore her hair in the latest bobbed fashion so that even though she was well into her fifties, she looked like she could run marathons, making others around her feel dismally aged.

'*Barre Jao!* Go to Mariam and she will give you some *mum-mum*,' Farida said to the dogs with the complete confidence that they understood Gujarati, English and any other language she may have been proficient in. 'Mariam!'

But it was Alnoor Samji, a boisterous, heavy-set, mustachioed man in a polo shirt and shorts who tromped in with his large, hairy open arms. 'Oho! Ravi-*saab, kem chho? Kem chho?* How are you? Oho, Suchitraben! By God, what a pleasure to see you both! Oh, so I see you have already met our children, Bubbles and Kiki, eh?'

Suchitra and Ravi exchanged a look.

'Yes, Alnoor. Just now only they were surprised by them,' Farida said, pulling a sympathetic face.

'Oh, the poor dogs!' said Alnoor and then broke into uproarious laughter.

Farida clapped her immaculately painted hand on her mouth, joining in on the joke. 'Oh, Alnoor! You are just too much some times!'

Right then Mariam appeared. From the look on her face, it was clear at least to Suchitra and Ravi that she was also entertaining heinous thoughts about the dogs. Kiki and Bubbles refused to leave the room, bounding around Farida and licking her bare legs liberally. Her leg kicked out ineffectually. 'Okay, okay, enough! Get out now and leave us alone for a while. Can't you see we are with our guests? Mariam, get them out of here!'

Mariam refused to move and Farida had to look over

her shoulder and throw Mariam a commanding look, after which the servant grabbed the thin leads and pulled them sharply, almost yanking the whining dogs out of the room.

'Poor little creatures,' Farida sighed, sitting on the edge of the bed, one tanned leg crossed over the other. 'What do they know but to just love, love and love?'

The Samjis returned dressed to the nines a few hours later, without the pesky dogs. Upon their insistence and much to Mariam's dismay, the Kapoors were whisked off to the Muthaiga Country Club, about a ten-minute drive from the city. It was made abundantly clear, when Ravi had attempted to offer an excuse of exhaustion, that this was not an invitation most people were fortunate enough to come by. As Farida had stared at the Kapoors in shock at such unthinkable impudence, pulling her red shawl tightly around bare shoulders, Alnoor elaborated with sweeping gestures, 'Hainh? What, are you joking Ravi? Do you know that only prime ministers, only presidents, the Crème de la Crème go here! Come on, come on! I am not going to let bhabhi and the kids suffer because you are so bloody lazy!'

As they approached the stately main building with its pink walls and bluestone pillars, nestled on fifteen acres of verdant tropical gardens, Alnoor exclaimed at the wheel, 'Ah, there it is! There it is! Old Kenya!' and one would have thought that the fat, perspiring man driving them in the shiny Mercedes was not in fact an Asian who at one time would have been booted out along with the howling dogs, but may have in fact played croquet with Markham, smoked a pipe with Finch Hatton, sipped gin and tonics with the Earl of Erroll, enjoyed bonhomie with the paragons of colonialism. 'Tch, you know this has become our home away from home now,' he admitted proudly. 'No, Farida?'

'Without question, darling. Tch, I so love this place.'

Pooja and Kiran exchanged a look, suppressing their laughter.

Naturally, since its opening in 1913, things at this legendary headquarters of Kenya's notorious 'Happy Valley' set had changed. Now one could even find a sprinkling of wealthy Kikuyus and Asians like the Samjis on its esteemed membership roster who were finally tasting the high-life and English traditionalism that had been denied to them as being far above their station and ethnic sensibilities.

The group was seated in a spacious wooden-floored dining room where a silver carvery trolley made its rounds sporting the finest meats. Between lavish servings Alnoor was filled with almost an eager self-reproach. 'Oh, bloody hell! Tch, if only I'd thought about it sooner, we would have reserved the private dining room, no Farida? Bas, next time, next time, by God!'

But this was already more than enough for Ravi who, glancing around a room still prominently occupied by Europeans, remarked, 'You've done so well for yourself, Alnoor, very, very well.' Ravi noticed Suchitra was shaking the life out of the salt shaker on her plate of tilapia and he put his hand out to her. She looked up, miffed, and reluctantly surrendered the silver shaker.

'Arre, it's all *mowla's meherbani!*'

Ravi was unable to hide how impressed he was. Underneath his cheer, envy gripped him. 'Still,' he said, a distinct tremor in his voice, 'In today's day and age, *this,* really this is just something else, Alnoor.'

Suchitra could not remember the last time she had heard her husband comment on the conditions in his beloved Kenya being anything less than optimistic and she stopped the vigorous spicing of her bland food to listen more attentively, as did Kiran and Pooja.

'Oh, come on now, Alnoor! Really, don't be so modest,' Farida jumped in, laughing almost lustily. 'He is *such* a genius, you know.' She affectionately touched Alnoor's sideburn with a long finger so manicured it looked as if it could slice flesh.

'Tch, but you see, Ravi, that's the good thing about our times, about this government,' Alnoor said, a little more softly. 'Here the colour of your skin, it doesn't count, not really, when you think about it. You know what counts? Only the colour green counts!' he said, rubbing his fingers together lustily. 'We Asians, we have but two options left to us now if we want to survive; either pack up and leave – go to Canada or London or back to India – or like Rahul, go to America, why not? Otherwise just shell out money and grease those hands.'

'I had just hoped there would be a different way.'

'What different way? You can't make money in this country and not pay the "big man". Not unless you want to end up at Nyayo House!' he said, referring to the notorious torture chambers in Nairobi that were allegedly filled with heinously tortured political prisoners.

Ravi, finding it hard to accept this grim reality said, much to his family's surprise, 'Ah, politics, it has always confused me.'

'But that's because you're a bloody idealist, my friend. Really, there's no need to worry about large, abstract ideas. Who here has the time? We are all just trying to survive, that's all. And if the man at the top wants to fatten his bank account, you just split some of your profits with him and then you can continue making more. Simple, no?'

'But then what does that lead to in the long run, Uncle?' Kiran jumped in, looking for support around the table at

Pooja, who was seated to her left, and her parents across the table. 'I mean, is that really the answer? More, more and more corruption? We have to all work together, save this country from the tyranny of greed and . . .'

'Oh, Kiran, how very silly,' Farida said, smiling. 'Who do you think elected Moi after all?'

'Work together?' Alnoor balked. 'These people don't know how to run companies, how to build businesses! Did you know, Kiran, that after independence there was a whole movement to Africanize everything, to take businesses away from Asians and give them to the Africans? Can you believe *that!*' Alnoor had no idea that the Kapoors were only too aware thanks to the tragedy with Suchitra's uncle, and nobody said anything, Suchitra just shifting uncomfortably in her chair. 'Tch, what do they know? And what did they do? They could not even manage. Bas, within six months, the Asians again owned those same businesses. That's why, my dear, no government now will dare to get rid of Asians, doesn't matter how they feel inside. We've become, what do they say? Tch, a "necessary evil".'

'But, Uncle, isn't it important that we start behaving like Kenyans first? Not Asians or Kikuyus or Luos or whatever you have?' Pooja said, her hand against her throat. 'After all, Uncle, we all fought for independence together, right? We all love this country. It's home to all of us.'

'No, no, no, Pooja. We do not *all* love this country. As for the people running it . . .' he grunted and then looked around the room furtively. When he had deemed it safe, he began elaborating on what Farida had touched upon moments earlier. 'Pooja, presidents like Moi are elected to safeguard the interests of the elite. And to a large extent, we have also benefited from this, don't you see?'

'Alnoor,' Farida intervened, touching him gently on his hairy arm and instantly placating him. She then turned to

Pooja and said with an even tone, 'Dear girl, in choosing who should run the country after Kenyatta, as if the needs of the Kenyan electorate were ever sought. It was the "white" settler community and the Kikuyus, the same ones that own land in the Rift Valley and who supported Moi and made sure he would be our second president so that their interests were protected, that had all the power. You think a radical like Odinga or moderates like Murumbu and Mboya would help those elitist bastards?'

Pooja and Kiran exchanged a look. Obviously the irony of her statement was lost on her.

'The appointment of Moi guaranteed that the "whites" and the Kikuyus could keep their privileges, and also it silenced other radical thinkers from Moi's own tribe on the issue of appropriated land,' Farida dispatched from her impressive arsenal of political knowledge. 'In a tyrannical regime, darling, competence in a deputy is a dangerous thing. Only interest matters.' She sat back, ever so slightly, a faint smile playing upon her immaculately painted face.

'Tch, but where do you think you are, beta? These ideas, all these lofty, lofty ideas you have, they all sound very great but you are not in America yet, are you?'

Pooja looked at him quizzically. 'But what does America have to do . . .'

'This is a one-party state. Just Kenya African National Union, bas! Sure, we're a democracy but in name only, nothing else. This one here is talking about, what is it? Tyranny of greed?' Alnoor was shaking his head and laughing. 'We live under a dictator, Pooja. Dictator! There is only KANU from now until the day we die. These lofty ideas you young people are having are better left here,' he said, jabbing at his head. Alnoor looked directly at Ravi. 'Come on now, Ravi. Are you telling me you have never given chai in your life, eh?'

Here nobody could deny what Alnoor was saying. Indeed Ravi himself had been guilty of using bribes to get things done, smaller things, like getting a copy of a missing birth certificate or expediting a passport, and had participated in the corruption he was so vehemently against. Certainly it was nothing compared to the Alnoor Samjis of the world who were immersed in murkier waters. It was a well-known fact that Alnoor was in cahoots with a Banyani tycoon who had the president's personal phone number and was rumoured to be responsible for an elaborate foreign exchange scheme. But in the end, these were all varying degrees of corruption, Ravi reminded himself as he quietly cut through the chicken on his plate.

And who could argue against Kenya's single-party system? He was only too aware that such systems of government often arose from decolonization because one party was credited with playing a dominant role in the liberation of the country, but that eventually the party became despotic; that single-party states just paid lip service to democracy and the will of the people. After all, without the choice of different parties, in a government where no opposition parties were allowed, weren't the elections just a joke? *How stupid am I?* Ravi chastised himself. *I have learnt nothing! Absolutely nothing!*

'Perhaps you are right, Alnoor,' Ravi conceded. 'What do I know?'

Alnoor looked at Suchitra. 'Where did you find this one, bhabhi? Disneyland?' And then he laughed some more, especially impressed with himself for having woven America in.

But Ravi's face fell from embarrassment and Suchitra was surprised because she thought she could see tears in his eyes. She smiled, keeping face, but inside she wanted to behead Alnoor Samji and his scrawny witch of a wife for trying to reduce her husband to a simpleton. Her husband was a good, kind man, one who saw beyond colour and creed and the Samjis of this world should never have the kind of power to reduce someone like him to a position of need and ignorance. She reached out to him, held his hand on the armrest but Ravi, confusing her gesture for pity, pulled his hand away and proceeded instead to drink deeply of his Scotch.

'You've heard the joke, na, about the Kenyan hell?' Alnoor said, and when everyone looked around blankly or shrugged, he launched away. 'So this big old bastard sinner dies and goes to hell, okay? And you know what, there's a different hell for each country. One for Britain, one for Australia, you know, one for each country. Naturally he decides he'll just pick the easiest one, the least painful hell to spend his eternity. First he goes to Germany's hell and there he asks the couple of people waiting in line, "What do they do here?" and he is told, "First they drop you into an electric chair for an hour, then they make you sleep on a bed of big, big nails for another hour and then the German devil comes in and whips you for the rest of the day." The sinner thinks, "*Arre baap-re!* Oh, this sounds too painful", and so he goes to the US hell. There he discovers it is exactly the same. So then he goes to the Russian hell and here also it's exactly the same. But then, he comes where? To the Kenyan hell!' he says, pausing for effect, eyes widened. 'And by God, there is such a long line to get in, he starts wondering, "Arre, what the hell is going on here? All these people waiting to get in! Why?" He's so amazed he asks one of the guys, "What do they do here, *bwana?*" And he is told, "Well, it is like this. First they put you in an electric chair for an hour, then they make you sleep on a bed of nails for another hour and then the Kenyan devil comes and whips you for the rest of the day." The sinner says, "Arre, but that is exactly the same as all the other hells. So why are there so many people waiting to get in here?' And the man waiting in line replies, "That's because in Kenya's hell, *bwana,* there's never any electricity, so the chair does not work. The nails were paid for but never supplied, so the bed is comfortable to sleep on. And as for the Kenyan devil, he used to be a civil servant, so he just comes in, signs his time sheet and goes back home for private business. So you see, it pays to be in Kenya's hell, *bwana!*"'

They were alone again, Pooja and Kiran in their own room, when Suchitra changed into a cotton nightgown covered with large hibiscus flowers and said to Ravi, 'Hai! Hai! God only knows who enjoys that sort of rubbish food!'

'English food,' Ravi mumbled.

'Yes, yes, I know,' she said, sticking out her tongue in distaste and making a sound of contempt. 'Boiled in water! No salt. No nothing! And those silly jokes!'

'It was rather funny actually. I really laughed.'

'Hunh!' she snorted in disdain. 'You! You laugh at everything!'

From where Rahul stood, almost at the edge of a precipitous cliff diving into the Indian Ocean, he could smell the sea. To his right sprawled out a lush golf course, its white flags flapping desolately in the strong wind. Behind him, across Mama Ngina Drive, which even at this time of night had an infrequent yet sustained procession of cars enjoying the cool air bounding off the ocean, was the golf club where the party was in full swing now – a double celebration for the Mombasa Cricketers victory over the Nairobi players and Rahul's bon voyage.

'Remember Hanif?' Rahul asked, taking the joint from Riyaz's hand.

'Come on, man. We should get back. It's almost midnight already.'

'You remember him?'

'Who, Hanif? Tch, *bwana,* why are you thinking about *that* one?'

'I don't know, maybe it's the ocean.'

'Can't even see it in the bloody darkness.'

'Just thinking, you know? Our lives just continue but his . . .' He took a drag, thoughts percolating. Although this wasn't where Hanif had drowned – it had been at Bamburi Beach, the island's touristy north coast – something about the water's presence beyond them made Rahul think of those who had been claimed by it, never to be seen again. He wished things had ended differently between Hanif and him, that the last time they saw each other Rahul had been anything but cold.

'It's been years, *bwana,*' Riyaz said, happy to let the passing of time somehow diminish the incident, its sadness. Then something, a memory, must have passed through his mind, a lash in his eye, because he grunted.

Rahul handed the joint back to him with a look bordering on disapproval.

Riyaz scratched the mat of glistening chest hair through a virtually unbuttoned shirt, obviously enjoying the breeze tickling through it. 'Tch, ah, come on now, *bwana,* you know I don't mean it that way. But you know, he was . . .' and here he assumed an exaggerated feminine pose, jutting his waist out to the side and batting his eyes at Rahul, and burst out laughing. 'Poor shit, man. Just went and drowned. Can you imagine? How does anyone born in Mombasa not know how to swim? Ridiculous!'

Rahul wondered what it must have been like. Had Hanif struggled, fought for life? At what point must he have released his grasp, given up, known it was futile, just surrendering to the tides? What if he had given himself up willingly, dipping into the lapping water, dead long before it invaded his weary lungs?

'*Bwana,* you know I really don't want to think about these kinds of things, okay?' Riyaz said. 'Tonight is a celebration, buddy, a happy occasion. Why you want to ruin it by thinking such things?'

But in his mind's eye, Rahul saw Hanif and himself facing the same ocean as they had perched atop Fort Jesus all those years ago. A late afternoon and although the scorching Mombasa sun had begun tempering its might, its light still suffused everything around them – the profusion of milky frangipanis fringing the fort, the azure waters of the Indian Ocean dotted with swimmers and dhows, the minarets and gleaming white houses at the shores on the other side. From below them, they could hear the laughter of children diving off ocean rocks and from a distant minaret somewhere, the muezzin's call to prayer.

Very slowly their knees began touching. Then Hanif had started to chat more animatedly – who even knows about what any more? The impending results for their A-level exams? Plans for a foreign university? That rascal headmaster whose tyranny they were finally free of? – and Hanif had grown more physical. Innocent little gestures at first, like squeezing Rahul's shoulder to express sympathy for something arduous, leaning into him and rocking from side to side as he bubbled with mirth, a flick at his earlobe when Rahul teased him. But then his hand landed onto Rahul's lap and stayed there. Rahul let it.

'Who knows? Maybe you would have married him instead of Pooja!' Riyaz said and started laughing so hard that he coughed up his inhalation.

'We weren't nice to him, man.'

Riyaz slapped his back. 'Nice? What nice, nice? Arre, *bwana,* what is all this sudden guilty nonsense, hunh?

Don't worry, I was very, very nice to him,' he said, making a crude masturbatory gesture and then chortling.

Rahul looked at him.

'What? What? Everybody did! Don't act so shocked! So what? It doesn't mean anything, you know that. I just sat there. *Bwana,* I still like chicks, okay? You've seen the fit girls waiting for me in there,' he said thrusting his head towards the party behind them. 'Anyway, what to do? Our girls, man, you know how they are. They won't do it. And a guy needs his release, no?'

Naturally he was right. It didn't mean anything. Shouldn't mean anything. Rahul knew for a fact that all his friends had dabbled in such experiences – handjobs, blowjobs, frottaging, and in rare cases, even actually fucking other boys just so long as they were the 'givers' – and that this was the norm, a rite of passage for boys, leaving not a smudge on their sexual identity. Ultimately, such encounters had served as outlets for oversexed boys in a conservative society where girlfriends didn't grant sexual favours. So when they weren't satisfying themselves, boys sought relief from either their other male friends – as long as this was never actually discussed afterwards and only alluded to when they needed indulging again – or paid a visit to the local African prostitutes at Abdullah's little shanty. But all of Rahul's friends had, in time, gone on to marry the childhood sweethearts who had denied them sex, or were now engaged to respectable women. In many cases, if the friendship had lasted, the male friend who had stood in for their bride now served as a kind of best man in the wedding.

Rahul felt Riyaz's hand on his back but instead of startling him from his thoughts, the warmth brought him safely back to the present. He started to breathe again, feeling Hanif vanish in the darkness of the concealed vast ocean in front of them, the features dissolving until it became tough to piece them back together. 'I'm going to miss you, man,' said Riyaz, and Rahul could have sworn he saw a glistening in his friend's eyes. 'You were always a little too *sidha-sadha*, so clean and proper, but man, I look up to you, you know.'

'Then can you do me a favour?'

'Favour? Arre, brother, anything you want, brother. Just ask! Just ask!'

Rahul pointed downwards. Riyaz looked confused. 'Can you be . . . nice to me also?'

Riyaz was caught for a moment and then he slapped Rahul's back. The two friends started howling away and with arms thrown around each other, made their way back to the club, trying to cull what they could from the joint's dying ember.

All night Pooja suffered her dreams. Many times she thought she had actually awoken from them only to realize, much later, that this too had been part of her dream. When she groggily walked into the dining room, yielding to Kiran's call, bits and pieces of her dream stuck to her like shards of glass in her hair.

The family had gathered around the table, feasting on an elaborate meal prepared by Mariam. The whole house, it seemed, danced in the smell of eggs and parathas fried in ghee and the incenses burning in a corner of the living room did nothing to douse their aroma.

'Aha! There is our *bitiya!*' Ravi announced, holding his hand up.

'These beasts wanted to wake you up! But I said, "No, no, let the poor girl sleep. Maybe she needs it for her little egg,"' Suchitra said, raising her eyebrows at Pooja a few times.

Pooja didn't have the energy or heart to tell her mother-in-law for the umpteenth time that she wasn't pregnant yet and when Mariam had deftly and quite unnecessarily dusted the vacant chair, she seated herself with an obligatory smile. She missed her parents. At a time like this, she wished she could have talked with her mother about the dreams. Very patiently they would have first pieced together and then dissected the dream, like a jigsaw puzzle, as they had so many times when she was a child. Suchitra, while superstitious herself, would have no patience for such analysis and might attribute it all to the ghastly house they were living in and which she hadn't stopped criticizing.

Pooja consoled herself by thinking she should feel fortunate. Most daughters-in-law didn't have such a good relationship with their in-laws. She knew for a fact that there was already some tension between Kiran and Lalita Jhaveri. Kiran had been quick to deprecate her haughty mother-in-law for slathering a good inch of butter on her toast before dunking it into her milky, sugar-laden chai and devouring it, and Pooja couldn't help but say, 'As if someone's gastronomy determines whether they are a good person or not,' to which Kiran had barked, much like her own mother, 'Ai-ai! Keep your big, big words to yourself, okay? But of course it does! As they say, Pooja, "You are what you eat," right? Too much butter equals *maha*-bitch!'

In the night, she had been transported back to her wedding. Everywhere she looked there had been friends and family, milling around in coloured silk and jewellery. Laughter, gossip, paternal admonishments and filmi matrimonial songs hung in the air as the soundtrack of celebration. But Suchitra Kapoor was griping away about someone wearing a black sari. 'What is wrong with her? Why is she here like this! Doesn't she know it's bad luck! Bad luck to wear black!'

Small coloured lights had been strung through hedges and rooftops and pillars and the Kapoors' garden was afloat with merriment. The mandap was in the middle of this garden, where a platform decorated with a profusion of flowers had been erected. The priests, chanting interminably in Sanskrit, sat around the ceremonial fire with Pooja, Rahul and their parents. The smoke from the fire began to bother Rahul, who started to cough a little. He covered his mouth with his hand and his eyes began to water. Pooja looked up at him quickly and with tenderness, concerned. His cough subsided. But was it just because he, like everyone else, had been distracted by that infernal sound coming from the heavens suddenly?

That sound, of crows cawing in the distance, grew louder and louder and she looked up, bewildered to see, through the brocade scarlet sari covering her face, that the sky was swarming with the descent of the dark, unruly birds until the chanting of the priests was drowned out and the sacred invocations ceased. The sky turned black. Pandemonium as people began screaming and running every which way. The fire, only minutes ago blazing, now fizzled and petered out and Pooja quickly thought that this was disastrous, if only because it had helped to keep the birds away.

Mariam stood over Rahul and Pooja and their parents, hollering and brandishing her *fagia* defiantly in the air as the birds dived upon them. She spun around the mandap, doing a strange, mystical gavotte, but soon fleets of crows were pecking away at the canopy, tearing it apart, and the tube frame, also adorned with vines of coloured lights, began to sway so that it looked like the entire mandap would capsize upon them. Mariam fell and didn't rise again.

Through all this, Pooja was the only one who did not scream. She stared, aghast, noticing that Rahul had pulled away from her. He was huddling with the rest of the family and blubbering priests, trembling like a petrified child. But she remained seated there, exactly where she had been before it had all been unleashed, paralysed. He was her husband, was he not? Then why wasn't he protecting her? Or, because the ceremony had been interrupted, they hadn't been wed after all.

Then she saw it, the lone, large crow, perched at the edge of the brazier where the fire once glowed but was now coughing up only wisps of ashen smoke. It transfixed its gaze upon her, its beady, haematic eyes blinking anticipatorily. It did not caw like its minions who'd been sent on their destructive mission. She saw two holes in its beak and she wondered if they were nostrils, if it actually breathed through them. It skipped from one forked leg to another, preparing. That's when Pooja let out a cry, awaking to the sound of crows in the compound outside.

'Tell her, to bring some food for Pooja.' Suchitra told Ravi and jerked her head in Mariam's direction.

But Mariam didn't need to be told again. She knew what was required of her and rushed hotfoot into the kitchen eagerly.

Suchitra leaned over the table, hooking one hand under the chin of her plump, already painted face and smiled deliciously at Pooja. 'So, Rahul called while you were asleep. He'll be here by this evening.'

First Pooja lightened up but then she looked even more distraught at missing his call, the pangs of wanting to connect with him searing. Especially now. If she could only see him, just talk to him, the dreams would disperse like a cloud. She couldn't help but moan with disappointment.

'O-pho! Look at her! Just look at her! He's not going anywhere, beti,' Suchitra said, slapping her wrist lightly. 'He's coming here, where else? Have something to eat, no? And then you can call him and talk to him all you want. But not all morning, okay, I'm telling you!' Suchitra raised one hand as if issuing an edict. 'We don't want to be late, you know. We're going to Woolworth's, that is if that good-for-nothing Salim comes back with the car! God only knows why I agreed to let him go with it.'

'Woolworth's?' Ravi said, incredulous, his hand stopping short of parcelling some yogurt-soaked aloo paratha into his mouth.

Suchitra looked somewhere up in the air, her eyes widening as if a portal had opened up in front of her. She could see the aisles and aisles of things she wished to possess and which she had lately felt deprived of. 'Oh! But of course Woolworth's! Where else?'

'Come on, Dad! Can't come to Nairobi and not go to Woolworth's!' Kiran baited him, nudging Pooja. 'Like going to Greece and not seeing the Pantheon.'

'Or India and the Taj Mahal,' Pooja chortled in.

Ravi grunted at the girls' implausible analogy even as he felt mildly relieved that his wife was feeling optimistic enough to consider any kind of expenditure. By the next day he hoped to take care of business and finalize the deal with the Samjis, putting an end to the tactile, touch-and-feel manner of conducting business that Asians were so fond of. Next to him, Pooja began to laugh. It was precisely because the Kapoors were so different from her own family, constantly bickering albeit innocuously, that she enjoyed their vaudevillian interaction.

Suchitra glared at Ravi. 'Hanh, hanh, you don't have to get an ulcer over it. All I want is to look, bas! Is looking a crime these days? Tell me!' She looked around at Kiran and Pooja for reinforcement. 'And anyway, at this rate, unless that buffoon Salim comes back from God only knows which relatives he has gone to visit, we can't even go somewhere.'

Ravi threw his hands in the air.

But what the Kapoors didn't know, as they began to prematurely celebrate the sale of the college and make plans about their day, was that by then the first gunshots of rebellion had already sounded in the city, and that in only a matter of hours, Pooja's convoluted dream would reveal its actual, more cataclysmic relevance in their lives.

By that morning in 1982, when Pooja struggled from her dreams and her mother-in-law fantasized about ransacking Woolworth's, President Daniel Toroitich Arap Moi had already reigned for five years as the second president of Kenya after President Jomo Kenyatta. Moi first entered politics when he co-founded the Kenya African Democratic Union, or KADU, defending the interests of Kenya's small minority tribes and rivalling the Kenya African National Union, or KANU, which was dominated by ethnic behemoths like the Luo and President Kenyatta's own tribe, the Kikuyus.

After Kenya's independence from British rule in 1963, Moi succumbed to Kenyatta's reasoning that uniting forces would achieve the decolonization process. The white man had been kicked out and now the Africans must unite for a better Kenya! So Moi's KADU collapsed into KANU, making Kenya a de facto one-party state dominated by the Luo and Kikuyu, who had played a pivotal role in ejecting the British from Kenya. But the minority tribes, from this point on, lost their voice forever. Having succumbed to Kenyatta, Moi was now rewarded for his loyalty and swiftly, the man from the Kalenjin tribe, one of the smallest, was promoted to vice-president.

Moi served his benefactor, 'the father of independence',

or *Mzee,* as adulating Kenyans called Kenyatta, with extreme loyalty. He faithfully executed the moderate policies of the Kenyatta era, even surviving several attempts on his office by the Kikuyus who refused to see him as anything but an outsider. 'The Giraffe' they called him, some affectionately and others only because they thought all he did was ravenously lick everything in sight like a giraffe does acacia trees. And then, when Kenyatta breathed his last, 'The Giraffe', over six feet tall and immaculately suited with the trademark rose in his buttonhole, lifted his *fimbo ya nyayo,* and led his country straight into the pits of hell.

Even in Kenyatta's time Kenya had never been free from corruption. By declaring KANU as the single effective political party, Kenyatta had already laid the foundation for a dictatorial regime where independent thought was heresy, and where the fate of over twenty million Kenyans lay in the grips of a couple of hundred elitists. But under Moi the beast of KANU grew bigger, receiving fresh and copious amounts of blood to escalate corruption. Unable to grasp the responsibilities vested in them as leaders of a country, its ruling elite morphed into an occupying force, thrusting the country into a kind of siege.

Opponents in thought or action were detained without trial, tortured, even eliminated without judicial process. Grand looting of state coffers became not only acceptable, but those appointed to positions were expected to contribute to the ruling party's war chest. A brotherhood of sycophants – Asians and Africans alike – became a channel for transferring resources from the poor to the rich, from other regions to that of the president, and finally outside of Kenya, into personal holdings.

That first day of August, a group of Kenya Air Force soldiers, already maltreated by seemingly endless shortages of essentials like food and shelter while the government sank its fangs deeper into the throbbing vein of the nation, decided to overthrow Moi, and rid the nation of its parasites. Kenyans awoke with the radio broadcasting messages by the rebels under Private Hezekiah Ochuka, interspersed with Bob Marley songs. Most of the army was manoeuvring in the northern country and absent from Nairobi. The country plunged into anarchy. The fires to burn away all that had ailed beautiful Kenya had been lit.

Old resentments were reignited.

The Asians, as many were known to say, had it a long time coming.

When Mariam hadn't returned with fresh parathas and fried eggs for Pooja in an instant, Suchitra grew agitated. 'Where is that woman? Is she laying the eggs herself? Poor Pooja hasn't even eaten yet!'

Not in the mood to hear her mother-in-law's fussing, Pooja rose from her seat. 'I'll go check. Although I really don't feel very hungry,' she said, touching her head.

Kiran, still working through an omelet, pushed her plate over. 'Here, here. Have some of this.'

'Not hungry? I really don't blame you. Who wouldn't lose their appetite after waiting for so long!' Suchitra snorted.

Pooja held her hand out and winked at Kiran who giggled. 'No, no, you need that now.' Last night Kiran had revealed to Pooja that she was pregnant. She was going to break the good news to her parents later that day, perhaps over picking out kitchenware at Woolworth's.

'Go, go! Quickly check on that lazy woman before she starves us all! Are you all right?' Suchitra asked, placing her hand over Pooja's forehead. 'There's no fever.'

Pooja, having no energy to explain, just smiled wearily. Talk of demonic crows and destroyed mandaps would only excite Suchitra more. As she walked away, she heard Suchitra call. 'And tell her please to bring some hotter chai as well. If it doesn't require her to go picking leaves for it!'

What most people didn't realize about Suchitra when it came to the servants was that underneath the armour was a large beating heart that only Ravi had been privy to, many times catching her handing out extra cash or salary advances to their servants. Why, hadn't she allowed Salim to take off with the car overnight so he could visit his city relatives? But, the model of race relations between Asians and their African labourers, just as it had been for the British with the rest of the coloured people at one time, was to act tough with servants; otherwise she would be perceived as weak and then they would walk all over her, wouldn't they?

Pooja found the main kitchen in the house empty with no sign of any food being prepared. An elaborate, imported stainless steel gas range sat untouched in its metallic splendour and expensive copper cookware hung around it from a rectangular ceiling rack. She reached up and touched a saucepan, sympathizing with its purposelessness, thinking, she would never let it go to such waste. The kitchen, like so much in the house, was primarily for display.

She wandered outside, hoping to find Mariam in the servant's quarters. She looked up at the sky, and the sun, as if on cue, broke through the clouds, suffusing everything with a golden glow but doing little to warm anyone. There was not a crow in sight and only the garbled sounds of transistor radio coming from Mariam's quarters filled the air. The cold flared Pooja's skin up in goosebumps. From where she stood, she could see that Mariam and the African man she had been flirting with earlier were standing and talking intently in her quarters, the front door ajar and opening into a dark, rather bedraggled room. She grew slightly irritated, thinking Suchitra might be right after all, that servants must be kept under control or they grew quite lackadaisical in their work.

Just then, Mariam and the African sensed Pooja and stopped talking abruptly. Pooja saw that panic was written all over Mariam's face, which she attributed immediately to her being caught at her neglectfulness. The African man, however, looked stonily at her. Pooja, fighting the urge to flee into the house, stood her ground resolutely, channelling a little of Suchitra.

'Mama, you need something?' Mariam asked, and then, without waiting for a response, turned back to the man and said urgently, 'You must go now! Just go, please, Njoroge!' But he hesitated, giving Pooja one last chilling look, and then dashed out of the property and through the open gates like a fugitive on expiring time, the sun pouring on him.

'Chai,' she said. 'We need some more chai please!' Her voice carried the palpable timbre of a command.

'Yes, yes, it is ready, Mama. It is too cold for you, Mama. You go in. I'll bring it in with some eggs,' Mariam said, and reaching somewhere behind her, silenced the radio and lifted out a checkered thermos flask she had already prepared and which she must have been bringing over before she was interrupted by Njoroge. Pooja, suddenly feeling guilty, crossed the gravel yard and went to Mariam's door so she could take the flask in herself and spare Mariam from encountering Suchitra. But once there, she couldn't help her eyes from being drawn into the dwelling, indeed as bleak and threadbare as she had imagined it from the outside. In contrast to the Samjis' home, this outbuilding was in a state of disrepair – rotting wooden doors and window frames, glass panes held together with packing tape.

'Sorry, Mama, I am so sorry, Mama,' Mariam kept apologizing as she handed the flask over to Pooja, who smiled appreciatively and with some guilt. Pooja could see a small unmade bed by the wall and a small window upon it faced the high, grey walls of the compound itself. It seemed that a small dresser upon which was perched a framed black-and-white picture of an African family and a scraggly money plant twisting out of a Gordon's Gin bottle were the only other personal furnishing. This scarcity broke Pooja's heart, filling her with resentment for the Samjis and even her own people.

'Your family, Mariam?' she asked, stepping into the room and pointing to the photograph.

Mariam grew excited, and fetched the picture. 'Yes, yes, Mama,' she said and began pointing out her husband and grown-up sons. 'Mohammad and Bashir both go to school. They're good children, Mama. Very good children. One day, Mohammad tells me, he will be rich enough to own the textile mill at Kangemi. Then I will not have to work any more. But I tell them, how can that be? They are my family too,' she said of the Samjis. 'And they need me.'

Pooja, choked up, put her hand on Mariam's and squeezed it, the picture and warming flask of tea between them.

Then they heard it, what sounded like an approaching mob outside the open gates. The voices of men continued to rise like a mounting wave and it felt like there must be a full-blown stampede closing in on them. There was the crashing of glass, then a piercing alarm followed by angry shouts going back and forth. Both Pooja and Mariam's hearts leapt. Someone cried out, followed by more sounds of breaking and crashing, as if demons had been unleashed. Both women looked out in the direction of the noise but Mariam, being closer to the door, spotted them first. There must have been at least seven of them, armed with *panga* machetes, invading through the open gates. Too late to send her back, Mariam pushed Pooja further into the room. 'Mama, you must hide!' she said, throwing the picture to the side, 'Toilet! In the toilet! Quickly!'

'But . . . they . . .' Pooja said, pointing towards the house.

'Go! Please, Mama, they mustn't find you!'

The flask escaped Pooja's hands but instead of crashing, it rolled out of the door. Mariam shoved her into the bathroom that was just to the side of the bedroom. She had barely pulled the door behind her when the men charged into her quarters. In spite of being brave, Mariam let out a cry when she saw the possessed faces. Pooja, crouching in the dark over a pit latrine, the stench of urine and unadulterated fear driving her to the point of nausea, could see through the slit around the door frame. A tall man came forward and seized Mariam by the neck, lifting her up mightily so that her feet almost lifted off the floor.

'You better stay away or we'll slaughter you, understand?' he bellowed in Swahili.

'Please, don't . . . don't hurt anyone,' she whimpered in his grip, barely able to look into his demonic, bloodshot eyes or breathe against the overpowering smell of *changa'a* on him. 'Take it, take what you want. We have nothing against you.'

Another man, a shorter, stockier one came forward and said, '*You* have nothing against us. But then, why would you? You are also one of us. But they, those people – they do! It's those Asian dogs that we have come for. Come on, *bwana,* tch! Why waste your time with this old owl? In there, let's go in there,' he said, eyes growing wild with excitement. 'That's where our business is!'

Some of the other men were already heading for the house. The others agreed with the stocky man vehemently, urging him on. The tall man, acting like the leader of the gang, released Mariam from his grip and she almost fell to the floor, coughing and gasping for air. 'If I were you, I wouldn't come in there,' he said and then they all turned around and left the quarters as quickly as they had appeared.

While Suchitra launched into her diatribe against Mariam's continued absence, Kiran, having force-fed herself, stood up from the table and serenely walked away to the living room, where a floor-to-ceiling window overlooked a verdant garden. The sun was bright, a shaft of its golden light pouring into the room and upon her. *What must Prashant be doing right now,* she wondered as her hand circumnavigated her still flat belly. In her mind's eye, she saw him behind the counter of the jewellery store, grandly displaying ornaments of buttery gold to clients doing their best to suppress their excitement over a piece and hoping to drive the price down.

She still hadn't told him that she was going to give them the most precious gift of all, holding on to the secret of the life growing within her belly for five weeks now, and only letting her dear Pooja in on it last night as the electricity returned and went away again. Would it be a boy or a girl, she wondered. It really didn't matter, the child would be coddled all the same by everyone. There were names to pick, birth charts to be divined. Just the thought of the fuss Rajanbhai alone would make over this new arrival as he stuffed samosas into his cavernous mouth made her burst into little giggles all to herself.

By the time they heard the commotion, it was too late to do anything. Suchitra rose from her chair. 'See? What did I tell you about this place! God knows what is going on out there. Quickly, let's get Poo –'

The sound of feet thumping through the house was followed by a jarring scream, and only then did Kiran turn around and realize that it was her father who had cried out. A gang of armed men in the middle of the room pulled him off the chair and threw him to the ground. Kiran shrank back and up against the windowpane, realizing all at once what was happening. Suchitra rushed to her husband's aid, falling next to him on the ground. The short, stocky man tried to pull her off him, but Suchitra struck out at him, slashing him on the cheek with the thick gold bangles on her wrist.

'You fucking cunt,' the man snarled as he saw the blood on his face and kicked out violently, hurling her to the side where she lay moaning in pain. 'We've suffered enough at your hands! No more! Shut up!' He kicked her again and again until she lay silently writhing on the floor. As Ravi tried to scramble to his feet, another man came forward and swung the butt of his machete at him, striking him in the head and drawing blood. He slumped to the ground and was silent and completely still.

Kiran, the only one left standing and facing the men, was shaking and sank to the floor, her hand clutching her belly. The tall, muscular leader took the first step towards her, his face breaking into a bloodthirsty grin, and the rest fell into step right behind him, hankering for a share of the prey.

When Ravi Kapoor came to, he felt as if his head had been seared by a branding iron. Moaning in pain, he began to slowly move his body on the cold floor, a mollusk pried off its shell and coiling into itself. Even before his eyes would permit light, he heard the sounds, not any of the screaming – his last memory before everything blanked out – but something much more racking; muffled sobs, whimpering smothered by raucous laughter and grunts.

Momentarily he thought he must be waking up from a dream, that he was still at home in bed and, as was characteristic of nightmares, he would awaken to the real world with the renewed gratitude and relief that a man who had visualized his personal Armageddon would feel. When the light bored into him at last, he wished he were dead.

Suchitra lay stripped and splayed on the dining room table in front of him, not a whimper from her bleeding lips. Her sari lay in a puddle of broken glass and food on the floor. Her disarrayed face was turned to him as if she had been waiting for the moment he would awaken and she would be helpless to shield him from what he would see. She remained expressionless, the light gone completely from her as if she were already dead, even as one man dismounted and another prepared to take his place. Her hair, always either oiled and rolled in a bun or plaited with a sprig of jasmine tucked into a tightly woven knot, now flowed over the edge of the table in a long, dark wave of black, emanating as if from the bruised vermillion mark on her forehead.

As more of Ravi's faculties mercilessly returned, bringing the house and the sounds being choked from it into focus, he realized also that the cries, like those of a wounded animal caught in a steel trap but still clinging to life, were coming not from his wife who lay in front of him, but from one of the bedrooms. He tried to clamber to his feet but managed only to crawl on the floor towards the sounds, his body leaded and revolting against his will. His only thought, however fantastical now, was that he could still do something to save his daughter from more pain.

He saw Suchitra's head slowly turn away from him and towards the wall on the other side, her body long having given up on resistance, still jouncing under the stranger, and it confirmed to him all at once that yes, she was still there, enduring all of this in the face of their complete powerlessness. Ravi's body went into convulsions. It was as if the mind, unable to accept what it was witnessing and having rejected the idea altogether, was now followed by the physical body also, so that there was nothing it could do but try and vomit the poison it had been administered. Spasms of gagging, each one a long, soul-excising retching, disgorged parts of him onto the floor. He had barely managed to crawl over his mess when one of the men, who had just buckled himself back up, strode forward, and, grabbing some artifact that lay in his path, swung it at Ravi, knocking him to the ground and banishing the light from his eyes.

Time was unfathomable. In times of crisis, it is said the consciousness focuses on a single point so intensely that even a moment can seem to last entire minutes, hours, a lifetime. Had she been there for hours now or a whole day? Paralysed by her fear, Pooja had no idea any more. She squatted in the dark, dank toilet of the servants' quarters; the stench now had no effect on her. She could hear only drops of water from a leaking faucet plopping into a wash cup somewhere beside her.

Drenched with sweat and trembling uncontrollably, she remained in that same fetal position long after she had heard the riotous sounds of the men swarming away from the house, their cruel, loathsome laughter, the vile, dissolute remarks about how they had violated the *muhindi* women who always thought they were too good for people like them. She prayed desperately, remembering the suffering of Draupadi at the hands of the Kauravas, how Krishna had thwarted her public humiliation by spooling out yards of fabric to keep her covered. *Keep your hand over me,*

Krishna. Don't let them find me. Preserve my honour as you did Draupadi's.

Why the same god or any one of his avatars hadn't come to the rescue of those that had been trapped inside the house she couldn't bring herself to question. Nothing could make her move, to come out from her hiding place. It was a decision that would come back to haunt her over the years because as she had remained there, clinging to life and safety, Suchitra Kapoor rose from the obdurate wooden table as if she had risen from death itself, and prepared to resolve their degradation the only way she knew how.

Covering her tortured body with the soiled chiffon sari from the floor, Suchitra managed her way out of the main house with determination, pausing just for a moment to look at the silent, humped, blood-soaked body of her battered husband only yards away and her whimpering daughter in the bedroom. It was this sight that almost brought her to the verge of feeling again as if her body had been impaled upon a wall of thorns. She had, after struggling mightily, yielded to their tormentors but Kiran had maintained her anguished pleas through much of it, like someone who, in her impossible innocence, still hoped to preserve or protect something of herself from complete annihilation.

Suchitra came out into the open where the sun had retreated behind a billowing rampart of clouds, plunging the earth into darkness. She could taste her own blood in her mouth as she crossed over to the garage. Stumbling, and falling once from the pain that seemed to cut her body into pieces, she thought of Pooja. Seeing no sign of her, she assumed that her daughter-in-law had suffered an even worse fate and been taken away by the men.

Upon entering the dark garage perfumed with toxic fumes, she found them lined up against the wall in the dark. Leaning over them, she felt around for the lightest one, choosing a can that was only half-full and easier to carry back to the main house.

Nobody can know of this. Not a trace can remain to taint the family name, she thought, tottering back to the house. *We are not the only ones who have endured. Even Sita had leapt into Agni's embrace to prove herself to Ram. We feel closest to God when tragedy strikes us. And in such times, His words resound within us like a temple bell, waking us up to action, to live up to the kind of heroic deeds that we have only read about and heard recitals of, stories which have become the foundations of our belief but which we, until faced with calamity, never thought we'd be called upon to re-enact.*

She was the strongest one of them all, Suchitra had always known, and she wouldn't let them down now that the time had arrived to summon courage.

She stopped in the kitchen for a box of matches before going into the room. Kiran lay in a fetal position upon the bed, a bloodstained sheet barely covering her naked body which heaved as she hiccupped as if still trying to urge the tears that might cleanse her.

'Stop crying, my child,' whispered Suchitra as she approached the foot of the bed gently. 'Soon the pain will end. I promise you it will. You will not have to endure this shame. Always you will remain the dutiful wife, the adored daughter, the protected sister, a joyful friend. I will not let them steal this from you. I am your mother. I can take away your pain.'

When she flipped open the plastic mouth of the can, Suchitra thought she heard a ravenous gasp escape its lips and saw plumes of trapped spirits escape into the air and float upwards to the ceiling. Slowly she hoisted the can up and as the first few drops fell upon Kiran's legs, searing the cuts on her flesh, her daughter cringed and looked up with terror.

'Ma!' she gasped.

Suchitra thought she saw her daughter hold up a protesting hand, her palm decorated with the rust filigree of henna, but she couldn't be absolutely sure. Because in her bifurcating mind she saw something else also. She saw Kiran being rejected by her husband and in-laws, felt her daughter's shame at being defiled by those men; she saw, like a film projected upon the screen of her mind, society's painful and certain repudiation of them all. And suddenly it became clear to her that her daughter had accepted her fate and was in fact offering up her palm print, like the Rajput satis who had left their marks upon the stone wall before climbing upon the pyre. Like Sita, who underwent the trial by fire to prove her virtue to Ram. Or Sati herself who had jumped into the fire of yajna so that she could be born again with dignity as Parvati.

As she struck the match, Suchitra's hands did not tremble, just as she did not hesitate from embracing her daughter as they were engulfed by the flames of purification.

Book Four

'Do you think that you shall enter the Garden of Bliss without such trials as come to those that passed before you?'

– The Holy Quran (2:214)

NO MATTER HOW he tried, Atif could not deny that his dream was coming true at a cost to others. But when a broken Rahul had shown up unannounced at his doorstep at night, as if having survived a violent accident, in his hands the same suitcase that had accompanied them to their retreat in Ojai, Atif enveloped him in his arms while silently thanking God for yielding to his prayers. And through his happiness, like drops of blood that had seeped through a bandage fastened to restrict its flow, some sadness of how he had won his desire stained Atif's elated heart.

Rahul sat on the leather reclining chair where they had made love so many times, wordlessly hunched over and looking into the ground as if he had lost something. It made Atif think of the Sufi parable of Mullah Nasruddin, who had lost a coin inside the house but was looking for it under a lamp post outside because the light there was so much better.

'I didn't know where else to go. I don't know what this means,' Rahul said without looking up, not wanting Atif to interpret this in any way as final, still grappling with his confrontation with Pooja.

'You don't have to,' Atif replied, kneeling down and squeezing himself between Rahul's legs.

'I'm sorry, I didn't want to be alone.' He covered his face with his hand.

'You're not.' Giddy inside, Atif tried to remain contained, another Urdu adage his father frequently employed streaming through his mind: *Never forget that serpents haunt even sandalwood trees.* 'And it doesn't have to mean anything,' he added, uncovering Rahul's face and taking it in his hands, hearing the lie escape his lips like beads rolling off an unravelling rosary.

Each day without Rahul felt like a lifetime to Pooja. A full week after the night Rahul had left, Pooja had driven out to his office in Westchester, hoping that the reason he had agreed to see her was that he had come to his senses and wanted to come back home where he belonged.

She had requested that he meet her outdoors, in the parking lot, where the planes descending upon the nearby LAX airport appeared so ominously close and cyclopean that they were like mythical creatures – Vishnu's mount Garuda or Ram's Hanuman – shaking the earth with a sonic boom and casting a penumbra over mortals. She had been uncertain if Rahul's co-workers already knew about their rift. Unprepared for the sympathy it would arouse or, even worse, the pretence required to act as if nothing had happened in front of obsequious employees like his assistant, she felt it was best to avoid going in altogether.

When she saw him approach her with that characteristic gait of uncertainty, his broad shoulders drooping lightly as if under the weight of his own strong physicality, she felt the conflicting forces of desire and anger arrest her. There was nothing she could do or say to convince herself that this man she had committed her heart and soul to, whom she had followed to the ends of the earth, wasn't still her husband and soulmate, that nobody could take him away from her. But having to see him here, in some parking lot instead of their home, made her want to scream. Ultimately though, it is impossible to shun those we love or to seek vengeance against those we pity.

They embraced – he tentatively, she ardently. If he had noticed how her anguish had begun to ravage her – the dark circles around her eyes, deeper lines cutting into her face and undisguised by make-up, the sheer nervousness of her being so that she appeared unstable between the love she still felt for him and the grievance it was also beginning to provoke – he said nothing. She looked up at him and although she wanted to touch his face she restrained herself, afraid that the gesture of affection would unravel her. 'How are you?' she asked, the words sounding hollow, absurd, as if it had been she who had left him and brought them to this place.

Rahul nodded, gave a tired smile.

At the neighbourhood pizzeria, he introduced her to the Italian owners without the slightest hesitation or awkwardness as his wife and when they excitedly reached over the counter to shake her hand, she caught a look, however fleeting, of pride and affection on his face. They had walked in right before the lunch crowd, sitting quietly at a corner table. She barely nibbled through a slice of thin-crust cheese pizza that the owner's son had chivalrously provided at no charge to celebrate meeting her. She watched Rahul's large hands as he salted and folded his slice before taking a healthy bite; strong fingers with neatly clipped nails, the tangle of veins, rising and falling beneath the skin matted with thick black hair as his fingers moved; she missed his touch. But then she thought about the boy, saw his face at the bookstore, considered how the same hands had touched him, were touching him, and the anger rose in her again.

Rahul sprinkled red pepper over his pizza and suddenly she found herself resenting even this quotidian act. How can his taste buds, like other aspects of his life – colour coordinating his clothes, dousing himself with his Jaipur cologne that even now made her spin with desire, shaving, breathing – not have lost their meaning in the aftermath of their parting?

She toggled back and forth between these two states – complete tenderness vacillating with abrupt corrosiveness. She loved him and now she was beginning to resent him because it seemed he didn't love her enough to fight for them, or even to appear disrupted. Watching him cater to his epicurean needs, she found that her love had commenced a frightening and irrevocable transition into something else, something darker, more alloyed with hate.

'How's Ajay?' he asked, his eyes protective, cautious.

She dabbed her mouth with a paper napkin. 'He thinks that all of this is his fault. He wants to know where you are. I didn't know what to tell him. I told him we were trying to work things out.'

'And in the meantime? Where did you tell him I was?'

'On a business trip.' Knowing this explanation would only suffice for so long, she looked up at him expectantly. Here was his cue to confirm what she had said, to impress himself back into her life.

Rahul put down the slice of pizza, struggling to come up with words. 'Could you tell him . . . Maybe tell him I'm staying with a friend, a room-mate or something?'

She looked at him, almost undiscerning for a moment, then made an exasperated sound. 'Room-mate? You want me to tell him his father has moved in with a room-mate?' She slapped down her slice on the plate and looked out of the window, beyond the parked cars. A moth clung to the pane of glass from the other side, inches away from her face. Its forewings were the colour of burnt leaves but there were startling markings in red, as if it was stained by its own blood. She thought of the countless poems and songs paying tribute to the *parwana* or *patanga*, which flung itself recklessly into the *shama* or flame, its passions overruling any concern for its own life. And this is just how she burned for him, wanting desperately to cling to him, to immolate herself into him.

'I'm sorry,' he said abjectly, realizing he was hurting her. 'Maybe I should talk to him. Explain . . .'

She looked at him, seized with sudden rancour. 'Talk to him? And tell him what? What are you going to tell him?' She turned away again, disgusted. How dare he? How dare he stoop to such filth and still have the temerity, the sheer audacity, to explain himself to his own son as if he had renounced his family to become some kind of selfless mendicant? All these years, they had protected Ajay from the ugliness of the past and now he wanted to expose their son to this? *He doesn't miss Ajay. He doesn't miss me. He wants to make this final.* This became evident to her now that Rahul was so willing to explain everything to Ajay. She couldn't understand how he could do without her, why he suddenly didn't need her, but because she couldn't bring herself to say this, she said, 'If I spend a little too long away from my son, I feel as if my life is going to end, like I'm losing my mind, and you, you make it seem like you can just . . .'

Rahul opened his mouth to say something, as if he was shocked she would even think such a thing – that this wasn't hurting him as much as it was hurting her – but then he just smiled sadly and looked away as if it was no use admitting how much he loved his son, how just because he was the cause of this, didn't mean it was any easier on him or that he relished seeing her in pain. When he looked back at her, Pooja thought she detected a glassiness in his eyes and she suddenly felt sorry for accusing him thus, even though hurting him made her feel good at least momentarily. Besides, wasn't she partly to blame for the distance between father and son? Looking back now, she realized she had been so possessive, so protective and readily available to Ajay, that it had left little room for Rahul to insert himself.

Some bystanders waiting for their order at the counter had started taking notice. Rahul smiled awkwardly at them as Pooja tried to rein herself in, again looking away into the distance as tears sprang into her eyes. The moth had fluttered away, not a mark left on the glass. She felt bereft, as if its departure also added to the betrayals.

'I think things, terrible, terrible things,' she spoke again, dazed. 'It's not like me to think these things. And yet, I don't know what to do, what's happening to me . . .'

He placed his hand gently upon hers as if to say, *everything that has happened to you has happened to me too,* but the warmth of his touch, the subtle pressure he applied in it, made her long for something more, a reaction far more impassioned than the one he could give. And suddenly she was able to recognize something she might always have known about the man she loved but which she had never acknowledged as a handicap – that a man caught in the traps of his own conflicts becomes inert and loses the capacity to feel himself as a moving force.

Rahul was always quite willing to answer any questions posed to him, but he felt lost when left to his own resources, as if his opinions, his own faculty of expression had been swallowed up by inner chaos. This detached, tormented, impenetrable part of Rahul was what had attracted Pooja to him from the very beginning, so it became painful for her to see now that the very thing that attracted her was the thing that eventually drove her away.

Rahul retracted his touch but her hand remained on the patch of cold Formica, fluttering as if something valuable had been snatched out of it.

'I want to say things, profound things,' she said, 'Something to make you stay. I know there are some words, there must be some words, no? Something? Something that can change . . . what you're doing to us.

But I feel the moment, it just comes and goes. And there are no words. They don't come to me. Nothing. I feel lost. Don't know what to say. Where are the words?' she asked, her eyes welling up.

He reached out, squeezed her hand again. Yes, she could see that it was painful for him to watch her like this but his pity, devoid of reconciliation, singed her and this time, she drew back her hand.

'I'm sorry. I should see him,' he said, nodding his head resolutely. 'I should talk to Ajay.'

'I'll tell him,' Pooja said, her hopes escaping in a tender sigh. 'I'll tell him you're staying with a friend. For now, the less Ajay knows the better.'

Having lived by himself for so long, Atif had grown accustomed to his space and freedom. Like someone who gets used to a physical defect, like the scar on his lip, he had made peace with his solitude, even grown possessive of it. So when Rahul moved in – first for a few days, which turned into a week and then, after Atif had convinced him to stay on, indefinitely – there came a period of adjustment, of the realization, not altogether hindering, that he had been delivered again to the world of familial ties and intimacy.

For the first time in Atif's life, space had to be made. In the hallway, so that much larger shoes, buffed to an immaculate shine and enforced with cedar trees, could park alongside Atif's sneakers and penny loafers; in the closet, where dusty, long forgotten, mustard-coloured pants and hooded flannel shirts had to finally be discarded in garbage bags so that tailored Armani suits and crisply pressed white shirts could also hang; in the bathroom caddy where the silhouetted bottle of light sesame oil had to sit next to a hulking can of shaving foam; on the sofa, where the left side offering the best view of the TV set was no longer Atif's for the taking; and the bed, where the middle, once just a spot from which its breadth seemed reduced and tolerable, where Atif could lie like a Vitruvian man and convince himself of spatial luxury, became the place where solitudes now melded as two bodies jostled together.

All these things he celebrated. In his mind he heard one of the few filmi songs that Zainab Aunty had enjoyed and which the iconic actress Nargis had sung to her real-life lover Raj Kapoor in the film *Awara*:

Ghar aaya mera pardesi,
Pyaas bujhi meri aankhiyan ki
Tu mere mann ka moti hai,
In nainon ki jyoti hai
Yaad hai mere bachpan ki
Ghar aaya mera pardesi

My lover has returned home
And quenched the thirst of my eyes.
You are the pearl of my mind,
The light of my eyes,
The memory of my childhood.
My lover has returned home.

These were the lovers' rituals Atif had been denied and which, after decades of yearning, he thought he would never share. Now they were his and he revelled in their mundane enchantment. He found Rahul, not just stealing hours from the day to be with him, but present without haste or negotiation. Atif realized that they had passed a kind of test. They were bound on a soul level, down to their very molecules and as such, he would never have to worry about the trivial inconveniences inherent in living together. These were negligible little thorns that had to be clipped off, overlooked, if flowers were to be enjoyed.

But somewhere in the back of Atif's mind lurked the fear that all this could be taken away from him just as easily. A marriage of decades, a grown-up son who carried Rahul's name, and a lifetime of conditioning still awaited Rahul on the other side. Atif did his best not to discuss any of this, as if even bringing up Rahul's family in a conversation was opening a door to them. For as long as he could, Atif would continue to pretend Rahul's decision was irrevocable, their future together sealed, inevitable.

Pooja saw that nothing ever dies. Everything that happens – all actions and emotions – is trapped in the walls, the spaces, furnishings, leaving *vasana*s, imprints that haunt long after the incident.

The possessed house drove her into the streets where at least momentarily, she found some solace in being one of the city's agitated drivers, unable to just drive off or away from her affliction. There were seldom any clear streets in Los Angeles and many times, clasped in the middle of traffic, on a street with no reason and among people who couldn't reconcile the city's congestion no matter how many times they encountered it, she found a strange comfort in their collective anguish.

Many times Pooja ventured to the bookstore as if by catching a glimpse, by observing the behaviour of the boy who had stolen her life from her, she might be able to understand more about the man she had been married to for more than twenty years, whose child she had borne, and who now remained a mystery to her.

Maybe, she excited herself into thinking, she could

reason with this boy, plead with him, appeal to his heart, some sense of justice, and make him see just how wrong all of it was. But every time she had been there, she could get no farther than the parking lot where Sonali must have caught them. Her own shame became so intense that her body began burning, her blood flooded with heat, and she drove back home to employ new words, fresh tears to plumb more desperate modes of emotional bartering to convince Krishna to come to her aid. She would give anything, do anything, endure anything if Rahul came back to her. It was not just her love that was being tested now, but her faith too.

After praying, whenever hope whispered, she remembered their meeting at the pizzeria, his resolve to come clean with their son, the complete lack of any regret in his voice or countenance, and she felt gutted until feeling itself abandoned her. From morphine numbness to terror, she shuttled back and forth, wondering if she was losing her mind, if it would be easier to just end her life. Then surely Rahul would suffer, he would mourn, the shadow of guilt would be cast upon his new life. But then she thought of Ajay and even though he was a grown-up man now, she knew she could never leave him with the kind of emotional legacy that Rahul's parents had bequeathed them.

Then one day Pooja saw the boy. It was a little past noon and from where she sat in the parking lot, she saw him walking back into the bookstore carrying a bouquet of tuberoses wrapped in brown paper like a baby in his arms. They must have come from the farmers' market nearby. She fought the urge to confront him, to tear the fragrant stalks into bits. *While he was perfuming his world with her husband,* Pooja thought, *her own world was being charred to ashes.* At that moment, she felt like her entire body was coated with salt so that every injury she had ever suffered in her life was inflamed. She stayed in the car and broke down crying.

Pooja's catering suffered. The last order of cashew marzipan that Parmesh had picked up had been made with too much sugar. Charlie had called to ask if Pooja was trying out a new recipe and if she could go back to the original recipe customers preferred. She no longer dolled herself up for appearances, caring nothing for the exoticism she once tried to impart. What was the point? While she had been simmering curries and chopping up almonds and cashews into a fine paste, her husband had found solace and shelter in another man.

The moment she had fallen to barely rinsing the basmati rice, to emptying jars of store-bought simmering sauces into the saucepans and using packaged spice mélanges instead of hand-picking each ingredient like selecting notes for a symphony, Pooja stopped taking even the few private orders from the loyal though infrequent clients in the Palisades. Why care? Would they know the difference? Apparently not. There had been no callback of any sort, no complaints. She had made her impression in the very beginning and now they subscribed to her unquestioningly, just as she had believed in Rahul and had continued to follow him through this thicket of betrayal.

It was only when she heard Ajay's Mustang pull into the driveway as he came home from hanging out with his friends or from researching colleges at the library that she bothered to pick herself up and make light-hearted banter to belie her incompleteness without Rahul. Even then, seeing the topography of Ajay's face so resembling his father's, she felt a stab of pain and she wanted nothing more than to be confined up in their room where she could mourn, beg, or remain inert.

At times, when she lay paralysed in her bed, she felt no different from when she had hidden in the dank bathroom all those years ago, too scared to face the world outside, a world without him. Except this time, Salim the driver wasn't there to find her and pull her out like a whimpering child to see the horrors of a mass crematorium, a house burned to its very skeleton.

She did notice, however, a change in her son. Almost overnight, Ajay seemed to have grown up, turned more sombre. He began spending more time around her, growing watchful, his eyes lingering upon her strained efforts to seem unfazed in her abandonment, and suddenly she wanted nothing more than for him to stay away as much as possible so that she could stop pretending. She could almost hear his mind, his emotions working up into a lethality that began with seeing his mother's pain and then, through it, reaching his own.

Ajay found that the homes of his American friends were always brimming with life. There was the uninhibited, boisterous conversation about politics, movies, ideologies, life. Sometimes he also became privy to the eruption of an untimely disagreement between Nicky and his divorcee mother Ro, who had a bottle of shelf gin attached to her like a limb, so that Ajay had to excuse himself from the scene while Ro called her son a 'good-for-nothing fuck' like his father and Nicky called his mother a drunken whore. Ajay was thankful that at least such things never happened in his home, but then again nothing else ever did either.

Apart from the confrontation Ajay had with his father late one night in the kitchen, most of the time the Kapoor household felt like an abandoned set, one upon which the drama had already unfolded but which had yet to be dismantled. The players, out of respect for a performance they had once banded together for, continued cordiality while moving on with their new lives – his father claiming to work obsessively at the bank and his mother left to confide in gods and cook curries. Whenever he did find his parents in the same room, there was always a marked composure. It was as if they were trying to keep their balance on the delicate bridge of glass between them, one that could easily be shattered with even the hint of a passionate outburst.

Now he felt he knew the real reason for this pretence. They had been deceived all along, forsaken long before his father had found the courage to move out and make it official. Remembering the time when he had confronted his father and been lied to knifed Ajay with the pain of betrayal. Witnessing his mother slip away into the depths of depression, no matter how hard she tried to appear unfazed, clutched him with a combustible rage, one that he tempered with the occasional hit of crystal Nicky provided for free.

It didn't matter what his mother said any more, about how people drifted apart; all that was just bullshit. It was clear as the dark crescents around her eyes and the whimpering that wafted from behind the closed door of her room through the night that this 'drifting apart' was not of her choosing. She was just trying to protect him from the truth – the well-intentioned yet dishonest act that parents became complicit in.

When Pooja opened the door to a nervous Sonali one morning, she was filled with a sense of relief she never thought she'd experience with the bearer of such bad news.

She smiled weakly, too drained to carry any grudges. Even the way she had responded to the door, without any urgency – because the person she really wanted was not going to show up anyway, so what was the point? – was indicative of Pooja's resignation.

'I'm only here delivering this package the UPS left at my place,' Sonali said quickly, defensively, one hand holding out a box and her body half turned away from Pooja in case of a brush-off. But it was obvious to Pooja that Sonali had dolled herself up in this buoyant yellow blouse, crisply pressed white pants and immaculate make-up and hair just to run this little errand in the middle of the day. In contrast, Pooja appeared downright bedraggled.

When she gently took the parcel from Sonali's hand and stepped aside to let her in, Sonali had a proper moment to take in Pooja's appearance. The look that washed upon Sonali's face was an undisguised combination of sympathy and concern, the likes of which Pooja had never seen.

'Please, come in, Sonali,' she said, opening the door wider. Sonali hesitated only momentarily, shifting from one foot to another like an apprehensive child before stepping in. Whatever Sonali Patel's faults, she was not to blame for Rahul's unfaithfulness, thought Pooja. Bringing this information to her had required courage far greater than the perverse joy Sonali normally distilled from other peoples' troubles.

Sonali settled gingerly onto the sofa while Pooja placed the package on the coffee table and went towards the kitchen. 'I'll just get us some chai. It'll take a minute only. Or do you want some lassi? You prefer lassi, don't you?'

'No, no, really, don't worry,' Sonali said quickly. 'Just some soda will do.'

Not used to Sonali being so amenable, Pooja paused suspiciously in the kitchen doorway. 'You sure? It's not a problem at all, really.'

'Oh, too hot for chai anyway,' Sonali said, tossing her head back and fanning her neck theatrically with her hand. 'Some cold-cold soda will do. Oh, but diet please! You know I have to watch my weight.'

Pooja returned with two glasses of cola with rocks of ice, and placed them on the coffee table without bothering about the coasters. Almost immediately a thick pool of sweat formed at the base of the glasses, threatening to destroy the teak's lustre.

'Ai! What, there's no coasters or anything?' cried Sonali. 'Put something quickly under the glasses. You'll ruin the beautiful table!'

But Pooja sat back in the armchair next to Sonali and smiled indifferently, as if this was her very intent, little acts of vengeance against the home that she had built with Rahul and in which he was no longer interested. This seemed to make Sonali even more cautious and she looked at the ordinarily sensible Pooja carefully, wondering what was coming next.

'Your package,' Sonali said, nodding her head at the table. Pooja just shrugged without any concern. Taking a sip of the soda, Sonali looked dreamily into space and broke the awkwardness. 'You know what I miss about Mumbai? Vadapav and Masala Coke! My God, sounds so ridiculous when you think about it, doesn't it?' she said, letting out a high-pitched laugh and putting an immaculately painted hand over her mouth. 'God, what an assault it is on poor Coca-Cola! I swear when the soda starts frothing up, it's because it feels assaulted! I tell you, Indians just can't stay away from their masalas.'

Pooja gave a short laugh, appreciating Sonali's attempts at lightening the situation. How it humanized her, she thought. Who would have thought the Sonali who boasted of her lust for beluga caviar, actually had secret and nostalgic cravings for the humble roadside food eaten mostly by slum dwellers? In the sudden lightening of that moment, she thought ruefully of just how much she missed the companionship of an adult, a familiar face with whom she wouldn't have to pretend sanity. In what had clearly been an exile no different than what Sita had endured with Ram, she could see that what she has missed most about being back home, in Kenya, was the company of her friends, lounging in the patio under the ylang-ylang tree, laughing, gossiping, talking about inconsequential things, dreaming, trying out clothes and jewellery, indulging in double entendres and lewd remarks. Despite everything, she was grateful that Sonali had done so much to recruit her as a friend, because America had deprived her of the friendship and warmth that emanated from people of the same country.

Pooja said with a melancholy smile, 'I miss roasted maize . . . with chilli and lime, and *mogo* crisps served in those large newspaper cones. We used to eat that every Sunday at the Lighthouse.' Almost instantly she remembered resting her head on Rahul's shoulders as they contemplated their future together while standing at the edge of the Indian Ocean. Her smile faded as if making way for the moisture in her eyes.

Sonali sighed powerlessly.

'I am so sorry for behaving the way I did, Sonali. It isn't your fault that this happened. It's just that I didn't know how . . . I still don't how to . . .'

'Oh, Pooja! I know what you must be going through,' she said, pressing her hand against her heart. 'I so wish I hadn't even been there, that horrible day. But maybe it was meant to happen, you know, so that you would discover the truth.'

Pooja started crying.

'Pooja, be strong.'

'It's just so . . .' She could not bring herself to speak.

Sonali made a sound, half impatience and half sympathy. 'Pooja, my darling, we women, we can't just give up. We cannot let these men destroy our spirit. We live for more than ourselves, do we not? You have Ajay to think about, that poor boy.' She unclasped her purse and fished out a pack of tissues and handed one to Pooja. 'Wipe your tears, darling. Oh, they really don't do any good. Trust me, I know. I know.'

And although she should have appreciated the sympathy, Pooja looked at her and felt the uncharacteristic urge to scream and shout and hit her. What was Sonali living for, her chimes? How could she have any idea of such suffering? After all, even her husband Sanjay had been a model husband and doted on Sonali until the day he died. 'I don't know what else to do,' she said, the tissue like a crushed gardenia in her hand. 'I've tried everything.'

'You can divorce him,' Sonali said, wagging her finger in the air vehemently. 'That's what you can do! Pooja, you know you'll be taken care of for the rest of your life. You know that, don't you? There's not a court even on Mars or Jupiter that will let him get away with this shamefulness!' But when Sonali saw Pooja shaking her head, the mere suggestion of such an act making her wince like someone was plucking the hair out from her skin, she clamped up. 'I'm sorry, Pooja. Oh, but what else is there to do?'

'You're trying to help, I know that, but I cannot hear of such things. No matter what has happened between us, we're married.'

'But is that what he wants?'

She looked away, remembering her last meeting with Rahul.

Sonali, seldom at a lack of words, tried, saying, 'Did you . . . I mean, were there any signs? Surely, there must've been.'

'No. Yes. I don't know,' she replied contemplatively.

'You've heard about how if you drop a frog in a pot of boiling water, it will jump out. But if you place it into a pot of warm water and then slowly turn the heat up, bringing the water to a boil, it will just stay there. Get boiled to death.' Pooja looked at her imploringly. 'Nobody must know, Sonali. Please, you must promise me! If anyone found out . . . if Ajay . . . Oh, God.'

'No, no, what are you saying?' Sonali said, leaning forward and squeezing Pooja's hand reassuringly. 'You have my word, darling. Nobody will know, absolutely nobody. Your secret, it is my secret. But,' she added emphatically, 'you can't go on like this. Oh, I can't stand to see you this way! At least for now, Pooja, you must promise me that you will go and see your doctor. Get something, some antidepressants or something? They will help, Pooja, really.'

But Pooja looked lost again, as if another life was being played out in her mind and her body was simply delaying following its thoughts into another realm. Sonali dipped into her purse again and pulled out her cellphone. 'I know your type,' Sonali said, punching a few buttons until she arrived at what she was looking for. 'You will do nothing, just suffer. I'm going to make your appointment with my very own doctor. I'm sure he'll take your insurance so don't worry . . .'

'No, no, Sonali!'

Sonali leaned back determinedly from Pooja, waiting to be connected. 'Come on, Pooja, we have a deal now and I intend for you to keep your end of the bargain. There was a time,' she said ruefully, 'when I should have done something but could do nothing. But now, yes, now things are very different indeed.'

Alone again. Her back propped up by the decorative pillows she had always been careful not to crush for fear of unravelling the delicate beadwork and embroidery, Pooja tugged the opening stub of the UPS box, only to find that it snapped midway. The beads on the pillow pricked her back through the thin cotton kurta, but she did nothing to avert the discomfort, remembering only how she had chided Rahul for plopping down upon them, how he had asked what was the purpose of such pretty things if they didn't at least provide some comfort?

She pulled from the other end of the box and lifted out a hardback wrapped in white tissue. Gently, she unwrapped it, found a hefty collection of poems by the Persian poet Rumi. She flipped through the book, glanced at the neatly compiled stanzas, and then back at the shipping label on the box, made out to Rahul. She had never known Rahul to enjoy poetry. At once, she knew this was intended as a gift for someone else, something ordered a while ago, while he was still here. Imbedded in the book, she also found a receipt with Rahul's Internet purchase transaction. She put the book aside, feeling the urge to cry.

It was then that she thought of the Internet and looked across the room at Ajay's laptop lying on the kitchen counter. Pooja brought the laptop to the couch. She flipped it open and was greeted by ethereal northern polar lights on the screen. The sky, lit up with green and red strokes, made her think of the gods in their heavenly abodes. She heard Ajay's voice in her head, asking her to verify the fan-like icon in the top margin of the desktop before clicking on the logo of an orange fox circling the globe to connect to the Internet. Pooja had used the computer occasionally to research recipes, read up on Kenya, Bollywood, but mostly when Ajay or Rahul had been around. It was the reason for her using it now that made her nervous this time.

She stared at the search engine, feeling like she was about to step into another dimension, one from which she may not return the same. Never in a million years would she have thought she would need a computer to better understand her husband, yet here she was, a book on Persian poetry lying next to her, Charlie's words in her mind.

She searched the words 'gay' and 'Indian' and was bombarded with hundreds of responses, the first one being a two-minute video of stand-up comedian, Vidhur Kapur. The last name, though spelt differently, panicked her. She clicked on him and was transported to YouTube, where Ajay had once surprised her with a selection of Bollywood videos. The bald-headed, animated man was armed with a microphone and pranced around the stage, bemoaning his fate as a gay Indian immigrant in America. Pooja found herself amused, even impressed momentarily, by his flawless imitation of old, gossipy Indian matriarchs. She confirmed to herself with some satisfaction that this was what a gay Indian looked like. Same last name or not, Rahul and he couldn't be more dissimilar.

Barely a minute into the video, Pooja used the go-back button and cut the comedian off, returning to the list of responses, all of them confirming India's disapproval of homosexuality. She tacked on various other identifiers: 'religious text', 'holy books', and even 'Is it okay to be', but each time the response was unequivocal and condemning. Then she remembered Charlie's mention of the *Padma Purana*. She searched again.

At the top, she was shocked to discover a gay and lesbian association for Vaishnavism, a monotheistic tradition of Hinduism that worshipped a supreme God who was known by different names according to his avatar or perspective. On this site, she also found a glowing review of a book about same-sex marriages. Discounting this as an isolated case, Pooja returned to the responses, searching deeper, and stumbled upon several Hindu-based sites that not only supported the gay lifestyle, but also provided caches of ancient texts to justify it. Among these, she found 'Behind the Veil', a thesis by two academics, Rani Seth and Vinod Basu, revealing the prevalence of homosexuality in their religious texts and culture.

Suddenly, Pooja found it difficult to breathe or believe her eyes as they fell upon an italicized fragment in the centre:

> *. . . And when Ashvatthama asked Krishna for his discus, Krishna replied: 'Phalguna (Arjuna) than whom I have no dearer friend on earth, that friend to whom there is nothing that I cannot give including my wives and children has never made such a request' (Sauptika Parva, XII).*

Pooja flinched, looking away from the screen, perturbed by Krishna's grandiose yet callous willingness to sacrifice everything for his friend. What kind of friendship – divine or otherwise – could take precedence over a marriage, children?

Like all devout Hindus, she knew only too well about the profound friendship between Lord Krishna and the Pandava warrior Arjuna, the famous pair on whose battle-side discourses at Kurukshetra the whole Bhagavadgita was based, but she had never encountered such ancient texts, never let them assume such personal impact. The Gita, the Ramayana and the Mahabharata were the foundation of Hinduism but what was all this? She read some more, about Krishna's last night at Hastinapur before returning to his city, Dwaraka:

> *'. . . all of them entered the respective apartments. Krishna of great energy proceeded to the apartments of*

> *Dhananjaya (Arjuna). Worshipped duly and furnished with every object of comfort and enjoyment, Krishna of great intelligence passed the night in happy sleep with Dhananjaya as his companion' (Ashvamedha Parva LII).*

I'm being stupid, Pooja thought, *taking all this so personally, reading so much into all this.* Often indivisible, Krishna and Arjuna were thought of as divine and human aspects of every being, born in the world to fight against unrighteousness. They were a metaphor, surely, for the love between God and his devotees.

She put the laptop aside, over the book, and leaned back into the sofa, its beaded thorns now abraded. She looked up at the white speckled ceiling, her confrontation with Rahul in the kitchen echoing. Could she have said something to change the way it had all turned out? What if she had maintained her silence, refused to confront him even when pressured to do so, would he still be here then?

For a moment all thoughts left her mind and the ceiling, an opaque sky that seemed to have suspended its fall just short of crushing her, offered her complete nihility. But the respite, like the elusive dip into infinity during meditation, passed and she wondered, as she often had as a little child, what the world would be like if it were turned upside down. If the chandelier, instead of hanging upon her, stood erect like a stalwart guard and she had to walk around it; if the ceiling offered ground and the ground provided shelter. If, instead of feeling pain as a constant, she felt more of nothing, a merciful numbness, and the pain became intermittent.

Where was her Krishna when she needed him?

Why hadn't he come to her aid?

He could give his friend Arjuna anything, including his wives and children so why couldn't he give her – his devotee – her husband back? *Why can't you help me? Why won't you give me what I want?* she demanded. *What else can*

I do? What words should I employ? And then, she thought about her mother praying in their puja room back home, of the countless heroines of Hindu lore that had been tested, and she thought, *I must remain strong. Miracles happen, intervention occurs, but so many times only at the very last second and not a moment before that.*

Lifting her head, her eyes fell on the lit screen again. She hesitated momentarily, placed the computer on her lap, scrolled down the page, found more:

> *'... My wives, my kinsmen, my relatives, none among these are dearer to me than Arjuna. O Daruka, I shall not be able to cast my eyes, even for a single moment, on the earth bereft of Arjuna ... Know that Arjuna is half of my body' (Drona Parva LXXIX: 153).*

Riled, she scrolled further down, trying to escape the electrifying declarations of ardour between the two superheroes of Hindu lore. And what of Radha? What of Meera? What of Rukmini? she wondered. Or any one of your sixteen thousand wives? Your children? You can live without them? Do they mean nothing to you? Why only him? How was she supposed to find solace in a friendship that discarded all other relationships?

Page after page, the thesis only confronted her with more of the same. Her eyes, trying to find something of the love between Krishna and Radha, or the ink-skinned god's love for his Gopikas with whom he had multiplied himself at the banks of the river, encountered only Krishna's passion for Arjuna and, in one startling passage, even the god's transformation into a woman called Mohini so that Krishna could marry the Lord Aravan and help save the world from another catastrophe.

This must be what Charlie was talking about; all this was nothing new, it had been there since the beginning of time, in us, in our gods. But what the hell did these people know? It was just like them, those daft white people, taking something sacred and twisting it to suit their own depraved thinking! The thought – no matter how well intentioned – that some ashram-trotting, nirvana-starved gora was manipulating the gods to justify Rahul's depravity, threw her into a furore. He could go and brainwash all those yoga-addicts with his exotic brand of Hinduism but she was not stupid. Somehow she managed to ignore the fact that the authors of the thesis were Indian, and diverted her anger to Charlie.

She clicked a button and closed the window, sending the information into a void. The heavens came back into view, her gods still hiding behind the aurora borealis. She shut the laptop and cast it aside, promising herself to give Charlie a piece of her mind, not even realizing that she was crying again.

Where was the Krishna chasing the milkmaids, loving the cowgirls, reuniting with the neglected Radha, rescuing Draupadi, giving his sermon at the battlefield, stealing butter?

This was not her lord.

That evening, Ajay returned to a home engulfed in darkness, his mother asleep on the sofa downstairs with her arm thrown across her face to shut the world out. She had been wearing that same dress for the last two days. She didn't even stir as he made his way through the living room and for a moment, it seemed as if life itself had seeped away from her. He stood over her in the dark and when he saw the almost imperceptible movement of her chest, he was relieved. Her face was turned away from him and into the sofa like that of a punished child who had cried herself to sleep.

Ajay had always known how much his mother loved his father, her demonstration of it as heady and potent as his father's was repressed and veiled, but this display took his breath away, and gripped him with red, hot rage. He hated himself for being unable to protect her and he hated her for her devotion to a man unworthy of it. Now, as he pulled the scarlet Kashmiri shawl over her, he was overcome with feelings so powerful and discrepant they were nearly primal, and he knew, in that instant, that he would do anything to protect her.

Who was this cunt that had bewitched his father? What did she look like? How had she made him forget all else?

While Ajay and his father had never spent as much time together as some of Ajay's friends did with their fathers – at Dodgers' games, throwing down beers, working around the house – he had never doubted his father's affection for him, that special brand of distant yet irrefutable love which was felt more than seen. But now that Rahul had moved out literally overnight without even telling him or expressing any regret, without giving Ajay the chance to tell his father how he felt, it became obvious to him that he and his mother meant nothing to Rahul, that his father's lack of demonstration was not just a personality trait but an expression of his inability to love them.

He looked at his mother one last time, then tiptoed his way quietly up the stairs to his room, determined to find out where and why his father was hiding.

For once in her life, Pooja wished that the person she was dealing with hadn't been another Indian. While the young, green-eyed, handsome Dr Arvind Patel did nothing to make her feel in the least bit self-conscious – none of the lingering looks that Indians gave one another or any kind of personal inquiries like what part of the motherland you or your family came from – she still felt embarrassed at being there. The fact that he shared her maiden name didn't escape her either, as if the moment he was done with her, he was going to get on a long distance phone to let everyone in the community know about her apparent breakdown. Being there, not for an infection or physical pain, but because she was unable to cope with her husband's abandonment of her, was a clear sign of defeat, a failure on the part of all the powers that were supposed to sustain her.

What would her own mother have said if she could have seen Pooja here like this, sitting on some examination table just because she couldn't stop crying? Why hadn't her fastidious upbringing buttressed her more? Why hadn't her prayers, if they couldn't move mountains, at least given her the strength of one so that she hadn't ended up here, crumbling and crying in a cold room with reproductions of Monet on the walls, as if the pale, sun-faded water lilies were going to bring her any kind of ease.

Dr Patel sat on a low stool and looked up at her on the table. As he spoke, asking general questions about her medical history that were obviously meant to elicit insightful responses as to her present malaise, Pooja noticed the chipped nail polish on her toenails and curled them into her sandals like snails recoiling from an attack. Dr Patel, noticing this, paused in mid-sentence only momentarily before catching himself, and then to prevent further embarrassment, continued, 'How's everything at home, Mrs Kapoor?'

She reacted ambivalently, shrugging and nodding at the same time as if her body was caught between two responses. Then, feeling awkward because of this, she managed to sound just as confused. 'Okay, I think.'

'How much sleep are you getting?'

'Some . . . well, actually none, not at night, none at all.'

'I see,' he said, forming a tight smile. 'And how are you feeling these days?'

She began to speak but then stopped, afraid her voice would break and that tears would gush from her eyes. She looked around the room frantically. Then she grew suddenly angry at his insipid questions. She was there, wasn't she? So shouldn't he know? What exactly did he expect her to say? 'No, no, this is all a mistake. I mean, I'm not even supposed to be here,' she said and started to get off the table, the thin tissue cover tearing under her.

Dr Patel raised his hand and said appealingly, 'Please, Mrs Kapoor, please just stay a few minutes. We're talking, that's all.'

She acquiesced and looked at him as if for the very first time. Too young to be Rahul and too old to be Ajay, Dr Patel was somewhere in between. *What part of India was he from,* she wondered. *Who were his parents? Was he married? And most importantly, how had it all turned out so right for him?* She noticed the gold band around his finger and decided that for no other reason than the fact that he was wearing it, he must be a devoted husband. Why, his very profession inclined him to be nurturing. And then just as quickly, she wondered if he, too, was harbouring some dark, shameful secret that his wife was unaware of, something that one day would tear them apart.

'You don't have to tell me anything you don't want to,' he said, and there was so much kindness in his eyes that Pooja's moistened up. 'But I may be able to help somehow, you know? If there's anything you're going through.'

'She told you, didn't she?'

'Who?' he looked around, confused.

'What did she say?' Pooja looked away from him, covering her face with her hand. 'We're going through a separation.'

'I see. Sorry to hear that.'

'But it's only temporary, you know,' she said quickly. 'Nothing we can't work out.'

'Of course, of course. Still, that must be hard.'

'You are married, doctor?' she said, jerking her head at the band on his finger.

He smiled. 'Four years now.'

'Children?'

'Yes,' he smiled even wider. 'One of each.'

Her head tilted up and she seemed to leave the room completely, the vision in her mind lifting her from all despair. 'I remember how it was at first,' she said, a tender smile on her face. 'We were so . . .' she could not bring herself to say it. In love. 'It's hard, yes, but I'll be fine. I will.'

'I have no doubts.'

'I just came because she insisted, you know? Sonali can be so persuasive, you know that, don't you? You're her doctor.'

He nodded with a smile. 'Everything's going to be all right,' he said, and this made Pooja smile. 'I'll prescribe something for you, just something for a week or so and then we can see about . . .'

'I just wish the pain would stop,' she said flatly.

'Well, it will help. But I would really like you to see a specialist . . .'

'No, no, not right now,' she said, waving her hand. 'This is enough for now.'

'Okay, we can talk about it in a week and decide then.'

Pooja smiled and fought a strange urge to touch Dr Patel. The crisp white coat, his lush dark hair, golden brown skin, the very scent and carriage of his youth made her yearn for a kind of transmigration to new beginnings. 'You are from . . .?' she found herself asking.

'Torrance,' he said, rising to his feet.

'No, I mean, where are you *really* from, you know, originally.'

'Torrance, California,' he maintained. 'I was born here.'

Her face fell. 'You're just like my son. No past.'

He looked at her strangely. 'But my past is here, Mrs Kapoor. Surely everyone has a past no matter where he's born,' and then, realizing that he may have sounded insensitive, added, 'But my parents, they were born in Uganda.'

'Uganda! In East Africa!' she cried, suddenly beaming.

'Yeah.'

'I'm from Kenya, you know?' she said excitedly. 'I was born there. My father also and his father before that. In Mombasa. We're like neighbours . . . I mean, you're not from there but still in a way we are, you know.'

'Yes, I suppose we are,' he acquiesced, smiling.

'Did they have to leave because of Idi Amin?' she asked, distressed.

'No, no,' he said, smiling as if he had encountered this assumption many times before. 'They left long before that tragic episode. They were lucky.'

'Yes, thank God,' she said. 'Many were not.'

'I want you to call me in a week, okay? Sooner if you need to and let me know how you're doing,' he said and then more emphatically, 'And I really want you to consider seeing that specialist.'

She nodded wearily as if the weight of the world upon her shoulders was being negotiated.

He paused at the door and looked back at her. 'I wonder what it's like, Uganda, I mean. I've never been to Africa. I'd like to go there some day, take the family on a safari or something.'

'We went, you know,' she said excitedly, 'On our honeymoon. So many people, they just want to go abroad to London, Canada but Rahul and I took a safari. After that we found out we had won the lottery to come here. I'm glad we did it while we could. You could live your whole life some place and still not know just how beautiful it is, you know? You'll love it, I guarantee it. The people, the country, the food . . . it's home, you know?'

But it was obvious Dr Patel couldn't relate to her attachment; he didn't point out that they were referring to two different places in Africa, neighbouring countries though they might be. Smiling warmly, he said instead, 'I'll be right back with some samples, okay?' and left the room.

Pooja looked at the Monet again, the two white water lilies floating alongside in a murky black pool even as time and the environment had stripped them off their brilliance. Still they remained, weathering all. Her eyes drifted past the walls and out of the window to the endless, pale sky dusted with so much smog that it too looked to her like a painting robbed of its colours.

Ajay reached the bank branch in Westchester a little before five p.m. in case his father left early. In the open lot, he parked a safe distance from the black Mercedes and guzzled down a can of Red Bull while listening to a Tupac collection, his fingers thrumming on the steering wheel.

As he waited patiently, eager to see his father, it occurred to him that Rahul had worked for the same bank for more than ten years now and that the last time he had visited him here Ajay had been only thirteen. One of his fondest memories was when, over lunch, his father had escorted him to the large department store across the street and indulged him in the trendy acid-washed jeans with the rip on the knee. He had clamoured for them but even Pooja, who normally gave in to all his demands, had stood firmly against this latest fad. 'This?' she had cried, pointing at a fashion magazine spread he had brandished to validate his taste, 'This is how you want to go out in public? In *fatela kapda*s? Well, then why don't you just bring me some scissors and I can cut out all your pants for you. No need to spend money just to look poor!'

Even the Garden Café – devoid of an actual garden – where Ajay and Rahul had eaten cheeseburgers on the patio was still there, still trying to compensate with plastic ficus trees and wall murals of tropical flowers. It made Ajay long for the rare and special times with his father and the feeling, instead of calming his rage, only intensified it.

A little after five-thirty, Rahul appeared in the parking lot, tall and majestic in a way that would make any son proud. Ajay lowered the volume on the stereo and studied his father almost clinically in the couple of minutes it took for Rahul to reach his immaculate car, throw his leather briefcase and jacket in the back seat and get into the driver's seat. He realized that he knew almost nothing about his father, this man who had given him life but whom he had admired only from an unbridgeable distance and as a result, had never wanted to imitate him, be like him, aspire to be him.

Yes, he knew that Rahul had been a heroic cricketer in his youth back in Kenya, the country that neither one of his parents ever wanted to talk about and which, even to Ajay, only meant what it did to most Americans – an exotic land known for its safaris and coral reefs. He also knew that his father, unlike most Indians who were mired in superstition and tradition, was an atheist; that Rahul, since arriving in America, had been a banker, one whose career had run the course from being a stellar salesperson to burning out in mediocrity. And he knew from the coy remarks of his mother that his parents had been in love when they had married.

Still his knowledge of his father amounted up to so little in the end, fragments that gave him clues but never constituted a full picture. How could one be born of someone, occupy the same orbit, breathe the same air, and still know so little about him? Could the link between father and son be this tenuous? Things that you always thought were eternal – your parents, the love between them, their love for you – could be lost overnight?

He followed his father on a thirty-minute drive, always keeping three or four cars apart, through Marina del Rey, past their street – Rose Bouleverd in Venice, where Ajay almost expected his father to turn – and into the heart of Santa Monica where the weather dipped a few degrees thanks to the Pacific's beneficence. He watched his father parallel park the car in a permit zone under a tree profuse with magnolia blooms and cross the road to a three-storey building.

Ajay, parked about a block behind, close to a church and on the other side of the street, was so overcome with the burning need to know more, to see the woman who was responsible for all this, that he didn't even think about how it would look if he were caught. He sprinted out of the car and to the building but Rahul had disappeared from sight by then. He foraged through the building, trying desperately to detect something, perhaps the voice of his father or that of his welcoming hostess, catch a glimpse of them through the vertical blinds of the apartments he tried to peer into, but he saw and heard nothing, only the insipid laugh track of a sitcom from someone's television set and the din of someone hammering away. His father, it seemed, had been transported into another realm, one to which his mother and he had no access.

Crestfallen, he began walking back to his own car when he noticed the parking permit hanging on the rear-view mirror of his father's car. That fact that it hung there constantly, indicating a kind of permanence, hurt him. He bent down and peered through the vehicle's tinted window. A forty-something woman walking by briskly in a sweat suit, sun visor, and gold crucifix pendant around her neck eyed Ajay suspiciously and for a moment, Ajay wondered if she could be the woman his father was seeing. When he stared back at her she picked up the pace fearfully and disappeared around the corner. On the plastic permit, under the holographic logo, he found what he was looking for.

Apartment #5.

After several indomitably foul-tasting shots of alcohol at a billiards bar in Santa Monica, Ajay and Nicky made their way through the traffic of Wilshire Boulevard to a trendy new bar in Hollywood.

Nicky's connections assured their unencumbered entrance into any hot spot roped off to most who weren't close to the managers, so they were in no rush to get anywhere on time. 'Fucking pretentious bougies,' Nicky would often say of the celebrities, the spoiled and mostly white patrons, and the club owners who called him incessantly for one party-favour or another, sanctioned his dealing in their clubs and secured his VIP status. 'They may have all the fucking chips in the world but they're nothing without me. Fucking crackies. I have no cheese but let me tell you, bro, I live better than they do!'

The mobile phone was still in Ajay's hand from when he had punched in an aggressive, inebriated girl's phone number at the bar as they had exited. When the phone both vibrated and emitted the current R&B chart-topper momentously, he thought that it might finally be his father. It was a blocked number. Assuming it was some girl stalking him, Ajay pushed a button and dismissed the call. The disappointment made his anger mount and he contemplated visiting his father at that very moment. He took more shots of the caustic, unpalatable booze, feeling his legs tingle and the world around him appear subterranean.

'So, has he called you yet?' Nicky asked, sensing his friend's preoccupation.

Ajay shrugged. Being familiar with Nicky's past, how his father had deserted them when Nicky was only four, he knew his friend had no faith in fathers or in familial ties. But this wasn't supposed to be happening to him. He had been brought up in a different world, one in which he had always felt protected by his parents, a world in which they had always been there for him and for each other; if the placidity of his parents' relationship had signified anything to Ajay, it had been their maturity, that they were a dutiful couple, far from the passionate, calamitous couples that ended up in divorces and cannibalized each other through attorneys. 'He'll call sooner or later.'

'So, he hasn't?' Nicky persisted, coming to a stop at the signal. A red Ferrari zipped past the red light and the traffic signal camera flashed twice. Nicky howled delightedly. 'Oh, shit! That wiseass is gonna' get a bitchin' surprise in the mail tomorrow,' he said, bursting into high-pitched hysterical laughter which was typical of him when he was high, but which was so incongruous with his tough, intimidating demeanour that even after all the years of friendship, it never ceased to startle Ajay.

'He's called a couple of times,' he replied miserably.

'Man, if he was *my* father . . . If I only knew where that

fucker was,' Nicky said contemptuously, his eyes still looking into the distance where the car had sped off while all sorts of violent thoughts boiled up in his mind, 'You know what pisses me off, man? It's not that he's not around no more. I mean I don't need his ass anyway, right? I can take care of myself just fine. It's just . . . you know, isn't he even curious to know what I look like? Who I am? Anyway, so what're you gonna do?'

The lights changed and the car resumed its trek through Westwood, past the National Cemetery on the left and the Federal Building on the right where crowds of protestors were picketing against Bush's foreign policy in Iraq. Some of the cars honked their endorsement and the bolstered crowd raised their picket signs higher and cheered in appreciation.

Ajay remained gripped by the thoughts of his suffering mother and selfish father. As hard as he tried, he was unable to squash the thought that in the end, his father was no different from Nicky's, that ultimately they had also been abandoned; only in this case, he actually knew where his father was, only minutes away, had access to him, could confront him, ask him why he didn't love them any more, ask him how it could be this easy to turn his back on his family, and suddenly he was not willing to let the bastard get away with it.

'This is why there's all this fucking traffic!' Nicky growled. 'Man, these assholes elected the retard, now they're all surprised he can't do shit right.'

'Take us back.'

Nicky looked at his friend, confused. 'Back? Where?'

Ajay, looking straight ahead but already immersed in the tumultuous, agonizing realm of his mind said, 'Back to Santa Monica. I want to see that son-of-a-bitch.'

It's rare to find unadulterated happiness because it is impossible to get what you want without hurting another, to gain for yourself without depriving another. *Such contentment,* thought Rahul, sitting on the couch and staring at the phone in his hands, *can only be achieved either through a complete excision of conscience, a disregard for everything but the object of your desire, or the expunging of all desire itself.*

What's the use of all this, he asked himself, looking around the living room which only after weeks had already started to feel like his own, *if I have to lose my son and quash Pooja, who has stood by me all these years? And yet, is there truly any way for me to go back to a life of make-believe?*

Having given him a few minutes to make his call, Atif came back into the room. He sat next to Rahul and put his arm around him. 'Give him time, Rahul.'

Rahul nodded catatonically and it was obvious he wasn't convinced that time would solve anything. Atif wanted to say more to make him feel better even though he also suspected the futility of this. As long as Rahul had to sacrifice his son and wife to be with him, he would always feel condemned and, to some extent, Rahul would remain inaccessible to Atif. As he rubbed Rahul's shoulder gently, he reminded himself that sometimes matters were in fact better left in abeyance, that the compulsion to solve everything in the present was an imperious, Western way of thinking.

He tried to take Rahul into his arms, but Rahul resisted, lost.

'I remember when Ajay was born,' Rahul said. 'It was only his mother and I. No grandparents or uncles and aunts, no one. Just Pooja and I. It was a difficult birth. He had to be pulled out with forceps. But he came out bellowing,' here he gave a short, proud laugh, acknowledging his son's fortitude and drive. 'After everything that had happened, he gave me a reason, you know? Life would continue through him, beyond us, and the past would . . .' he flinched. 'But he's had a lonely childhood. Pooja grew so protective of him. And I kept thinking I'd hurt him somehow, I don't know. I haven't been a proper father to him,' he said sorrowfully.

'No, no, no,' Atif said vehemently, touching his face and making him look up. 'You've been a great father, Rahul. And I'm sure he knows. I'm sure of it.' Atif thought of his own father, the phone call that never came, and he thought, *I wish you had been my father*. 'But if you *really* want to do this, Rahul, why not go and see him? Trying to do this over the phone . . .' he trailed off.

'Because I'm afraid. There will be more questions. Questions I don't know how to answer.' Rahul looked at Atif, the fear apparent in his eyes. 'How do I tell him about myself, Atif? About this? I don't have a road map for something like this . . .' Rahul remembered his conversation with Ajay in the kitchen, the disgust in his son's voice when he had described how he beat up some guy for making a pass at him. How could Rahul tell his son he was no different?

'Sooner or later, maybe, maybe he'll . . .' but then Atif remembered his own situation, how his parents had been unable to understand or accept, and suddenly his faith in other peoples' tolerance evaporated.

Rahul attempted to clear his throat but then he buried his face in his hands and hunched over in his grief, beginning to cry. As the tears washed through him, his body convulsed. Atif took him in his arms. *There's so much you can tell about a man from what breaks him down*, he thought. For his own parents, it had been the abject humiliation of being cursed with a son who would not live up to their expectations or be admitted into their very discriminating version of heaven. For Rahul it was the loss of one love to gain another.

Though Rahul was right there, Atif grew afraid that he would lose him again and that this time, no prayer or promise would bring him back. A reservoir of fear pushed against the walls of Atif's ribcage, agitating him, making him so nervous that he wanted to hold on to Rahul and never let him go. He could smell Rahul's odour, and felt so affected by it that he leaned into Rahul, began kissing him, but Rahul resisted, steeped in pain. Atif persisted more gently, rubbing Rahul's broad back, kissing his ears, neck, eyes, offering intermittent assurances that everything would be all right.

Finally, Rahul grew aroused by Atif's affection and yielded, pushing him down on the couch with force, covering Atif's body with his own. They did not kiss, their love-making impassioned but choleric. And as Rahul drove himself deeper, like a man evading the tyranny of his conscience, Atif tried to convince himself that their love story had triumphed.

By the time Ajay had climbed up the flight of dimly lit stairs to where he expected to find his father and the woman who had taken him away from them, he had missed Rahul by just minutes. Having picked up on his smoking habit again, Rahul had walked over to a liquor store a few blocks down the street for a fresh pack of Marlboros.

Ajay used the cat-knocker to rap on the door a few times even though he noticed that the door was in fact ajar. Looking back at Nicky, he said, 'Maybe you should wait in the car,' but then they were both startled when the unmistakable voice of another man from the inside groaned and then called out, 'Oh! Did you close it? I told you to leave it open. Hang on, Rahul.'

For a fleeting moment, hearing a man's voice relieved Ajay of all his suspicions. Perhaps his father was staying with a friend, someone he knew from banking, and all his fears about another woman would be unfounded. He pushed the door open and stepped into a chimerical apartment dancing in the light of candles and the perfume of flowers. The floor under his feet was strewn with clothes – men's underwear, boxers, socks, undershirt and white button-down dress shirt and, further away, glowing iridescently at him like a snake in the carpet, his father's opulent paisley tie, the same one his mother had given to his father and which they had joked would be Ajay's inheritance some day.

Stepping further in, his eyes took in the spray of tuberoses on the coffee table, the yards of books on shelves and against the walls and his father's weathered leather briefcase, which could no longer be found by their door where Rahul would discard it after a hard day's work, but here, in its new place by a desk in a strange apartment. And there were pictures, framed and placed strategically around the well-designed apartment, of his father with another man against scenic backdrops in moments of amusement and leisure.

Nicky stepped in behind him. 'What the fuck?' he said with a shocked, mocking laugh.

'Rahul?' Atif came out into the living room just then, stark naked. Finding the two strangers in his home, he first looked confused and then shrank back, horrified. 'Who are you?' he cried, bolting back into the bedroom.

Ajay remained frozen, as if an invisible hand had assembled the pieces of a jigsaw puzzle and revealed to him his worst nightmare. And even as he stood stationary, the room, indeed the whole world, seemed to spiral off its axis and overturn. 'Impossible . . .' he gasped. He didn't feel his friend tug at his shoulder, didn't hear him say, 'Ajay, let's get the fuck out of here, man.'

His body moved almost robotically towards the bedroom from where he could hear the boy talking to someone frantically behind the closed door. He pushed against the door and even as Atif tried his mightiest to hold himself up against it, he was no match for Ajay's barbarous strength and was eventually knocked to the ground, the phone tumbling from his hands like an ineffectual toy and vanishing somewhere under the disarrayed bed.

'Please, don't hurt me,' Atif said, scrambling to his feet and cowering back against a wall at the end of the room. 'Just take whatever you want, okay? Please . . .' He grabbed a red and orange towel from the floor, the same one he had blanketed over his belongings in the suitcase when coming to America and which, for some inexplicable reason, Rahul and he used to wipe themselves up after sex.

'Where is he?'

'Who?' Atif cried, noticing that the boy's face looked strangely familiar. Was he – could he be – Indian? And then, like seeing a Rorschach image revealing itself through the thick brows, intense eyes, flaring nose and full lips, realized that he was looking at a version of Rahul. He turned to the other boy, pleading, 'Please, please just take him and go.' But here again, as if by a bizarre coincidence, he recognized another face, felt a chill of dread go up his spine. 'You,' he said, pointing at the towering companion, 'I . . . I know you . . . Nuru! You know . . .'

The blow struck him with such force and speed that Atif didn't even see it coming and, his mind suddenly a blank sheet of pain, he fell backwards and onto the ground. 'Shut the fuck up, you fucking faggot! You don't know nothing!' Nicky roared. He turned to Ajay almost frantically now, rubbing his knuckles in the palm of his hand. 'Come on, man, we gotta bail! Now!'

But by then Ajay, who had been standing still, his mind taking in more of the universe in which his father had been only minutes ago – the soiled sheets like frozen currents of what had undulated between his father and this guy, more pictures of them intimate and blissful, his father's leather sandals – one turned upside down – at the foot of the bed – found himself possessed of forces beyond his control. 'You,' he said, his voice subterranean in his own ears, 'you did this to us.'

Atif struggled to his feet, tasting the salt of blood in his mouth, holding his arms up in anticipation of further assault. 'Please, we didn't mean to . . . he didn't . . .' but there were no words that could convey the regret about how much pain had been caused, the inevitability of what had already happened. In that moment, Atif wished he could have found a way to comfort the person who not just resembled, but came from the man he loved. He wished that rather than defending himself, he could have allayed his assailant's pain. But something, a long-suppressed suspicion of how his luck would eventually run out, his own distrust of life or just the pure, unalloyed hate in Ajay's face told him that things would not work out well. 'Please, don't . . .'

Ajay, white-faced, his eyes like coals from a brazier of rage, barely mindful of the terror in Atif's eyes or his crying, grabbed his slender neck and started shaking him violently.

Atif choked, his hands flying up to his neck as he struggled to free himself from Ajay's hands. For an instant, he thought that this wasn't really happening, that Rahul would be back any moment and rouse him from this nightmare, that perhaps his total disbelief could make them vanish. Miraculously, he broke free. Gasping and coughing, he tottered further back into the room only to find himself cornered against the wall. Another blow from Ajay crushed the air from his trunk, sending him reeling. He almost slumped to the ground but was held up by Nicky as Ajay emptied himself out like a cauldron of fury.

He cried out in pain, blood spilling from his mouth, but was only hit harder, in his face, his belly, his kidneys, his legs, until he no longer knew where to put his hands because his whole body howled out in pain.

Released, he finally tumbled onto the floor. He scraped against the unyielding wall, emitting a great gush of spittle and blood, and begged, but remained a trapped animal. 'Come on, man! Let's get the fuck out of here!' he heard someone say but when he looked around, he found he could see almost nothing, all sight blocked from his swollen eyes. He began groping in the dark, put out a hand pleadingly.

> Against a blood-soaked sky the sun dipped into the Arabian Sea; the sound of rickshaws and cars and humans and animals on the streets grew to a deafening cacophony as deformed beggars and street urchins with plaintive glances and carefree smiles deftly manoeuvred their way through it all; his mother and Mrs Vaid hung washed, colourful bed sheets over a line flapping with laundry on a latticed balcony, clothespins in their mouths; he saw the ecstasy on the face of his lover, the pearls of perspiration rolling to the tip of Rahul's nose and dropping upon his own face like raindrops on parched earth.

It was then that Ajay grabbed a heavy metal candleholder from the bedside table, the candle toppling off and drizzling melted wax that had not congealed, and delivered his next and final strike, swinging with both hands from the right down to the left and smashing it against Atif's head which collided with the wall like a clay pot.

They scrambled down the stairs, steps at a time, and by the time they landed on the street it seemed to Ajay in some erroneously preternatural way that they might still be able to get away. But by then, the 911 operator had recorded the entire episode – the gruesome cries, the violent clamour. Next door, Nona, labouring away in chat rooms, had grown alarmed by the sounds coming through the walls and made her own frantic call to the police. An alert tone had been sent over the radio frequency and multiple police cars had already descended upon the block and surrounded it.

Ajay and Nicky bounded to the right of Montana Street, neither one noticing that the area had been sectioned off with armed police officers poised strategically around the block and alley. Three more officers had swarmed the apartment and found Atif's bloodied body. Nicky, a few paces behind Ajay, was the first to hear, 'Police! Stop!' and froze at once but Ajay heard nothing and continued to sprint towards a church, its steeple piercing into the night sky, still clinging to the bloodied candleholder under his arm. By the time he heard the warning for the first time as it was repeated, he had reached almost the end of the block.

He continued to run, envisioning only a vacant street around the corner and driven now not by the unearthly rage that had possessed him only minutes ago, but by the terror of his deed. His mother's admonishment of his unrestrained temper over the seemingly trivial incidents in the past now gained the full power of their prophecy and flashed through his mind even as he recognized the irrevocability of what he had just done.

An officer, his gun at Ajay, appeared from around the corner and onto the pavement like an apparition and commanded him to stop. His mind a blank sheet of terror, Ajay decelerated, his arms flying up reflexively. But then the candleholder escaped him and Ajay swooped his right arm back down and under his side in an attempt to catch it. A thousand spikes of light pierced him from behind, stealing his breath, pinning him in the air. He crumbled to the ground where the candleholder had rolled away from him, staining the magnolia-strewn cement with blood.

A small crowd of bystanders had gathered behind the barricade of police cars and bright yellow tape – neighbours who had left their TV shows halfway and rushed out onto the street to investigate the commotion, pedestrians who had paused on their way to a nearby pub so they could view the public spectacle of private disaster, and at least one bedraggled homeless person who had hitched up his overloaded grocery cart of brown paper bags by the curb to survey the scene with the look of indifference only a person on an intimate basis with tragedy could muster.

Rahul came down Montana Avenue and approached the barricade slowly, smoking his cigarette. At first it all felt distant, like he was part of an audience witnessing a tableau of crime in the movies, but with each step he took towards the apartment building he had left only minutes ago his eyes fixed upon the landing behind the cordoned-off area where ambulance men, investigators and police swirled in a flurry of activity. His heartbeat quickened to a frenzy. He tossed away the smoke and manoeuvred his way through the crowd until he got to the front where he dipped under the yellow crime scene tape to cross the barrier. He was immediately forced back by a burly mustachioed officer.

'Wait, but I live here,' he protested, pointing at the building.

'I don't care where you live,' the officer responded gruffly, pushing him back behind the tape. 'Nobody's going anywhere right now.'

'But what's happened? What's going on?'

'Sir, we'll let you know as soon as we're giving interviews, okay? Please get back!'

Rahul checked his pockets for his cellphone and was dismayed to find he had left it in the apartment. He looked around frantically, feeling helpless and not seeing anybody in the crowd he recognized. He asked around the crowd in case someone knew what had happened and was told by a woman in a pink housecoat with rollers in her hair that apparently someone had been robbed and attacked but that thankfully they had caught the assailants.

He walked over to a pay phone on the corner of the street, from where he could still keep an eye on the scene, and called the apartment with the loose change from his cigarette purchase. There were a few eternally long rings, during which he found himself desperate enough to pray that Atif would answer the phone; by the time someone finally answered – a strange male voice – Rahul's eyes had spotted something else through the filigree of commotion across the street. He could see the strangely familiar, slumped figure of the person they had apprehended in the back seat of the police car parked in clear sight all along. The prick of recognition made his stomach lurch and the receiver, still emitting the sounds of someone from the other end, escaped his hands and thrashed against the brick wall.

He started walking back to the scene, his eyes fixed on the hulking person over and through the band of bystanders, as terror webbed up his legs and covered his entire body. Each step turned the axis of his world upside down. He pushed through the crowd roughly, his only thought to get to the car and nullify the vision forming in his eyes.

A detective bounded over and grabbed him before Rahul could tear past the yellow tape and reach the car. Although Rahul couldn't hear anything as he struggled against the detective holding him back, he felt that he must have been calling out because just then Nicky turned around and looked over his shoulder through the rear window at him. In that look of fear and penitence before Nicky turned away and hung his head low as if on the lunette of a guillotine, Rahul knew that all was lost.

He wished it were day instead of night. Somehow, the rays of sunlight, while not easing the pain, might have helped to at least provide a less morbid setting for it. God alone, if he even existed, thought Rahul, knew what still kept him on his feet – moving, speaking, breathing – even as he desired nothing more than to stop living. Perhaps it was the duty of this final act – of unleashing this catastrophe upon her – that prevented him from any kind of escape. After he had identified both Ajay and Atif, their bodies had been taken in for autopsies. By the time he used his keys and entered the house undetected to the sound of women laughing, it was past midnight.

She was in the kitchen, enjoying a late night cup of chai with Sonali when he showed up. It was good, he thought, that they had patched things up. They had bridged their separation and were talking about Greg's obsession with Hinduism. Sonali was making a joke, how in Mumbai a cow may be elevated to temple worship but if it dared filch even a red onion from the street vendor, an avalanche of sandals would descend on its big rump, holiness be damned. It had been so long since he had heard Pooja laugh so openly, without the burden of pain that occluded mirth's boisterousness, and he realized how precious it was. In all the years he had known her, she had never laughed so loudly, so openly, as if doing so connoted some flaw in decorum.

He walked straight into the kitchen, startling them.

Seeing him, Pooja drew in her breath sharply. The room froze, both women surprised. For several seconds Pooja sat still on the wooden stool and looked at him, smiling uncertainly. He thought he detected a spark in her face, hope rearing its head, and before she could react more fully, he wanted to lift up his hand and stop her from coming to him and putting her arms around him, to tell her not to rejoice. It would make everything he had to say that much harder. He wasn't coming back. He was not there because he missed her, just to snuff the last flicker of hope from an existence already labouring in the winds of life's cruel vicissitudes.

As was typical of her, Sonali was the first to speak. 'Okay, well, maybe I should go,' but she made no move to do so; this was much too juicy an occasion for her to miss unless she absolutely had to. She didn't have to worry because Pooja put her hand out, asking her to stay if only to show her resoluteness. A coward who had managed up to this point, but unsure if he was equipped to handle the grief of a mother, Rahul was secretly thankful.

'Pooja,' he said. 'Something terrible has happened.'

She slowly rose to her feet. The dread from his face seeped into hers, covering it like a shroud. He looked into her wide, trusting, amber-coloured eyes, and felt a protective instinct so strong – even though ruthlessly delayed – that he could only compare it to what a mother must feel for her child. For a moment he saw her again as she was all those years ago, unsullied by his faithlessness, the woman he had systematically destroyed; then just as quickly the image vanished, and as a single tear spilled over and onto his cheek, he saw fear ripple across her upturned face.

'What is it?' she asked, touching his arm.

'He, Ajay, he went to see Atif, Pooja,' he said carefully, as if gathering shards of glass from the floor. 'Something terrible . . . there was an accident.'

'Where is he?'

He shook his head, unable to look at her. 'They're both . . . gone.'

Sonali grasped his meaning but Pooja remained only dimly aware of what he had said. 'Gone? Gone where? I don't understand.'

Rahul, his head hung low, wished he could have given up his own life to prevent this moment. But it was too late now.

'Rahul?' she said, shaking him by the arm. 'Is he okay? Is Ajay okay?'

He shook his head, the words stuck in his throat.

'Where . . . what . . .' she glanced at Sonali, back up at him, terrified.

'They're gone, Pooja,' he said, his eyes finding her again. 'They're both dead.'

Slowly she pulled herself away from him. She felt completely removed from everything around her, as if she was from another dimension and the burden of emotion was the misfortune of an alien race. There were muffled sobs from someone standing somewhere behind her, the sound of a neighbour's dog barking way in the distance as it was being taken for a night jaunt, and a name she felt she must respond to being repeated over and over again by the man in front of her. Then, the merciful hand that had plucked her out of the tableau of grief dropped back into it, and as her bones began liquefying, Pooja felt herself sinking to the ground.

Outside their bedroom window only the faint rustling of the jacaranda tree could be heard. It was quiet otherwise, almost four-thirty in the morning according to the digital clock on the nightstand to which he used to wake up each morning. Rahul sat by Pooja's side as she lay lifeless but for the breath that moved her body almost imperceptibly under the red Kashmiri shawl. The room, stiflingly hot in the middle of July, did nothing to quell the iciness of her silence or how she felt within.

Even after Sonali had left, Pooja hadn't asked how it had happened, as if by some uncanny sixth sense, she had already envisioned it, and had now, drained of all hope, slipped into the underworld where she must echolocate through permanent darkness. In time, she would want to know everything, every detail, but for now, she had entered that black hole of grieving into which all questions are devoured and answers, in their futility to reverse disasters, become insignificant.

When he had tried to explain to her that he hadn't been there to prevent it, she had turned her head away to the other side of the bed and held up a shaking hand not to him, but to her own mouth, in the process silencing him, afraid that disrupting the silence of her grief with unavailing words might at once force her into complete disintegration before she could see her son again.

He remained by her side, minutes stretching into hours, wondering how he could have seen this coming, how he might have been able to barter his life for theirs. When she finally spoke with a flattened, shell-shocked drone, she said, 'Take me to him.'

An image of Ajay, covered in blood, flashed through Rahul's mind and he couldn't bear the thought of letting Pooja see their son that way. 'Tomorrow. Right now they have to . . . they're taking care of things,' he said.

She looked up at him and the pain in her eyes revealed her estimation of how gruesome it must have been. 'The boy . . . Atif, is it? Does he have anyone?'

'No,' he said, her kindness cutting deep into him.

'Then you must take care of everything.'

When they stood side by side over their son on a cold, metal table in a mortuary across town, Rahul thought that he heard her breath stop for what seemed like an eternity.

For minutes Pooja refused to move, her body moored so that the tides of her grief wouldn't carry her away and sink her, and her eyes were unable to tear themselves away from the face in which so much of them both now lay frozen. Then, slowly she lifted a trembling hand and ran it over Ajay's thick black hair, afraid yet hopeful that her touch would somehow revive him. She bent over his face – eyes still dry – and kissed him on the lips. His skin felt chilled, as if he had been out in the cold too long.

She looked at Rahul but he remained absolutely still. Something told him that he should move, express, utter something, but he found himself unable to react. In front of him was not just a son he had loved all his life yet never known, but also one who was lying there lifeless because of him. Pooja had been right all along, that he would hurt their son. And now here he stood, a bereaved father, a penitent killer.

Even in her grief, Pooja understood the currents of Rahul's heart, so she touched him. When Rahul clasped his son's hands over the white sheet, he thought about how small they had once been. Yet he couldn't remember ever holding them, whether to cross a street safely or teach him how to play a sport. *These may have been the hands that cudgelled the life out of Atif,* thought Rahul. *But I moved those hands. I did it.*

Later, in a modestly appointed office in another wing of

the mortuary, the young, well-mannered funeral director told them that he had experience with Hindu cremations and that the funeral home had recently accommodated special requests such as allowing community priests to say prayers, tying sacred threads to the body, letting a relative witness the actual injection of the body into the retort.

Pooja sat quietly through it all. Before leaving, she and Rahul thanked him for his thoughtfulness, told him they would get back to him. When they had made their way out of the building and into the blinding sunshine that seemed to mock them, they were fully aware that along with their son, both had left something vital that was necessary to live a functional life behind. She said, 'No ceremonies, Rahul. Just bring him to me when they're done.'

The next day he drove to Atif, lying in a room smelling not of the tuberoses that he had enjoyed but formaldehyde and antiseptic. When the white sheet was pulled from Atif's face, for a moment Rahul thought that by some miracle, he might actually start to breathe again. That everything that had happened, that was bound to happen, would be overturned. He thought that if he could only touch, stroke, lick, caress the flesh that once burned against his own, in which he had found and to which he had once given pleasure, it would stir to life. Surely lovers had a memory of each other, one that transcended time and even death.

But the black and purple lesions, the history of bruises on Atif's body belied this fantasy. All of Atif's spirit, the love and yearning, and the memories stored in the meridians of his body, had been scourged from it. Rahul couldn't be sure how long he had stood there alone as the vengeances, memories, wishes – some of which had come true and those that now never would – passed through his mind. In them he saw the tender smiles in which Atif had suppressed his pain, and heard his crying, the undignified pleading when they had been apart, the ecstasy with which he called out Rahul's name when they made love, the gravelled voice with which he recited Rumi. What must have been the last thought that went through Atif's mind? Did he beg, try to reason with Ajay? Did he recognize the end, give in to it like Hanif with the tides?

Rahul clasped his hands together and pressed them against his mouth, more from grief than the intent to speak or pray. He would have liked to pray but the words, quelled for decades, did not spring to his lips automatically. He would have liked to apologize, but the regret, impotent in bringing his lover back or reversing the suffering, felt trifling in the face of such loss. Instead he thought, and almost said, 'I love you,' and heaved into tears. Then he prayed silently for the first time in decades, asking that if there was an afterlife, they would meet again, that Atif would find a lasting love, a loving family.

Slowly, he touched the scar on Atif's upper lip, realizing now that he had never asked its origin. He bent over Atif's face so that their lips were a hair's breadth apart, and caressed his thick black hair. He delivered a favourite poem that Atif had recited on their nights together, his words crackling and bruised by the force of his anguish:

If anyone wants to know what the spirit is,
or what God's fragrance means,
lean your head towards him.
Keep your face there close.
Like this.

With that, Rahul kissed him one last time on the lips, a tear falling upon Atif's cheek.

All day she slept in Ajay's room, unkempt, a mother in mourning. For periods of time she pretended to herself that nothing had changed. Her son was just away with that friend of his, perhaps a new girlfriend, and with the night he would return with that sheepish face that could melt a mother's heart, his red mobile trilling away incessantly at the hip. She would insist that he eat and when Ajay would ask for the flavourless slabs of chicken breast, dusted with salt and pepper, or his protein shakes, she would make a needless fuss only to prepare him just what he had asked for.

But then, as the hours crawled by in his room where Pooja stared endlessly at the basketball trophies, collection of CDs, hamper of soiled clothes, she realized her son was not coming back. Her eyes would never rest upon his magnificent form nor would she hear his robust laughter or catch the potent smell of his sweat mingling with deodorant when he playfully hugged her. All that had already been reduced efficiently through a furnace and pulverized into the ash that his father had brought home and placed in a corner of the room like an unobtrusive artifact to decorate the home.

For two days, Rahul placed little plates of food that he had thawed from the freezer on a tray and tried to talk her into eating something but she wouldn't. Once, she looked up at him and nodded with a smile, the delicately shaped face now so arrested by grief that her deep eyes looked like they had been reduced to impassive motes in a statue, but when he returned hours later, the plate remained untouched. When she finally ate a morsel or two, at the end of the second day, she did so grudgingly, contemptuous at every grain that sustained her. On the third day, he heard the bedroom door creak open. He heard the doggerel of existence – Pooja blowing her nose, the water running, flushing, little knocks and thumps. Then she descended, like Ganga rebuked, broken, but unlike the river, without the strength to bear up under the weight of man's transgressions.

She appeared in the unlit living room, ghostlike. It was dusk but Rahul had not yet bothered to turn the lights on, knowing that mourning a loved one required a gloomy setting. Lights were the emissaries of celebration. Even in the dark, he could see her suffering. Holding together a body, one in which grief had taken up residence was a long, arduous process. In time, the body would adjust to its inhabitant, form some sort of alliance, but until then, it would impinge upon the new terrain. Rousing from the sofa, he reached out for the lamp on the side table but she held up a hand, stopping him. When she turned and looked at the urn on a table against the wall to her right, he said, in a broken voice, 'I'm sorry.'

It took a minute for her to face him, for his words to reach her. 'Sorry?' she said, looking at him wildly.

He dropped his eyes.

She walked away from him, went in the direction of the kitchen but the pain must have been so strong that she stopped by the dining room table and leaned against the chair for support, grabbing the edges so tight, her knuckles went white. 'You must leave,' she said, not turning around. 'This time, don't come back.'

'Pooja, I . . .'

But she shook her head, stopping him. She continued looking out through the window but she was much, much farther away than Sonali's house. 'There's nothing here any more for either one of us, Rahul. Whatever there was, you've already destroyed,' she said, her voice stony now, devoid of the tinder and debility of mourning. 'You brought us into this exile. Then you betrayed me. Now Ajay . . .' her voice was derailed momentarily. 'What else is there for you to do?'

And only now, as she turned around to look at him, the light from the kitchen illuminating her face spectrally, could he see that not only had she been crying but it also looked like she had been beaten physically so that he could barely recognize her. He would have liked to think that if he could have only reached out and touched her, placed his hand on her arm, taken her into his own, then all this would be erased. But it was too late for that. That was the remedy for another time, one that had come and gone. He rose to his feet and when she saw him approach her, Pooja shrank back. He touched her anyway. She threw her weak fists at him repeatedly, struggling to break free form the embrace she once sought.

'No!' she cried. 'You did this. You took my son away!'

He overpowered her blows, clung to her.

'Bring him back! Please bring him back!'

'I wish I could, Poo. Please . . .'

'I want him,' she said, her nails digging into his arms, her eyes struggling to look away from the urn. 'I just want my son back. I want Ajay back. Rahul, please bring him back!'

'I can't bring him back,' he said, his tears escaping him. 'I can't . . .'

'He's everywhere. Everywhere. If I close my eyes, I can hear him calling me. If I shut my ears, I can feel him kicking in my womb. It's not natural, Rahul. It's not natural for a mother to outlive her son. It's not natural that I should live without him. Why won't you listen? Why won't they listen?' she said, looking in the direction of the kitchen altar.

Her mouth opened again but no sound escaped her. It was as if she was summoning all the uncried moments of her life from that hidden, secret place in her heart. The gravity of grief pulled them both to the ground as she buried her face lifelessly into his chest, covering it with tears and spittle, and finally let out a howl as if a thousand arrows had felled her.

As a child, her mother had told Pooja that our perceived misfortune was an inability to sense the wisdom behind God's plan, a short-sightedness; we couldn't see the better ending that was being prepared for us because we were too attached to maya, illusion.

As a grown-up woman, this understanding had morphed into blind faith, something stronger so that Pooja, even after experiencing the horrors in Nairobi and the loss of her in-laws, believed in God's mysterious ways. When Ajay had been born, so shortly after Rahul and she had come to America in a state of such devastation, she had in her own way, interpreted this as divine benefaction. Nothing would change the past but at least they could see the future.

But now the future had been expunged. At least Parvati had Shiva to reanimate their slain son with the head of an elephant that would then live on to even greater glory and be the scribe of the Mahabharata. But Rahul and she were mortals and in as much as she had accepted him as her god incarnate, he was helpless in bringing her son back to her.

She grew tired of the games her mind played, dreaming that Ajay had come back alive and well at the end of the day, only to awake to a nightmare. She hovered around the aromatic altar of the nectareously smiling gods, growing resentful at their indifference, their seeming impotence. Her pain coiled around her neck, chest, torso, and pulled so tight, like a compactor, that it became hard for her to breathe, the pressure so unbearable and oppressive. Ajay's birth had been so painful that Pooja remembered it as if it was only yesterday, but nothing could compare to the pain of his passing.

In the morning she bathed, letting the scorching water slough away the grime of memory. She made a phone call to her parents but a new male servant answered and in her now-broken Swahili, she began to leave a message but then changed her mind and hung up. She thought momentarily about calling Charlie but couldn't think of what to say and didn't want to hear what he might say. Sonali had left a couple of concerned messages but Pooja felt resistant to any consoling. She had reached, even if only temporarily, a state of darkness in which she felt too numb for pain, too cold for rage, yet depleted of all verve.

When she came down to where Rahul had spent another night on the couch, she insisted on his leaving. He looked at her pleadingly, unable to summon words from the depth of his guilt. When he opened his mouth, she shook her head decisively, cutting him off. He packed up some of his remaining clothes, and told her he would come back the next day. He asked her to call him if she should need him but she smiled back at him calmly and even that faded almost as soon as it appeared on her face.

Before he walked out through the door, he paused to look back at her and she considered him one last time, broken just like her, only intermittent flashes of the man he once used to be, the one she had fallen so devotedly in love with, falling in and out of her view like quantum particles torn between two realms. She walked up to him as he lingered by the door frame, still hoping she would ask him to stay. They had been on similar terrain before, where loss and grief cried for companionship and support. In spite of herself, she found some sympathy stirring within her. But it was an impotent kindness, one that permitted her to go no further than to acknowledge his torment. He had lost a son too and in time, if not now, would castigate himself for Ajay's death. For Rahul, who had already known so much loss, the trial would continue.

She reached up and touched his face gently, the stubble prickling her fingers, and looked into his bloodshot eyes. They stood there only for minutes but entire lifetimes passed between them. Together they had traversed the terrain of life, its peaks and valleys, a youth full of promise and an aging filled with loss and despair. As a Hindu couple that had circled Agni's fires, they may be bound together for six more lifetimes but in this one, she knew, the journey had come to an end. And it broke her heart to look at him and know that Rahul didn't see this, that he was still clinging to the hope that in a few days, they would pick up and begin again, that now that they had lost everything, they might still have each other.

'Go,' she whispered.

When the house had been plunged into its familiar tombal silence, Pooja slowly and silently went to her son. Her hand touched the cold marble of the urn and she tried to listen for a sound, a breath. Her eyes fell upon a framed picture next to it – a plump, five-year-old Ajay gregariously posing on his new tricycle, one arm raised in the air at the photographer, who had been his father. He had ridden the red toy engine so vigorously that within a year, the front wheel rolled off its axis and threw him to the ground. Hearing his cry, Pooja had hurtled down the flight of stairs from their old Culver City apartment and thank God, he hadn't been hurt. The memory made her smile to herself but then black tears bubbled up her throat.

She picked up the urn, took it into her arms. It was lighter than she had expected it to be, most of its weight in the marble and not the remains of her once robust son. She carried it upstairs to his room and placed it gently on the nightstand, next to his iPod, gym wristwatch and a workout magazine with Herculean models on the cover. Suddenly she thought about his cellphone. Where must it be? Are people still calling it? Who would tell them?

She went into her bathroom and from the medicine chest, pulled out an amber-coloured plastic container and twisted off the childproof cap. She emptied its contents into the palm of her hand, and cupping the glistening capsules to her mouth, wondered if there was enough there to take away the pain. All the pain. Life could hold no meaning any more and although she could walk, talk, eat, breathe, it was all just empty ceremony like the bindi on her forehead and the vermillion in the parting of her hair. She turned on the faucet and cupping water into her mouth, swallowed the pills a few at a time until they were all gone.

She returned to Ajay's room and stripped away her clothes. She lay down in his bed where she could no longer even smell him, traces of him already wiping out from the log of atmosphere. What she wouldn't do to birth him again, to feel him kicking in her stomach, hold him swathed in the yellow cotton blanket in the hospital bed, feel the pressure of his gums around her nipple, each tug bringing forth his nourishment, to spend long soporific afternoons of storytelling and find him looking up at her with those wondrous black eyes. If she had created him once from her own primordial substance, couldn't she conjure him back into life again like Parvati who had longed for a son and had sloughed the dirt and ash from her skin to create Ganesha?

She opened up the urn and dipped her hand into it,

feeling the cool ash. Slowly she lifted a grey mound of his remains in the palm of her hand and closing her eyes, began rubbing it over her face, her neck, her shoulders, her arms. Her eyes burned and tears ran as the ash of bone and flesh rolled off her and fell to the side of the bed. She reached in for more, now covering her breast, her stomach, her thighs and the space in between from where she had once portalled him into life with the dust of his existence.

Then she closed her eyes.

She waited.

Acknowledgements

A GREAT NUMBER of people have assisted me in various ways and this list in no way includes all of them.

To my mother, whose blind faith gives me strength, and my father from whom I first learned to create.

My special thanks to my agent and friend, Deborah Ritchken whose passion for books is inspiring, and who has nurtured and enabled me to stay true to my vision; Karthika V.K. at HarperCollins, India, for getting behind this novel and bringing it 'home'; Adrienne Brodeur, for shaping the novel in such a fundamental way; Don Weise, my US publisher at Magnus for embracing the novel, the invaluable guidance, and for being such a class act; Sarah Van Arsdale, for the astute copyediting.

I am blessed with my family of friends who have stood by me through the ups and downs of a writer's journey. Victor Riobo, for being a confidante and patient sounding board, Corky Velasquez, for being my bulwark and providing unwavering support. Elena De La Cruz, for her kindness and love. My writing comrades – Shilpa Agarwal, Bhargavi C. Madava, and Francesca McCafree – for their solicitous readings and suggestions, and for getting me to the finishing line.

In researching this book, I am especially indebted to the staggering amount of information provided by Ruth Vanita and Saleem Kidwai, and Stephen O. Murray and Will

Roscoe. To Coleman Barks for introducing me to Rumi; Lieutenant Frank Padilla at the Santa Monica Police Department for patiently explaining procedure; Vikram Doctor for teaching me Bambaiya Hindi and always opening doors. Vikram Phukan and the dedicated folks at *Bombay Dost* for getting the word out.

Craig Kirkland and Robert Martinez – thank you for understanding the importance of balance and enabling it. To the many others who have offered me support: T. Heather Ho, Jeremy Kinser, Sandip Roy, Jitin Hingorani, Myna Mukherjee, and David and Paige Glickman.

Finally, my thanks to the readers who come to my readings; to those who took the time to write to me and demonstrate how far and wide a novel can travel – your voices provide encouragement when I'm struggling, and conviction when I'm in doubt.

Thank you.